SNIP SNAP

Jane Holland

CHAPTER ONE

'I want to be young again,' Mrs Walker says. 'I want to look fifty. Sixty, at a push.' Her rheumy, bloodshot eyes meet mine in the salon mirror. 'Can you do it, love?'

'Of course.' I plump what's left of her dyed platinum blonde hair with one assessing hand. 'Give me an hour, you'll be walking out of here looking like Dolly Parton herself.'

'Isn't she dead?' Mrs Walker looks suspicious.

'Not yet.' I smile and breeze off to make my customer's obligatory cup of coffee. White, two sugars.

In the back room, I check the wall clock over my shoulder.

Half past eleven.

Another hour, and my morning stint at the hairdressing salon will be over. My feet are aching. I decide to stop off at Simon's place on my way back and check how he is, poor soul. He told me he wouldn't be going into work today, what with his mum's funeral to arrange, so odds are good he'll still be at home. Unless he's gone down the pub.

I just hope he'll want to see me. I'm not sure I can handle another knockback. Not right now.

'Come on, Melanie, spill the beans.' Cheryl, folding white towels fresh out of the drier, gives me a knowing wink. 'How did it go with Simon last night?'

My heart contracts at the question, the same uncomfortable feeling I had on first waking this morning. It's the tiniest twinge, like somebody sticking a pin in my chest.

Wincing, I put that twinge down to the booze I consumed last night, though it really didn't seem that large an amount at the time. Two or three glasses of wine, perhaps? Maybe I'm no longer used to drinking much and my body isn't coping well with the detox. My mouth is dry and my head is still feeling a little delicate …

I fix Mrs Walker's coffee. 'Usual second date stuff.'

'And?'

'And nothing.' I shrug. 'I went round to his place. We had a Chinese takeaway and a bottle of wine.'

Something in my voice must have given me away.

'Tried it on, did he?'

I pull a face. 'He got a bit handy, yeah.'

'I hope you slapped him down.'

'We had words.'

'Quite right too.' Cheryl stops folding and looks at me more closely. 'Hey, you okay?'

'Bit tired, that's all.'

'Are you going to see him again?'

'Why not?' I shrug. 'So we had a fight. That's hardly the end of the world. Besides, he's missing his mum, poor thing. She only died last week. No wonder he's on edge.'

Stirring two sugars into the coffee, I add, 'In fact, I'm going round to see him when I finish my shift. Maybe drag him out for a burger or something. I know he's a bit older than me but older men can be fun. And I need a little fun right now.'

'That's the spirit.' Cheryl grins at me, and then frowns. 'How much older?'

'That would be telling.' I bite my lip, pretending to be coy.

'What are you, twenty-two?'

4

'That's what it says on my passport.'

With a chuckle, she glances past me into the salon. 'I see you've got Mrs Walker again.'

'She likes me. And she tips well.'

'That's because you humour her. Okay, what does she want this time? To look like Marilyn Monroe?'

'Dolly Parton.'

We both laugh, but guiltily.

These old ladies need their daydreams every bit as much as we do.

I walk back through a lingering cloud of hairspray, its cloying synthetic taste at the back of my throat, and pop the coffee down in front of Mrs Walker.

'Now,' I say as my hands begin to work their magic, 'just you relax, Mrs Walker, and tell me more about that great-grandson of yours.' I smile at her in the mirror. 'He sounds amazing. Has he started school yet?'

There's a parcel sitting in the open front porch at Simon's house when I turn up at lunchtime, and the milk hasn't been brought in yet.

I ring the doorbell, but there's no reply.

His car's still in the drive.

I eye it thoughtfully. Maybe he's gone for a walk. Down to the pub, perhaps. He's 'between jobs' at the moment, as he put it the other night. Unemployed, in other words. Though it's early, even for him. Barely one o'clock.

'Simon?' I call through the curtained windows downstairs. 'It's Melanie. You in there?'

No reply.

I collect the parcel and the pint of milk, and head down the shrub-lined path to the back of the house.

The back door is unlocked, so I let myself in. The remains of our meal are still where we left them last night. Two plates of Chicken Chow Mein. Stained

5

brown paper bag and plastic tubs from the takeaway round the corner. The smell of stale food on the air.

'Messy pup,' I say under my breath.

I close the back door and stiffen, hearing voices in the other room, followed by the closing theme tune of a daytime soap.

Simon must be watching the telly.

I put the milk in the fridge, feeling awkward now. He must have heard me come in, surely? Is he ignoring me? Or maybe he fell asleep in front of the telly after I'd gone last night, and hasn't woken up yet.

It was a late night, after all, and we were both the worse for the wine.

'Simon?' Tentatively, pinning an apologetic smile to my lips, I carry the parcel through to the living room. 'I hope you don't mind; I let myself in …'

I stop dead in the doorway to the living room, staring.

At first, I don't understand. Then my brain starts to take in what I'm seeing. And my throat closes up in horror, my breath choking.

There's blood everywhere.

Dark brownish-red spatters of it up the cream walls, over the thick-pile cream carpet and the white leather sofa. And there's a body too.

Simon is lying crumpled face-down, at an angle, dried blood caking the back of his neck and white shirt. He's between the sofa and the television stand, as though he was kneeling and then tumbled forward.

A pair of scissors is sticking out of the back of his neck.

They've been plunged in about halfway up the shaft, presumably stopped by hitting the bones of his spine, his vertebrae.

They look like my black-handled hairdressing scissors. The ones I used on him earlier in the evening, before we'd eaten.

He'd asked for a quick trim, since I'm a hairdresser and he didn't want to go to his mum's funeral with untidy hair. Afterwards, I remember putting the scissors down on the side table while he got up to check his reflection in the silver-edged oval mirror that hangs opposite the sofa.

'You're good,' Simon said, turning his head from side to side.

I laughed. 'I know.'

'What else are you good at?' He looked round with a sly grin. 'Do you do massages?'

I'm still holding the parcel.

I look down at it in a daze. It's addressed to Mr Simon Conway.

My fingerprints must be all over it.

I look up again at the body, the white sofa, the television remote control on the floor. What did I touch last night? What didn't I touch?

I slip the parcel into my capacious shoulder bag, and force myself to move. I stand over the body, staring down at his remains in a dizzying wave of nausea. For an awful moment, I think I'm going to faint. My vision blurs, then miraculously clears again.

I bend and drag my hairdressing scissors out of his neck.

It's not easy; the scissors are wedged in there pretty tight. The soft, wet, sucking noise as they eventually work free is horrendous. It's a struggle not to retch.

I back out of the room.

Careful to avoid touching anything else, I collect the brown paper bag from last night's Chinese takeaway, drop the bloodied scissors into the bottom, and leave the bag on the table for later.

I find kitchen roll and anti-bacterial cleaning spray by the sink. Painstakingly, meticulously, I go around the downstairs of the house, cleaning up after myself: door handles, walls, sofa, coffee table, glasses, plates, cutlery. When I'm done, I force the spray bottle and used wads of kitchen roll into the paper bag, take a deep breath, and leave Simon's house in the same unobtrusive way I'd arrived.

Clutching the bulging paper bag, I stroll back up the garden path and continue along his street at a nonchalant pace for two interminable blocks until I reach the first corner. Now I'm out of sight of his neighbours and can stop tensing my shoulders, constantly expecting to feel a hand there or to hear a shout ordering me to stop.

There's a bin outside a newsagent's shop opposite.

Trying to act casual, I cross the busy road as soon as it's clear, push the spray bottle and kitchen roll into the already overflowing bin, and then continue on my way, walking more briskly and with purpose now, as though late for an appointment.

It's only on reaching the relative safety of my flat that I realise I should have wiped down the milk and returned it to the doorstep too.

Now they'll know somebody was there today and didn't report his murder.

They'll know *I* was there.

I double-lock the door to my flat and bolt it, put the paper bag on the table, and cross the living room to close the curtains. It's a two-bedroom flat on the second floor, but you can still see in from the street below. The outer fringes of South London are full of anonymous little flats like this. I knew it was perfect as soon as I saw it. I didn't choose it, of course. But whoever did had chosen well.

Returning past the table, I notice a red stain beginning to bloom through the paper sides of the takeaway bag.

Simon's blood.

I avert my eyes, heading into my bedroom. There, I drop onto all fours beside the unmade bed, the duvet still crumpled from where I crawled out for work early this morning, feeling like death.

I put my pounding head and fuzzy memory down to too much booze the night before. But was there another reason? What exactly did I get up to last night?

Murder.

I ignore the traitorous little voice in my head. I have no proof that I did anything wrong, and indeed I do vaguely seem to recall Simon kissing me goodbye on the doorstep before I made my unsteady way home, weaving a little due to the wine …

Unless I imagined that. The guilty mind creating false images to help me cope with what I've done. Again.

Lowering my chest to the carpet, I reach under the bedframe, feeling about blindly for what I know is taped there.

My fingers find it.

I wrench at the tape keeping it hidden and secure, and the phone comes loose. There's a charging cable in the bottom drawer of my bedside cabinet.

I charge the phone for ten minutes while I nip for a wee, splash cold water on my face, and stare at myself in the mirror. Then I go back and sit on the bed, phone in hand, charging cable still attached so it won't conk out on me partway through this.

There's only one number saved on the phone. It was pre-programmed when I got it.

I hit call and wait.

It rings and rings, but nobody answers. Though that's not a surprise.

Nobody ever answers.

I tap out a brief message instead, and send it.

It's happened again.

Five minutes later, I get a reply.

Does anyone know?

Not yet.

Address?

I close my eyes briefly. I don't know the postcode. But maybe that won't matter. I type in Simon's house number and street address, and hit send.

The reply comes almost immediately.

Are you there now?

No, I'm at home.

Does anyone know that you were there?

I frown, thinking.

I nipped into the off-licence alone last night while Simon went round the corner to the Chinese takeaway. It's possible we may have been seen together, walking to his house. But it's not far, only a few streets, and it would have been late by then, gone ten o'clock at least.

Then I remember the conversation this morning with Cheryl.

Someone at my work.

There's a long wait for the next response. I begin to get scared it will ever come. That the police will make enquiries and eventually turn up at my place, and then –

Stay where you are, pack your bags and await further instructions.

I put the phone back on charge, wrap the paper bag containing the blood-encrusted scissors in a plastic bag and hide it at the bottom of my wardrobe, and leave the flat.

I'm not going anywhere without Charlie.

CHAPTER TWO

'Mummy?'

Charlie makes an unhappy sound under his breath, dragging on my hand, and I realise with a shock how fast I've been expecting his little legs to walk.

I slow down, shooting him a harried, apologetic smile, and say, 'Sorry, darling. Mummy's in a hurry, that's all. Are you all right?'

Charlie nods, his smile returning.

He's a typical three-year-old, rising four: thatch of dishevelled fair hair, big blue eyes, flushed cheeks like two rosy apples either side of a mouth that can grin broadly or dip in sudden, inconsolable unhappiness.

And I love him more than anything else in the world.

The thought of him being ripped away from me by the police, by social workers, while I'm investigated for a murder I didn't commit, knowing how incriminating that scene was, how it would look to the authorities, that I have no possible way to prove my innocence ...

No, I can't bear to put Charlie through that. Rather the difficulty of sudden, irrevocable relocation. At least then we would be *together*.

The staff looked at me oddly when I collected Charlie early from nursery. Perhaps they could see the guilt in my face. Or perhaps I simply failed to hide my anxiety.

'We can't reimburse you for the last week of term, I'm afraid,' the nursery director told me, when I explained we were going away and wouldn't be back until after the end of term, which is just over a week away.

'That's fine.' I knelt to help my son on with his outdoor shoes. 'I'm sorry for any inconvenience, but .... Well, it can't be helped. It's for a family funeral.'

'I see.'

I saw her brows drawing together, and improvised. 'The funeral's being held abroad, so I thought we might as well stay on for a few extra days afterwards.'

She nodded. 'I'm sorry for your loss.'

'Thank you.'

One of the other pre-school staff came hurrying up to hand me an armful of Charlie's outwork, accumulated over the term, and I accepted the pictures with an awkward smile, folding them into his rucksack.

'Better say goodbye to your friends, Charlie,' I whispered.

He ran about the small room, cheerily waving goodbye, while my heart hurt to see his smiling face.

He'll miss his pre-school companions, I think, who would have been moving with him into the first term of infant school next year. Now he'll never see them again. But I have little other choice, do I? Not if I want us to stay together, to be a family.

We're not far from home now.

'Nursery,' Charlie says indistinctly, gazing up at me.

'I'm sorry, darling. You're going to miss your friends, I know. But we have to go away ... for a bit.' *Forever*, I'm thinking, but dare not voice the word. The look in his eyes tells me he's been knocked off-balance by being taken out of nursery early, and he wouldn't understand anyway. 'You'll need to pick out a few favourite toys when we get home, while I pack up your best clothes. Can you do that for Mummy?'

He nods enthusiastically.

Back at our small flat, I draw the curtains and send Charlie running to his bedroom to collect his top toys, the ones he simply can't be without.

Then I call Kriss at the hairdresser's, using my usual mobile phone. He's astonished by my apologetic request to take a few days off work - it would be too dangerous to admit that I'm leaving for good - because Charlie isn't well.

I feel awful using my son as an excuse, but I know the family funeral story won't wash with Kriss. My boss is immovable about staff absences and would ask to see actual proof that a close relative has died. But I know he's got a soft spot for little Charlie, who's come to the salon a few times with me, usually when I'm covering for a Saturday morning stint.

'I'm terribly sorry,' I say into the silence that follows my request. 'The nursery called to ask me to take him home early. He's already thrown up and is running a fever. I've given him some liquid paracetamol, but I may have to call a doctor out if I can't lower his temperature.' I inject a note of frantic concern into my voice. 'God, I only hope it's nothing ... serious.'

'So do I,' Kriss agreed, immediately smooth and professionally reassuring, in that deep, charming voice that keeps the pensioners coming back week after week. 'Not a problem, love. I'll ask Carmen to cover your shifts. She's been asking for more hours anyway. You stay home, look after your boy.'

After the call, I twitch a corner of the curtain and peer out cautiously. The sunlit street with its rows of tight-packed cars is empty of people. Light bounces off a dozen windscreens and metal roofs, dazzling me.

I blink and step back, shaking my head, then look again.

There's someone walking along the pavement opposite. A man in a black jacket, despite the summer heat. I can't see his face; it's hidden by the baseball cap drawn far down, casting deep shadow. His head turns towards our building as he passes, his steps seeming to slow. I drop the curtain in fright and stand there a moment , listening hard, my heart thudding. But there's no sound of footsteps, and after another minute or so, I dare to peer out through the gap between curtains.

The street is empty again.

I hurry to grab an overnight bag to hold Charlie's clothes, and head into his room. He's on his knees, scrabbling about under his bed for a soft toy he's suddenly decided is indispensable. As I roll up pastel T-shirts and several pairs of shorts, plus as many changes of socks and underwear as will fit into the bag, I talk to him in a quick, breathless way that tells me how scared I am.

'Are those all the toys you want to bring? Oh, darling, I don't think Shaun the Sheep can come. No, I know you love him. But there simply isn't enough space.'

All the time I'm talking, I'm thinking at the back of my head, over and over, like a nervous tic, what else did I touch in Simon's house? The obvious stuff, of course. But I cleaned most of that. Oh, but then I used the upstairs toilet too. Door handles, taps, towel. The banister rail.

I have a brief memory flash of Simon standing beside me at the base of the stairs, pointing the way to the upstairs toilet. 'First door on the right.'

I really liked him. His pleasant smile, his wide, guileless eyes ...

Was it me?

My heart races and stutters, and I stop, momentarily clutching my chest as the obscene thought batters at me again. God, was it me? Did I kill Simon and then blank it all out? Am I a killer?

'Mummy? Mummy?'

I look down in a daze. Charlie is tugging on my sleeve. He holds up a large plastic xylophone.

'This too?'

'No room, darling,' I say automatically, shaking my head. 'I'm so sorry.' I sit heavily on his toddler bed, and feel it creak under my weight. 'I'm so, so sorry.'

'Don't cry, Mummy,' he says, frowning with almost adult concern, and lays his fair head in my lap.

He's right, I realise, lifting a stupid hand to my face. Tears rolling, my lower lip quivering. My mascara will be ruined.

14

'Oh, darling.' I cradle his head, stroking his fine hair. 'I love you so much.'

Last night, while I was out with Simon, a neighbour a few houses along babysat him. Joan's a cheery mum in her thirties who often comes in the hairdresser's for a trim or new coppery highlights in her lustrous brown bob. If the police do manage to track me down as the last person to see Simon alive, they'll find out about Charlie and talk to Joan. They'll ask what kind of state I was in when I collected him last night. They'll start to piece together a picture of me, their prime suspect.

I can't even remember what state I was in last night. Which is strange. I wasn't *that* drunk, I feel sure. Mildly tipsy at worst. But maybe it's the sheer terror of what's happening that's blocking everything else out. All I can think is, what's next?

Somewhere, a phone rings faintly.

I sit up and put him gently from me. 'Put your toys in your rucksack, sweetheart. Take out the drawings first. You can leave them for ... for later.'

Hurrying into the living room, I root for the burner phone in my handbag. It's the usual number. Only it's ringing this time. It's not a text.

Putting the phone to my ear, I find it hard to breathe, lungs burning as though I've been inhaling smoke.

'H-Hello?'

'Do you know St Peter's?'

No greeting, no small talk. Just straight down to business. The voice sounds robotic, like it's being fed through some kind of distorter before coming to me. All the same, I'm pretty sure it's a man.

'The church?' I blink, visualising the place. 'Of course, it's only a few streets away.'

'At seven o'clock, go there and wait to be picked up. I'm sending a car for you and the boy. Wait in the car park at the back of the church. Try not to be seen.'

'Who are you?' I ask in a rush.

15

'Seven o'clock,' he repeats in that robotic voice. 'Once you've left, turn off your usual mobile, and don't use it to make any calls. Don't use any bank or credit cards either. Don't buy anything online. Don't tell anyone what's going on or where you're going.' I don't know where I'm going, I think rebelliously, but say nothing, listening to his rules. 'Trust nobody. And make sure this phone is kept on and charged.' A moment's hesitation. 'It will be a long journey, I'm afraid.'

That unexpected touch of humanity at the end emboldens me.

'I have a bag in my wardrobe. The scissors are in it. The ones that were used to … ' I grimace. 'What should I do with them?'

'Leave them where they are. They'll be taken care of. Just like last time.'

'Why are you helping me? Please … I don't understand.'

'Lock up the flat as usual when you leave and take the keys with you. You can throw them away later.'

'But – '

'Have you changed the locks since you moved in?' The question was abrupt.

'No.'

'Has the lock on the front door been changed?'

'No.'

'Good. Then our business is concluded.'

The line goes dead.

I glare down at the blank screen, furious and helpless.

I'm tempted to ring the man back, whoever he is, and demand an explanation. He seems to know everything while I know nothing.

Don't I even have a right to ask questions?

Or I could turn the burner off and call the police instead. If I tell them everything I know - which admittedly isn't very much – maybe they'll understand why I panicked and left Simon's body there. I'm innocent, after all. I could show them this burner phone as proof. For all I know, the man on the other end may be connected to Simon's death, and the police may have ways of tracing the call back to him.

16

But as I come back to the moment, I'm aware of Charlie in the doorway, watching me with solemn eyes.

And while the police investigation was going on, I remind myself, what would happen to my son?

He'd be put into care. Temporarily, it's true, but what if my explanation doesn't hold up and the courts find me guilty of murder? I've seen enough TV crime shows to know that miscarriages of justice like that happen all the time.

I might never see Charlie again.

And how would that affect him? I had an horrific childhood in care myself, passed from foster parent to foster parent. What chance would my son have for happiness, growing up with an imprisoned murderess for a mother, and as for his father ...

Pushing aside my doubts, I stuff the burner phone back into my bag. 'Are you all packed and ready? Clever boy. I've just heard it's going to be a long car ride.'

'Where?'

'I don't know. And we'll have time for a hot meal before we go. We'll use up what's in the fridge. But I know you get hungry on long journeys.' I hold out my hand. 'So let's make snacks for the journey, shall we?'

'Sa'dwiches!' he manages excitedly. 'Juice!'

'Tuna or ham sandwiches?'

He considers that solemnly. 'Tuna.'

'I'm sure we can manage that. Though not too much juice. I don't know if there'll be any chance of a toilet break.' He runs to me and I crouch down, embracing him fervently. 'This is quite an adventure, isn't it? Our very own secret adventure.' I feel his arms tighten compulsively about me. He's afraid and uncertain. And he's not alone. But I need to be strong now, for his sake. 'Don't worry, Charlie bear,' I whisper into his hair. 'Mummy's going to keep you safe, I promise.'

To my disbelief, the 'car' sent for us turns out to be a limousine with smoked-out windows. We've been waiting in the quiet back car park of St. Peter's for about ten minutes when it pulls up in evening sunshine with a quiet swish of tyres across gravel.

There's little time to stare, shocked as I am. The driver's door opens almost immediately, and a heavy-set, liveried chauffeur gets out. He studies me and Charlie, and the collection of bags at our feet. Then, without a word, he turns to the back door and opens it for us.

An act of invitation.

For a moment, I can't believe what's happening and wonder if perhaps there's still time to change my mind. But Charlie tugs on my hand, dragging me towards the car with a muffled cry of, ' 'Venture! 'Venture!' and, reluctantly, I go with him.

I hadn't expected a limousine. It smacks of money and privilege, the kind of power that does whatever it wants, takes whatever it desires, and doesn't care whose lives it ruins in the process. The deep sense of foreboding inside me twists and ramps up. Accepting this help feels like I'm sticking my head in the lion's mouth.

But what choice do I have? It's either get in this car, or take my chances with the police and social services.

'Excuse me,' I say to the chauffeur, a middle-aged man wearing dark sunglasses, who inclines his head. 'Can you tell me where we 're going?'

He doesn't answer this, merely takes the heavy bags away from me without a word. He walks around to the boot, which has opened automatically. Once the bags are safely stowed away, he gestures me to follow Charlie inside; my son is already bouncing gleefully on dark blue leather seats in his dusty trainers.

Intimidated, both by the chauffeur's silence and the expensive limousine, I climb inside and drop my bulging handbag from my shoulder with relief.

The heavy door closes behind us with a thud.

I shiver, my skin chilling, and wish I'd kept a cardigan with me. But all the clothing is in our bags, in the boot now. The car has air-conditioning, and after the sunshine beating down on us during the ten-minute trudge to the church, my body is having trouble adjusting to the drop in temperature.

'Sit down, Charlie.' I help him on with his seatbelt as the car pulls smoothly away, and then fumble with my own. 'Here we go.'

While Charlie colours in a picture of a fairy-tale castle with his thick wax crayons, I watch the streets and signposts as they pass, trying to glean a sense of which way the car is going. After a few miles, it becomes obvious we're leaving the outskirts of London and heading west instead. South-west, I guess, as the driver merges onto the M4 motorway, heading towards Bristol.

I have no idea of our final destination. But every mile takes us further away from poor dead Simon and an accusation of murder, that's all I know, and all I should probably be focusing on right now.

But I'm afraid. Deeply, mortally afraid.

I stare out of the smoky-glass windows of the limousine, and my hands clench as I try to control my breathing, fingernails digging deep and painfully into my palms.

Yes, I needed to escape London, and in a hurry.

But have I made a fatal mistake, trusting that robotic voice on the end of the phone? I know nothing about him, after all, except that last time this happened, somebody - presumably him - helped me get away and relocate under a new identity. I was sick and confused, going through severe mental stress, and in the early months of my pregnancy with Charlie - though I wasn't aware of that at the time.

This feels different.

Before, it all kicked off with a mysterious burner phone arriving on my doorstep, followed by text messages telling me what to do and where to go. I'd been so relieved and thankful to have someone - even an anonymous someone with uncanny insights into my life - on my side that I hadn't questioned it much, simply obeyed, and fled my old life like the devil was at my heels.

That probably saved my life.

But now, this immaculate, expensive car, the unspeaking chauffeur in his smart livery and peaked cap, and this 'long journey' ahead into unknown territory ... Where the hell are we going now?

CHAPTER THREE

It's late at night when I wake with a start to find the car is slowing to a halt. I sit up, check that Charlie is still asleep. He finally nodded off after a tearful episode that ended in a toilet break for both of us in a discreet, wooded layby off the motorway. I had been unable to persuade the driver to stop at a service station, so had made do, reluctantly. Perhaps he'd been ordered not to let us out anywhere near CCTV cameras. Or, and this was a more sinister possibility, to let us out of the vehicle anywhere that might enable us to slip away unnoticed. Because it strikes me how vulnerable we've become.

Are we actually *prisoners* now?

In an effort to protect my son from the fallout from Simon's murder, I've put us in the power of an anonymous voice on the other end of an unregistered phone. I've spoken to nobody else, as instructed. And that means nobody can help us. Because nobody knows where we are. Including me.

I stretch uncomfortably and stifle a yawn, peering out at what appears to be pitch-black countryside, not a single light visible.

I press the intercom button, which is the only way I have of communicating with the driver, separated from us by a glass partition.

'Where are we?'

The chauffeur glances at me in the rear view mirror but doesn't answer. Seconds later, the car stops, and the purring engine falls silent at last.

'Hello?' I feel panicked, still unable to see a thing out of the window. Apart from the bright headlights of the limousine, illuminating a narrow lane with grass banks on either side, we seem to be surrounded by complete darkness. 'Is this it? Are we here?'

Still no reply.

I sit forward to look at the clock illuminated on the dashboard. It's almost eleven forty-five at night. We've been driving for hours.

I glance around anxiously at Charlie, but he hasn't stirred, slumped motionless against the leather upholstery, his soft breathing audible in the silence.

The chauffeur clears his throat, puts his peaked cap back on, and gets out of the limousine. I watch in breathless apprehension as he walks to the rear of the vehicle. The boot is opening automatically, I realise, craning round to see what's going on. A moment later, my door opens and the chauffeur is there, gesturing me without speaking to get out of the car.

I hesitate, and then scramble out onto the roadside, clutching my handbag and Charlie's rucksack. But the most appalling scenarios are racing through my head. What is about to happen? Is someone meeting us here, at almost midnight in the middle of nowhere? The person on the other end of the phone, for instance?

Where the hell are we?

I try to glean any clues I can from the chauffeur's face, to gauge his intentions. But it's impossible. The sunglasses have gone but his face is unreadable in the dark.

'Wait, my son is asleep.'

I lean back inside and unfasten his seatbelt, then lift Charlie tenderly out of the car. His face is flushed, his eyes still closed; he clings to me sleepily, and lays his head on my shoulder.

I look around, still dazed and off balance, trying to get my bearings in the dark. My eyes are slowly adjusting to the low light. I can't see much but there are high grassy hedgerows on either side of the narrow lane, and I can smell a distant tangy scent on the air.

The sea?

We're in the middle of full countryside here. Hence no lights to be seen. But there's a faint glow to my left, beyond what looks like a short stretch of woodland, which does suggest buildings of some kind.

The chauffeur closes the door and then nods to my luggage, watching me with that strange, impassive expression.

I suddenly realise what he's waiting for.

He's abandoning us.

'Wait.' I'm horrified. 'I've no idea where we are or what's going on. And my son's only three. You can see how tired he is. He needs somewhere safe to sleep tonight.' I've raised my voice, trying to sound firm and in control. Which is a joke, given how shaky I feel. 'I know that you can speak and that you understand me. So quit messing around. Where are we supposed to go?'

By way of reply, the chauffeur merely picks up the heavy bags and hands them to me, one at a time. I can scarcely manage them now that I'm also carrying Charlie, his weight balanced on my hip. But he seems oblivious to my problems. He indicates the lane ahead, and in the car headlights I see a name on a road sign about three hundred feet ahead.

Darkling Moreton.

I've never heard of the place and, frankly, it doesn't sound particularly pleasant.

Perplexed, I look back at the chauffeur.

'What, am I supposed to go that way? Is that what you're saying?' Abruptly losing my patience with this dumb show, I snap, 'For God's sake, can't you just speak? Just once? You can't dump us on the side of the road like this. Tell me where I'm going.'

The chauffeur mimes putting a phone to his ear and then points to my handbag.

'What on earth are you trying to say?' I demand, frustrated and weighed down with bags. 'That I'll get another phone call?'

He points towards the signpost to Darkling Moreton again, climbs back into the limousine, and a moment later starts the powerful engine again.

'Fine, okay.'

I'm angry, but there's no point arguing with nobody. Moths and tiny flies dance and swarm in the bright, ethereal beam of the headlamps as I grip Charlie more tightly, and start to walk forward, the handles of both bags clasped in one hand, a bulging rucksack and my handbag slung awkwardly over the other shoulder.

It's slow going, but what else can I do? Short of having an attack of hysterics in the middle of the road, that is. And that won't help Charlie.

Our bags knock painfully against my knee with every step. As we pass the village signpost, the beam of light that's been illuminating my path shifts and wheels to one side, moving away from us. I look back and feel a sudden stab of abandonment.

The limousine is backing into what looks like a gateway, presumably onto a field, as though turning around in the lane. Which is exactly what it's doing, in fact. As I watch, the long, graceful body gradually noses the other way, and then finally accelerates; the red points of its rear lights shrink between the hedgerows and disappear.

Then we're alone.

In the silence, a ping sounds in my handbag.

I start, my heart thumping, and put down the heavy bags to fumble in my handbag.

It's a text.

3 houses past the pub. Red front door. Go to side, door is unlocked.

I stare down at the cryptic message on the screen, baffled, my skin creeping. Is this a trap of some kind? Is the burner phone guy waiting for me in this house with the red door?

But if so, why couldn't the chauffeur take us straight there? Why leave me and Charlie to walk the rest of the way? Unless they didn't want the car to be seen arriving at the house; a horribly sinister thought that, once in my head, refuses to be dislodged.

I look about us at the empty lane, the silent fields plunged in warm darkness, and a slight wind lifts my hair. Again, I catch that vague alluring scent of the sea, and wonder how close we are to the coast. And which coast, exactly?

The last road signs I remember seeing before I dozed off were for towns in Devon and Cornwall ...

I've never been to the seaside. Not that I recall, at any rate.

And yet that tang of salt seems oddly familiar.

Charlie stirs at last, blinking and lifting his head. He peers about at the dark lane, then looks up at my face. 'Mummy?'

'Hush, that's a good boy.' I try to sound reassuring. 'We're nearly there, sweetheart. Go back to sleep.'

But Charlie is already wriggling free, his movements restless. Gently, I put him down and gather up the bags.

'You want to walk? All right, but no noise, okay? It's very, very late and most people will be in bed.' And I don't want anyone to see us, I think, my nerves prickling as I recall what we left behind, that awful scene in Simon's house, and realise that the police may have found his body by now and already be asking questions about who saw him last. 'Which is where you ought to be. Fingers crossed there's a bed waiting for you.'

'Rucksack,' he says, holding out his hands for his bag, but I shake my head.

'I'll carry it. You're too tired.'

'Not tired.' He trots confidently along beside me. ''Venture.'

'Yes, we're having a nice adventure, aren't we?'

I grimace, but luckily he doesn't notice the irony in my voice. We round the corner and enter Darkling Moreton, which turns out to be a small village with one main street.

On our left, we pass a church surrounded by leafy trees, its grey stone tower picked out by a spotlight - the glow of light I'd seen from the lane, no doubt. A few houses cluster around it, detached, exclusive-looking residences with large, walled gardens and tall iron gates. Beyond the church, on the right-hand side of the road, is a small shop with dusty windows lit up by one of only three visible streetlights in the village; there are example postcards for sale in the window, and a sign advertising, 'Hot Cornish Pasties.' We cross the road and I study the postcards, which feature picturesque Devon coastal resorts like Ilfracombe and Clovelly.

Presumably that's where we are, then.

Devon.

I've never been here before, but I know it's a very green and rural county, with sandy beaches and great stretches of moorland.

We keep walking.

The pub, about a hundred feet up ahead, is The Last Trump; it stands silent, its painted wooden sign showing an apocalyptic scene.

There's nobody about anywhere. No light either - apart from these few street lamps - no sound, and no movement. It's like a village of the dead.

Shakily, I stop and count three houses past the pub, all detached, all in darkness, while my son waits beside me in weary silence.

One, two, three.

The third house has a red front door.

It's a two-storey former shop of some kind, judging by the large front window, which is shrouded in thick dark curtains, and the raised outline of what must once have been a shop sign, now long since removed.

There's a narrow alley beside the property, walled and in darkness.

'Come on,' I whisper, and we walk on towards the house with the red front door.

Outside, I put down our bags and peer down the alleyway, horribly uncertain now that we're here. Am I doing the right thing? My heart is beating fast and erratically, and not just through the exertion of carrying these heavy bags. Goosebumps rise on my arms.

26

Charlie looks up at me questioningly. 'Wass matter, Mummy?'

I want to say, 'Someone just walked over my grave,' but he wouldn't understand.

'We've arrived,' I tell him instead, and struggle to pick up the bags again. 'I think they may have left the side door open for us. Shall we go and see who's inside?' I take a deep breath. 'I only hope there'll be something for you to eat. It's been hours since you finished those sandwiches. You must be starving.'

'Starvin'!' he agrees cheerfully, and follows me down the alleyway.

The side entrance has one step up to a solid wooden door with a Yale lock. I dump the bags again beside the step, my hands aching, and knock tentatively, not really sure what to expect. When there's no reply, I risk turning the handle.

The side door is unlocked, just as promised.

It swings opens onto a black space.

I glance up and down the alleyway. Nothing but long, menacing shadows further on, and dim lighting from the street the way we came. Something rustles in the darkness. A rat? Or somebody watching us?

Fear propels me up the step and inside the house. 'Keep close,' I tell Charlie, who follows with solemn eyes, watching me all the time. Even he can tell there's something wrong.

'Hello?' I call inside.

No sound.

I hesitate and then grope along the wall, my fingertips hunting in blackness, my heart banging against my ribs, until I feel cool plastic and a switch.

I flick the light on, and blink in sudden illumination. It's a small kitchen: pale lemon-and-white lino flooring, oak-look cabinets, sink and draining board, fridge, washing-machine and oven. It smells of disinfectant, which is vaguely comforting.

The doorway opposite yawns into darkness; light spills over a patch of beige carpet in the hall. It looks freshly hoovered. Brand-new, even. An ordinary enough house, I think, staring about the place; nothing sinister here, nothing to worry me.

'Hello?'

27

There's still no reply. But we're here at last, wherever 'here' is.

We've made it.

I dart back outside for our bags, shut the door against the darkness outside, and belatedly discover a key in the other side. I turn the key in the lock, draw the sturdy-looking bolt across too, and double-check the door is secure before turning to Charlie with a brisk smile.

'There, all safe and sound.' We both glance at the dark, silent opening into the hall, and then away. 'Shall we see if there's any food in these cupboards?'

Charlie nods, but he's yawning and swaying on his feet, and by the overhead lights I can see how flushed and sleepy he is. That short walk took it out of him. He needs to go to bed more than he needs food, I decide. Besides, I need to take a proper look around and check we're definitely alone. For that, it would be better if I'm alone.

'First, let's find you somewhere to sleep, little man.' I reach out and he tucks his small hand in mine. 'You look all done in.'

'Not ... not ... tired.'

I smile at this weary protest, and brave the rest of the house. Finding the hallway light, I flick the switch, and feel relief to find merely another empty space waiting for us. It's a narrow hallway, with a door to the left, which presumably leads to what was once the 'shop' area, and a cupboard with stairs above it.

'Come on, let's go exploring.' Having found more light switches, the two of us creep upstairs to find two closed doors and one ajar, that reveals a decent-looking bathroom with a lemon bath suite. The lino is the same as in the kitchen, matched by lemon-and-white tiles around the sink and bath with shower attached. Occasional tile squares are decorated with a bright lemon. There's a small plastic duck on the bath surround, which is somehow comforting.

'Duckie!' Charlie whispers.

'Need a wee?' I ask my son, aware of the way he's been hopping about since we entered the house, and he nods, looking anxious.

I help him, and then he washes his hands.

28

To my relief, there's a water heater concealed in a cupboard, along with laundered and folded towels and linen on shelves. There's even a fluffy white towel already hanging on the bathroom towel rail, fresh soap in the dispenser, and a white bathroom mat on the floor.

There's a smell of bleach up here, and a hint of lavender furniture polish too. The mirror above the sink still holds a few smears of glass polish.

Someone must have been in here recently, cleaning the house in readiness for our arrival.

But who?

I find it hard to imagine the owner of that robotic voice turning up with cleaning sprays and cloths, hoovering that immaculate beige carpet downstairs, and wiping down the surfaces in the kitchen.

Afterwards, we check the other rooms, the ones with closed doors.

One door turns out to be padlocked, so I leave it alone. The other room contains two beds - a double and a single, both made up with clean white linen and light summer duvets with yellow duvet covers. The matching yellow curtains at the window have been closed already. The overhead light has a pretty, yellow shade. There's a framed painting on the wall, depicting a seafront with Victorian children playing on the sand with buckets and spades, and donkeys in the distance, parading along the promenade. It's all very pretty and homely, and yet somehow impersonal too.

Like the kitchen and bathroom, the bedroom is spotless. There's a large set of pine drawers against one wall for our clothes, with a hairdryer in the top drawer alongside sweet-smelling cloth sachets of lavender.

'This place is like a holiday home,' I mutter, turning on the lamp beside the single bed and then turning to help Charlie remove his shoes and socks. 'No, pet, don't worry about pyjamas tonight. It's so late already.' I strip him down to underpants and T-shirt, and steer him into bed. 'We'll unpack our bags first thing tomorrow, how's that?'

Stifling another yawn, Charlie slips under the duvet without comment, his head nestling on a deep white pillow. His eyes are closed even before I bend to kiss him goodnight.

Poor little soul. What a day he's had!

But at least we're still together, I tell myself, pushing aside the terrible memory of what drove me to flee my home.

My son still has his mother. That's what I need to focus on right now.

Clicking off the main light, I leave the bedside lamp on, just in case Charlie wakes up at some point and is scared to find himself somewhere unfamiliar. Luckily, the lamp has a dimmer function, so I turn it right down to its lowest setting, creating a soft golden pool around his bed.

I stand a moment, listening to the silence in the house. Then some small noise outside tugs at my attention. Crossing to the cheerful yellow curtains, I open them a crack and glance down into the street.

There's a man outside the house, staring directly up at the bedroom window. His face is in shadow but I catch the gleam of his eyes.

He's a silver-haired man in rolled-up shirt sleeves, maybe six foot, walking two dogs who are trotting a few feet ahead in deep shadow. It's too hard to make out his looks accurately, the nearest streetlight some distance behind him, not close enough to illuminate the man's features but lighting up the back of his head like a halo.

I lock gazes with him for two, maybe three seconds, and then shrink back, dragging the curtains shut again in a panic.

My heart is racing, though I don't know why. The most logical explanation is that this villager was passing the house with his dog and stopped in curiosity, seeing an unaccustomed light at the window, or perhaps the brief movement of the curtains. If I'm right and this is a second home or holiday let, perhaps it's empty more often than not.

Though this is mid-summer, almost the school holidays. So, there's no reason for him to wonder at the house being occupied, is there?

I snap off the bedside lamp to avoid being backlit, count to five in my head, and then peer cautiously out of the curtains again.

The village street is empty. The man and his dog have vanished.

But it's too late, and I know it.

I've been seen.

CHAPTER FOUR

Downstairs, I explore the rest of the house, still suspicious there might be somebody else there. Though last time we had to relocate, the flat was empty and well-kept, just like this one, and nobody ever contacted me again once we'd moved in safely and started our new lives.

Things feel different this time, maybe because he spoke to me on the phone, whoever 'he' is. He never did that before. It was only ever text messages, and once, a padded envelope of money and documents that landed on the mat - hand-delivered, clearly, though I never saw who brought it.

It doesn't take long to master the layout of the place and lay my fears to rest. Besides the kitchen, and a large cupboard under the stairs, there's only an open-plan living room, and nowhere for anyone to have concealed themselves.

The window facing the street is vast, almost floor-to-ceiling; it was clearly used as a shop front originally, though is now draped with thick-lined curtains, carefully closed to keep out prying eyes, and what was presumably the shop floor has been carpeted in neutral beige and reconverted for use as a living space, with a sofa and an armchair, and a small dining area near the window.

There are faint indentations left on the white-washed walls from fixtures and fittings, now long since removed. Something about the marks strikes me as oddly familiar. But I'm too tired to think clearly, pushing that thought aside for later.

The front door, fitted with a wire basket below the letter box, has a key in the lock too. There's no bolt. As with the side door, I check it's all secure before turning to the coffee table, where I can see various items laid out, presumably for my attention.

I spot the scissors first. And shudder.

There's a typed note.

There are food supplies in the kitchen, fresh and store cupboard, enough for several weeks. The local shop also sells bread and milk, and a few other food items. There is a supermarket in town, and the bus stops right outside it. See the bus timetable.

There are several packets of hair dye, a pair of scissors on the table, and glasses. Cut your hair short, choose a new colour, and dye your hair straightaway. The glasses are plain glass, not prescription. Wear them whenever you leave the house to alter your look.

To remind you of the rules, which must be strictly adhered to:

1. *DEACTIVATE YOUR SMARTPHONE AND THROW IT AWAY.*
2. *NO SOCIAL MEDIA. NO SIGNING INTO OLD ACCOUNTS. NO LAPTOP USE WITHOUT A VPN.*
3. *CUT UP ALL PREVIOUS BANK AND IDENTITY CARDS. (NEW CARDS WILL ARRIVE SHORTLY.)*
4. *DO NOT SPEAK TO ANYONE IF YOU CAN AVOID IT.*
5. *DO NOT CONFIDE IN ANYONE OR LET SLIP YOUR PREVIOUS IDENTITY.*
6. *DO NOT FORM ANY ROMANTIC ATTACHMENTS. (YOU FAILED TO FOLLOW THIS RULE LAST TIME, AND LOOK WHERE IT'S GOT YOU.)*

You are now Sylvia Smith, relocated from Milton Keynes, a divorced mother looking for a better life in the country. You fled an abusive marriage and don't want to talk about it. The house is a former holiday let; you are renting it through an agency for the summer but may move on if country life doesn't suit you. You have private means so do not require employment. Avoid answering all other questions.

I stand there, reading and re-reading this note in silence for maybe ten minutes before I finally drop it to the floor and give into a fit of body-wracking sobs.

I've been struggling not to cry ever since I walked into Simon's house and found him dead. It's been less than twenty-four hours since that awful moment, and yet how long ago it seems now. I don't bother trying to stop or pull myself together, but fall to my knees on the carpet and sob with all my might. A dam has burst in my head now that we've finally stopped running, and it feels like this flood of tears is inevitable, even cathartic.

I'd built up a new life for myself at the salon, made friends, given birth to Charlie, raised him as best I could on my own, and he'd only recently started to enjoy going to nursery and seeing all his friends ...

Now, I have to start all over again, in a brand-new place with a new fake identity. Only this time, I have Charlie to protect from discovery as well as myself.

And all because I stupidly thought enough time had gone by, that it must be safe to date again, to live freely again.

I'd forgotten my promise.

And this is the result. Poor Simon brutally murdered, and me and Charlie on the run.

Why though?

That's what I can't understand.

Who killed Simon, and why?

After half an hour of vigorous weeping, I roll onto my back and stare up at the white-washed ceiling, my eyes and nose sore, my whole body shaking.

I push aside the obvious answer, but it keeps coming back.

I killed him.

Because I'm mad. Because there's something deeply wrong with me. Only I don't know what it is. Because I can't actually remember killing him.

But it had to be me. Didn't it?

No, I tell myself feverishly, and stagger back to my feet.

34

I'm not a killer.

I catch my reflection in the oval wall mirror opposite. I look a complete mess. An emotional wreck with streaming eyes and nose and a quivering chin. There's definitely something wrong with me. But I don't look like a murderer.

I need to cling to that. Because it's the only logical explanation for what's happened to me. Twice now.

Last time, it was a man with curly dark hair and a winning smile. He had a motorbike and took me out on the back, riding pillion. His name was Kurt, and I knew him through my hairdressing course at college. In fact, he was one of my tutors.

With difficulty, I push his memory aside, and force myself to check in the envelope - it contains at least a thousand pounds in ten-and-twenty-pound notes, I realise, giving up on counting after about five hundred - and study the bus timetable, with the supermarket stop circled carefully in red, and the map, which shows the village of Darkling Moreton, also circled in red, and the surrounding area.

As I suspected, we're in rural North Devon, smack bang in the middle of what appears to be a network of rough moorland and narrow lanes, a few miles inland from the coast.

There's a helpful box of tissues on the coffee table. My guardian angel appears to be prescient. I dry my eyes shakily, and get up to explore the kitchen instead. The note said something about food, and I realise with a start how hungry I am. I'd let Charlie eat my sandwiches in the limousine, not having much appetite at the time, but now my stomach is growling like crazy.

The cupboards and fridge are well-stocked. It's almost two in the morning by the time I sit down to a simple meal of beans on toast with a cup of strong tea. Afterwards, I work out how to operate the water heater, take a quick hot shower in the comforting yellow-and-white bathroom, and then tumble into bed a few feet from Charlie, deep in slumber, and am soon lost in sleep myself.

When I wake up, there's light in the room and Charlie is sitting cross-legged on the carpet, playing noisily with his toys. Deliberately noisily, it strikes me as I surface from sleep. How long has he been waiting for me to wake up?

'Wake up, sleepyhead!' He jumps up and comes running to the bed, looking as fresh as a daisy. 'Breakfast! Breakfast!'

On checking the cupboards last night, I was relieved to find boxes of cereals he might like, as well as staples like bread and jam, so I nod sleepily and roll out of bed.

'I'd better get dressed first though,' I say, glancing with surprise at the bedside clock, which tells me it's gone eight o'clock in the morning. 'And you should probably put some clean clothes on,' I add, as he's still only wearing underpants and T-shirt, and ignore his protests. 'Let me sort some out for you; it won't take long.'

As I drag suitable clothes out of our luggage, I'm amazed at how heavily I slept, not least because I'm usually woken up by Charlie and his antics at the crack of dawn. But yesterday was one of the most exhausting and stressful days of my life, so my body and brain obviously needed to recharge.

It's another sunny day July outside, and the sun is full on the east-facing front of the house, already warming the room. I pull on jeans and a blue vest top, and sort out shorts and a clean T-shirt for Charlie. Luckily, I thought to bring a few changes of shoes, and choose light summer sandals for myself while letting Charlie run about in socks.

After filling the kettle at the sink, I risk opening the blinds.

'There's a garden out the back,' I say, and smile when Charlie's head whips round enthusiastically. 'Not very big, but it's fairly long. With a lovely view, too.'

Charlie clammers to be lifted up to see, so I perch him briefly on the cold side of the sink and he stares out wistfully.

I know how he feels.

There are a few trees down the bottom of the long, narrow stretch of lawn, bordered with flower beds crowded with large, perennial shrubs at the back and annuals in straggly rows towards the front. I spot orange marigolds, here and there, amid sprinklings of bright pink geraniums. I've never been much of a gardener, but lately I've been starting to appreciate the joy flowers can bring. And there's something about this garden that makes me feel welcome, somehow.

At the end of the garden, beyond a wire fence, lies a wide open space, green-and-brown moorland, craggy and with clumps of low, windswept trees. It looks lonely out there, I think, and cold, even in the sunshine. I can imagine it coated in crisp white snow, the mysterious lumps and bumps just begging to be explored ...

There's a low, sturdy-looking plastic slide nearer the house, perfect for a little boy of Charlie's age. It's hard not to suspect it was put there especially for him. But that would indicate rather too much forward planning, given the short notice of our need for new accommodation.

Charlie's already spotted it. 'Slide!' he cries, pointing eagerly. 'Want to play!'

'We'll go out and explore soon,' I promise, letting him back down to the floor and gently nudging him back towards the breakfast table. 'After you've finished your breakfast.'

A knock at the side door freezes me in sudden panic.

I look at Charlie with apprehension, but he doesn't seem to have heard, settling to eat his cereal without comment.

Should I answer or pretend not to be in?

The knock comes again.

Then a high-pitched female voice says, through the door, 'Hello? I'm so sorry to disturb you. But I saw you arrive last night, and you seem to have dropped something on the way in.' There's a long pause as I stand in silence, wondering what on earth she can mean. 'I think it must be your handbag ... If you're missing one?'

Oh, God!

I gaze about myself wildly, and only then realise that I didn't check my handbag at any point last night, in all the confusion and weariness, and that I haven't seen it since we arrived. Belatedly, I recall putting all those heavy bags down several times on arrival, and then gathering them up afterwards. But it's possible my handbag slipped off my shoulder during that process, and in the dark I didn't notice.

Stupid, stupid, stupid!

'Hello?' calls the voice again, and it's obvious she's not going to give up easily. But she may have been standing outside there some time, listening to us talk. So there's really not much point pretending not to be in.

Hurriedly, I turn to Charlie, bending to his ear. I hate doing this but what choice do I have? 'Mummy needs to tell people her name is Sylvia. Mrs Sylvia Smith. Okay? It's … part of the adventure. So Mummy's name is Sylvia now, okay?'

He nods, looking up at me dubiously. 'Not Melanie?'

'Not Melanie. Not anymore. That was my … my old name.'

Except Melanie isn't my real name either. But it's the only name he's used to hearing people call me.

'Okay?' I whisper.

''Kay.'

Unlocking the side door, I force a smile and peer out into sunshine, not really sure what or who to expect. Abruptly, I recall that I was instructed to cut and dye my hair before showing my face in public again and to wear my glasses.

But it's too late now.

CHAPTER FIVE

Our unexpected visitor is a middle-aged woman in a chintzy blue knee-length dress with frizzy, blonde shoulder-length hair, straight out of a box by the looks of it, with brazen highlights. Her creased eyelids are daubed with olive green, her lipstick a garish pink, a little too young for her age, and one front tooth is chipped.

But her smile is genuine enough as she holds out my handbag. 'This is yours, dear, isn't it? I didn't make a mistake?'

'No, it's mine.' Uneasily, I take it from her. 'Thank you.'

My handbag is still zipped shut. But I can't help worrying that she may have peeped inside to see who it belonged to, perhaps innocently hunting for some ID, and studied some of my personal documents, or one of the cards in my wallet.

'It was just lying there on the path,' the woman says, nodding behind her vaguely. 'I spotted it earlier when I nipped to the shop. Of course, I'm sure you would have missed it sooner or later, and come outside for a look. But I know I'd be panicking if I thought I'd lost my handbag, with all my precious bits and tricks, so I thought I'd better knock and ...' She peers past me at Charlie, who has crept to my side with fascinated interest, and her eyes widen in obvious delight. 'Hello, young man. You look like you're dressed for an outing. Isn't it a lovely day for a walk?'

When Charlie says nothing, but shrinks closer to me, the woman laughs unconcernedly. 'Look,' she says, addressing me again, 'please don't think I'm interfering, but I see you don't have any transport at the moment. If you need a lift into town or to the supermarket, you only have to ask. I'm Patricia Eagleton, and I live next door,' she says, holding out her hand to shake mine, indicating the posh house beside ours with a jerk of the head. 'It's wonderful to have someone in here at last, the place has been empty for months. And nobody likes an empty house.'

'Thank you,' I say, not sure how to respond to this outpouring. I pause, glancing back at Charlie guiltily, as I haven't had time yet to warn him of my change of name. 'I'm Sylvia, and this is Charlie.'

'Very pleased to meet you both. Are you on holiday, Sylvia?'

'No, actually. I've just relocated from Milton Keynes. We're renting this place for a few months.' I hesitate, struggling to remember my new cover story. 'I'm divorced.'

It feels like I'm reading from a cue card. But to my relief Patricia doesn't seem to notice my wooden, faltering delivery.

'Oh dear, that's too bad.' She gives me and Charlie a sympathetic smile. 'So, you're all on your own with this charming young man?'

'I'm afraid so, yes.'

'I'm all on my own too. My husband Ken passed at Christmas.'

'I'm so sorry.'

'Thank you. It was a sudden thing. So, I'm only just getting back on my feet after that shock. It's not much fun being alone, is it?' Her eyebrows rise sharply and her intent gaze swivels back to Charlie. 'Here's a thought. Did you notice the church when you arrived?'

I nod, not sure what's coming next. I've never been a church-goer and have always a been a bit suspicious of religious people.

Patricia continues, 'We have quite a lively Sunday school group at St. Hilda's these days. Ten-thirty to twelve, while the adults are in church. Charlie would be welcome to join the other little ones.' She beams at us. 'And I'll be happy to look after him myself any afternoon when you need some time alone. Just say the word.'

'Oh, I couldn't possibly.'

'Nonsense, I'm sure he's no bother. I'm a grandmother of three, and I know what it's like to have a youngster running you ragged. Though mine have all flown the nest. Literally, I'm sorry to say. My daughter emigrated to New Zealand last summer, took her whole family there. Now I have a house full of pre-school toys and nobody to play with them. I had been thinking of packing them up and donating the good ones to a charity shop. But if Charlie would like them ...' Patricia laughs, showing the chipped tooth again. 'Not the dolls, perhaps. But I have plenty of trucks and action men, and there's even a wooden fort with soldiers. If he's not too young for all that.'

I bite my lip, tempted. That's an offer too good to pass up. We had to leave most of Charlie's toys behind, of course, in our mad dash to leave, and this morning I could see that he was pining for them. This might cheer him up.

'That's very kind of you,' I say shyly. 'Though only if you're sure.'

'You'll be doing me a favour, frankly. But I'm sorry, I can see I've interrupted your breakfast.' Patricia shakes my hand again, her grip light but energetic. 'Why don't you come round for coffee tomorrow morning, shall we say at eleven? Then your boy can choose what he likes. Take them all if you like. My youngest grandchild is almost six now, so even if they come back for a holiday, those toys won't be wanted again.'

I don't feel I can refuse, not least because of how suspicious it would look. So, I smile and thank her again and agree to go around for coffee tomorrow, but my smile feels about as fake as it's possible to be.

When she's gone, I close and lock the door again.

I check everything in my handbag; it all seems to be in place. Then I make myself a cup of tea and watch Charlie finishing his soggy cereal with apparent pleasure, no doubt looking forward to the treat of getting his pick of some other kids' toys tomorrow.

DO NOT SPEAK TO ANYONE IF YOU CAN AVOID IT.

I know the consequences if I break the rules, and they terrify me.

41

But part of going unnoticed in a new community, as I learned last time round, is behaving in an ordinary, unremarkable way.

It's being the loner, the odd one out, that attracts people's attention.

'Finissed ... Play now?' Charlie asks eagerly, looking round at me, his spoon dripping milk across the table.

I fetch a cloth to wipe up the spills, and remove his breakfast things.

'Of course you can play now.'

Turning to wash my hands, I glance out at the garden, and feel again that strange frisson of fear. What on earth's wrong with me? It's just an ordinary back garden. Or is that view of the wild moorlands, stretching into the distance beyond, that's making me uneasy?

'Then you can watch telly, if you like, while I spruce up my looks. Which colour would you prefer Mummy's hair to be?' I ask him. 'Red, blonde or black?'

'Red!' he shouts, and we grin at each other.

In the back garden, Charlie plays on the slide for a few minutes and then discovers a small plastic ball in one corner, which he tries - not entirely successfully - to kick about the long, overgrown grass.

It's not quite as idyllic outside as it looked through the kitchen window. For starters, the narrow lawn badly needs to be mown, and the flower beds on either side could do with being weeded, as too many of the bright summer annuals are peeping through clumps of dandelions. There's a small shed down the bottom of the garden, where I may find a lawn-mower. Though at the moment Charlie is in seventh heaven and doesn't seem bothered by the untidiness of his surroundings. There was no garden at the last place, so the local park and the back of the nursery were the only green spaces where he got to run about freely. But keeping the lawn mown and the garden weeded would be another way to avoid unwanted attention. 'Hey, I'm just like everyone else,' would be the message generated by a tidy back garden.

I stroll about the place while Charlie's playing, my hands thrust into the back pockets of my jeans, trying to get a feel for the place and my new neighbours without making it too obvious that I'm studying the backs of their houses.

There are a few houses and then the pub and shop to my right. That's the way we walked into the village last night. The other way, which we haven't yet explored, has only two big houses and then nothing. A roadway, perhaps?

I really need to study the map and get my bearings. Just in case we need to make a hurried escape. Though where on earth I would run to next, I can no longer imagine.

Perhaps Patricia was right to suggest a walk for me and Charlie. It would be an ideal way to explore where we've ended up without arousing suspicion. The sun is strong today but so long as we avoid midday, and aren't out longer than about forty minutes, it should be all right. Thankfully, I threw a bottle of kiddies' sun block into my bag during that frantic packing scramble yesterday, so Charlie, whose skin is sensitive, shouldn't get burnt.

At the very end of the garden, I stop and look out over the waist-high wire fencing at rough moorland, sunlit clumps of green and brown tangled undergrowth, with low, stunted trees and thorny shrubs here and there.

I can't see the sea from here, but there's a sense of wide-open space and expansiveness, something I never experienced in London. In the far distance, which I can only make out by shielding my eyes and squinting, the land just seems to stop, and there's a hazy blue border line that lightens into white higher up. Is that the Atlantic Ocean or merely more sky?

When I turn to glance back up at the house, perhaps moving too quickly, I suffer an unexpected attack of dizziness. It's like the whole world shuffles sideways, like a horse shaking off flies. I stagger with it, struggling to stay upright, the sun suddenly too bright.

Vertigo.

Charlie is shouting something, but my head is spinning and his voice sounds oddly muffled, as though I'm listening to him underwater.

'Mummy! Mummy!' His voice is so familiar, so high-pitched ... I blink down at him, confused and off-balance. But there's no time to take apart what I'm thinking; Charlie's found me and is tugging on my hand, desperate for my attention. 'Mummy! Found something! Found something!'

'What ... What have you found?' I ask automatically, though I'm a little nauseous and am having trouble focusing on the blurred pale oval of his face.

My chest feels tight too, and it occurs to me that perhaps I'm having a panic attack. Though why now is beyond me; I've been in far worse situations recently and not panicked. Perhaps this is my body finally rebelling against the insane stresses of the past twenty-four hours. That would certainly make sense. Though maybe it's just this hot, dry weather, taking its toll on me at last. We haven't had rain in several weeks and, while summer is my favourite season, the unrelenting heat has grown unbearable these past few days.

'Come see,' Charlie says indistinctively, dragging me forward. I stumble after him, trying to shake off my strange dizzy fit. 'Quick, quick, come here!'

Near the back of the house, he drops to the ground beside an odd lumpy shape in the grass. I can tell he's already been tearing at it; there are wisps of straw-like grass everywhere, the turf disturbed. Beneath a shroud of woven grass, a dark shape partly shows through, curving in its moulded burial-place, hard edges gleaming in the sun.

I know what it is before he finishes uncovering it, some sixth sense guiding me. A child's tricycle, the once-red frame peeling, the wheels sadly deflated.

'Bike.' Charlie looks delighted, despite the tricycle's poor condition. He tugs but it's caught fast in its shroud. I help him, breaking the stringy grass with an effort, and finally, with one last, breathless pull, both of us trying together, the rusty old thing is free. He kneels back and wipes green-stained hands on his T-shirt, a satisfied smile on his face. 'Mine.'

'Oh, darling, I don't think you'll be able to ride it.' Studying his buried treasure, I shake my head regretfully. 'Look at all that rust. And the wheels are bent out of shape. It could be dangerous. No, it's only fit for the bin.'

'No,' he wails, and starts to cry.

'Hey, don't be silly, it's not the end of the world.' I hug him, loving how Charlie's small body melts instinctively into mine, seeking solace, his fair curls tickling my chin. I hate seeing him so upset, especially when it's my fault. 'Listen, maybe I could buy you a tricycle when we go to town. There must be somewhere local that sells them.' I think of the thick wad of notes inside that envelope on the coffee table. No good for online deliveries, but perfect for untraceable cash payments. We might even be able to pay to get a tricycle delivered, which would save me a lot of bother. 'A shiny new one. Would you like that?'

He nods enthusiastically, his tears rapidly drying.

I glance about this overgrown area of the garden, assessing its potential. Maybe I could find a garden centre locally and buy some plants and seeds too. I'm sure they would deliver. It would be good to try my hand at tidying up the garden.

'This place could do with a bit of attention. Would you like to help me do some gardening?' I ask, and laugh when he jumps up, instantly ready to start digging and weeding. 'Not right now. It's a bit too hot, don't you think? And I'll need to buy you a trowel.'

When he runs back to his slide, my gaze moves to the rickety old shed. Maybe there are tools in there. In fact, I'm willing to bet there are. I can imagine them now. A dusty lawn mower, along with an assortment of ancient spades and garden forks, buckets, twine ...

The image is so strong in my mind that when I open the door – thankfully not locked – it's almost a shock to find the place empty, except for a newish-looking, electric strimmer.

'Oh.' I pick up the strimmer, flecked with dried grass and with an impressively long cable, and examine it. 'Hmm, seems simple enough to use,' I say, mostly to myself as Charlie is no longer listening. 'Probably need to plug it into the kitchen and run the cable out of the window.' I glance back at the house in that moment, and sunlight bounces off the dusty top window at the back. The window to the padlocked bedroom. I blink, dazzled, and shield my eyes. 'God, that sun ... I feel so ... '

I open my eyes to find Charlie bending over me, concern in his flushed face. 'Mummy? Mummy, you all right?'

'What?' My mouth is dry and I feel truly peculiar; I'm on my back on the grass, staring up into a cloudless blue sky. How the hell did I get here? One minute I was looking at the strimmer, and the next ... Actually, I can't remember what I did next. 'What ... what happened?'

'You falled over.'

'Oh my God.' I struggle to sit up and he crouches, watching me, his eyes wide. 'I'm sorry, sweetheart. Don't be scared. Mummy's just tired, that's all.'

Though in fact I slept heavily last night. The deep, dreamless sleep of the exhausted.

'Time go bed?'

I laugh shakily, pulling a stray leaf out of my hair. 'No, I'm fine, I don't need to go back to bed.' Then I see his worried expression and bite my lip. 'It's okay. I'm feeling better now.' I get up and replace the strimmer – lying beside me; I must have dropped it when I fell – in the shed. 'Maybe we should go back indoors. It's ridiculously hot out here and I imagine we could both do with a drink.'

Charlie nods, pulling a face. 'Thirsty.'

'I saw chocolate milk in the fridge. Let's pour you a nice big glass, shall we? And I'd better make myself a coffee. I could do with a pick-me-up.'

Back inside, I soon feel better after a sit-down and a strong coffee. Remembering the parcel that I'd collected from Simon's front step, I leave Charlie watching cartoons on the television, and go upstairs to find it among our luggage.

Sitting on my bed, I tear the package open and stare down at a small plain black box. No note, no accompanying letter. Gingerly, I open the box and find a cheap mobile phone inside. Not in its packaging. No charging cord either. Just a phone.

46

I drop the open box on the bed and stare down at it in horror. It's clearly a burner. What the hell? Why was Simon getting a burner phone delivered?

I pick up the phone and study it, but don't turn it on. I would probably have a heart attack if it began to ring.

Replacing it in the box, I push it under the bed, and sit a while staring at nothing. I have no idea what to think. But I'm shaken.

Stumbling into the bathroom with my washbag, I cut and dye my hair, thankful that I brought my own salon scissor kit with me. It serves to distract me from Simon's inexplicable phone delivery. An hour or so later, with my newly cut hair blow-dried and gleaming red, I go downstairs to show my son.

Charlie glances round at me as I enter the room, and then stares at my red hair, temporarily distracted from the cartoons.

'What do you think?' I twirl about, letting him see my new look. 'You like it?'

He nods, but I can see he's unsure.

'It's very different, I know,' I tell him reassuringly. 'But you'll soon get used to it.'

Charlie says nothing but returns to watching the telly.

I look at myself in the wall mirror.

The difference is astonishing, I think, studying the new hairstyle with its feathery layers. I look like a completely new person. Even the other girls at the salon might struggle to recognise me on the street. Which may feel strange but is kind of the point of hiding in plain sight.

I feel relieved by this drastic change in appearance. It feels as though I've drawn down another blind against the world.

Finding the large-framed tortoiseshell glasses provided by my anonymous protector, I balance them awkwardly on my nose and return to check my reflection in the mirror.

I pull a face at myself and toss them aside.

47

Maybe it's insane of me, given that I may be wanted for murder, but I draw the line at having to wear grim plain glass spectacles to change my appearance. Besides, the tortoiseshell frames clash horribly with my red hair, and they look stupidly large now my hair is shorter. They'll only draw more attention to me.

If I get worried that the police are closing in, I can put the glasses on whenever I leave the house. As an extra disguise.

For now though, it's hashtag #nothankyou.

I tweak my feathery layers and turn this way and that, considering my reflection. I look pale, despite a new cluster of freckles across my nose, and start to wonder about my overall health. I can't help worrying about my flaky behaviour earlier too. That dizzy feeling of vertigo.

Did I actually faint out there on the lawn? I've never fainted before in my life and it's unnerving. Is there something *physically* wrong with me? That would be too awful. Right now, I need to hide out and keep Charlie safe. I can't risk registering with a doctor or going to hospital. Being unwell is out of the question.

Though it could be a *mental* illness rather than a physical one.

'No,' I mutter.

I'm not suffering from a psychosis.

But my eyes, meeting my unfamiliar reflection, don't believe me.

I didn't do it, I tell myself with silent force. I didn't kill Simon and blank it all out afterwards.

It's simply impossible.

CHAPTER SIX

Patricia Eagleton's house is immaculate, almost intimidatingly so, and decorated in muted and coordinated shades of white, mushroom and beige. It's like a show home. Nothing out of place. Its tidiness doesn't seem to suit her personal appearance, in fact, which is slightly dotty as before; too much eye-make-up and a strident red lipstick that doesn't match her pink, creased cotton dress. But she's pleasant and reassuringly ordinary, leading me into the conservatory with a beaming smile for Charlie and a promise to show him 'lots of lovely toys'.

The conservatory looks out over a neatly-kept garden – I guess she gets someone in to tend it for her, as the lawn is perfectly manicured and the bright summer bedding stands in regimented lines – bathed in sunlight for about the sixteenth day in succession. The marble-look flooring is spotless, like you could eat your dinner off it, and I feel almost guilty as Charlie drags toy after toy out from the treasure chest of goodies she shows him, scattering them about her tidy conservatory.

While she's in the kitchen, I spot a Daily Mail on one of the wicker conservatory chairs and grab it up, flicking frantically through the pages for any mention of Simon.

It's yesterday's newspaper, so early days yet. And I'm not sure what I expect to find, anyway. 'GRUESOME MURDER OF HAIRDRESSER'S BOYFRIEND' perhaps.

But there's nothing.

Of course, it's not that big a story. People get murdered quite frequently in London. It might make a local online newspaper, but not one of the nationals.

Not yet, at any rate. Not until they have someone to hunt for the murder, I'd guess.

Which would be me.

Last night, I finally gave into temptation and broke the rules by turning on my laptop. Using my mobile hotspot and a VPN, which allows me to browse 'privately' so nobody can find my location or identity – though, frankly, I'm not convinced that any online search can ever really be completely secure – I scoured online news reports and forums for murders in London, recent deaths, even obituaries. It's unlikely the news would have made it into the public domain so quickly, but it can't be long.

Unless nobody has found him yet.

The thought of Simon's body sitting undiscovered in that silent, empty house fills me with horror. It's so disrespectful, somehow. His body ought to be cared for, cleaned and buried, presumably by his family. Not that he ever spoke to me about his family, apart from his recently deceased mother. I hadn't liked to pry and, besides, we had already known each other so briefly.

Having searched unsuccessfully for any evidence that Simon's remains have been found, I then took a few minutes to google our immediate area, just to see what kind of shops we have in the nearest towns. It's a bit of a lean area where shopping is concerned, but it seems Barnstaple is the nearest large town, and it's possible to catch a bus from the village that eventually ends up there. Though the journey looks over-long for a restless three-year-old.

She brings us fresh-brewed morning coffee on a tray with a plate of biscuits, plus a carton of juice for Charlie. 'How are you settling in, dear?'

'Very well, thank you,' I say with careful restraint.

I have to stop breaking the rules.

DON'T TALK TO ANYONE IF YOU CAN AVOID IT.

Patricia pours the tea and passes me a cup with a saucer, all very quaint. 'There you go, dear.' Her gaze rests on my red hair again, which she'd studied without comment on finding us on the doorstep. Now she nods, smiling. 'I love your new look. That's the spirit. New place, new you. And you've cut it very professionally.'

Without thinking, I say, 'I'm a hairdresser,' and then fall silent, wishing I could bite my tongue out.

She catches my stricken look and misinterprets it. 'Didn't go well? Don't worry, you're so young, there's plenty of time to start again in a new career. When I was about your age, I got in a muddle too. It took me ten long years to find out what I wanted to do with my life. But I got there in the end, and managed to enjoy two more decades of productive work.'

Hurriedly, I switch the focus to her, smiling. 'What kind of job did you do? I mean, I presume you're retired?'

'Oh yes,' she agrees, settling back in her wicker chair to watch Charlie play with a yellow plastic truck, her look indulgent. 'I have a reasonable work pension, and this house is all paid for. I worked as a civil servant, you see. A government employee.' She sees my look of surprise and laughs. 'I know, it does sound rather boring. But I wanted to do some good with my life. To be of service.' She pauses, then adds more gently, 'That's why I enjoy helping out at the church, I suppose. I may be retired, but I still want to help people.'

'I'm not much of a church-goer, I'm afraid,' I say awkwardly, not wanting to be rude to this woman in her own home. Not when she's been so kind.

'Of course not. So few young people are these days.' She reaches across to hand me the plate of biscuits. 'To be honest, I'm not a believer myself.'

'Sorry?'

She laughs again at my expression. 'I know, crazy, isn't it? I would never say that to any of the others, of course. But it's about community. That, and being of service to others. The God stuff I can live without, between you and me. But it comes with the territory ... ' She tails off, her gaze on Charlie's curly fair head,

51

bent now as he rummages in the depths of the toy chest. Her sigh is heartfelt. 'It's so lovely to have a child about the house again. Makes me feel years younger. You will tell me if you need a babysitter, won't you? I promise I'm not an ogre or a child-snatcher. I'll take good care of your boy.'

'Of course,' I say automatically, though I'm still not sure about her.

'It's funny, you being a hairdresser,' she remarks in an off-the-cuff way, and sips her tea contemplatively, still looking at Charlie.

I smile. 'Oh?'

I'm half-expecting her to ask for a haircut, or advice on her current styling, as this is one of the most frequent responses to me telling people I'm a hairdresser.

'It used to be a hairdressing salon,' she says, nodding through the conservatory windows in the direction of our house. 'Where you live, I mean.'

'*What?*'

She looks at me then, perhaps startled by my tone. 'Erm, yes. Now, let's see ... We moved in about fifteen years ago, and the sign above the shop was still up then. About a year later, it was renovated. The owners turned the place into a holiday home for a few years. And the sign disappeared. But yes, it was a salon once. Odd coincidence.'

I stare at her in disbelief, my brain clicking through what she's said and what it could possibly mean. The house used to be a *salon*?

'Yes,' I manage, and feel myself shiver despite the hot weather. 'Very odd.'

'I seem to recall there was some kind of bad business around the time it closed. But I don't know any of the details.'

I say nothing, still struggling against the shock that's creeping slowly through my bones now like ice-water.

A moment later, Patricia changes the subject, asking what kinds of food Charlie enjoys, and talking cheerfully about her own grandchildren, and their funny little likes and dislikes.

But it feels again like someone's walking over my grave.

It's hard not to become a little paranoid, given the circumstances. I've always resented the power the unknown person at the other end of the phone holds over my life, even while I acknowledge how vital a role he's played in keeping me and Charlie safe and together.

Perhaps it is that rare thing, a genuine coincidence. But to my bewildered brain, this seems more like a cruel joke at my expense. Or a message of some kind, perhaps.

Though if it *is* a message, what is my guardian angel trying to tell me?

As soon as I kick the side door shut behind us, I know that something has changed during our absence. The house is somehow different, yet I can't see anything out of place.

Has someone been here while we were out?

I stand motionless in the kitchen, peering warily about while Charlie deposits his favourite new acquisition–a large plastic dumper truck–on the floor with a clatter. He turns, holding up both arms, and requests the two boxes of toys Patricia pressed on us when we were leaving her house.

I place the toy boxes on the floor beside him. 'Have a look see what's in there,' I tell Charlie with forced cheeriness, and then walk into the living room, hoping he won't follow.

The curtains are still shut tight, as they have been ever since we arrived here, the living room shrouded in a glimmering half-light, strange bulky shapes littering the place.

My heart thuds.

'Hello?' Tentatively, I click on the light.

There's nobody there. But the living room is full of black binbags and taped-up cardboard boxes, none of them marked or identified in anyway.

I rip off the brown tape sealing one tall cardboard box, open it, and peer inside. I can see plates, cutlery, kitchenware, all partially wrapped in newspaper for safety.

Our possessions have arrived from the London flat.

This delivery must have been coordinated while we were next-door, having coffee with Patricia. Which confirms my suspicions that somebody is watching the house. Or has been, at any rate. Otherwise, how would they have known when to get in and out unseen?

And whoever it was has a key.

Trying not to dwell on that terrifying fact, I tear open one bulging black binbag and instantly recognise shoes and clothes inside that belong to Charlie. His Spiderman pyjamas and matching slippers have been rolled up with one of my old winter coats. Below these are some jumpers and a pair of jeans that I couldn't fit in my overnight bag.

As I'm sorting these out, Charlie comes running into the living room and stops dead, staring in wonder at this treasure trove of bags and boxes.

'Wow!' This is his new favourite word since Patricia said it several times while he was demonstrating how to kick a football. 'Wow!' His eyes widen, and he dashes forward, pouncing joyfully on his alternative pyjamas and slippers. 'Piderman!'

'Yes, all our things have arrived from London. Isn't that nice?' Since he doesn't seem curious about how they got here, and I have zero explanation for it myself, I don't comment further. 'All this may take a while to sort out, I'm afraid. Will you be all right to play with your new toys on your own in the kitchen? Just while Mummy takes these clothes up to the bedroom.'

He nods without concern, holding up a commando figure in military gear donated by Patricia. 'Action man!'

'Lovely,' I say, chewing on my lip.

It's probably too sophisticated a toy for a three-year-old, besides being a bit macho for my tastes. But trying to part him from it would only risk hysterics, so I smile and let him keep the action man.

Better to remove it later while he's sleeping or distracted by something else, and hope he forgets. Though maybe I'm worrying too much.

While Charlie is busy enacting war games in the kitchen, I carry up several heavy bags of clothing to our bedroom and begin putting them away in our designated drawers. All the time though, I'm wondering who collected and packed these things from our small London flat? Who let themselves in with their own key and did anyone see them do it? And how would they have explained who they were and what they were doing if spotted and interrogated by one of my nosy neighbours?

There was no landlord or landlady to contact when I left the flat, of course. Nor any utility or other bills to finalise. Ever since the incident in Coventry – which is how I prefer to think of the first time this happened – the anonymous person on the phone has taken care of all such details for me. Perhaps they even own the flat in London. That would make sense.

Once, I did try to find out who they were, when an errant bill for council tax came through the door during the first month after I moved in. But all it got me was the name of a random limited company, and I quickly chickened out of digging any deeper, in case they found out and punished me somehow.

When you live as a fugitive under an assumed name, you're always looking over your shoulder and fearing discovery. I've grown scared of spurning the safety and financial security that's been provided for me free of charge, even if I can't understand the motivation behind it.

Whoever my guardian angel is, they hold my life – and Charlie's life too – in their hands. And though I may struggle with that knowledge and curse my utter lack of agency, living this shadowy half-life is better than being separated from Charlie, possibly forever. Isn't it?

It's only much later, sitting down at last with a cup of tea and the last of the chocolate biscuits – we'll need to take a trip into town soon for more supplies – that I reach for my laptop, and realise it's not on the coffee table where I left it this morning.

Perplexed, I head back upstairs to look in the bedroom, and then check in the kitchen too, just in case I moved it without remembering.

While hunting for it in vain, I discover that my smartphone – the ordinary Pay As You Go mobile, not the special burner that I use to communicate with The Voice, which is still in the house – has vanished too. My handbag is still on the coffee table where I left it. But my mobile isn't in there anymore.

Someone has taken my phone and laptop.

And when I check under the bed for the burner phone delivered to Simon the day after he was murdered, that's gone too.

I don't need it spelled out to me further than that. I get the message. No contact with the internet.

Or else.

CHAPTER SEVEN

On Sunday morning, I take Charlie to join the playgroup at the parish hall. I don't like to think of it as Sunday school, though I know that's what it is.

It's important for us to fit in here, to not arouse suspicions.

Besides, now the initial shine of a new place has worn off, Charlie is getting bored and restless, kicking around the house and garden all day with only me for company. Since I started full-time at the salon, he's got used to seeing his little friends at nursery every week day, and I know he misses them. A boy his age needs to run about and play, and meet others like himself. Socializing, it's called. And I don't want him to miss out just because of what I ...

I stop and push that thought aside again.

I didn't kill Simon.

Or the other one. The one whose name still brings back night terrors. One minute we were laughing and kissing, the next I was waking up in his bed, only to find him dead in the next room.

He'd been murdered.

A pair of scissors plunged deep into his throat, just like Simon. Blood everywhere, just like Simon.

Only they weren't my scissors. I'd only just finished my training course in hairdressing at the time and didn't own any professional-level scissors. Though he did, of course. He was one of the hairdressing tutors on the course. So perhaps they were his, and an unknown assailant had broken in and killed him with his own scissors. That's the best explanation I can manage.

Kurt.

That was his name.

I was still eighteen at the time, and very shy after a hellish childhood in care. Kurt had been my first boyfriend since school, and the first man I'd ever let take me to bed. Though I don't think of him as a boyfriend now, if I dare think of him at all. It hurts too much to remember.

The whole class had piled into the pub that night to celebrate graduation. As the crowd broke up, Kurt unexpectedly asked me back for coffee.

I didn't intend to go that far, not with someone I'd only just met. But he was so charming and persuasive, and not bad-looking either.

I have no explanation for what happened to Kurt that night. I was a little tipsy and exhausted, and I slept all the way through after we'd made love ...

I've clung to that truth ever since.

Patricia meets us at the door to the parish hall, greeting Charlie with huge pleasure. 'Come in, both of you, please.' She ushers my son into the hall, where a small play area has been set up, with a plastic ball pit and a large floor puzzle, plus the usual trucks and boxes of toys, and a pile of kiddy picture books. 'Why don't you go and join the others, Charlie?'

He glances up at me for permission, and I nod.

'Go on, sweetheart. I'll come back for you in an hour or so.' I bend to give him a quick hug. 'Don't worry, it'll be just like nursery.'

Extricating himself from my hug, Charlie runs off at once, and I watch him with some trepidation, hoping that I've made the right decision in bringing him here.

There are seven or eight young kids already playing some kind of 'tag' game, laughing and screaming and running about the hall. Their high-pitched voices bounce around the open space, hurting my ears. Charlie joins them and the others accept him with barely any hesitation, just a few curious glances. Then the screaming and laughing begins again.

'So, you're coming into the church service with us, dear?' Patricia asks me, smiling broadly, and I feel embarrassed, having to shake my head and say no.

'Actually, I thought I'd take a quick walk about the village instead. Try to get some exercise and get a feel for the place at the same time.' I hesitate. 'I'm sorry.'

'Oh goodness, Sylvia, you have nothing to apologise for. I'm sure I wouldn't want to be cooped up inside on a lovely day like this, either. Especially when you've finally got some time to yourself.'

Patricia introduces me to two fresh-faced girls, aged about sixteen, who are tasked with looking after the juniors during the service; they assure me breathlessly that they will take good care of my son.

'Beth and Pippa are both trained in basic first aid, and Mrs Bloxley is always here in case of serious incidents.' She points out a grey-haired woman seated apart and reading a book. 'She used to run the local infant school. Headteacher, you know. It closed down years ago, of course,' she adds in a whisper. 'But she's a safe pair of hands.'

'All the same, I'd better give you my mobile number,' I say, automatically reaching for my back pocket.

But my mobile phone's not there; it was taken while I was at Patricia's house, leaving me only the burner phone that connects me to my protector. And my instinct tells me it wouldn't be safe to share that number with anyone.

'Damn,' I finish lamely, 'I left my phone at home. Perhaps I should stay with him.'

'No, go out and enjoy your walk. He'll be fine.'

I'm reassured by the sight of Charlie helping another small boy drag a piece of giant floor puzzle into place. He looks flushed and happy, and though I could stay and watch him for the whole time, I know there's really no point.

Anyway, Patricia is right; as a single mum, it's important to take advantage of this opportunity to be alone, if only for the sake of my mental health.

'Hello,' says a deep voice, and I turn to find a vicar – dog collar and all – looking me up and down with interest. 'I'm Reverend Shearsman. You must be Sylvia.' He's a lean, energetic man, somewhere in his forties, I'd guess, with short dark hair slicked over his scalp like it's been painted on, and eyes like shiny black currants. He holds out both hands in welcome. 'I've heard all about you from Patricia.'

'Goodness, Reverend, you make it sound like we've been gossiping.' Patricia gives me an embarrassed smile. 'We haven't of course. I just wanted to check it would be all right for young Charlie to join the gang here on Sundays.'

I say hurriedly, 'I'm very grateful to you both. Running about with other kids his age will help shake off his fidgets.'

The vicar pumps my hand with a firm, two-handed grip. 'Well, I'm very glad to meet you. It's good to have someone new in the village ... Someone who isn't just passing through, that is. Fresh blood is always welcome.' He has a strange, flickering smile that makes me doubt his sincerity. 'So, will you be joining us in church this morning?'

'Sylvia's not a believer,' Patricia tells him in a hushed voice, glancing nervously at the children as though this terrible admission might somehow corrupt them.

'Sorry,' I say, feeling something is needed.

'I see.' The vicar looks me up and down. 'I hope you won't be offended if I suggest a small donation towards our fund, then?' He nods at a collection box on a side table near the entrance. 'We're collecting towards repairs to the church tower. We need twenty thousand pounds, and only have seven so far. But we'll get there.'

'Of course.' I push a ten-pound note into the collection box, and the vicar's smile switches on fully.

'Thank you for your generosity.'

If only he knew where that money had come from, I think, he might not be so happy.

We follow Reverend Shearsman out of the parish hall. Several cars have pulled up in the car park under the shade of purple-headed buddleia, their sprays of tiny flowers dotted with bees and butterflies. A small plane is passing overhead, far above us; its faint, throbbing drone fills the air. I shield my eyes and squint up into the sky, the sunshine strikingly hot on my bare arms and shoulders after the cool interior.

'I hope you'll reconsider joining today's service,' the vicar says. 'It's a good way to meet new people in a small place like this.'

I look away, not sure how to respond. The last thing I want to do is meet new people. Equally though, I don't want Charlie to become a hermit.

'Maybe next time?' Patricia offers helpfully, smiling at me.

'Yes, maybe.'

Apparently satisfied by this, the two head away towards the church, already discussing today's service.

More slowly, I cross the car park in their wake, having decided to take a shortcut through the tree-lined churchyard to where a footpath begins that should lead around the back of the village. Churchyards always give me the chills, so I'm not keen on walking past the grim, straggling rows of gravestones and lichened statues of angels. But it doesn't make sense to detour along the main road simply to avoid them. Besides, it's the more recently deceased who are haunting me, not the long-dead buried beneath these barely legible Victorian and wartime memorials.

In the sticky shade of the church tower, I halt a moment to remove a hand-drawn map of the village from the back pocket of my jeans and study it.

Before my laptop was taken, I'd thankfully made a few notes on the general layout of the village and what lies immediately beyond the village boundaries, and this map is the result. I intend to use this time alone to explore Darkling Moreton without Charlie in tow. It's always a good idea to scout out the area, just in case Charlie and I ever need to leave here in a hurry, or find somewhere to hide around the village.

High above, the church bells begin to ring with an eerie clanging.

Startled, I glance up at the tower, wondering if the bells are automated or have real people on the other end of them. Campanologists, I think they're called. Bell-ringers.

As I peer up at the grey stone edifice, its square rise pointing upwards into an unblemished blue sky, my head begins to spin. I look away quickly and nearly fall, clutching the nearest gravestone to steady myself. It's the same vertigo I experienced in the garden. What's wrong with me? Is it this relentless heat? Or am I developing some kind of illness?

I blink and stumble on between the trees, fighting nausea, the map crumpled in my fist.

There are people walking towards me through the shady churchyard, presumably heading for the service. A middle-aged couple, striding briskly, followed by two elderly ladies moving at a gentler pace, heads together, chatting as they support each other.

I flick back my hair, feeling flushed and embarrassed now, my forehead damp with perspiration. Did any of them see my funny turn when the bells rang out?

I step onto a sunlit patch of grass to let the churchgoers pass, trying not to appear queasy. The middle-aged couple, in smart Sunday clothes, say nothing, though I catch a sideways glance from the woman before she looks hurriedly away. But the two old ladies are more friendly. One asks, 'Are you all right, dear?' while the other makes a sympathetic noise and smiles at me.

'Thank you, it's just the heat,' I say, smiling in return.

At last, I spot the pathway I'm looking for at the rear of the churchyard; it's overgrown and lushly green, a few feet beyond the entrance to a quiet sunlit lane. The lane is hedged with high grass banks and barely wide enough for a single vehicle. I'm pretty certain it snakes around the back of the church, past a few outlying houses, before eventually curving back to meet the main road into town where the limo dropped us off.

There's a man on foot, ahead of me, turning into the churchyard from the lane.

Again, I stop to let him pass.

He looks to be in his late sixties or early seventies, very upright and smartly clad in a cream-and-blue striped jacket, cream-coloured trousers and a Panama hat. Although he walks with a stick, I get the impression it's more for show than necessity.

To my surprise, the man turns his head to look straight at me. He's wearing dark glasses, so I can't see his eyes. But he's unsmiling.

'Good morning,' he says, in a deep, cultured voice that raises the tiny hairs on the back of my neck. 'Beautiful morning, isn't it?'

With a muttered, 'Yes,' I leave him and the churchyard behind, and follow the footpath into a green dazzle of sunlight as the bells peal out behind me.

My chest is tight, and my heart is thumping like a wild thing in a trap. I can't seem to catch my breath. I look ahead and see nothing but light.

That old man has no idea who I am, so why am I reading more into that simple greeting than is probably there? What's happening to me? Am I losing my mind? It wouldn't surprise me; things have been super-stressful since I found Simon's body and we had to flee London. But I can't afford to crumble under the pressure. Not now that it's not just myself. I have to hold it together for Charlie's sake.

That's why I'm here in Darkling Moreton, after all. To keep Charlie safe. To prevent the two of us being split apart by the fallout from Simon's murder.

Though if I'm really to blame for murdering two men now, is it such a good thing to keep Charlie close?

What if I'm like Jekyll and Hyde?

What if I have an alternative personality buried deep inside myself?

I don't remember much about my birth parents or my early childhood. Just vague memories. Flashes of light and colour. All I know for sure is that I've spent most of my life either in care or with foster parents. Something may have happened to me as a small child that made me a killer. Only I don't know anything about it, because whenever I try to remember, my brain blocks it out.

Which means, I could get triggered to flip personalities at any moment, blank out again ... and *kill my own son*.

Shivering inside, I push that old fear away again, determined not to give into dark, sinister suspicions that make no sense.

I didn't do it. I didn't kill either of them. Not Simon. Not Kurt.

I feel it in my bones.

I'm innocent.

But somebody murdered them, that's not in dispute. I saw their bodies; I removed the bloodied scissors and disposed of them, afraid they might eventually lead the police back to me. And whoever his killer was, they must know that Charlie exists.

If they've been watching me closely enough to spot when I'm dating again, how could they not know about my son?

Or that Kurt was Charlie's father.

Dead Kurt.

Kurt with the hairdressing scissors in his throat ...

CHAPTER EIGHT

The footpath winds its narrow way through greenish-brown, idyllic countryside, rough moorland stretching as far as I can see on one side, and the quiet, tree-shrouded village on the other.

Darkling Moreton.

I look back at the village, unable to shake off my bizarre and enduring sense of unease. Why bring me somewhere like this? Somewhere so small and claustrophobic?

It's a question that's been bugging me ever since we arrived, and it's growing more insistent by the day. The outskirts of London felt like a logical choice after the incident in Coventry; harder to find someone in a big city, easier to blend in and disappear. But there'll be no 'blending in' here. So why deliberately choose to rehome me somewhere so parochial and insular that I'm immediately conspicuous as a newcomer? Or is this considered 'hiding in plain sight'?

Of course, it's possible the police haven't yet made a connection between me and Simon's death, just as they failed to do when Kurt was murdered. At least, I never found any evidence online that they considered me a suspect back then. Though that may have been because I found no mention of his death, over months of searching the internet, or even of his presence on the hairdressing course.

Kurt had simply ceased to exist online, even while his baby grew inside me, a constant reminder of the mistake I made that night …

There must be a reason I've been brought here to Darkling Moreton, of all unlikely places to conceal a suspected double-murderer.

I just have no idea what it is.

A short walk from the church, I come across a narrow stream half-hidden by foliage. I stop and sit there for a while in the shade of a gnarled old tree, watching the water glide by, its treacly surface speckled with white blossoms. I can hear birds calling to each other, and the faint chirrup of crickets all around me, and I realise how long it's been since I was alone. Properly alone, with not even Charlie to look after.

It's so peaceful, the horror of what happened back in London begins to feel unreal and far off, like it can't touch me here. I close my eyes and try not to think too hard, just to be in nature and let the tension drain out of me.

Eventually, feeling calmer and more centred, I get up and continue along the dusty footpath. Without my phone, I have no idea of the time.

There's a wooden stile ahead, close to a thick patch of woodland. I clamber over it and follow the winding footpath through trees, glad of the cool from their leafy canopy.

After about five minutes' walk, a high wall looms to my right, roughly eight foot in height and topped with jagged glass. I catch glimpses of roofs and more walls at intervals beyond it. Somebody's house, I guess, though it looks to be like quite a large property. The path runs alongside this wall for a few hundred feet before emerging abruptly into full, bee-rich sunshine, where I stop, blinking.

I must have circled back to the single-track lane I saw before.

I hesitate, unsure of the time and whether I should head a little further out in the direction of the main road or return to the village.

Taking a few steps across the lane into shade, I produce my crumpled, hand-drawn map once more and begin to study it.

An explosion of barking behind me makes me jump and whirl around.

The high wall on my right has ended in a pair of tall iron gates, closed against intruders. Behind these gates, two large and bristling German Shepherds have appeared, barking at me with ferocious intensity. My heart thuds fast and I can't help backing away slightly. One of my foster dads bred Rottweilers, and after I'd been bitten a few times, I learned to avoid them. I don't mind dogs though, in general; even guard dogs can be perfectly friendly once assured you're no threat.

All the same, I check the gate warily, hoping the dogs can't get out, or that their owner comes out to control their behaviour.

'Good doggies,' I say in a light voice, and grimace when the German Shepherds simply snap their jaws at me.

Putting away the map, I decide to head back to the heart of the village. It's been nearly an hour and I think that's long enough for Charlie to be socialising, especially on his first time without me in a strange place.

I glance curiously through the iron gates on my way past.

The first thing I register is how immense the house is; very posh and intimidating, it's built of old red brick with a mass of chimneys and windows, like a stately home in miniature. The porched entrance has three broad white steps up to the front door, supported by two ivy-smothered columns. A charcoal-grey BMW sits on the gravelled drive beside a jumble of terracotta pots and urns filled with tumbling pink, white and red geraniums. On the top step of the porch, a black cat stares at me unblinking, its tail wrapped about its paws.

The snarling dogs are not outside alone, I realise with a start.

There's a man in the garden too, on his knees in dark overalls and an apron, weeding a summer border thick with riotous colour. He's heavy-set and balding, only a few strands of hair covering a sunburnt scalp. He turns, no doubt to see what the dogs are barking at, and shields his eyes with a gloved hand to stare at me.

I stop awkwardly, thinking he's about to say something, and sunlight flashes off glass as a window opens, high up on the second storey.

I glance that way automatically.

A figure ducks out of sight as soon as I look up at the window. I catch the quick movement and the sway of curtains, but nothing more.

Was somebody up there also watching me? Weird. But I suppose Darkling Moreton is a small, rural village and there aren't many strangers to gawk at here.

'Good morning,' I say to the man in the garden.

He doesn't reply, still staring at me from behind a raised hand while the two dogs snarl and bark through the iron bars of the gate.

I walk on, uneasy.

For the last half-hour of the session, I sit and watch Charlie play at the Sunday school, and afterwards thank the helpers for looking after him. Walking home, my son seems happy but tired out, stumbling occasionally, his fair head hanging and his arms limp.

'Did you enjoy yourself playing with the other kids?' I ask. 'Was it fun?'

'Fun,' Charlie repeats, nodding, but his feet are dragging.

I head for the village shop on our way back, intending to do some shopping for lunch. But although it was open earlier in the day, presumably to sell Sunday newspapers, it's shut now. So I'll need to drop in there tomorrow instead to top up our basic supplies: bread, milk, eggs.

Charlie, spotting a shiny red football in the window, perks up. He's also keen to visit the shop, no doubt hoping I will buy it for him. 'Please, Mummy? Please?"

Kicking a ball seems to be his new thing, so why not? I love to see his face light up with delight whenever his foot makes contact with a ball; not so long ago, he used to miss the football completely and get so frustrated, poor little man.

I say, 'All right,' and he smiles up at me innocently. 'Tomorrow, when it's open.'

I'm not hungry, but I cook Charlie a lunch of fishfingers and chips with peas, all taken from the freezer, and insist he eats it before taking his afternoon nap.

While he's picking at his meal, I wander into the gloomy living room and stand looking at the permanently closed curtains across the shop window facing the street.

These curtains have kept us safe so far from prying eyes.

But we can't live in darkness forever.

I drag the curtains open, dazzled by the sunlight pouring in. The village street outside is silent and empty, not a soul in sight. Even those who were at church this morning have gone, the last of their cars passing us as we walked home. Everyone is at home, no doubt, eating Sunday lunch. Or enjoying a day out in this glorious sunshine.

Once my eyes have adjusted to the brightness, I look around the room and for the first time see the marks on the wall properly. Distinct blemishes and indentations where there had been units once. Shelves and mirrors and even a single basin with plumbing, judging by the shape. The shop walls must have been papered over years ago. Somebody slapped fresh paint on top later. But with sunlight drenching the room, I can still see the scars. I walk around, slowly running my fingers over the old marks, ridges and bumps in the wall that tell me so much.

Patricia was right; this place almost certainly used to be a hairdressing salon. One of those bijou village salons run by one person, probably with the help of an assistant or apprentice. Haircuts by appointment only. Which might seem innocent enough to most people. Hairdressers are considered cheerful, chatty people. Except I'm a hairdresser, and both Kurt and Simon were stabbed to death with a pair of professional hairdressing scissors. So we're not all harmless gossips.

Why bring me all the way out here, only to hide me in a former salon?

Is this a sick joke?

That night, I have an incredibly vivid dream, all the colours popping, the sound realistic, and a strong sense of genuinely being there. I'm at the bottom of a long, narrow flight of stairs, gazing up into semi-darkness. Something seems to be

69

calling me to go up, so I start climbing the stairs, slowly and with painstaking care, my gaze fixed on my bare feet.

At last, I reach the top, and look around, and that's when I realise where I am.

I'm standing alone on the upstairs landing in the house at Darkling Moreton. I can even hear Charlie's soft breathing from the bedroom behind me.

Only I'm facing the wrong way.

The locked room is ahead of me, at the far end of the landing.

Except the door's not padlocked anymore.

In fact, it's not even shut, but slightly ajar; an invitation the dream-me can't turn down, where the awake-me would definitely manage to resist.

As I creep towards the room, the door creaks slowly open, like something from a horror movie. There's a hooded figure on the threshold, and as I watch, they hoist something in the air. Something that gleams in the half-light through the landing window. I can't see it properly but my instincts tell me what it is.

A pair of scissors.

I back away, screaming and screaming, but as usual in nightmares, I can't seem to make a sound or escape. The figure comes towards me inexorably.

I can't see the face under the dark hood. It's just an empty space. But they're going to kill me, I know it.

My scream goes on and on, and eventually turns into a more familiar sound.

It's the ring tone of the burner phone, sitting on the bedside table a few inches from my pillow.

I sit up, breathless and sweating.

It's already light outside, and Charlie isn't in his bed any more.

I must have overslept.

Still disorientated from my nightmare, my mouth and throat dry as sandpaper, I snatch up the phone. 'H-Hello?'

'Turn on the news.'

It's the robotic voice again, my anonymous guardian angel.

70

The line goes dead.

What the hell?

I drop the phone and stagger downstairs, barefoot and still in my PJ's, noting on my way that the other room is shut, padlocked and secure. Just as it was when I went to bed.

I find Charlie on the floor in the living room, bashing two of his new dumper trucks together while making noises like a growling diesel engine.

He looks around at me in surprise. 'Hello, Mummy.'

'Morning, sweetheart,' I say, rummaging urgently for the remote control among the debris on the coffee table.

'Breakfast time!' He jumps up.

'In a minute, darling. Hang on.' At last, I locate the remote control. 'Mummy has to check something on the television. Then toast and jam, how about that?'

'St'by jam?'

'Yes, strawberry jam. Not a problem.'

The place is a mess and my head's pounding. Among the items in the store cupboards, I'd found various bottles of alcohol – wine, gin and even some expensive Russian vodka, along with mixers. After several sleepless nights, I'd helped myself rather liberally to some gin and tonic yesterday evening, once Charlie was safely in bed. I'd watched some soppy black-and-white film from the Forties, and then staggered up to bed in the wee small hours, leaving everything on the coffee table, not drunk but 'relaxed' enough to fall asleep straight away.

It's nearly nine o'clock in the morning, I realise, with a stab of guilt. Too much gin last night, coupled with a very late night, and it's small wonder I overslept.

Bad Mummy!

Mentally apologising to my son, who's probably been up since dawn on his own, I flick through to one of the news channels, where they cycle through the same headlines every half hour, and listen impatiently to the first few stories, all largely political.

While the presenter drones on about government issues, Charlie presents me with his top three favourite trucks, and I murmur dutiful praises about each one in turn.

Then, just as I'm beginning to wonder if the anonymous voice on the phone is playing another mind trick on me, the beautifully-coiffured news presenter turns serious.

'In Breaking News,' she says sombrely, looking straight into the camera, 'the remains of a body discovered in a burnt-out car at a Surrey beauty spot three days ago have been identified as those of missing Private Investigator, Tim Shaw.'

A photograph of Simon–or the man I previously thought of as Simon–flashes up on the screen, formal in a dark suit and tie; he's smiling and shaking hands with a middle-aged woman at some kind of public event.

My heart thumps painfully at the mere sight of him.

'Mr Shaw, who was twenty-eight and a former police officer, is believed to have been working undercover on a case at the time of his disappearance last weekend. Police say investigations into his death are ongoing.'

I turn off the television as the news moves on to foreign affairs, and sink down onto the sofa, staring at the blank screen in a state of numb terror.

I barely register the relocation of his body – clearly, it was moved and incinerated to prevent suspicion falling on me. My guardian angel, hard at work again. But something must have given his identity away. Dental records? Or perhaps it was his own car that had been left to burn with him inside it. That would have been a swift way to identify him.

All I can focus on is the revelation that Simon lied to me.

He lied about everything: his name, his job, perhaps even about his elderly mother having just died. I'd only recently met him, of course, so I'd taken everything he told me at face value. But he seemed so friendly and so vulnerable too. If that was an act, I totally fell for it. He had me fooled, good and proper.

Mr Shaw, who was twenty-eight and a former police officer, is believed to have been working undercover on a case at the time of his disappearance last weekend.

When we first met, Simon told me he usually worked as a Human Resources consultant but was between jobs at the time, having taken a few months out to care for his sick mother while she was dying.

Instead, he was a former policeman and private investigator. But who on earth was he investigating when he was murdered?

It couldn't possibly be me.

Could it?

Police say investigations into his death are ongoing.

Those final words are branded into my memory in letters of fire. I keep thinking of the phone, the one I found in the parcel delivered to him on the morning after his death. Who sent it to him? Perhaps his employers or a colleague. A burner phone that he could use to exchange secret messages with someone about the subject of his latest undercover investigation.

Was that me?

My heart thumps erratically and I can't seem to relax, not even when Charlie tugs on my arm and asks me to make his breakfast.

'Hungry, Mummy.'

'Sorry, darling, yes,' I tell him, and stumble into the kitchen only to remember that we're out of bread, because I haven't been to the shop yet. There's no milk for cereal either. 'How about bacon and eggs instead?' I ask him, peering into the fridge. 'I've got plenty of that.'

Charlie's lip quivers. 'Toast and st'by jam.'

'Well, if you wait fifteen minutes while I get ready, I can pop to the shops for bread and milk.' I force myself to smile, to sound normal, though my mind is racing. 'You'll have to come too, of course.' When he claps his hands excitedly, I add, 'We'd better change into outdoor clothes, then. Can't be seen wandering the village in our jim-jams, can we?'

Charlie giggles and runs upstairs ahead of me.

Nauseous and light-headed, I lean over the kitchen table and struggle to get my breath back.

It didn't feel real before.

Finding Simon dead like that. Packing up our things in terror. The seemingly endless limousine drive into darkness. This empty house in a quiet Devon village.

A fresh start in a new place.

All over again.

Only this time, they're going to find me, aren't they? I feel it in my gut. The police won't stop looking. It's not like it was with Kurt, where his entire existence was simply spirited away, no questions asked. Simon – or rather, Tim Shaw, according to the news - used to be one of them, and the police always look after their own. They're going to track me down and arrest me, and then lock me up for murder.

Nobody will believe I didn't do it.

Because I ran.

I fled immediately after a man's violent murder, leaving no trace behind, and somebody else disposed of the body for me.

It won't matter what I say or how I try to explain my actions. As soon as the police catch up with me, I'm going to look guilty as hell.

And the most frightening thing out of all that?

It's just possible I am.

CHAPTER NINE

When we leave the house, there's a well-built bloke I don't recognise whistling as he pushes a bicycle a few hundred yards down the street. He looks to be delivering leaflets out of a bag strung over his shoulder. While Charlie crouches to pick a dandelion, I pause to check what the stranger is up to. He drops his bike to the ground, heads through the gate into the posh, faux-Tudor house that calls itself The Grange, and pushes a leaflet through the letter box, seemingly unfazed by the dog barking ferociously inside.

The other way, a large, dark SUV is parked near the turn to the church. It's got blacked-out windows, so I can't see if there's anyone inside. I glance at the car curiously in passing and then look away, trying to pretend I haven't noticed it. There's no point drawing attention to myself.

Probably just someone visiting the church, I tell myself. But I can't help feeling uneasy.

I take Charlie to the village shop and ask the beaming woman behind the counter if she can fetch the football from the shop window for us. While she's getting it, I grab up a wholemeal loaf and some full fat milk, a selection of fruit and salad vegetables, and a few other fresh food items we might need.

One of the tabloids on the newspaper stand has the same photograph of Simon on their front page they showed on television last night.

My heart racing, I snatch it up, fold it over so the photo isn't showing, and bundle it into my wire basket with the rest of the shopping.

'Here you go, my love,' the woman says in a warm Devon accent, coming back with the football. She hands it to Charlie with a smile before slipping back behind the counter. 'On holiday, are you?'

Briefly, I explain that we've just moved to the village. But when I mention the former salon, her smile fades and her gaze runs over me in undisguised hostility. 'Tenants, is it?'

'That's right.'

Her eyes narrow on my face. 'You got work in the area? Is that why you're here?'

'Not yet.'

'I see.' She rings up the items and tells me the cost, her tone definitely unfriendly now. 'Will you be needing one of our bags-for-life? The cost two pounds, made of jute.' When I nod, she hands me one, her gaze on Charlie now. 'Your boy must be coming up to school age. We don't have an infants school in Darkling Moreton anymore, so he'll have to bus into town every day.' She pauses, looking back at me keenly. 'Or are you not planning to stay that long?'

'I'm not sure,' I say, in a hurry to leave, packing my bag as quickly as possible. I'm dreading any further questions. Like, *where have you come from*?

When we head back out into sunshine, the SUV with the blacked-out windows is still there. I try not to look that way, monitoring Charlie as he carries the shiny, red football proudly before him, like a trophy. 'Careful not to drop it,' I warn him, but I'm distracted. The man with the bike has reached our house; he's bending to push one of his leaflets through the letter box.

Charlie fumbles the ball and it rolls into the road. Instantly, he runs after it, shrieking with laughter.

'Charlie, no!' I cry, panicking, and drop my shopping bag to run after him. 'Come back here at once.'

He pays no attention, toddling along at his usual reckless pace, his entire focus fixed on the still-rolling football. Thankfully, there are no cars coming in either direction. But it's still horrifying to imagine what might have happened if this had been a busy street.

'Oh no, you don't.' I manage to grab his hand and pull him reluctantly back to where I left my shopping. 'What have I told you about not running into the road?' I feel shaken and exasperated. My heart is still thumping violently as I scoop up our shopping bag, still holding his hand tightly so he can't run away again. 'You could have been killed.'

'Ball,' he cries, pointing.

The man with the bag of leaflets has strolled into the road and picked up the red football. He's fair-haired and well over six foot, in blue denim jeans and a plain green T-shirt. I guess him to be in his late twenties. He's muscular too, his biceps bulging. All the leafleting, I think, and suppress a smile.

He comes our way and presents the football to Charlie. 'There you go, son.'

'What do you say, Charlie?' I prompt him.

'Fank you,' Charlie says almost inaudibly, clutching the ball to his chest with obvious relief. I see him eye the man with a certain wariness, perhaps because of his height and physique.

I thank the man too. 'What are you delivering?'

Smiling, he hands me a leaflet. It's a glossy, brightly coloured advertising flyer for a handyman. NO JOB TOO SMALL. His name and mobile number are along the bottom.

'Thanks, John Foreman,' I say, reading out his name. He seems like an okay guy. No alarm bells are ringing for me, at any rate. 'You live locally, do you?'

'Not quite,' he admits, grimacing. 'I'm mobile at the moment, you could say.'

'Sorry?'

'My wife kicked me out a few months back. Now I live in a camper van. Move about, take jobs all over the county.' He gestures over his shoulder. 'I'm parked in a field the other side of the village at the moment. I know the owner, he only charges me a few quid a week. I've got some jobs lined up in the area, so I'm getting about by bike wherever possible,' he added, 'and when those jobs are done, I guess I'll move on again.'

'Living in a van sounds a bit uncomfortable.'

'It isn't one hundred percent wonderful. Especially when it comes to my shower, which is a bit on the temperamental side.' His smile turns rueful. 'But it's all I've got at the moment, so I'm not complaining. And I can always pop into the pub for a pint and a hot meal when I can't be bothered to heat myself beans on toast for the twentieth time. One of the beauties of being parked up for a few weeks ... I can have a drink in the evenings and not worry about driving. Have you been in the Last Trump yet?' He nods towards the pub. 'They have a pub quiz on Fridays. Why don't you come along?'

'Oh, I can't leave Charlie alone,' I begin to say, and then remember Patricia. 'Though I might be able to arrange a babysitter.'

'Maybe see you there, then,' John says cheerfully. We walk back towards the house, and he collects his bike. 'I don't suppose you have any odd jobs you need doing?' he adds, eyeing the facade speculatively. 'Any repainting? Plastering?'

I hesitate. 'How are you at plumbing?' When he raises his eyebrows, I explain my thought. 'This place used to be a salon, and I ... I happen to be a hairdresser.' No 'happen' about it, I think darkly, but keep that suspicion to myself. 'I was wondering if it might be possible to reconnect the plumbing. Maybe start up the salon again.'

John cups his hands to peer dubiously through the front window at what used to be the village salon but is now part of my living room. 'Bit beyond my pay grade,' he says frankly. 'Though if you want my advice, you might do better keeping your business mobile, like I do. It's so much cheaper. Hardly any overheads, and you can set your own working hours.'

'I don't understand.'

'You could offer to go to clients, do their hair at home. That's quite a popular service out in these remote Devon villages.'

78

I don't have a car, of course. Nor even a licence. Though it's possible I could find a few clients in and around Darkling Moreton, and walk to their houses, or take the bus if it's a little further. Or even get a bike and cycle around, like John does. If we were to stay here long enough …

I thank him. 'I'll think about it.'

He heads off with his bike and his bag of leaflets, and I watch as he pushes one through Patricia's letter box, and then her neighbour's, and then crosses the road.

I hesitate, still watching him, still a little wary. The car with the blacked-out windows hasn't moved. John walks past it without a single glance, gets onto his bike and cycles off down the lane towards the church car park, presumably heading back to his camper via the narrow lane on the other side of the church grounds.

Perhaps the SUV belongs to one of the villagers and I've never noticed it before. Perhaps someone who's been away since we arrived and has only just returned home.

Charlie is already in the back garden, kicking his football through the unmown grass with cheerful little cries of triumph. I'm reminded of the dire need to strim the lawn and am almost tempted to call John back and offer him the job. We've got plenty of cash, after all.

But John was a little too nice. I don't want to risk making friends again.

Not after what happened to Kurt and Simon.

DON'T TALK TO ANYONE.

'Come on,' I call to Charlie, unlocking the side door into the kitchen. 'Toast and strawberry jam for breakfast, with a nice cup of cold milk. How does that sound?'

After breakfast, Charlie goes back out to kick his new football around, and I make a cup of tea and sit down to study the newspaper story about Simon. The photograph is only accompanied by a caption and a few lines, with the main story continued inside the newspaper. Feverishly, I tear my horrified gaze from his face and thumb through the pages to find the rest. Essentially, it's the same story from the news last night. Except with a little more detail about his background, and a few quotations from the Met police team running the investigation.

'We're appealing for anyone with information on this man or anyone who might have known him, or seen him about, to contact us,' the detective's comment reads, along with a contact phone number.

I go through the article three or four times, feeling numb inside. Then I turn back to the front page and study Simon's face and the caption below, *Private Investigator, Tim Shaw, whose body was discovered in a burnt-out car. Police appeal for witnesses.*

I get up and pace back and forth, cradling my lukewarm tea. If I didn't need to look after Charlie, I'd be gulping down a glass of gin about now. Or a whole bottle.

Police appeal for witnesses.

I'm panicking now and can't think straight. Last night, it had all seemed so surreal, not touching my reality. I'd felt pretty certain I was safe enough, that nobody would put the two of us together. But is that true? And what about at his house? Someone might have seen me leaving the property, especially if I'd been looking as terrified as I'd felt inside.

Then there's our hurried departure, achieved in daylight. Could someone have seen Charlie and me walking to our rendezvous with the car that day? A limousine would have been a fairly remarkable vehicle for that area. It's possible someone might have noticed us getting into such a striking car and being driven away. A woman and a small child, with luggage.

Could the police trace the movements of a car like that, using CCTV footage on motorways? We stopped for a wee once in a wooded layby. I hadn't seen any other cars and it had been getting dark by then, but I can't be absolutely sure.

I'm washing up later, still worrying about the chances of someone having seen me and Simon together, when somebody knocks at the front door.

Knock. Knock. Knock.

Three perfectly spaced raps on the door, like a code or a pre-arranged signal, followed by silence.

My heart thumps, going into instant overdrive, and I stand motionless, holding my breath, staring into soapy water while I listen for any sound of movement.

The tap drips.

If it was the police, I would have heard a car, maybe a police radio. This is someone on foot. Someone who has come to my door quite deliberately. But it could still be a completely innocent visit; someone selling merchandise door-to-door or touting for business in the area, like the handy man, John.

I reach for a tea towel and dry my hands, still listening. Irritably, I tell myself to calm down. I'm safe enough; the front door is locked and whoever it is will go away eventually if I don't respond. I'm panicking for no reason.

But I'm wrong.

My visitor comes to the unlocked side door a moment later, knocking again and calling out, 'Hello, Sylvia?' in a friendly but determined manner.

It's a man's voice, deep, rasping and vaguely familiar too, though I can't immediately place it.

There's a long silence when I don't respond, followed by, 'I know you're there; I can see your son in the back garden.' An even creepier pause, then he asks softly, close up to the door, 'Won't you let me in, Sylvia?'

CHAPTER TEN

As I stand there in horrified silence, the visitor knocks at the door again, more insistent now. 'It's Reverend Shearsman,' he continues in the same familiar, rasping voice, as though well aware that I'm standing right on the other side of the door, listening without opening up for him. 'We met at Sunday school. You brought Charlie to us for a few hours. Do you remember?

There's no point continuing to pretend I'm not in the house. Not when he's already seen – or more likely heard – Charlie playing in the back garden.

Taking a deep breath, I pull open the door and look out at him, a fake smile ready on my lips. 'Oh, hello,' I say, screaming inside at this intrusion. What does the vicar want with me? I'm hardly one of his local flock of believers. 'Of course I remember. It's nice to see you again. Sorry about the delay opening up.' My hand tightens on the door handle as he waits expectantly for my explanation, his brows raised. 'I … I couldn't hear you over the running water.'

'No problem at all, dear lady.' Reverend Shearsman looks past me towards the sink, which is full of soapy water and dishes, and nods benignly, as if this pathetic excuse is somehow believable. Today, he's in a light blue shirt with an immaculate white dog collar, a faint sweat on his gleaming forehead. 'So sorry to disturb you.' He holds up an old biscuit tin. 'Raffle tickets.'

'Raffle tickets,' I repeat blankly.

'We're raising money for repairs to the church tower. You were generous enough to donate before, if you recall.' I'd forgotten how intent his eyes are, small and dark as currants. 'We're still short of our target and thought a raffle might help galvanise fresh interest. Two pounds a strip. Or three for a fiver.'

I nod automatically, wondering how soon I can get rid of him. 'It sounds like a good cause. When's the draw?'

'Sunday mornings after church. We plan to draw a winner most weeks. This time it will be a fresh fruit hamper, courtesy of Sheila at the village shop.' He waits, watching me. 'Are you interested?'

'Of course. Hang on.'

I turn to fetch my purse, and realise he's followed me inside without waiting to be invited.

'You don't mind my calling round like this, do you?' The vicar sits down at the kitchen table with a sigh and pushes back slick dark hair before prising off the lid of his tin. Inside are several books of coloured raffle tickets, pens and money bags. He removes some, glancing up at me. 'Be honest, now.'

'Not at all,' I lie shamelessly, handing over a five-pound-note. 'Three strips, please.'

'Excellent, thank you.' He folds three strips and begins to write on the back of them. 'Sylvia, isn't it? Forgive me, I'm not sure of your surname.'

'Smith.' I watch as he writes it down.

'I don't meet many Smiths,' he remarks, 'which is odd, isn't it? Given that it's such a common surname.' He tears off my part of the raffle tickets and hands them over. 'Patricia mentioned that you've moved down from Milton Keynes.'

'That's right.'

'How marvellous. Whereabouts were you based, exactly?' He smiles at my blank look. 'I know the town quite well. My sister lives there.'

I stare at him, caught in the treacherous dark web of the lie that's been spun for me by the stranger who dictates my every move. I've never been to Milton Keynes in my life.

'I … erm … ' Reaching for my cup, I manage to deliberately knock it over, the last third of my now cold tea running across the tabletop in a pale brown streak and dripping onto the linoleum floor. 'Oops.' I turn, hunting for a dishcloth to mop it up, and when I return, he's packed away his tin of raffle tickets and has picked up the newspaper to avoid it getting wet. 'Sorry about that.'

'Not at all. Accidents happen.'

I'd hoped to distract him with the spilt tea. But, to my horror, Reverend Shearsman glances at the newspaper, still lying open at the page I'd been reading earlier, showing the article about Simon's body discovered in the burnt-out car.

His expression changes. 'Dreadful story, isn't it?' His gaze meets mine as he passes me the newspaper. 'Poor man. I suppose they burnt out the car to conceal their crime.'

My chest is tight, my heart thumping. I can't seem to say a word, though I try to nod my agreement, to seem unaffected.

'Thank goodness that kind of thing never happens around here.' The vicar studies me, his brows tugging together as I stare back at him in silence, then his gaze drops to the spilt tea dripping noisily onto the lino. 'Your floor ...'

Hurriedly, I crouch to mop it up. 'Silly me,' I manage to say in a strangled whisper, keeping my head down. His shoes look new; they're so shiny with black polish, I catch my reflection in them, a reddish shadow without features.

'Are you all right, Sylvia?' His voice holds a vague hint of suspicion. Or is that my paranoia on overdrive again? 'You seem nervous. Are you upset about something?'

'Only about making an idiot of myself by spilling the tea.' I straighten, the soggy dishcloth dripping, and somehow dredge up a smile for him. 'Can I get you something to drink? Some fresh tea, perhaps? I should have offered before, I'm sorry.'

'No, that's very kind, but I must be on my way. More doors to knock on, more raffle tickets to sell.'

To my relief, Reverend Shearsman turns at last to leave. But he doesn't make it, hesitating on the threshold.

My nerves scream again as he glances out of the kitchen window. Charlie is still at the far end of the garden, kicking his football and shouting, 'Goal!' at the top of his voice whenever he makes contact. Which is thankfully not at every attempt.

'You're sure there's nothing you want to talk to me about?' He adds, more gently, 'Vicars aren't simply for Christmas and Sundays, if you know what I'm saying.' He looks round at me, his small eyes sharper and shinier than ever. 'I can hear your confession, if you'd like.'

'Confession?' My voice is breathless.

His smile gleams at me, almost conspiratorial. 'The act of confession isn't common in the Church of England. More of a Catholic thing, I grant you. But it is offered to those who ask, and personally, I like to get in deep with my parishioners. Really wrestle with the soul, and all that. Totally confidential, of course. You can trust me with *anything*.'

He waits, watching me as though hoping for more, but then shrugs in a disappointed manner when I say nothing.

'Well, the offer stands. Raffle draw after church on Sunday, remember. Take care of yourself, my dear.' He pauses, his smile somehow sinister. 'And little Charlie too.'

Once he's gone, I close the side door and lean against it, numb and exhausted by fear.

I can hear your confession, if you'd like.

It's too much of a coincidence, an offer like that, given my situation, my inner turmoil. What does he know about me? Does he know about my past? The killings? The body in the burnt-out car? Did he come round here deliberately to frighten me into a confession he could then use to threaten or destroy me?

No, that's impossible.

He's just the vicar, I tell myself.

Reverend Shearsman.

I see again his polite, smiling face in my mind's eye, the gleaming forehead, his surprise when I spilt the tea …

I'm going mad, that's what it is. I'm seeing enemies on every street corner, suspicion in every face. The vicar merely spotted my nervousness and misinterpreted it, thinking I have something on my mind. And he's not wrong.

I sag against the door, trembling as my unused burst of adrenalin slowly drains away. I can't go on like this, hiding away from the world like a pariah, constantly pretending to be someone I'm not, and jumping every time there's a knock at the door.

Wouldn't it be easier simply to give myself up?

One phone call to the police and all this would be over. Though then I would have to explain what had happened, face any number of terrifying interviews and court proceedings, and probably jail time too. And if they found me guilty of murder, even though I have no memory of killing anyone, I could end up behind bars for years, perhaps even decades. A dangerous criminal. A murderess.

I'm crying, I realise, and choke down a sob. My ears are buzzing and the world feels very far away. What's happening to me? It feels as though I'm falling apart, piece by piece …

'Mummy?' I hear Charlie crying for me, his voice high and panicked.

I dash a hand across wet cheeks and hurry outside, berating myself for not being with him, for forgetting even to watch him out of the window.

He's not safe in the back garden, not on his own.

Charlie is bending over, examining his bare leg. His fair hair flops forward to hide his face. When he looks up, his lip quivers; he's been crying too.

'Baby?' I snatch him up and cuddle him. 'What's the matter?'

'Knee,' he says indistinctly, a wobble in his voice.

I check, and sure enough, there's a nasty graze on his knee. 'Oh no,' I say instantly, and carry him inside to the first aid kit. 'Did you fall over on the path?'

He nods mournfully.

'Never mind,' I tell him, trying to sound positive and cheerful, though my heart is aching. 'Mummy will soon get you patched up. I think we have sticking plasters with teddy bears on them. Would you like that?'

I'm smiling and making soothing noises all the time I'm cleaning his graze and gently applying antiseptic cream before rummaging in the first aid kit for the child-friendly teddy bear plasters. But my mind is elsewhere, in a dark and lonely place.

I can't ring the police and hand myself in as a potential murderer. How could I do that to my son?

Charlie would be taken into care.

The thought of my darling boy being sent to live with complete strangers turns my stomach. I grew up in care, and I'm not going to inflict that same horror and torment on my own child. Not while I have breath in my body.

The stranger on the end of the phone will keep me and Charlie safe, I tell myself, and try hard to believe it.

All I need do is to bloody well stop deviating from their instructions.

It's late afternoon when a black motorbike pulls up noisily outside, disturbing the village peace, and a man in leathers and closed visor comes to the front door.

'Special delivery,' he shouts indistinctly through the letter box. Unsure whether or not I should respond, I wait a moment out of sight, and he thumps on the front door with a gloved fist, repeating, 'Special delivery for Ms Smith.'

I unlock the door and stare at him, bemused.

Sunlight bounces off his visor as he holds out a small, plastic-wrapped package. 'Ms Smith?'

I nod and take the package.

The delivery rider strides back to his bike without another word, and within seconds has roared out of the village again.

I glance up and down the street, but nobody is about. The car with the blacked-out windows is still parked near the church.

I close the door, lock it again, and tear open the package. The contents spill out across the living room carpet. A passport in my new name. And more cash. I crouch, gathering it hurriedly together. There's at least a thousand pounds there, mostly in twenty-pound-notes.

I flick through the passport, pausing at my photograph. The same one as in my original passport, and my birth data is the same too. Thankfully. At least I don't have a new lie to commit to memory. But I'm in awe at the speed and apparent ease with which a fake passport has been fabricated for me.

Who could have done this? Who has the resources and contacts to organise this? Who's pulling the strings of my life, and why the hell am I considered worth protecting?

I check the packaging carefully before throwing it away.

There's no accompanying note, of course.

There's never a note.

I wake up in the dark that night, Charlie breathing softly and rhythmically close by, and sit bolt-upright, abruptly sure that there's somebody downstairs.

I pick up the torch on my bedside cabinet and slip out of bed. Creeping to the bedroom door, I open the door. It creaks slightly and I freeze, holding my breath.

There's no sound from below.

Perhaps I imagined hearing someone in the house.

Or perhaps I didn't.

There's an infinitesimal noise downstairs. Like someone taking a few steps across the living room in exactly that spot where the floorboards creak.

The hairs rise on the back of my neck. I fight the urge to turn and barricade myself in with Charlie. But that would make no sense. This isn't someone here to attack us, otherwise they would have come in hard and fast. And whoever this is got into the house without making much noise. Which suggests they have a key.

So this is something else. *Someone* else.

I tiptoe across the landing and down a few stairs, and then stop, my ears straining for any noise, however tiny.

Then I hear it.

The sound of breathing.

Someone is standing in the shadowy hall below me, not moving, but listening to me exactly as I'm listening to them.

My protector?

In one swift movement, I lean over the balcony and switch on my torch, shining a beam of light down into the hallway below.

I catch a split-second glimpse of someone all in black, a balaclava covering their face; only the glint of narrowing, startled eyes staring up at me.

Then the intruder turns and flees.

Shocked by the realisation that perhaps, after all, Charlie and I have been in real danger – since I don't get the impression that, whoever my protector is, they would turn up wearing a balaclava in the middle of the night – I stand motionless for what feels like ages, the torch beam focused on empty space. Then I creep down the stairs, not wanting to risk a confrontation but keen to ensure our visitor has definitely gone.

I put all the lights on.

To my relief, there's no intruder, but the front door is wide open. Taking a deep breath, I step out into the street and peer around. The road is dark and empty.

I turn and study the door. No sign of forced entry.

Hurrying back inside, I lock up again, even though it seems kind of pointless under the circumstances.

Unfortunately, there's no bolt on the front door to secure it more thoroughly. No doubt that's deliberate, to allow Balaclava Man or whomever to enter the house at will, using only a key.

After a moment's thought, I carry a kitchen chair through and prop it under the handle of the front door.

That should give any intruder pause, key or no key.

After running back upstairs to check on Charlie, who is still fast asleep, his breathing deep and even, I wander back downstairs in a slow weary daze, pour myself a stiff drink and collapse onto the sofa.

I'm afraid and confused and completely at a loss.

Whoever the intruder was, they must have a key, or they couldn't have got inside without forcing the door.

So it must have been my protector.

Only that doesn't make sense.

If the voice on the other end of the phone needed to speak to me, why not message me as usual, via the burner? They already specifically warned me to keep a low profile, not to draw attention to myself, and not to talk to anyone. Why risk all that by coming here in person?

It was different when someone came in and took my laptop and old phone, as well as Simon's burner parcel.

I'd broken his 'rules' by using the internet and potentially giving away our location, assuming anyone in the police is actually monitoring my sign-ins and online activity. But why bother coming back again?

Unless that wasn't my protector but somebody else entirely. Someone who just happens to have a key to this house. And if so, what were they looking for?

CHAPTER ELEVEN

My neighbour Patricia cheerfully agrees to babysit Charlie on Friday evening while I head rather uneasily down the quiet village street to the pub. I do trust Patricia to take care of Charlie – her tenderness with him is rather touching – but it's rare for me to leave him with anyone in the evening, and I have no idea how he will respond to 'bedtime' in a strange house. But I need answers and the only way I'm going to get any is to go out and ask questions.

The Last Trump is one of those small country pubs where you can imagine how everyone's head must turn each time the door opens. Tonight though, it's busier than I expect, no doubt due to the Friday Night Quiz advertised in bright colours on the chalkboard outside, along with various drinks offers.

Pushing through the old wood-panelled door into the saloon bar, I feel ridiculously exposed as people look my way, their scrutiny pointed as soon as it's obvious I'm not a regular. For tonight's outing, I've chosen a tight T-shirt paired with a knee-length black skirt instead of my usual jeans or leggings. Last time I wore it was to my hiring interview with Kriss at the salon. Not that he was ever interested, for which I was deeply grateful.

It's not particularly comfortable to be stared at, but as I scan the faces, I spot several that are familiar to me: the Reverend Shearsman sitting with Mrs Bloxley, the shop owner with a man I don't recognise, and to my relief, John, who lifts a hand in greeting.

'You made it,' the handyman says, coming across at once with a ready smile. 'I hope you're going to join my team. We desperately need a third.'

'We?'

He indicates a heavy-set man in a baseball cap standing at the bar. 'Robbie.' When I glance that way, he adds in a lower voice, 'I wasn't sure you were going to show, so I asked him to team up with me for the quiz tonight.' He grins. 'Hope you don't mind.'

'Not at all.'

We find a table and John politely offers to buy me a drink. I ask for a glass of dry white wine, though I'm determined not to drink too much tonight.

While he's gone, I study Robbie covertly. There's something familiar about him.

'Have we met?' I ask.

'I don't think so.'

His voice is deep and gravelly, somehow matching his burly figure. He removes the baseball cap with a rough, calloused hand and slicks back a few thin strands of hair that have slipped forward, exposing a balding head. Both his forehead and scalp are mottled with red blotches and darkened patches, suggesting someone who spends a great deal of time in the sun.

That's when I recognise him.

'I saw you,' I blurt out, 'in the garden of that big house at the other end of the village. Out towards the main road.'

He meets my eyes briefly, and then looks away, picking up his pint glass. 'Oh, yes?' He downs some of his pint and then wipes his mouth with the back of his hand.

I'm curious now. 'Is that your house? You live there?'

Robbie gives a short hoarse bark of laughter. 'Me?' He shakes his head. 'I wish.'

'You work there, then?'

He hesitates, looking at me, then says flatly, 'Gardener.'

'Right.' I smile up at the quiz organiser, a middle-aged woman with pink-streaked hair, who's just dumped sheets of paper and three pencils on the table. 'Thank you.'

The woman grunts something, eyeing me curiously, and then moves on.

John returns with my wine and his own drink. 'We all set? They'll be starting any minute.'

'What's our team name?'

John grinned. 'I thought, what with my handy-man status, Robbie's job, and you living in an old salon … The Clippers?'

My breath stalls in my throat. Talk about hiding in plain sight. But I manage to keep my smile steady. There's no point arousing his suspicions by drawing attention to his choice of a team name.

'Why not?' I say easily, and reach for my wine glass, wishing I'd ordered gin instead. I need something stronger than wine to steady my nerves. But I also need to keep my wits about me. I've caught Robbie eyeing me sideways a few times when he thought I wasn't looking, and I'm not sure I entirely trust him. Or John, if it comes to that. I mean, what do I really know about any of the people in this isolated little Devon village?

The quiz starts, and it's surprisingly fun to take part, racking my brain for answers. Names of pop artists. Politicians. Chemical compounds. Far-flung parts of the globe.

Mrs Bloxley and the Reverend are on the same team, just the two of them, heads bent together as they work out the answers. No Mrs Reverend that I can see.

At the end, we swop sheets to mark them, and there's a short wait before the winners are announced.

I offer to buy the next round and head for the bar. The landlord is a large fellow with a protruding gut and a cheery smile. I order another glass of white wine for myself and stand waiting while the lads' pints are poured, glancing about the saloon bar.

The quiz organiser is studying the team sheets. Behind her, three white-haired old ladies sit nursing tall glasses of something blue – gin, perhaps? – and staring straight at me, chatting busily amongst themselves. From the way their eyes widen and they look hurriedly away when I glance their way, I guess they are talking about me.

'Here you go,' the landlord says, setting the last pint in front of me on a tray. He names a figure and I pay in cash. His smile seems genuine enough as he asks, 'Anything else?'

An idea strikes me. 'I don't suppose you know anyone round here who owns a large car with blacked-out windows? One of those big recreational vehicles with huge tyres.'

He hands me my change. 'Can't say I do.' Scratching his head, he turns to the two men on bar stools at the end of the counter. 'Geoff, Paddy, you know anything about a big SUV with blacked-out windows in the village? Lady here's asking about one.'

The two men look puzzled and shake their heads. 'Sorry.'

But a comfortably-built blonde also behind the bar – possibly his wife, as they look to be about the same age – comes forward, carrying a tray of freshly-cleaned pint glasses. 'An SUV? Is it a black one?' When I nod, she smiles, beginning to put the pint glasses away on shelves under the counter. 'I've seen that car a few times myself. The driver parks up in the Sallies. I meant to mention it to you the other day, love,' she says to the landlord, confirming their relationship, 'but it slipped my mind.'

I frown. 'The Sallies?'

'Big house down the way.' She puts down the tray and gestures vaguely behind me. 'High brick wall, stone lions. Belongs to the Duckworths.'

The landlord gives her an odd look. 'Can't be Derek Duckworth driving it. They've gone out to America for the summer to visit his parents.'

His wife tuts, unpacking the tray of clean glasses onto the shelf. 'I didn't say it was Derek, did I? That's why I was going to mention it to you. The house is

94

standing empty. But whoever's got that damn great SUV keeps parking in their drive.'

'Maybe a friend of Derek's checking on the house for him,' one of the men on bar stools suggests.

They all nod wisely.

'That'll be it, I expect,' the landlord says, and nods at me. 'There you go, Miss. What did you want with the driver, anyway?'

'Oh, I just ... ' Everyone at the bar is looking my way and I feel utterly exposed. 'No reason. I was just curious.'

But he's studying me now. 'You that new tenant moved in next to Patricia Eagleton, then? In the old hairdresser's salon?'

Small villages. Nothing much happens here without everybody knowing, I think grimly.

The other people at the bar keep their eyes fixed on me as though whatever I say next may decide the fate of the entire western world.

'That's right.' My tone is noncommittal. I pick up the tray of drinks, balancing it carefully. 'Thanks.'

'We've got a photo of it, in case you're interested. From back when it was still a salon.'

'Sorry?'

He nods to the wall near where I'm standing. There's a framed photograph hanging on the wall, its colours faded.

'Photo of your house.'

I stare at it, the glasses rattling on the tray as my hand begins to tremble, one of the pints spilling a few golden drops down the side of the glass.

It's the house where I live, a snap-shot taken from across the street. The layout of the building and the little patch of lawn out front is unmistakeable. Except in this photograph it's still a hair salon with a fresh coat of paint and the shop sign – now missing – hanging above the front window.

The salon sign reads, NATASHA CUTS

There's a woman pictured in the shop doorway. A tall, shapely woman with sleek blonde hair hanging past her shoulders, one hand raised as though the sun was in her eyes. The hand slightly obscures her face.

Natasha, presumably?

There's another figure in the photograph. A small child in shorts, riding a red tricycle across the lawn. Probably a girl, judging by the slender build, but her back is turned to the camera and it's impossible to be sure.

'Oh yes, that's very interesting.' My voice is husky. 'Thanks again.' I throw the landlord and the others a quick smile and continue back to the table. 'Here you go,' I tell the other two, sliding the tray onto the table, 'drinks all round.'

'Thanks,' Robbie says, reaching for his pint.

John has been watching me, it seems. 'What was Ben saying to you?'

'Ben?'

'The landlord.' John jerks his head towards the photograph on the wall. 'Something about that picture, was it?'

'Oh.' I take a sip of my wine and lean back, crossing my legs, my air nonchalant. I see his eyes dart towards the slight glimpse of thigh revealed as my skirt rides up a notch. 'He was pointing out a bit of village memorabilia. You know how local pubs love that kind of thing.'

I glance about the saloon bar; sure enough, the walls are crowded with framed photographs, all candid snaps of Darkling Moreton buildings and residents taken over the years, some black and white, the more recent ones in colour. There are even a couple of sepia prints which look Victorian.

'It's just an old photo of the house I'm renting,' I finish with a shrug. 'You remember I told you it used to be a hairdresser's …'

'Of course.' John raises his glass, apparently having lost interest in the subject. 'Well, thanks for this. Cheers, team Clippers. Let's hope we've won.'

'Cheers,' Robbie grunts, and drinks deep.

I murmur, 'Cheers,' and take another good gulp of white wine, letting it pool in my mouth a few seconds before swallowing, enjoying the crisp, cold feel of it against my tongue and palate.

My gaze strays back to the photograph on the wall opposite our table. The pub spotlights glint off it, making it hard to see any details. But that doesn't matter; I took it all in during that one quick glance, knowing I might not have another chance to study it closely. Not without giving away my morbid interest in this place and its history.

NATASHA CUTS

So that's what the salon used to be called. Not a terribly original name, I consider, downing more wine with a sudden thirst for it. It's a bizarre choice, really.

Most salons go for something quirky or amusing, wanting to be memorable or seem more client-friendly. A pun or a joke.

Was this a joke too?

But the name Natasha had been in larger, bolder letters than 'cuts,' which suggests that the main draw for the salon had been the hairdresser herself, Natasha. Maybe she'd trained somewhere important or influential, a top-name salon in London or Birmingham, perhaps, or maybe somewhere closer like Bristol or Plymouth.

Or perhaps it was her striking looks or personality that had drawn customers to the salon. A tall, elegant blonde …

Yes, that might have been it.

The quiz organiser picks up her microphone, taps it noisily a few times to quieten down the buzz of conversation, and begins announcing the results.

I zone out, concentrating on finishing my wine in a series of restless little sips. The hairdresser was a mother too, presumably. Just like me. That child in the photograph had been playing on the lawn right outside the house, after all. Though the little girl might have come along with a customer, I suppose, and been left to play in the quiet village street while her mum got her hair done.

I wonder how old the photograph is and long to ask the landlord. But I dare not give away my interest.

Maybe on another visit to the pub, when it's quieter, I can sneak a closer look at it. There might be a date at the bottom of the picture or written on the frame. It would be good to pin down the dates when the photo was taken and discover when exactly the salon closed – and why.

'The Clippers' take second place in the quiz, which is a tin of chocolates and three free entries in the next church raffle. Robbie waves away the chocolates, looking annoyed that we didn't win the top prize, pockets his raffle ticket and bids us goodnight without a second glance.

Reverend Shearsman and Mrs Bloxley – team name 'The Tombstoners'– take First Prize.

'Typical,' a woman mutters on the next table to us.

Mrs Bloxley accepts the prize, which is cash and a bottle of whisky, and hurries back to the table. I watch in interest as she divides the cash between herself and the vicar, and then drags on her jacket and leaves, hugging the bottle of whisky close to her chest.

The vicar only stays a few minutes after she's gone, shaking hands with a few people and thanking the pub organiser. Then he too slips out into the night, after an odd glance back towards our table, his expression unreadable.

John finishes his pint and looks at my glass. 'Another?'

I check the clock behind the bar. It's gone half past ten. 'I'd better not,' I say, regretfully, as I've enjoyed the evening.

I'd forgotten how good it is to spend time with other adults. But now the quiz is over, I'm aware of a few niggling fears at the back of my mind; fears that I need to deal with alone.

Besides, I don't want to encourage him to see more into this evening at the pub than a friendly gesture.

That could be dangerous. And not just for me and Charlie.

'I left my son with our next-door neighbour. She asked me not to be back too late, as she's not much of a night owl.'

To my relief, he doesn't seem too bothered by this awkward brush-off. 'Okay, I'll walk you back then.'

'That's very gallant but you really don't need to. It's only a few hundred yards down the road.'

'All the same.' John gets up, nodding to the people at the next table who are also leaving. 'This is Darkling Moreton,' he added, shifting his gaze to mine. 'You never know what wild beasts or evil entities might be out there, roaming the streets.'

I follow him to the door, the tin of chocolates under my arm. 'Evil entities?'

'I had to think of something.' John shoots me a twisted grin, holding the door open for me. 'I've got my reputation as a travelling handy-man to keep up. Couldn't risk that lot knowing you'd shot me down in flames, now could I?'

CHAPTER TWELVE

Outside in the village street, the sky is close to darkness, that soft velvety dusk of a late summer's eve, just a few brush-strokes of orange light fading in the west. A few birds are still awake and singing, but in a defiant way, as though complaining that it's bedtime.

Moodily, the church clock chimes the last quarter of the hour from somewhere behind a cloudy mass of trees. Above their leafy branches, the church tower itself stands in stark, bold outline against a rapidly darkening charcoal sky.

As I look up, a lone rook flaps away into the dusk, cawing.

One of the group who left the pub at the same time as us calls out, 'Goodnight,' before getting into a small Renault across the road and driving off. The others are nowhere to be seen. Already on their way home, presumably.

John and I head down the street together at an easy pace, shoulder-to-shoulder, hip-to-hip. I'm aware of his hand occasionally brushing mine and jerking away, almost like it's an accident, though I'm not sure it is.

It's very quiet, oppressively so.

After the heat of the day, the evening air is still and balmy, rather too warm to be comfortable. I can already tell it's going to be the kind of night where I can't sleep for the prickling heat and usually end up opening the bedroom window and kicking off the covers to cool down.

When we reach the house, I hesitate, looking up at my dark bedroom window. 'Well, here we are. Thanks for a great evening. I'd better pop next door to collect Charlie.'

John slips an arm about my waist. 'Do you have to? Right now, I mean?' He's standing very close, his face inches from mine. 'I could … I dunno, come in for a coffee?'

I wonder if anyone's watching us. We're quite a distance from the nearest streetlight here, and it is almost full dark. Even so, we're not hidden from view. It crosses my mind that someone might be spying on me. On us, in fact.

More paranoia?

I shiver. 'Yeah, probably not a good idea.'

'I don't see why.' He leans closer. 'Maybe I'm being cocky. But I get the impression you quite like my company.'

'I do. But I'm not ready. Sorry.' My smile feels fixed and artificial.

It's suddenly very tempting to bury my fears with this man, if only for a few hours. Wine, a few kisses … Why the hell not?

John is right. I find him easy company. Easy on the eye too. But there's Charlie to consider, and rather more unpleasantly, the knowledge that boyfriends of mine tend to come to a sticky end. Often after only one night with me, like I'm a kind of Black Widow spider who sucks the life from her lovers, even while they're mating with her.

I couldn't go through that again. Not the desperate aftermath of another murder, I realise, but the loss of life. The sheer horror of it, my hands stained with their blood for years afterwards …

'Okay, no worries.' John releases me and steps back. 'I'll help you carry Charlie back home. He'll be asleep by now, I expect.'

'I can manage.'

'After two large glasses of wine?' He raises his eyebrows at me until I laugh, giving in.

'All right, yeah. Why not? Thanks for the offer. Charlie's only little but he can be rather heavy when he's asleep. Especially when I'm also carrying chocolates,' I add, nodding to the tin we won. 'You sure you don't want these?'

'God, no.' He pulls a face. 'I was holding out for the First Prize of cash and the bottle of whisky.'

I knock quietly at Patricia's door, and she opens it a moment later, ushering us inside with a warning finger at her lips. Her eyes widen, seeing John at my elbow. But she's too polite to pass comment.

'Hope you had a good evening at the pub,' Patricia says with a smile, closing the door behind us. 'He's been a little angel ... Though he only went to sleep about half an hour ago, I'm afraid.'

'I'm so sorry.'

'Don't be silly,' she whispers, showing us Charlie flushed and asleep on the sofa, the television still going quietly. 'I've had the most marvellous time, making things with Lego and watching cartoons. I've missed having my grandchildren around since they all went out to New Zealand. This has been an absolute treat.'

'Thank you, Patricia.'

'I told you, I'm happy to look after him whenever you need some free time. Your boy is a darling.'

I follow John to the door, who has scooped Charlie up in his arms, ready to carry him home for me.

I give Patricia a quick hug, genuinely grateful to have such a generous neighbour. 'Honestly, thank you so much.'

'See you at Sunday School, I hope,' Patricia says meaningfully, and glances curiously at John again before shutting the door.

Back home, I fumble for my house key while John waits patiently on the step, studying his sleeping cargo with an amused look.

Once Charlie is safely tucked up in bed, I go back down to find John lingering in the kitchen, checking his phone. His face looks sombre in the light from its screen, but he quickly turns it off and shoots me a warm smile.

'Right, I'll be off, then,' he says, with a quick, speculative look at my face. No doubt he's hoping that I've changed my mind about that 'cup of coffee'.

'Thanks, John,' I say firmly. 'For such a lovely evening and for helping me with Charlie.'

'Any time.'

John heads out the side door and stops on the step, his gaze shifting to the street, where a car is passing slowly.

It's a large car, one of those expensive recreational vehicles with blacked-out windows and huge tyres. The same SUV I've been seeing parked up outside the house during the day, I'm convinced of it. It's impossible to see who's driving it, but the car is moving at such a crawl, it's as though they're looking for something, maybe a house number or name.

John doesn't move, also watching the car.

The SUV stops.

Standing alongside him, I stare at the stationary car, my heart thumping, my mouth suddenly dry.

'That's odd,' I say, since remaining silent seems almost like an admission that I'm not surprised to see a car like that stopping dead outside my house at this late hour, as though the occupants are checking to see what I'm up to. 'I guess they must be lost.'

Though I *am* surprised, to be honest. And frightened too. And unsure what it means. But I can't let him see any of that.

John makes a non-committal sound under his breath and takes a few steps down the path towards the car.

As though in response, the big car revs and takes off at speed, tyres squealing aggressively on its way out of the village. I don't move, my heart rate spiking, my body trembling with a familiar rush of adrenalin as I listen to the engine roar fade into the distance.

His face in shadow, hands in his jeans pockets, John turns to look back at me. I have no idea what he's thinking but I'm too badly shaken to trust myself to come up with even a halfway decent lie to cover what just happened.

'Goodnight,' I stammer and close the door.

I stand a moment, listening warily.

To my relief, John takes a hint and I hear the receding sound of his footsteps as he heads across the road on his way home. Which was a camper van parked in a field around the back of the village, as I recall. No doubt he'd been hoping for a more comfortable bed tonight.

Perhaps I ought to have said yes.

I would feel safer in the house with another adult here, after all, even if only for a few hours. Especially now I know somebody out there has a key and can let themselves in whenever they like. But that would be against the rules.

Besides, Charlie would be sure to see John in the morning, and my son could do without that kind of emotional confusion in his life.

Once everything outside is quiet again, I splash my face with cool water from the tap and pat it dry.

Then I reach into the cupboard under the sink, take out a flathead screwdriver from the toolkit stored there, and tread softly upstairs with it to the padlocked room.

Years ago, I had to pry open a padlocked shed for an elderly neighbour who'd lost her key. So I know it's possible when there's a latch attached to the door first, and the padlock hooks onto the latch. It takes me a few attempts to loosen the tightly-embedded screws that hold the latch attached to the wall, but eventually I feel the lock mechanism give way under my slow and patient ministrations, and then I'm able to release the padlock along with the latch.

The door creaks open and I breathe stale air, like opening a tomb after many centuries. Clapping a hand to my mouth, I stand on the threshold and peer dubiously inside.

This must have been the back bedroom of the house once. In fact, there's still a wardrobe in one corner and a wooden-frame single bed pushed against one wall to make way for storage chests and other debris. Everything looks dusty and forgotten. Several larger items are covered with sheets, as though to protect them.

I flick the switch back and forth.

The bulb doesn't work.

Hurrying downstairs, I find a spare bayonet-style one under the sink and go back up, balancing on a chair to switch bulbs.

The lit bulb swings as I jump down and stare about the bedroom. I pick my way across to the window; a closed blind covers it, and I pull on the drawstring, dragging a few blinds up. It's dark outside, nothing to see.

The room has been papered with tiny rosebuds, dusky pink. There are some marks in the paper a foot or so under the windowsill. I crouch to examine the marks. Blue crayon, by the look of it. Not a word but a few squiggly lines with a rough circle on top, also coloured in with faint waxy blue.

I trace the odd shaped drawing, not sure what to make of it.

A child did this, clearly.

But what was it supposed to represent?

There are a few scratches and gouges on the painted sill too, as though someone in the past played here with metallic objects. Cars and lorries, perhaps, with wheels that dug into the paint and left marks. Charlie had done that once with a toy double-decker bus and I'd had to cover the scratches in the paint with a strategically-placed pot plant.

I remember the photograph on the wall in the pub, and the skinny child on the tricycle. So maybe I'd been mistaken. Maybe that had been a little boy, not a girl. Though I'd played with a few toy cars myself as a kid, remembering times in the children's home when the other kids had mocked me for behaving like a tomboy. It doesn't necessarily mean anything.

Dragging a dust sheet off a large, rectangular item on the floor, I realise it's the old shop sign.

NATASHA CUTS

It's in good condition; barely any fading, and the phone number on the lower right-hand side of the sign is still perfectly legible.

I open a packing crate and rummage inside through protective bubble wrap and paper, uncovering knick-knacks and mantelpiece ornaments. There's also a stylish set of hairdressing combs, brushes and tools, still in their double-layered box, everything used but clean and serviceable.

The largest pair of scissors is missing. The empty moulding where it used to nestle on black velvet seems to mock me.

Hunting through the other crates, I find more tools of the trade. Multiple hairdryers, straighteners, crimpers and curling sets, towel bales, boxes of pins, rusty old cans of hairspray, bottle after bottle of salon shampoo with sticky lids.

I leave the packing crates and head for the large wardrobe, curious to see if there's anything left inside.

The wardrobe is unlocked.

I open the door and find a row of women's outfits hanging up inside. Flicking through a few hangers, I blink in surprise at the slinky dresses and silk-lined jackets. I don't know what I was expecting but definitely not this … A hoard of expensive, designer clothes. Somewhat dated in style, true. But still impressive.

I hook one dress out. It's a black, clingy number with double spaghetti straps and a faint glittering sparkle to the fabric. Entranced, I hold it up against myself for measurement; it falls right to my ankles. The kind of evening dress that requires very, very high heels.

I stare down at myself, almost in awe. I own nothing this expensive, and for good reason.

I've been a low-wage hairdresser since leaving college, a poor single parent with a young child, unable to afford anything but the most basic outfits from charity shops.

Though even before I fell pregnant, I was never much of a night owl, preferring my own company to bellowing above loud music in a club or sweating it out on a dance floor until the early hours. And after Charlie's birth, I rarely went out to pubs or wine bars, clinging to my baby's company instead, knowing he was the only family I had in the world. So, I stayed in instead, except for those strangely exhilarating times when I was actually *dating* someone. Though finding them horribly murdered afterwards has tended to put me off the whole idea of having a boyfriend …

For all those reasons, my usual wardrobe consists of jeans, vest tops and T-shirts, plus a few leggings and exercise tops. I've certainly never found an occasion to wear an outfit this stylish and feminine.

This gorgeous dress must have belonged to Natasha, the hairdresser who lived here once. There's no other explanation.

Sighing, I carefully hang the dress back inside the wardrobe and run my hand along all the other beautiful outfits, loving the feel of their rich, silky textures under my fingertips. There are a few pairs of high heels on the wardrobe floor too. I pick up a classic black stiletto and turn it over, intrigued to find it's my own shoe size. The clothes too are not far off my figure, though I'm maybe a little shorter and less willowy than Natasha in that photograph. Too many nights of pizza and chips for tea, I think ruefully.

Why on earth would any woman leave such a treasure trove of expensive outfits behind for so many years? Patricia said she thought the salon had been closed since before she arrived in Darkling Moreton, and that was nearly two decades ago, wasn't it?

Closing the wardrobe door with a quiet click, I look around the room at the dusty crates and boxes. None of them look like they've been opened before tonight. Not since the day they were packed up and left here in a locked room to rot.

I can think of only one reason why the hairdressing salon owner had never come back for her possessions.

Natasha is dead.

CHAPTER THIRTEEN

Sunday morning, I'm up insanely early, determined to do some more digging among the chattering busy-bodies at church. I still have so many questions and only the vaguest answers, none of them fitting together, like different puzzles mixed up in the same box and me, like an idiot, fumbling to force them together to make a picture.

I shower and pull on a light summer dress; the material is cheap and cheerful, picked up from a market stall ages ago, purely on a whim. I don't know much about church-goers but I suspect it's the only thing I own that won't look out of place in a Devon village congregation.

'Come on, sleepyhead,' I tell Charlie, and drag him out of bed for a quick wash before breakfast. He groans, but without much real aggro. I can tell he's happy about the idea of seeing other people for a change, and he certainly enjoys playing with the toys and other kids at Sunday School.

Which reminds me; I'm going to have to get him into school locally if we stay here. Yet everything is still so uncertain. I hardly dare plan a day or two ahead, let alone look forward to the start of the autumn term.

Home schooling wouldn't be a major problem for us, assuming I can get another laptop. I quite enjoy talking to Charlie and helping him with sums and forming letters, and he's always eager to learn more about the world.

However, I worry what it's doing for his mental health, being stuck home permanently with a slightly manic mum. If I were more able to get out and socialise myself, that might be different. But given our dangerous situation, we rarely even leave the house. How can I properly mix with others in society when I've been warned not to speak to others?

Patricia is in the church hall, speaking to Mrs Bloxley, who turns to look at me with her usual cool expression.

It's not an ecstatic welcome, at any rate.

My neighbour, on the other hand, welcomes us with open arms, literally, crouching to hug Charlie before he squirms free and hurries across to join the other kids. Her beaming smile transfers to me instead. 'Sylvia, how wonderful to see you here again. I hope you've settled in now.' Patricia hesitates, as though sure of a refusal. 'Will you be joining us in church today?'

I'm probably the least religious person it's possible to be. But I need to start insinuating myself into this village if I'm to discover more about the house I'm occupying. I need more information.

'I thought I'd give it a try, yes,' I say, and her beam widens.

'How lovely.' She takes my arm, nods to Mrs Bloxley, and guides me out of the hall. 'We can sit together. We are next door neighbours, after all. And if you're at all uncertain of what to do, I can whisper in your ear. Does that sound good?'

'Thank you, yes.'

We arrive first and sit at the front in a polished, dark wood pew. Stained glass windows ahead of us show colourful scenes from Scripture. The altar is draped with an immaculate white cloth bordered with a green-and-red line and decorated on either side with vases of beautifully arranged flowers, filling the old building with the fragrance of summer meadows.

Looking back at some noise, I see others arriving and recognise the middle-aged couple from the churchyard, who are speaking to a few others loitering in the doorway.

Then someone else enters, a man in a cream suit and Panama hat, and the others fall silent and shuffle aside to let him through. They exchange greetings in hushed, reverent voices, and leave a respectful space before following in his wake.

It's the old gentleman who spoke to me on the footpath behind the churchyard.

He comes to sit a few rows behind us.

Our eyes meet, and he lifts his hat in a gesture of greeting, then removes it completely and places it on the bench beside him.

'Good to see a new face in church,' he says in that rich, deep voice I remember, watching me steadily, and I mumble something polite in return before facing front again.

My neck prickles with apprehension again, just as it had when I last encountered him. What is it about him that seems to flick a switch deep inside, causing … What? Panic? Suspicion? I can't work out what I'm feeling, and that alone disturbs me.

The church service seems to stretch on unrelentingly. My attention drifts to the stained glass windows, a wall cloth embroidered with dark holly leaves and berries interwoven with ivy strands, and the plain cross on the altar itself, gleaming by the light of two tall candles in polished silver sticks. The church isn't grand nor is the service particularly ceremonial, but the simple ritual is rather comforting, even though I don't fully understand it. And Reverend Shearsman is wearing a green and purple robe – to celebrate some special day in the church calendar, Patricia explains, whispering in my ear when she catches me staring – and looks far less sinister and intimidating than when he came round to my house on the pretext of selling raffle tickets.

After all the muttered prayers and 'Amens,' we all shake hands and I then find myself the focus of fascinated interest.

'So you're the new lady,' one woman says, looking me up and down with a smile. 'The one with the little boy.'

The smart, middle-aged couple who passed me in the churchyard introduce themselves. 'I'm Laura,' the woman says, shaking my hand. A small gold cross on a chain nestles in the folds of her ruffled white blouse; her neatly-cut dark bob holds streaks of grey. 'And this is my husband, Paul.'

111

The man leans across in turn to take my hand. His hair is more silvery, his angular chin slightly stubbled; he looks like a business executive, someone used to being deferred to. But his smile is friendly enough.

'Pleased to meet you,' I say, keeping my head down, my eyes lowered too; I'm not shy, but it's always better for me and Charlie if I pretend that I am. Fewer questions, less chance of me saying something indiscreet by accident. 'Such a charming village. We love it.'

'Isn't your husband going to join you?' an old lady from the back pews pipes up. Despite her age, which might be early eighties, she has a vaguely malicious air, head tilted like a sparrow's as she waits for my reply. There's an empty wheelchair waiting at the end of the pew. Hers?

'She's divorced,' Patricia replies for me, looking embarrassed, and shoots the old lady a warning look. 'I told you, remember?'

'Oh yes.' But I can tell from the old lady's smile that she hasn't forgotten. She just wants to make me feel bad about my lack of a husband. Nasty piece of work. 'Of course. Well, not all marriages work out. Especially when people marry so young these days.' Her thin brows soar. 'You barely look old enough to be out of school, let alone the mother of a child.'

'I'm twenty-two,' I say defiantly, and then wish I hadn't said anything.

DO NOT TALK TO ANYONE.

Did I just allow this old woman to irritate me into breaking cover? When will I learn to put my personal feelings aside and follow the rules?

'Twenty-two,' she muses. 'And how old is the boy?'

My face hardens and I refuse to answer her. I won't drag my son into this. Besides, one or two innocently stated facts, like our ages, and I could be accidentally exposing my true identity, my hiding place, ruining everything …

I fold my arms and look away. 'I should go,' I mutter to Patricia. 'Charlie will be missing me.'

All this time, the elderly man in the Panama has been deep in conversation with Reverend Shearsman. I glance that way and the old man half-turns, as though

112

sensing my gaze. A shudder runs through me and I look down, pretending to check in my handbag, my heart thudding almost painfully.

Why on earth does he disturb me so much? He's just an old guy like any other, though a little more expensively dressed than most old guys I've known.

'What's the house like inside these days?' Laura asks curiously.

I turn to her at once, keen to hide my response to the man in the hat. 'Sorry? What do you mean?'

'The old hairdressing salon,' Laura explains, and smiles when I stare at her blankly. 'I had my hair done there a few times when I was a teenager. I do miss it. It was so nice to have somewhere in the village where you could go for a simple haircut. Wasn't it, Glenda?' She turns to the old lady who baited me. 'Nowadays we have to drive miles into town just to get our roots retouched.'

'Or take the bus,' Glenda agrees, a touch of bitterness in her voice. 'Some of us don't have a licence anymore.'

'Of course, I was forgetting.' Laura tuts. 'Such a shame they took it away from you, just because of a few accidents. But I suppose you are in your eighties now.' She shoots her husband a quick, ironic look that totally undermines her faux sympathy, but continues with a pleasant smile, rounding on me again, 'Anyway, I was simply wondering what it looks like now. Inside the house, I mean. It was only a small salon, a couple of sinks and chairs, some mirrors on the wall. But I presume all the fittings have been removed now.'

'Yes, to make way for my sofa and coffee table,' I joke, and everybody laughs, the sound echoing about the church interior.

'Well, I suppose they had to close it, really,' Laura adds, pulling a face. 'After what happened.'

Everyone else is leaving the church now. The Reverend solicitously helps Glenda into a wheelchair and pushes her after the others. We too begin drifting automatically towards the door in their wake.

'Sorry?' I frown, not sure I've understood. 'What do you mean?'

'The dead man, of course.'

113

I stop, my throat suddenly convulsing. 'Dead man?'

Laura looks at me oddly. 'You didn't know?' She gives a tiny shrug and looks towards her husband again, who's pulling on his jacket by the door, his air unmistakeably impatient as he waits for us. 'Ancient history now, I suppose. All water under the bridge.'

I grab her sleeve, and she stares at me, surprised.

'Tell me,' I say urgently.

'I'm afraid there's not much to tell.' She frowns. 'There was a man found dead here, that's all.'

'*Here?*' My chest tightens. 'You mean, in the church?'

'Oh yes, it was quite a scandal at the time.' Laura drops her voice to a whisper, as though unsure whether we ought to be discussing this at all in the church itself. 'They say he was found right over there,' she added, pointing back down the aisle, 'on the steps beside the altar.'

'When was this? What year?'

'Not sure. Years ago now. You'd have to check in the church records or maybe ask Mrs Bloxley. She's the real expert, knows everything about the history of this old place.' She flaps a hand, and her rings gleam in the warm coloured light filtering through stained glass. 'The real scandal, of course, was that he didn't die of natural causes. He was *murdered.*'

I can hardly breathe, gulping at the air, my lungs burning.

'Who … Who did it?'

'They never found out. Nobody even knew who he was, as I recall.'

'So what did his death have to do with the hair salon?'

'Oh, didn't I say?' Laura looks uncomfortable. 'Well, it was really rather nasty. He'd been stabbed with a pair of scissors, you see. A pair of *hairdresser's* scissors.' She looks at me anxiously. 'I'm sorry, I can see I've upset you.'

'No.' I struggle for self-control. 'Please, go on.'

She gives me another worried, searching look. 'There's really not much else to tell. They closed the salon. I'm not quite sure why. I was in my teens at the

114

time, still at school, and my mother never told me about anything even remotely exciting, God rest her soul. Like I say, you'd need to ask someone else. Maybe the vicar?' She glances towards her husband again, who's shuffling his feet now and clearing his throat. He even checks his watch, to make it obvious he's bored. 'Sorry, I should go. Paul hates me hanging about after church. He's likes to mow the lawn on a Sunday afternoon.' She rolls her eyes. 'I'm always telling him, it's meant to be a day of rest. But he won't listen.'

She chatters on as we leave the church. The couple make their way across the car park, Laura looking back with a cheery wave.

In a daze, I stumble around to the hall to collect Charlie. He's playing with a couple of other kids, too absorbed in their game to even notice me arriving. The two teenage girls have disappeared, presumably gone home.

But Mrs Bloxley is still there with her usual lapful of knitting. Thick scarlet wool this time, long needles clacking away as she watches the children intently, a fat ball of wool shaking and unwinding at every few stitches.

Patricia has got there ahead of me and is beginning to pack away the Sunday School toys and books.

'I'm glad to see you're making friends,' she says, smiling. 'Laura's a dear, but she does talk rather a lot. Hard to get a word in edgeways. I imagine that's why Paul says so little. What was that I heard her telling you?'

'She said there was a murder here once,' I mumble, feeling numb and off balance. 'A murder in the church.'

Just saying those words make me want to grab Charlie and run back to the house, lock all the doors, and sit holding my son tight while I try to work out what I need to do.

It was an idle conversation between two women after church, I tell myself. And a freak coincidence. Two freak coincidences, actually: one, that my new home was a salon once, and I'm a hairdresser. And two, that someone was murdered in this village once with a pair of hairdressing scissors. Just like the people I allow into my life have a tendency to be.

115

Packing a bag and escaping is at the forefront of my mind. Getting as far away as possible from this place. But the voice on the other end of the phone would not approve. My protector.

He sent me here deliberately. To this village. To that house. He must have a reason for those choices. And his plans have always worked flawlessly in the past. I need to trust him now. Because if I don't and he chooses to abandon me …

I try to smile, to stay light, but panic has set in, fluttering like a wild bird in my chest, beating its wings against my rib cage.

Patricia is staring up at me, consternation in her face. 'A murder? In our little church?' She straightens, discarded plastic food from the toy oven in her arms. 'Are you sure that's what she said?' She sounds hesitant. 'Laura can be a bit funny sometimes. Maybe she was just pulling your leg.'

I shake my head. 'A man was stabbed with a pair of scissors. Left by the altar. She seemed to think his death had something to do with the salon. And that's why it closed.'

'My goodness. Of course, I did hear that something bad had happened in the village, and the salon closed soon afterwards. But I had idea the church was involved. Do you know anything about a murder in our lovely little church, Mrs Bloxley?' She frowns, glancing back at me. 'When did she say this happened, dear?'

'Years ago. That's all she could remember.' I call to Charlie, but my voice is too high and thin and he doesn't hear me.

Mrs Bloxley has put down her knitting at last. She gets up, her voice sombre. 'The killing. Yes, I remember that. A dreadful time. We don't talk about it.'

The killing.

That seems an odd way to refer to the shocking and unexpected murder of a total stranger in their quiet Devon village. To my ear, *the killing* makes it sound more like an ancient ritual. Like something dating back to the pagan era, in fact.

'We don't?' Patricia is looking surprised.

Mrs Bloxley shakes her head, her mouth set in a hard line. 'People don't like murder here. It's not a nice subject.'

Murder. Not a nice subject.

Or perhaps Mrs Bloxley is simply one of those rural conservative women who've been steeped in disapproval so long they are no longer able to feel or express empathy.

'Doesn't really fit the village image, does it?' My smile feels utterly false. 'But it's so bizarre. In such a quiet, off-the-beaten-track place like Darkling Moreton …' I pause, thinking back over what she said. 'Who do you mean by "people"?'

Mrs Bloxley merely shakes her head, gathering up her wool. 'Time I was going.'

Two other women trail in to collect their children, and Charlie finally tears himself reluctantly away from the play area, rushing up to show me a picture book he's been admiring.

'Good boy.' Unsteadily, I take his hand and check he's got everything he came with. 'I expect you'll need a lie-down before lunch.'

And I need to escape.

Patricia comes after me as we walk through the car park, heading back home. She calls out, 'Sylvia, please wait … I've something important to tell you.' I keep walking, my head buzzing, but it's impossible to ignore her. She's trotting now to catch up with me, her voice breathless. 'Sylvia, dear? Didn't you hear me?'

Reluctantly, I turn and wait for her, forcing myself to behave politely though my heart is banging away under my ribs.

'I'm so sorry about that,' she rattles on. 'I had no idea about the murder, honestly. All before my time, of course. I did know there was something not quite right about the history of the salon, but murder? Oh dear.' She peers at me, concerned. 'Are you all right?'

'Of course.' My answering smile is fake and horribly rigid, but there's not much I can do about it.

I want to scream and tear my hair. I want to weep loudly until my eyes turn red and raw, and I beg someone to save me from this nightmare that's become my life. But I have to keep it all inside until we're safely back at the house and I can shut out the world. If anybody knew …

We walk on again in the direction of the main street, Charlie humming and dragging his feet wearily.

'Well, look,' Patricia says, touching my arm gently, 'I asked Mrs Bloxley just now if she knew who your landlord was. I remember you said you didn't know. That the agency hadn't told you?'

I wonder where the hell this is going and hope she hasn't thrown me to the wolves by interfering. Though part of me hopes she can shed light on something that's been bothering me ever since we arrived in Darkling Moreton, which is who owns the former salon and whether it was chosen for my hiding place coincidentally or as an ironic joke.

'And did she know who the landlord is?' I ask.

'Yes.' Patricia beams; her air is triumphant, like someone producing a rabbit out of a hat. 'She told me it's *Sir Philip*. Fancy that, eh?'

I turn my head to stare at her, feeling like I'm going mad. 'I'm sorry, I have no idea who that is.'

'Sir Philip.' When I merely shrug, Patricia smiles and rolls her eyes. 'Oh, I'm so silly. Of course you don't know who he is. Why should you? You've only just arrived.' After a quick glance around, her voice drops conspiratorially. 'Sir Philip Janus is the elderly gentleman who was at the church today. The man in the wonderful Panama hat. You must have noticed him, I'm sure. He does look so dapper in it.'

She's laughing but I can't join her, transfixed and staring at her with my mouth open.

Hurriedly, she adds, 'You see, I thought if anybody would know the history of your house, it must be the landlord. Because Mrs Bloxley says that nasty business happened a very long time ago. Before you were even born, I should imagine.'

My mouth is dry but I manage to say, 'Did she know anything else? I mean, whether the murder was connected to the salon or not?'

'If she did, she refused to talk about it. Can't say I blame her. Such a horrid business.' She shook her head. 'But if you're still curious, you just need to ask Sir Philip. I'm sure he'd be delighted to tell you everything he knows about it.' She puts a reassuring hand on my arm. 'Don't be put off by the title. He's the most polite gentleman you can imagine, not at all snobby or stand-offish, and so refined in his speech. He was knighted by the Queen, you know. With a sword. Such an honour.' Her eyes glow. 'Our very own local celebrity. I'm such an idiot for not mentioning him to you before.'

I stop dead in the middle of the street. 'Wait, Sir Philip lives here?' My voice is hoarse and urgent; I see her staring and clear my throat, trying for a more casual tone. 'I mean, in the village itself? Here in Darkling Moreton?'

'Why yes, in the big house – '

I interrupt her, my eyes widening. 'With the dogs. The German Shepherds.'

'That's right.' Patricia laughs at my expression, nodding. 'You've passed his gate before, I take it?' Her smile broadens. 'And been thoroughly barked at, I suppose?'

'Yes.'

She misinterprets my stillness and my whispered response. 'Oh, are you afraid of dogs? I'm so sorry, that's awful … And I'm afraid Herod and Caesar do make an awful racket whenever people go past. But I suppose Sir Philip needs a serious deterrent to keep out the burglars, not just an alarm system.' She gives me a wink. 'Though he has one of those too. State-of-the-art, they say.'

I look at her sideways, wondering what she means.

'He has rather a grand house, you see,' Patricia goes on airily, 'and so many precious antiques and artifacts in glass cases. The church group meets there sometimes in winter when the hall is too cold, so I've had plenty of opportunities to admire his lovely home. And I daresay the dogs are a necessity, even if they can be a bit noisy.'

She pauses, biting the tip of one fingernail. 'You know, I wonder if Sir Philip even knows that you're his tenant. The agency who put you in there may not have bothered to consult him. It wouldn't be that odd. Sir Philip owns a lot of property around the village, and further afield too. In the olden days, I expect he would have been Lord of the Manor, or something like that.' She laughs, again seeming to find this funny. 'He probably has an assistant or a solicitor who handles all that business for him.'

I don't find any of it even remotely amusing but I nod and jerk my mouth in a mimicry of her laughter. I dare not make her suspicious. Not when she seems to have the ear of Sir Philip, this wealthy man who owns the very building I'm living in.

Charlie has had enough of our boring adult conversation. He looks up and tugs on my hand, flushed and tired.

'C'mon, Mum. Home now.'

I repress a burning impulse to rush round to Sir Philip's big, forbidding house with the guard dogs, right on the picturesque edge of the village, and demand to speak to my privileged, well-to-do landlord. Though that might be the most dangerous thing I could do under the circumstances. For all I know, this Sir Philip may be perfectly well aware who I am.

A terrifying thought, and one that brings me to my senses.

'Of course, darling.' Checking his forehead, I'm alarmed to find it's warm and clammy. Is he feverish? Or just tired after a busy day. 'You've overdone all the running about today. Let's get you back to base.' I stroke his hair and try to push my panic aside and focus on my little boy. 'Mummy thinks you need a nice cool drink and a nap.'

'Telly,' he whines, dragging me along.

'Nap first,' I say firmly.

Patricia gives a heartfelt sigh, smiling down at Charlie's weary figure. 'What a sweet little poppet he is. And you're such a good mother.' Embarrassment flits across her face. 'I'm sorry about Glenda, by the way … Such an unforgiveable thing to say to you. But she's always been a bit catty. The vicar's mother, you know.'

'No, I didn't know.'

'Oh yes, the Rev quite dotes on her. Though she's bedridden, poor old thing. I suppose it's not helped her temper.' She pats my arm reassuringly. 'Best just ignore it. Forget all about her.'

'Already done.'

'That's the spirit.' We reach our respective houses, and Patricia heads down the path to her front door. 'See you later.'

Indoors at last, I lock the door, hurry around to check all the downstairs windows are closed, and stand listening to the silence.

The house feels empty, but it's a reassuring emptiness. The wolves are all outside right now: unseen and mostly unknown, but definitely there, watching.

Inside feels safe: no enemies here. Just me and my boy.

Charlie picks up the television remote control but I pluck it away from him and ruffle his hair.

'Nap time first, remember? Then lunch a bit later than usual. After that, telly, and only if you've eaten everything on your plate.'

He moans but doesn't resist as I guide him upstairs and into our shared bedroom. His eyes have closed before I've even pulled his shoes and socks off.

I drape the covers lightly over him so he doesn't overheat and draw the curtains against the afternoon sun. He doesn't seem as hot now, but he's clearly very tired. Maybe he's sickening for something.

Pulling the door to behind me, I stand on the landing for a moment, looking at the door that used to be locked. The forbidden room.

My mind flicks through the things I found in there. The wardrobe of fabulous clothes. The box of dusty knick-knacks. The fixtures and fittings from the former salon, including the shop sign that said NATASHA CUTS. None of it taken away to be sold, thrown in a skip or recycled but collected together and stored up in that spare room as though for future use.

Which means, whoever left those things here, presumably Natasha herself, intended to come back for them. Either to set up the salon again or start a new business elsewhere.

Yet she never returned to retrieve her possessions.

I thought it had to be because she'd died. But now I wonder if there might be another explanation.

How is it possible that someone in this village was murdered in exactly the same way as Simon and Kurt, but years ago, perhaps even before I was born, as Patricia suggested? And now I'm living in the actual salon where the murder weapon may have come from?

I remember the case of hairdressing tools I found, and the empty space where the largest scissors ought to have been stored.

And someone broke into the house.

Someone in a mask.

'Oh, God.' Feeling oddly light-headed, I steady myself against the nearest wall. 'Get a grip, Sylvia.'

What's the connection? What's the bloody connection? Why put me here? Why this place and why now?

I feel like I'm going mad.

My head shifts again, almost a hundred-and-eighty degree reversal. I'm back in the church hall, listening to Patricia as she tells me about my landlord.

Sir Philip Janus.

The man in the Panama hat. The man with the barking dogs guarding his large, impressive, gated home. So elegant in his stylish cream suit, with that natural authority, the way the others moved aside for him without question. But I suppose he's like a miniature God in this quiet village.

He was knighted by the Queen, you know.

Why?

What did plain Philip Janus do to be elevated to the knighthood?

And if he owns the house I'm standing in, why did he leave the dusty contents of the back bedroom untouched, padlocking the door against intruders instead? Why not simply throw those old things out when it became a rental?

More importantly, does Sir Philip know anything about me? About what I've left behind, what I'm fleeing?

I remember his well-turned out, authoritative figure in church and can't believe that he does. A man like that, so upright and respected, knowingly harbouring a fugitive from justice in a building he owns?

What did gossipy Patricia say about him? *Sir Philip owns a lot of property around the village and further afield too. In the olden days, I guess he would have been Lord of the Manor.* Not someone who would ever stoop to acknowledge a lowly tenant, in other words. Especially not an unemployed single parent who may not even be staying that long in his precious country village.

No, my neighbour has to be right. That's the logical thing to assume.

Sir Philip is a wealthy man. He knows nothing about me as his tenant or about my dodgy past. Someone else will have arranged my tenancy through the agency that handles all his other properties too. The voice on the other end of the phone would have made the calls, paid the money, filled out the forms …

Yet I can't shake the feeling that our high-and-mighty 'Lord of the Manor' knows rather more about me than is entirely comfortable.

CHAPTER FOURTEEN

The next week goes quietly. No more night-time intrusions, no more cars parked outside. Charlie and I travel to the nearest town on the bus and wander about the shops, buying new clothes and shoes for both of us, plus a few toys for Charlie. It's a dull day, thankfully, as I'm wearing a hoody the whole time, pulled low over my face to avoid any CCTV cameras picking me out of the crowd.

Charlie loves the unfamiliar excitement of the bus journey, chattering most of the way and smiling at other passengers, saying, 'Hi, hi,' with a friendly wave. Most of them smile and wave back, charmed by the little fair-haired boy with the beaming face.

I'm glad to see him so happy, and burn with guilt at how I've ruined his life; if it wasn't for me, he would be living like a normal boy, surrounded by friends and enjoying as many outings as we could afford. Instead, he has a mother who dare not stir from her house most of the time and has to go partly disguised if she does, while he will need to start at another new school this autumn or put up with me teaching him from home.

I stop in a bookshop and, while Charlie is looking at picture books and jigsaw puzzles, browse a few home-schooling resources like textbooks and worksheets for early reading and writing, as well as forming numbers and simple adding up.

Come September, if things still feel unsafe out there, I may have to teach Charlie myself, rather than run the risk of being seen and recognised if I need to go to the school in person.

If he attends school, he would probably use the school bus with the other kids, thankfully. That's one advantage of living in a remote Devon village.

But what about parents' evenings, sports' days and school productions? I can't simply *never* attend one. It wouldn't be fair on Charlie and I can't bear to think of his disappointment, eagerly hunting for his mum in the audience and never seeing her face.

But for all I know, I'm a wanted person. There may be posters of me up in shops where I used to live, or on the police database.

Last time, there was less to tie me to the crime. I only had to lay low for a few months and that was largely out of choice.

Not that there was an actual crime, with Kurt.

No body, no crime.

Kurt just disappeared off the face of the earth after that night, or appeared to, from what I could glean via online searches at the time. Did the person on the other end of the burner phone dispose of his body and clear up all traces of my presence too? The incredible resources that would take, the knowledge and expertise, the determination ... and all to conceal a crime I may or may not have been involved in.

It makes no sense.

Unless I'm missing a vital piece of the puzzle.

I see John a few times during the week, cycling by in the village street. Once, I take Charlie to the shops and find John there too, halfway up a ladder with a soapy bucket, cleaning windows.

He raises a hand in greeting but I only say, 'Hello,' in an offhand way and duck inside the shop after Charlie.

I like John.

But I can't risk starting a relationship with him. Not when it's only too possible that whoever killed Kurt and Simon is still watching me. It seems incredible. But I have no other explanation for the intruder, the car with the blacked-out windows, the occasional figure watching from the shadows across the street … Those have to be related to the way men keep dying when I'm foolish enough to spend the night with them.

The alternative theory – that I'm the killer, that I'm the one who stabbed them with the hairdressing scissors – is not one I can even countenance. It makes me close up in horror whenever my head goes there. Me, a cold-hearted killer? No, it can't be true. I refuse for it to be true. Yet the possibility still haunts me.

Either way, I can't bear the idea of having John's death on my conscience too.

I resolve to be more careful, to stop going out of the house, to avoid speaking to anyone at all.

We spend long, lazy days in the garden, and like a blessing from heaven, the weather stays dry most days, though the intense heat has mercifully abated for now. In the evenings, I sit and study the items in the back bedroom, investigating boxes I haven't previously opened but never finding much of any use, only more ornaments and random personal possessions, old books and pointless knick-knacks.

By the end of the week though, I'm already starting to fret again. The little house is a prison and I long for another few hours away from Charlie, much as I love him, even just to stretch my legs on my own. Whenever we go for walks about the village, we can't go far, as his little legs won't carry him much over a mile before he gets tired. So we take the usual circular route, mostly round the church buildings and through the meadow beyond, then back past Sir Philip's grand house. It's called 'The Old Manor,' I note as we trail past on our first walk out that way, trying not to make my interest too obvious. But there's never any sign of anyone in residence, and the aggressive dogs are locked up inside, judging by the muffled barking audible from the road.

I walk over to Patricia's early on Friday afternoon when the sun has just come out again, burning away the morning haze.

The large car with the blacked-out windows is parked a little further down the street, but as soon as I stop and glance their way, my eyes narrowed against the sun, the engine starts up and the car takes off at once, soon disappearing around the bend.

I ring Patricia's bell and am relieved to find her at home.

'Any chance you could look after Charlie for a couple of hours while I go for a proper walk? He's had his lunch and a run-around outside, and is usually a bit quieter at this time of the afternoon.' I smile hopefully and hold out some home-made biscuits wrapped in clingfilm. 'I brought a little bribe.'

'Are those gingerbread biscuits?' She smiles at Charlie, who nods. 'Well, what a coincidence. They're my favourite.'

'Me make,' Charlie tells her proudly, tapping his chest.

'You made them? What a clever boy?'

'Wi' Mum,' he admits.

'Ah, but I bet you did all the hardest work.'

He nods vigorously.

'Excellent.' She opens the door wide and he runs inside. 'Are you going to be a chef when you grow up?'

Charlie nods back at her, though I'm not sure he knows what a chef is.

I thank Patricia profusely for agreeing to look after him, but she shakes her head, her eyes shining.

'No need to thank me, please. I was so bored today, and this is just what I need. Come in, see him settled before you leave.'

I follow her into the living room, feeling awkward.

'It's very kind of you,' I say. 'I honestly wouldn't have asked, but I'm dying to stretch my legs with a long country walk. Charlie does his best, poor thing, but he starts to flag after about twenty minutes. We haven't even managed to walk beyond the village yet.' I watch uneasily as he throws open the toy chest in the

127

corner and starts playing with one of her grandchildren's toys, a red plastic trumpet. 'Not so loud, Charlie.'

'Nonsense, he can make as much noise as he likes. Nobody will hear.' Patricia offers me tea, but I shake my head. Her smile is indulgent. 'Well, you take your time, dear. Come back when you're ready.'

I thank her again and say a quick goodbye to Charlie, hurrying out before he can miss me.

Outside, the sun is beating down again, soon warming my bare arms and legs in the white vest top and shorts I've chosen for today's outing. It looks like being a real scorcher this afternoon.

I've got a plan.

The village has few passing places for cars, and almost no parking areas. The verge is too narrow for people to park for long without causing an obstruction. And yet the owner of that large, dark car with blacked-out windows keeps sitting outside our house for hours – the only part of the village where it's wide enough to do so safely – or crawling along the street at intervals, as though keeping a close eye on the property.

Where does it go when it's not outside my house?

According to the pub landlady last Friday, she's seen the car parked up at the Sallies, where the owners have gone to America for the summer.

The Sallies is a large, new-build house with a high brick wall and white stone lions, a place I've spotted since on my walks with Charlie but not dared stop to study it, and never when the SUV was actually parked up there.

My plan is to look for the SUV, either at the Sallies, or on the drives of local houses where the occupants might be out most of the day, or in one of the few side-streets in the village. I also know there are some outlying homes beyond the boundary of the village, some of them with long, dusty driveways. Maybe the car could be parked up discreetly in one of those driveways, lurking and waiting to swing by for another look.

Close-up, I might be able to get a glimpse of who's driving it.

I deliberately don't think beyond that. To what might happen if the driver got out and spoke to me. To what would be the consequences for me and Charlie if the driver turned out to be the voice on the other end of the phone. Or if it was the police watching me.

All of those possibilities scare the hell out of me.

But I have to do something.

I can't sit in that house like a terrified child and do nothing, say nothing ... Just wait for my fate to unravel on its own.

That's not who I am.

At least, I don't think so. That's not who I was before all the people around me started winding up dead.

The driveway on the Sallies is empty. I stand staring at the house and garden for a moment, almost relieved to find nothing. I was dreading having to confront the driver if the car had been parked there. But I'm disappointed too. All these maddening questions buzzing around in my head like a black swarm of flies and not a single answer to be had for any of them. Just bits and pieces, fragments of information and random comments, and none of them making no sense.

I keep walking, looking from left to right as I pass other houses, other driveways. There's no sign of the SUV.

It's hot and sunny. I pull my baseball cap down to shield my eyes and begin to wish I'd applied more sunscreen, especially to my arms and around my neck. Ahead, the lush green of Devon fields stretches for miles in a sun-baked patchwork of hills and valleys, melting to a soft, blurring heat-haze on the horizon. The countryside feels alien but I have to admit it's easy on the eye, and I do love the fresh, clean quality to the air, nothing like the polluted lungfuls I used to breathe in on a daily basis when we were living in London.

All the same, the complete absence of people, of buildings, even of streets ... It's somehow sinister.

129

My ears catch the deep note of a car approaching. It's going slow, somewhere behind me. Then it stops, the engine still idling.

I keep walking.

The car behind me starts moving again. It even sounds like it's speeding up. Usually, when a car approaches, Charlie and I step onto the verge and the car sidles past at a wary distance. So I don't panic, merely shift to the side of the road and wait there for the car to pass.

There isn't much of a verge on this stretch, just a narrow strip of grass below the hedgerow that runs between village properties. I have to squash in against the bushes to make room for the vehicle, a few spiny thorns scratching my arms and legs. I keep my head down, the baseball cap hiding my face. The instinct not to be seen is very strong, even in this remote spot.

But the car doesn't slow down. Instead, the engine revs and the driver accelerates toward me down the lane.

I turn to stare at last, alarmed.

It's the dark SUV with blacked-out windows. Sunlight reflects off the windscreen, blinding me.

The driver is aiming straight for me, I realise, with a shock that starts my heart pounding like crazy.

I take to my heels, sprinting close to the side of the road, the big car racing its engine behind me all the way; after what feels like an age, but is probably closer to fifteen seconds, I spot an opening and dart sideways, forcing my way through dense bushes.

There's a field behind the hedgerow here, not a property, and I make for that, bending almost double under low-hanging tree branches and paying no attention to my flesh tearing on thorns.

Behind me, the car has stopped. I hear a door open and shut, and shouts. Then the sound of someone pursuing me through the bushes.

Abruptly, the bushes end and I'm out in the field, running free across dried patches of earth and thin, green grass studded with wildflowers. At the far end of the field, what looks like a large bull lifts its head from grazing to stare at me, but I pay no attention. There's no time to worry about the bull and his response to someone invading his field. I'm focused on running for my life, lungs burning, a stitch in my side, blood streaks down my arms and legs from the thorn bushes I tore through …

The car continues, and I remember too late that the road divides into two just ahead of where I was walking, one side heading out to the main road, the other, narrower and more overgrown, curving back round behind the houses in a single-track lane.

There's a five-bar gate ahead at the other side of the field; I've been making for it instinctively. But it gives onto the lane the big SUV is even now travelling, faster than I can possibly run.

And behind me I can hear someone running too, thudding across the low-cropped grass, breathing heavily.

I can't risk falling, so I haven't looked back and I've been keeping my eyes mainly on the ground at my feet, looking out for hidden hazards. But the sound of a speeding car behind hedgerow somewhere to my right reminds me I need to find a new escape route or it's all over.

There's another thick, spiny-looking hedge to my left too, this one dotted with white flower-heads and running the width of the field. As I glance briefly that way, I see the hedgerow break for a few yards of fence and a wooden stile, mossed and half hidden by bushes, leading into yet another field.

Beyond that field, the church tower rises above the trees. Seeing it, my eyes widen.

The church.

It represents safety; not simply the traditional sanctuary of hallowed ground but a good chance of being *seen* by someone. The vicar, a dog-walker, anyone with a pulse, really … Because my instincts tell me whoever this is on my trail, they won't want to be spotted pursuing me.

Skirting an old water trough, I swerve sideways towards the stile, one foot skidding through dusty, uneven ridges of mud.

I clamber over the stile without looking back and drop into thicker grass, ankle-high, golden buttercups glinting here and there among the grasses. The ground is softer too, yielding underfoot. No animals have grazed here for a long while.

Heading for the church, I keep running, and at long last dare to raise my head from the ground for longer than a second or two.

Up ahead, I see an old camper van parked up in the field. There's an awning shading the side door, which is closed, and a deckchair set out beneath it.

John's camper?

I put on a spurt of speed, though my legs are tired and my heart is thudding so violently I'm afraid I may actually have a heart attack. I'm panting by the time I reach the camper van and fling myself against the door, pounding on it with both fists and yelling in a hoarse, breathless voice, 'John? For God's sake, help me, you've got to help me!'

I risk a glance back at last, and see a burly figure on top of the stile, climbing over. My hair is in my eyes and I'm gasping for breath, but I'm pretty sure that it's a man. Well-built, in dark clothing, with short dark hair. He jumps down into the field, landing heavily.

'John?' I cry out, thumping on the door so hard it shudders under my blows. 'Please, open up, open up!'

'Hey, what's all the panic about?'

The voice is behind me.

I whip around, shaking with adrenalin, but it's only John, standing there with a shocked look on his face.

'Oh, John,' I cry, and stagger towards him. 'That man over there. He's been chasing me.' He catches me in his arms and I feel like sinking to the ground, resting against him as I get my breath back. 'Thank God … I'm so glad to see you.'

132

'Hush, you're okay now.' He rubs the tops of my arms reassuringly, studying my face, and then peers in the direction I've been pointing. 'Someone was chasing you, you say?'

'Yes, he's right behind me ...' I turn, but the field is empty.

There's no sign of the burly man in dark clothing that I saw jumping down from the stile. I look around, confused, wondering where on earth he could have hidden, given the lack of trees and bushes this side of the fence.

'I don't understand.' I'm stunned. 'He's gone.'

'Well, that's a good thing,' he says sombrely. 'Otherwise I would have had to call the police.' He studies my flushed face. 'Unless you'd like to call them anyway?'

'I ... ' I bite my lip furiously, my fists clenching.

Of course I don't want the police called. That's the last thing I want. And whoever was chasing me knows it.

'No,' I say lamely, and turn away from the empty field. John is staring at me and abruptly I can tell what he's thinking. That I'm a flake, or worse, that I made up a pursuer in order to get his attention. 'I must have imagined he was after me. Maybe he was out jogging and I heard him coming up behind me and thought ... Well, you know what I thought.' I manage a wan smile. 'I'm so sorry. You must think me a complete idiot.'

'Not at all.' He unlocks the camper van door and gestures me up the steps and inside. 'You did the right thing. If you hear some bloke huffing and puffing behind you in a lonely spot, you need to assume the worst. Especially out here in the countryside, where there's no one to hear you scream.'

It's meant to be a joke, I can tell by his half-smile, but I don't find it very funny. Still, if it hadn't been for John and his camper van, I might have been killed or bundled into that bloody SUV by now.

I have no idea what those people in the SUV want with me. But I'm happy not to have found out the hard way.

'I'm sorry,' I say again, swallowing. My heart rate is finally returning to normal but I feel shaken and exhausted after that tremendous sprint, my legs like jelly. 'Yelling like a maniac. And your door … I gave it a bit of a pounding, I'm afraid.'

'Forget it.' He clears space for me to sit on a padded bench behind a narrow, melamine table. 'Please, sit down. Make yourself at home.' He winks as I look about, curiously taking in his homely but messy interior. 'Welcome to my humble abode. It's not the Ritz but …'

'I love it,' I say decidedly.

He inclines his head with a smile. 'Can I get you a drink of some kind? Something alcoholic, maybe?'

'Not for me. I'm feeling a bit too shaky.'

He picks up the tin kettle and fills it from the tap. 'Cup of tea, then? I have fresh milk.'

'Sounds perfect, thank you.' I watch as he lights the gas ring. 'You know, I can't remember the last time someone made me a cuppa. The hazards of being a single parent, I guess.'

'Well, you're always welcome to drop in anytime.' John pauses, looking round at me a little wryly. 'Or whenever you're being chased by a dangerous jogger.'

I force a laugh. 'Don't, I feel stupid enough as it is.' There's a box of tissues on the table. While he's finding clean cups and tea bags, I take a tissue and wipe my sweaty face and neck with it. 'I'm so glad you turned up when you did, though. I thought I was going to burst a blood vessel.' I lean back against the padded seat, taking a deep breath. 'Your timing was magnificent.'

'Wasn't it just?' He grins, fetching milk from a small fridge tucked in under a counter.

'Where were you just now? I mean, where had you been?' I recall him saying he still had some odd jobs to do in the area. 'Working, I suppose?'

'Actually, I don't have any new jobs on until Monday. I just popped out to the shop for some cigarettes.' John pulls a folding chair into the narrow space opposite the bench, sits down and places his mobile face-down on the melamine table between us. 'Nasty habit, but I do sometimes indulge.'

'I didn't realise you smoked. I would never have guessed.' I'm rambling, not really thinking ... I glance towards the far end of the camper, where a pull-out bed is still in situ, covered with a crumpled duvet and tossed pillows. 'So this is where you hang out. Your home sweet home.' I drop my face into my hands, suddenly trembling and nauseous. Belated shock, I suppose. 'Oh God ... That was all so horrible. You know, I don't usually smoke either but I could really do with a cigarette about now.'

'Ah.' John sounds regretful, and I look up to see his gaze steady on my face. 'I'm sorry. By the time I got to the shop, I'd changed my mind. I promised myself weeks ago to stop smoking but ... It's easy to get tempted, living on your own.'

'No, of course, I understand.' I smile, though my heart is beating fast again. 'I didn't really want a cigarette anyway. Like you say, it's a nasty habit. A cup of tea will be fine.'

The kettle is boiling. John gets up to make us tea, and I stare blindly out of the camper van window at the quiet, empty field.

He's lying.

He didn't go out to get cigarettes.

I can't imagine why on earth John should feel the need to lie to me about such a mundane thing but it's disturbing. Rather like turning around to find him right there when I needed him, while the man who'd been chasing me simply vanished into thin air while my back was turned, like a conjuror's trick.

CHAPTER FIFTEEN

John insists on walking me back to the house, and I don't argue. That SUV is still out there somewhere, and while I'm not entirely sure I can trust him, I don't think John's one of the people who's been following and watching me. So he lied to me about going to get cigarettes, or it seems likely he did. That doesn't necessarily make him an enemy. I lie about stuff all the time these days. But only to protect my son.

On reaching my house, I don't immediately go next-door to collect Charlie from Patricia's, feeling too sweaty and done-in to cope with a manic three-year-old. At least I know he'll be safe with my neighbour for now, and she won't be expecting me back for a while yet anyway.

At the side door, John hesitates. 'Well, I'll see you around.' His eyes meet mine. 'Unless you invite me in for that coffee now.'

'Tea at yours, coffee at mine? People will talk.'

He laughs, but his gaze still holds mine. 'Seriously though, I'm happy to hang about for a bit. In case whoever that bloke is happens to have a go at you again.'

'I told you, it was most likely a misunderstanding.'

'Like the other night, you mean?'

'Sorry?'

'With that car that was kerb-crawling. Stopped outside your place there,' he says, nodding down the path to the street, 'and then drove off, tyres screaming. Definitely a misunderstanding.'

I study him for a moment, and then shrug. 'All right, why not come in? Though I'm afraid you'll have to make your own coffee or wait twenty minutes. I desperately need a shower.'

'Yes,' he says, with a speculative sniff, 'you do.'

'Hey!' I mock-punch his chest and am taken aback by how muscular he is. My fist makes zero impact. I noticed his muscles the first time I saw him but his chest is genuinely iron-hard. 'You work out?'

John laughs but shakes his head. 'It's the day job, actually. I'm always carrying heavy loads, digging holes or diving up and down ladders. Far better than a work-out. Plus, I get paid for doing it.'

I let him in and close the side door, locking and bolting it carefully behind us. He watches but I say nothing.

Let him think I'm a crazy security-obsessed lady. It doesn't matter. He clearly knows the driver of the SUV the other night was watching the house, following my movements … So he's not a fool. But I'm not prepared to discuss my business with him.

I don't know enough about John, and besides, the voice on the other end of the phone was explicit.

DON'T TALK TO ANYONE.

I leave him in the living room while I go upstairs for a quick shower, sure there isn't anything lying about that might incriminate me. I always make sure I hide anything important, aware that at any moment there may be another intruder or even a visit from the authorities.

When I come out, he's waiting for me in the bedroom, staring down at the street below.

I stop in the doorway, still wrapped in a towel, surprised to see him in my bedroom and not sure I want things to escalate this quickly. Not least because I don't want to find him tomorrow with a pair of scissors sticking out of his body.

'I thought you were making coffee,' I say lightly.

John turns and smiles. 'Yeah, I suddenly wasn't thirsty.' He comes towards me, his eyes on my body, partially exposed by the skimpy towel. 'Wow, you're really very beautiful.'

He bends his head and kisses me, his mouth warm and confident. After the initial shock, I jerk away hurriedly, shaking my head.

'Not yet, okay?'

To my relief, he doesn't push it, holding up his hands in a gesture of surrender. 'Okay, no worries. Sorry if I misread the signals.' The towel has slipped, exposing rather more breast than intended, and I see his eyes widen. Not quite touching me, his index finger traces a small, silvery scar there, more of an indent with raised pinkish edges. 'Is that what I think it is?'

'Cigarette burn.'

His eyes lift to mine. 'Christ.'

'I was thirteen. My foster dad did it. He said afterwards that I provoked him.' He frowns, waiting, and I finish softly, 'By not doing what he asked.'

'And what was that?'

'I don't think you want to know, actually.' My voice is suddenly hoarse. 'But it wasn't very nice.'

I turn away, pulling up the bath towel to hide myself. My heart is thumping and I feel light-headed, like I'm going to faint. The heat, no doubt. Or a delayed reaction from today's insane chase across the fields.

It's odd how his hands aren't calloused, I think. Considering that he works as a handyman.

'Sorry, I need to get changed,' I tell him, my tone cool and business-like. 'Do you mind?'

'Of course not.'

138

He vanishes downstairs without another word, and I stand there in my towel, unmoving, listening hard. After a minute or so, I hear cups clinking and the sound of the electric kettle.

I close the bedroom door and drop to my knees on the rug beside Charlie's bed, trembling with reaction. That damn cigarette burn scar. What on earth made me tell him about that? Or even remember that terrifying night, all these years later, when I thought it was buried under all those other times and places when I was in a bad spot and couldn't get out?

I rock back and forth, my mouth open on a silent cry of anguish, my eyes filling with tears …

By the time I go back downstairs, dressed and with a faint sheen of make-up to cover my blotchy cheeks, I'm back in control.

John has made coffee and is waiting in the lounge area, standing up, looking out at the back garden.

'I didn't know if you take sugar.'

I shake my head and scoop up the mug, cradling it in my hands. It's only instant coffee but it smells good.

'Thanks.'

He watches me, his brows still drawn together, his eyes frowning. 'Did you report him to social services? This foster dad who … did all that to you?'

'Eventually. It wasn't that simple.'

'I don't understand.'

'I had a reputation. For telling lies.' I sip my coffee, not looking at him. 'After a while, people tended not to believe me.'

'But the burn scar??'

'Self-harm.' I take another sip. 'This coffee really is good.'

'Sylvia… '

'Honestly, it's fine. It all happened a very long time ago. And it's something that happens to a lot of kids, especially in care. It was nothing special.' I give him a brittle smile. 'I am nothing special.'

'Am I allowed to disagree?'

I sit down on the sofa and gesture him to join me. 'It's an old story. I try not to think about it anymore. But Charlie ... That's where my focus is. My own child. And never wanting him to go through what I did as a kid, to suffer at the hands of... ' I stop and sink my teeth into my lower lip, hard. 'People who were supposed to be looking after me.'

John comes to sit beside me. Not too close, our thighs not quite touching. All the same, I freeze, very aware of him.

'I understand now why you didn't want me to call the police.' His gaze is steady and serious. 'You don't want to risk Charlie being taken into care too.'

'Never,' I agree. 'Not even for a day. It would kill me.'

'I get that now.' He puts down his mug on the coffee table. 'But you're the victim here, Sylvia. You were the victim both as a child and today. The police wouldn't take Charlie away just because you thought you were about to be assaulted.'

'I have no witnesses,' I point out. 'You didn't see anyone. They might think I'm mentally unstable, and then I'd lose Charlie for sure.'

'I suppose that's a possibility.' He leans back against the sofa cushions, looking at me. 'How long were you in care?'

'For as long as I can remember. Let's see...' Memories flash through my head, dark and golden. 'I was probably about five or six when I was taken to Broadfields. That was my first children's home,' I add when he frowns again. 'It was an okay place. Nice enough people. The other kids could be shitty at times, but ... I got used to it.' I put my own mug next to his. 'Then I got fostered. And that was not a great experience. They brought me back within a few months. I had another two or maybe three foster parents before I was eleven. Then I was back in care for a couple more years. Then Mary and Froggy fostered me.'

'Froggy?'

'Yeah, he had long, funny-looking legs and a big, wet mouth, so I called him Froggy.' I suck in a sharp breath. 'He was the one who … ' My voice breaks and I reach for my coffee again, holding it against me like a magical talisman. Something to ward off evil spirits. 'He, erm… ' I clear my throat but struggle for the next words.

'You don't have to tell me if it makes you uncomfortable.'

I nod and take a gulp of coffee; it isn't so hot now. 'I've never told anyone else, really. Except the social worker and she didn't believe me. Not until I got the burn marks.' She heard his intake of breath and nodded. 'Though even then, Froggy swore I'd done it to myself. He was very good at that. Lying about me, I mean. It took social services another two years to work out what was going on and pull me out of there.'

He runs a hand through his hair. 'You poor kid.'

'I grew up fast.'

'I bet.' John leans forward. 'But what about your real parents? How did you end up in care?'

'I told you, I don't remember. Except one thing … I have a memory, and I'm not sure if it's real or made-up, but it's me sitting in some kind of waiting room, maybe at a railway station or a bus station, and the hours ticking by … And people kept asking, where's your mother? Where's your father? And I always said, they're coming soon, they're coming back for me. And then eventually I realised nobody was coming.' I swallow a sudden rush of bitterness that I didn't even know existed until now. 'So I went to someone and told them I was alone, and … that's all I remember.' I sigh, closing my eyes. 'Just the sitting and waiting for hours, and the longing.'

I feel his hand take mine, and I open my eyes.

'I'm sorry,' he says, like it was his fault.

'Thanks.' A tear rolls down my cheek and I brush it away impatiently. 'Yeah, it wasn't the best start in life. But now I have Charlie, and I'm determined to keep him safe. To be a good mother and never leave him waiting somewhere, not knowing if I'm ever coming back for him.' I sit up with a violent start, my gaze flying to the clock on the wall. 'Shit.'

He sits up too. 'What is it?'

'Charlie.' I jump up and instantly feel dizzy. Today's excitement was definitely not good for me. 'I forgot to pick him up from Patricia's. How bloody ironic. She's had him nearly three hours now. Some mother I am.'

'Hey, don't beat yourself about it. Not after the shock you've had. These things happen.' Helpfully, John gathers up the coffee mugs and follows me into the kitchen. 'Can I do anything to help?'

'No,' I say, shooting him a smile. 'I have to go, I'm sorry. Look, thank you for seeing me home and making that coffee. It was great.' I pause. 'And for the chat. I actually needed that.' My mouth twists. 'I didn't know I needed it, but I did.'

I watch John head off back to his field and his camper van, making sure he really is leaving, and then hurry next door to collect Charlie.

'Thank you so much,' I tell Patricia, who's tidying away a plate of snacks they've been enjoying together. 'I'm sorry I took so long.'

'It was no problem,' she says, and smiles indulgently. 'To be honest, I love the company. Never get old, Sylvia. It can be a very lonely existence.'

'Mummy.' My son holds up his hands, grinning, and I lift him into my arms, hugging him tight.

Today, I crossed a line without even realising.

I left myself wide open to whoever is out to get me, and nearly never saw my little boy again.

I must never, ever, *ever* do that again.

CHAPTER SIXTEEN

Charlie is drowsy and heavy-eyed but insists on watching cartoons. I sit him in front of the television with a tumbler of juice and some chocolate biscuits, which he seizes on with a glowing face. Most days, I try to give him healthy snacks. But as everything seems to be going to hell in a handcart, I let him have the much-prized biscuits and even take a few from the packet myself.

While my son is preoccupied, giggling over his favourite cartoon show, I grab the burner phone and text an urgent message to my protector, whoever that is.

Chased by a man from an SUV while out for a walk. Got away but I'm scared. What should I do?

I wait a long and agonizing twenty-three minutes before a reply finally comes. In that time, I double-check all the doors and windows are secure, scan the road outside several times, and wipe chocolate off Charlie's mouth.

'More,' he chants, grinning. 'More. More. More.'

'No.'

'More. More.'

'You'll only be sick.' I help him with his juice. 'I think you're tired.' His face falls. 'Time for another nap, maybe.'

My son folds his arms and shakes his head, mouth set in a mulish line, and throws himself back among the sofa cushions.

'Telly,' he insists. 'Toons.'

'Only if you sit quietly,' I warn him, but gently, knowing how weary he is.

Charlie gives a fervent nod and fixes his eyes on the television screen. All the same, I can tell how much today's outing to Patricia's has tired him out, poor little man. Nap-time looks like an inevitability. Though it might be a good idea to let him fall asleep on the sofa and then carry him upstairs later. Whenever he does that, he always seems to sleep longer than when I enforce a nap-time on him.

The mobile finally buzzes while I'm rinsing out his juice tumbler. Quickly, I dry my hands and pick it up.

Keep the door locked. Speak to nobody. Don't leave the house. Await further instructions.

I stare at the message in growing frustration. Is that it? That's all my so-called guardian angel has to say, after I was chased by a man across several fields, in fear for my life? How about some kind of explanation?

I ring the only number in the burner phone memory and wait. It takes about ten rings, then someone answers it. Only they don't speak. I stand in the kitchen with the phone against my ear, listening to silence.

'For God's sake,' I hiss into the phone, 'I thought he was going to kill me. Do you get that? Do you understand? I was terrified.'

Silence.

But he's listening, I'm sure of it.

'Tell me what you know … Who was that man? Was he from the police? Is he something to do with the … the deaths?' Even on this private burner phone, I can't bring myself to say their names out loud or detail what I really mean. 'Do you even know what's going on?'

The silence continues.

The skin crawls on the back of my neck, and I shudder.

'WHO THE FUCK ARE YOU?' I yell into the phone, shaking with pure mindless fury.

The phone cuts off, and I drop it, staring down at the mobile like it's a snake that's bitten me.

He hung up on me.

I yelled and my protector cut me off.

Christ.

I sink onto the kitchen floor and wrap my arms about myself, rocking back and forth, tears spilling down my cheeks. It feels cold and dark in the little house, though it's bright sunshine outside.

I'm so alone, I keep thinking, rocking and holding myself. So alone, so alone, so alone …

A little hand strokes my hair.

'S'okay, Mummy,' Charlie pipes, sounding both sympathetic and frightened at the same time. 'Don't cry.'

I grab my boy and half-laugh, half-groan, my whole body shaking as we cling together.

'I'm sorry,' I babble. 'Don't worry. Mummy's not … not sad. Just a bit tired. I'll be better in a minute.'

'Bedtime,' he suggests solemnly, and clasps a sticky hand to my damp cheek. 'Nap?'

'Yes, I'll take a nap soon. But first Mummy has a few things to do.' I stumble to my feet and take his hand, forcing a cheerful smile to my face. I don't want him to be scared. Right now, I'm scared enough for the both of us. 'But you should go up to bed. How about I tell you a bedtime story and then you can have a nice nap until tea-time?'

He nods enthusiastically, clearly relieved that his mother is no longer in a helpless puddle on the kitchen floor.

I take him upstairs, tell him a rambling bedtime story with a deeply unsatisfying ending, and then tuck him in, all the time my attention half on the sounds of the street below the bedroom window.

I catch the occasional rumble of cars coming and going, voices, laughter, noises that suggest activity outside the house.

But nobody comes to the door, and it's with a slowing heartbeat that I finally trail downstairs again and sink onto the sofa with the silent burner phone to wait.

But wait for what?

When I wake up, it's late afternoon. The light is no longer so sharp but has segued to a soft golden mellowness, filtering through the curtains that mask the large bay windows overlooking the back garden. I blink the sleep away, staring sideways at the blank television screen.

I must have fallen asleep while waiting for the burner phone to buzz again. It's in my hand; I check my messages but there's still nothing new from my protector. Assuming he is my protector and not someone controlling me, jerking my strings from the shadows.

So what woke me?

I listen but there's still no sound from upstairs where I left Charlie deep in slumber.

Then I hear it. A gentle *tap-tap-tap*.

I sit up, my heart revving.

Someone is standing in my back garden, tapping on one of the windows. I stare, bolt-eyed, at the closed curtains. There's a vague shape just visible through the thin fabric, one arm raised to tap on the glass.

Tap-tap-tap.

Who the hell is it?

Someone, for starters, who doesn't want to be seen visiting me, so has crept around the back for added secrecy. Except there's no way around the back of these houses unless you come via the wild moorland that stretches seemingly forever at the bottom of the garden. Which somehow makes this visitor even more scary. Whoever it is must have come creeping from God knows where through acres of coarse dry grasses and scrub bushes and gnarled trees, and climbed silently over the fence, slowly slinking up to the house from the bottom of our long, long garden …

I get up, breathing fast and shallow, my chest tight. Should I ignore the tapping? Or pull back the curtain and see who's there?

I suppose it's possible whoever it is came to the side door and knocked there while I was sleeping, and continued on round into the back garden when they received no answer.

But I doubt it.

The hand raises again, refusing to be ignored.

Tap-tap-tap.

That's not the knock of an ordinary visitor. It's not Patricia or John or the Reverend. It's someone new.

Slipping the burner phone into my pocket, I take a few unsteady steps towards the back window and rattle the curtain across.

There's a figure there in a black hoody, face obscured.

I jump back with a gasp.

'Christ…'

But my instinctive urge to run isn't needed; this isn't the well-built, dark-haired man who pursued me across the fields earlier.

This person is shorter and less bulky, and as the hand at the window is slowly withdrawn, I catch the glint of silvery-pearl varnish on each well-manicured fingernail.

It's a woman.

Her features are hidden under the dark, over-large hood, but I see fine strands of blonde hair peeking out – the kind of too-strong platinum blonde that only comes from a bottle – and am aware of the glint of teeth as the woman smiles.

She points to the side door and then places a finger against her lips.

Unsure what to do, I nod and make my way to the side door, thinking all the while. I shouldn't let her in, should I? She's a complete stranger. But she's also a woman, which seems less of a threat.

Is my protector a woman?

I was so sure the voice on the other end of the phone sounded male, but she could have been using software to disguise her voice, deliberately making it sound like a man's to throw me off the scent.

Or perhaps this is someone he's sent to help me, because he can't make it here in person himself.

But if it's a trick, a trap …

I unbolt the side door and open it a crack, and she's there suddenly, pushing it wider and slipping inside like a ghost.

'Hey,' I say, but it's too late, she's in the house.

The woman closes the door, turns the key in the lock and bolts it too before turning to look at me. She's breathing quickly, her chest rising and falling, more blonde hair showing, and now I can see more of her face.

For a moment, neither of us speak.

Then she pushes back her hood and stares at me. She's slightly taller than me, though our figures are similar, and she has fine, sculpted features, full lips with dark pink lipstick, and large blue eyes outlined with thick black kohl, her lashes darkened with mascara too. Her blonde-from-a-bottle hair falls to just below her shoulders and is well cut in a classic style.

That's when I realise why she dyes her hair; she's not as young as I'd thought at first. The slender figure and lithe, graceful step had confused my senses. How old exactly, though? Late forties? Early fifties?

'You are Sylvia,' she says hesitantly, looking me up and down.

I nod.

'You know who I am?' she asks, and there's an odd accent behind her question. Guttural, foreign.

Before I can answer, there's a buzzing from my front jeans pocket. A text. We both look down at it.

'See who it is,' she instructs me softly. 'But don't reply.'

I don't argue. After everything that's happened today, I'm willing to take a few things on trust if it will keep me out of danger and with Charlie.

Someone's coming to help you once it's safe. Stay where you are and wait. They'll knock three times. Let them in.

148

I had assumed, on first looking at the blonde, that I'd been wrong to imagine she was my protector. But this message confuses me.

I shiver, feeling like someone just walked over my grave. It's not the first time I've felt that since coming to Darkling Moreton, to this strange little house that used to be a salon. All the tiny hairs on the back of my neck and on my arms are prickling …

'What does it say?' the blonde demands.

Silently, I show her the screen.

'Ha,' is all she says on reading it, but studies my face, her eyes narrowed. 'Who sends you this message?'

'I thought it might be you.'

She is blank. 'Me? No.'

'A man, then. My protector.' I see her face and add, 'That's what I call him. He's like a guardian angel. He looks after me when I get into trouble.' I don't know why I'm admitting all this to a complete stranger, but it just feels so natural. 'That's why I'm here. He told me to come here. To this village.'

Her eyes narrow again. 'Why?'

There, my nerve fails me. 'I'd rather not talk about that.' I put the phone away without replying, chin up. 'Why are *you* pretending?'

The woman frowns. 'Pretending?'

'Not to know who the message is from.' I point at her. 'You knocked three times. My protector sent you here. Didn't he?'

She says nothing, tilting her head to one side as she watches me. Her face is hard to read.

'Come on, admit it. You know who he is.' I'm not going to let her off the hook, even if she has come to help me. I'll keep asking until she's honest with me; I've had enough of all these lies and subterfuge. 'Tell me the truth, for God's sake.'

At last, she nods. 'I know who he is.'

That accent again. I can't place it but I know it's familiar. So familiar, it makes me feel light-headed listening to her.

'Thank you for being honest.'

'Honest?' The woman's gaze falters at last and she looks away. There's a flush along her strong cheekbones. 'Come, we sit down and talk properly.' She opens a cupboard without asking where the alcohol is and gets out the bottle of expensive vodka, fetches two small tumblers from the glass shelf and nods me toward the living room. 'Woman to woman.'

CHAPTER SEVENTEEN

The platinum blonde spins a dining chair around and straddles it, facing me across the dark wood table we hardly ever use, preferring the more homely pine table in the kitchen instead. With a steady hand, she unscrews the vodka bottle lid, flips it away into a corner, and pours two generous helpings of vodka into the two tumblers. No mixer, I note, and am unsure I'll even be able to manage a mouthful.

She puts the bottle down, pushes one tumbler towards me and takes a large gulp of neat vodka.

To my relief, she makes a disgusted noise and pulls a face. Maybe now she will ask for a mixer.

'We have a litre bottle of lemonade,' I begin hesitantly, but she glares at me, her face still screwed up as though she can smell something awful.

'Never pollute vodka with lemonade. Never. You hear?' She takes another long swig from her tumbler, and this time I realise it's a look of contempt on her screwed-up face, not disgust. 'This should have been kept in *fridge*. In *fridge*, yes? You cannot drink vodka if you keep it in cupboard.'

'You're Russian,' I say, suddenly understanding both the accent and the way she's downing the vodka as though there's no tomorrow.

'Of course I'm Russian.' She slams the tumbler down on the table and a little vodka sloshes out, pooling under the glass. Her stare challenges me. 'You know who I am, *Sylvia*.'

The way she drawls my name gives me the chills. It's as though she's mocking me with it. As though she knows it's not my real name but is playing along for her own amusement.

Exactly how much did my protector tell her about me?

'Yes.' I had recognised her face as soon as she dropped the hood. 'You used to run this place. You were the hairdresser, Natasha.'

'Natasha Cuts,' she agrees, nodding, and then laughs grimly. 'Natasha. Cuts.' More vodka and she almost growls. 'He thought it was good joke. Ha ha ha … ' Her lip curls, the laughter dying abruptly. 'Not for long, though.'

'He?'

But she's noticed I haven't touched my own vodka. 'Drink, drink,' she urges me, pushing the tumbler closer to me. 'It will put heart in you.'

I raise the tumbler to my lips and shudder as the fiery liquid bathes my lips. 'Sorry, I … I'm not a big vodka fan.' I see her outrage and add hurriedly, 'Not when it's neat.'

Natasha looks disgusted again. For real, this time.

'You said, he …' I try to distract her, though I also want answers. 'Who is *he*?' She says nothing, so I take a shot in the dark and suggest, 'Sir Philip?'

She's playing with her glass, turning it round and round, but stops and sucks in a sharp breath at this suggestion. 'Janus,' she corrects me. 'That is his name. That is what I call him.'

'Well, that's who I meant. Sir Philip Janus.'

I try not to show how shocked I am by this confirmation of my suspicions. I was sure it couldn't be a coincidence I'd been brought here, to this former salon, to Darkling Moreton, considering my history. But this crazy unexpected visit from the former owner, who may or may not have murdered a man in the church twenty-odd years ago, has blown my mind.

So, I was right. The older gentleman in the stylish Panama hat is connected to what's going on here.

But how?

'Drink.' Her eyes narrow on me.

'Look, I'm still struggling.' I pretend to drink, just wetting my lips with the horrible neat vodka again, though only to placate her. 'What's Sir Philip's connection here? Can you explain it to me?' I'm thinking hard, trying to sort out my priority questions so I ask them in the right order, at least. 'I mean, I know my protector sent you to me, but I don't really understand – '

'He did not send me.'

My heart begins to race again. 'What?'

'Your "protector" did not send me. I come here because I want to see you. To talk to you alone.' Natasha raises her gaze from her glass, slowly. She seems reluctant to say more, but after a brief hesitation adds grudgingly, 'And ask for your help.'

'*My* help?' I'm utterly at sea now. I can't imagine being able to help this woman who, frankly, scares the living daylights out of me. 'I'm sorry but you've lost me.'

The glass, on its way to her mouth, pauses. Her blue eyes widen and fix on me intently. 'I have *lost* you?'

'As in, I don't have a clue what you're talking about.'

'Ah.' She throws back her head and gives a real laugh then, her whole body shaking. Then she tips the vodka bottle and refills her glass almost to the top. 'I need more vodka, in that case.'

I watch her drink.

'There was a man found dead in the church here,' I begin warily, poised to leap back if she attacks me. 'Two decades ago. He'd been stabbed with a pair of scissors. Maybe a pair of hairdressing scissors.'

'And you want to know, did I kill him?'

Her blunt demand stops me partway through my meandering lead-up to exactly that question. All I can do is nod, watching her in trepidation.

'That man, hmm.' Natasha sips her neat vodka, her eyes half-closed as she seems to savour the fiery taste on her lips. 'What you must understand... He was sent here to kill me.'

'*What?*'

'He came to Darkling Moreton to kill me.' She shrugs, unmoved, as though this is somehow commonplace. 'That's what he was. Assassin. He was doing job. Nothing more, nothing less.' She sips again, this time without immediately swallowing, seeming to savour the heat of the neat vodka in her mouth. 'I had no choice, see? It was kill or be killed.'

She seems to be waiting for an answer, so I shrug too. 'Of course.'

Her eyes are unfocussed, as though looking back on that day in her past. 'Girl was not here. I was alone in house. There was nobody to help. I run to church to see if ... ' She frowns and corrects herself slightly. 'To hide there. But he finds me. We struggle, we fight ... I kill him.' This time her shrug is eloquent. 'I leave body in church, pack bag and leave village.'

'You ran away.'

Again, she shrugs. 'If you like.'

'And the hairdressing scissors? Is that what you used to kill him?'

'I forget.'

I don't believe her nonchalant loss of memory over that detail, but I can't see what good it will do to press her on the subject.

'Okay.' I'm piecing the situation together in my head but there are still huge parts of the puzzle missing, gaping holes where I can't make any logical connection. What *isn't* she telling me? 'But if that's exactly what happened, Natasha, you wouldn't necessarily have been blamed for his death. If he came here to attack you and you could prove it was self-defence, why not just stay and explain all that to the police?'

'*Police?*' She is staring at me in blank astonishment, and then shakes her head, her mouth quirking in a crooked half-smile. 'No police, no thank you.'

'But – '

'Have you talked to police?' She leans forward as though interrogating me. 'Have *you* told them about all bad things that happen to you?'

I can find nothing to say in response to that, but look away guiltily, my heart hammering.

Natasha was definitely sent by my protector, whatever she may say. She must have been, I tell myself. She knows about the deaths. She knows what's happened to me. What else can she mean by *bad things*?

'You see? It is not so simple.' She is nodding. 'Sometimes, there is no way to explain to police. Only jail cell.'

There's a sound elsewhere in the house. The faint creak of floorboards, and then a door opening slowly. Somewhere above our heads. I glance up with sudden apprehension.

Someone is moving around upstairs.

Natasha jumps up from her seat, staring wide-eyed at the ceiling as though expecting masked men to come crashing through it with guns. 'Who is it?' she asks me in an urgent whisper. 'Who is up there?'

'Calm down, it's only Charlie. My little boy. I left him sleeping upstairs.'

'Ah.' Slowly, she lowers her gaze to my face, and then nods. 'I had forgot…You have son.'

I'm surprised. 'You knew about Charlie?'

'Of course.'

She says 'of course' as though there's nothing this woman doesn't know about me, right down to my shoe size.

It's disconcerting.

A sudden realisation strikes me. 'You're Balaclava Man.'

She stares at me blankly.

'You came here in the night, wearing a balaclava. You had a key.' I blink, remembering the figure I'd half-seen in the hallway. 'I thought you were a man.'

She shrugs, not denying it. 'Yes, I still have key. I just wanted to … look around.' I get the feeling she's lying about that. But an odd smile lifts her lips, distracting me. 'I thought locks would be changed. Huh.'

More creaks from upstairs. She glances up at the ceiling again, frowning.

'I expect he's woken up and needs the toilet, that's all.' I half-rise and she watches me, eyes narrowed. 'I … I should go up and help him.'

At that moment, we hear the toilet half-flush several times, worked by a small and inexpert hand, and then the sound of Charlie tottering across the landing on his way downstairs.

I get up and head for the stairs, eager to keep Charlie away from her. 'Sorry, I'll make sure he goes back to his room.'

'No,' she says sharply, and drains her glass with a decided air. 'I want to meet this boy. Let him come.'

I hesitate in the doorway, uneasy.

I don't like the idea of introducing Charlie to this woman. By her own admission, she's a murderer, even if it was self-defence as she claims. And given the particularly brutal method she used to kill that man – with a pair of hairdressing scissors, which she hasn't denied – there's a faint but crazy possibility in my head that she may also have been behind the deaths of my boyfriends. Though why and how is beyond my understanding.

But I'm not sure I have much choice at the moment. I'm alone here with Natasha and I'm suspicious she could force me to do whatever she wants. Better, perhaps, to play along for now and avoid outright violence.

'Hello, darling.' I go to meet Charlie at the foot of the stairs, my heart thumping wildly. 'Did … Did you wash your hands after going to the loo?'

Still flushed from sleep, Charlie holds up both hands to show me they're still damp from the tap. He's smiling.

'Wishy-washy,' he chants. 'Wishy-washy.'

'Good boy.' I take his hand, which is indeed still moist and clammy, and lead him halfway towards Natasha, stopping in the middle of the open-plan living area.

'This is a friend of mine. She's just here for a quick visit.' I look at her with a challenge in my face. 'Aren't you?'

'We will see,' is all she says, not looking at me but at Charlie. She crouches and beckons him. 'Come, let me see you.'

Charlie wriggles free of my hand and runs towards her. He's usually quite shy with strangers, so this surprises me.

I watch in trepidation.

'Hello,' he says, and holds up his hands again. 'Wishy-washy. All clean.'

'I'm glad to know this,' our visitor says soberly. 'Dirty is not good.' She looks him up and down. 'He is big boy. Very fine. How old?'

'He's nearly four,' I say quickly, and come to scoop him up in my arms. 'Too young for this conversation though.'

'Toons?' Charlie suggests hopefully, looking towards the television. 'Biccies?'

'You'll spoil your tea,' I say automatically and shake my head. 'You can watch cartoons, but no snacks. You have to wait until tea-time.'

'Fruit,' Natasha says forcefully, and strides into the kitchen as I seat Charlie in front of the television and turn it on for him. She returns with a small apple from the fruit bowl. 'This good for you.' She hands this to Charlie with a grim nod. 'Eat.'

Eyes widening at her stark tone, he nods and bites into it. 'Fanks,' he says indistinctly through a mouthful of apple, and then turns his head as one of his favourite cartoons comes on.

Natasha watches him eat for a moment, an odd expression on her face, and then takes a deep breath. 'Now, we talk again,' she says under her breath, and heads back to the table to pour herself another large glass of neat vodka. 'Come, come.' She points to the chair I'd vacated. 'Sit, we drink together.'

'I'm fine, thanks.' I cover my glass as she approaches it with the bottle. 'I need to stay sober. For the boy's sake.'

'Huh.' But she doesn't insist, putting down the bottle. 'Okay, I know how it is.'

I wonder how she's able to stay upright after all the alcohol she's consumed, and am glad to see her only sip at it this time, her mind clearly on other things than getting drunk.

'You had a child once, didn't you?' I ask, looking at her curiously.

Her eyes shift to mine, fixed and intent. 'How do you know this?'

'There's a photo of this house in the pub. Back when it was still a hair salon. You're standing in the doorway over there,' I say, jerking my head towards the entrance of what used to be the salon, 'and there's a child on a bike out front.'

She nods slowly. 'Ah, I remember that photograph. That day. A long, long time ago.'

'What happened to the child?'

Her face is abruptly cold. 'I … *lost* her.'

I'm not sure what she means, exactly. So, she had a daughter. But whether the girl is dead or genuinely lost to her, I can't tell.

'I'm sorry.'

'And him? Charlie?' She pronounces my son's name with difficulty. 'Where is his father?'

There's no point lying. Not to this woman.

'Dead.'

Her eyes narrow on my face. 'Huh.' She sips at her vodka, looking down into her glass and repeating slowly, 'Huh.'

'By the time I realised I was pregnant, it was a bit late to do anything about it. And I've always thought …' I hesitate.

Her brows rise. 'Yes?'

'That people should live by the consequences of their actions, I suppose. I was careless. In return, I got Charlie.' I smile and take a deep swig from my vodka glass before realising what I'm doing. My mouth burns, my eyes smart, and I finish breathlessly, choking, 'Not a … bad … bargain, really. I love him to bits.'

'To *bits*?' She looks scandalised.

'It just means I … love him a great deal,' I explain between coughs, wishing I could rush to the kitchen and consume half a gallon of cold water.

But she seems to understand, nodding. 'A dangerous thing.'

'Love? Yes.'

Our eyes meet, and I get the oddest sensation. That old 'someone stepping on my grave' thing, or maybe a wave of nausea after all that neat vodka.

She begins to say something softly, almost under her breath, but stops dead at a sound from outside. A rattling crash, and then running footsteps down the side alley.

Someone bangs on the kitchen door. Loud, urgent. 'Sylvia, let me in! Quick, hurry up!'

It's John.

CHAPTER EIGHTEEN

I head for the side door, reaching automatically to unbolt it. Natasha is quicker though, slapping my hand down, her whisper urgent in my ear. 'No, don't.'

'It's only John. He's a local, a friend of mine,' I whisper back. She shakes her head, not seeming to understand what I'm saying. 'I should let him in.'

'No,' she mouths at me, stubborn.

The panic that seized me when I first began to realise she might not have been sent by my protector comes back in a wave of fear, rather like a spasm in my gut, everything inside clenching hard. I feel lost and helpless, as though Natasha is the adult here and I'm the child. Perhaps sensing this, she throws an arm across my chest and forces me backwards, but silently. Her gaze locks with mine the whole time, as though daring me to disobey.

'For God's sake … ' John bangs on the door again, sounding increasingly desperate. 'Open up!'

'Take the boy upstairs,' Natasha says into my ear.

I stare at her. My heartbeat thuds loud as a drum, my breathing ragged.

'It could be the visitor I'm expecting. Remember the text? I was told to wait until someone knocked three times, and then let them in.'

'This one, he knocks six, seven, eight times,' she points out, her eyes mere slits of derision. 'Take boy upstairs.'

'But why?' I ask, also keeping my voice down, her caution infecting me too, though I really don't know why I don't call out to John to help us, that we're being held hostage by this crazy individual.

'Do what I say.' She shakes my arm. 'And make no noise, yes?'

There's an unmistakeable threat in her face now.

Uneasily, I take a few steps toward the living room, still unsure whether I should rush to the door and unbolt it or think of Charlie's safety first and hurry him upstairs to that locked room as fast as I can. But my brain is jammed with contradictory messages.

Why does she think John might be an enemy?

She doesn't even know John.

But once Charlie is safely stowed upstairs, perhaps I can come down and let John into the house anyway. Yes, that's the sensible thing to do. Especially if he was sent here to save me.

As I reach the threshold into the living room, I glance back to see her slip a black, snub-nosed pistol from the bulging pocket at the front of her hoody and walk purposefully toward the side door.

For a split-second, I'm frozen, watching her. Too horrified to process what I'm seeing. Then reality hits.

'No,' I gasp, and run back.

Natasha stops, her hand raised to the bolt, staring round at me. 'I tell you, no sound. And take boy away.' She seems astonished rather than angry. 'Go.'

'No, it's John,' I repeat, breathing hard. 'You can't shoot him, for God's sake. He's a friend, and I trust him.' I glare at the gun. 'Where the hell did you even get that? Is it real?'

She makes a snorting noise.

'Sylvia?' John is thumping on the door again, calling my name, his voice suspicious now. 'I can hear voices.' Pause. 'Who's in there with you? Are you in trouble?'

'Look, how about you go and hide,' I tell her softly, 'while I find out what he wants? Maybe there's been some kind of accident and he needs help.' I see her eyebrows flick upwards in derision and add, 'I won't tell him you're here, I promise. Put that gun away, for goodness' sake.'

To my relief, she pockets the gun again. But her expression is sulky and rebellious. Is it the vodka making her behave so wildly?

'This not end good,' she mutters.

Charlie is standing in the doorway to the kitchen, TV remote control in hand, watching us with obvious dismay.

'What wrong, Mummy?' he pipes up.

There's a short tense silence.

'Nothing, little boy,' Natasha tells him, her unwavering gaze still on my face. 'Aunty Natasha sit with you. Five minutes. We watch cartoon, yes?'

'Yes!' Charlie exclaims, his face brightening, suddenly enthusiastic.

'No, Charlie, you come here and stay with me,' I begin, frightened for my son. I don't want him alone with a madwoman with a gun for five seconds, let alone five minutes. But Charlie has already seized Natasha's hand and is dragging her towards the living area.

'Toons,' he insists cheerfully.

John is still banging on the door and calling my name.

It crosses my mind that my protector may have sent him. Sent him to protect me against Natasha.

I unbolt the side door with shaking hands, turn the key in the lock, and open the door a crack, peering out. John's hand slams against the wood, pushing me aside as he shoulders his way inside.

'Hey,' I protest.

How many more people are going to insist on coming into my house today?

He pays no attention, stalking about the kitchen like a caged animal, stopping to stare out at the back garden as though expecting to see someone there. He's flushed and sweating, dark stains under the armpits of his blue polo shirt.

162

'What the hell, Sylvia … Why didn't you open the door before?' John demands, wiping the back of his hand across his forehead. 'Didn't you hear me shouting? And who were you talking to?'

No more Mr Nice Guy, it seems.

I watch him, disturbed. Perhaps my protector didn't send him to look after me. Or Natasha is far more dangerous than she looks – she does have a gun, after all – and John is reacting out of fear rather than anger. Either way, I can't believe his turning up here right now and in such a storming panic is a coincidence. This has to be connected to Natasha's visit, doesn't it?

'I was talking to Charlie,' I say lamely, unsure now whether I should mention my visitor or not. After all, she has a gun and she has Charlie. Crazily though, John's erratic behaviour is worrying me more than the armed Russian hiding in my living room. 'He was being naughty so I … I sent him to watch telly.'

He looks unconvinced by my lie, turning towards the living area as though to check my story.

I try to distract him. 'What was all that yelling for, anyway? I thought there must have been an accident in the street, the way you were going on.'

I start to open the outside door, and he comes dashing back to slam it shut, holding it closed with one large hand.

We're standing very close. His chest is heaving and he's very red in the face. I don't like the look in his eyes.

'John,' I say carefully, 'what's going on?' I take an unsteady breath, meeting his angry gaze. 'You're scaring me.'

'I know you probably won't believe me,' he begins.

How ironic. 'Try me.'

'People are coming to hurt you. To hurt you and Charlie.'

'People?' When he says nothing more, his gaze fixed on my face, I say more cautiously, 'Why would someone want to hurt us?'

'I think you know why.'

Catching my breath, I hold it, staring at him blankly. I recall how I fled across fields and straight into John's arms, turning to find my pursuer had vanished. Mysteriously, but to my great relief too, so I hadn't questioned it at the time.

Now I'm suspicious.

Softly, I ask, 'Where are they, John? These "people" who want to hurt us?'

'Outside.'

'You were running from them?'

He nods.

'What now, then? We can't stay here forever, and if they're waiting outside, we can't leave either.' I decide to test him. 'Perhaps we should call the police.'

He smiles then, and I feel my skin crawl.

'I don't think calling the police would do any good, would it? The only thing we can do is leave together, right now, in broad daylight, and call their bluff.'

'And go where?'

'Let me take care of the details.'

From the other room I hear the theme tune of one of Charlie's favourite cartoon shows. It's loud, like he's just cranked up the volume. Though of course Charlie is unlikely to have done that. My unwelcome guest has been playing with the remote control, I guess.

His head turns that way, listening. 'Get Charlie,' he tells me, his voice hoarse and urgent, 'and we'll walk out of here right now. Before they think to call for back up.'

'Back up?'

'There are only two of them. Sitting out there in their damn SUV. Easier odds.'

Now I understand. He's talking about the watchers in the black SUV. The men who tried to run me down and then gave chase across the fields.

But something's still wrong here.

I shake my head, taking a tentative step backwards. I'd half had it in the back of my mind that my watchers must be undercover police, that they had found me in Darkling Moreton, despite my protector's help, but perhaps wanted to make sure they had the right person before making a move. But now I'm confused and unsure.

The police might understandably want to arrest me for suspected murder. But I doubt they mean me actual physical harm as John is suggesting. Or Charlie, in fact.

'John, what do you know about them? Who are they?'

'The least you know, the better,' is his abrupt answer.

John grabs my arm before I can move out of his reach.

'Look, just get Charlie now,' he orders me, 'before they decide to rush us.' His eyes narrow on my face. 'Do you think I don't know what you're doing, trying to delay me? You'll only end up getting yourself and your son killed.'

When I flinch, he nods, looking almost satisfied. 'Yes, not a nice thought, is it? Stop messing about and do exactly what I tell you.'

Before I can react, I see John's face change and his eyes widen. His grip slackens and he stares over my shoulder at the kitchen door. 'What in God's name ...?' His body turns rigid, the flush leaving his cheeks so rapidly, it looks like he's about to faint. 'I don't believe it.'

I turn my head, not sure what to expect.

Natasha is standing in the doorway.

Our chat about the gun has clearly been forgotten, because she's taken her weapon out of her hoody pocket and is pointing it straight at us.

At John, in particular.

On her other side, she holds Charlie by the hand, and it's clear they've been busy since she went to sit with him. My son is all set to go outside, wearing his trainers and baseball cap, but shows none of his usual excitement before an outing, staring transfixed at her weapon instead.

'Gun,' my little boy points out, unnecessarily.

165

That Charlie even knows what a gun looks like, at the tender age of three, chills me to the bone. But my focus right now is on Natasha. That's where the danger lies.

'Please,' I say, holding out a placatory hand, 'put that away. You don't need it. I told you, he's a friend.'

'A friend who want you dead,' she said succinctly.

'Of course he doesn't.' I struggle to stay patient. 'Listen, you don't understand. He says there are people out there, people watching the house, and we need to get out of here before they can call for … Well, more men.'

She gives a laugh. 'Oldest trick in book.'

'Now you're just being ridiculous.' I glance back at John and see something in his face that alarms me. 'Tell her, John.'

Before I know what's happening, John has me by the throat, spinning me around in the same violent movement to face Natasha, with him safely behind me.

Now I'm facing Natasha's gun head-on. He's using me as a human shield.

Shocked, I give a muffled exclamation and try to wriggle out of his grasp. But it's no good. His arm is clamped across my throat.

The more I struggle, the harder his arm presses down, cutting off my ability to breathe.

'John,' I gurgle, thrashing about as his grip tightens.

Natasha takes a step towards us, teeth bared, gun pointing at us both. 'Let her go.'

'Stay exactly where you are. Or I'll break her neck.'

I can't move.

I stare helplessly up at the ceiling, my head forced back by his arm.

'Mummy,' Charlie whimpers.

I want to speak to my son, to reassure him, even if it's not true. But I can't make a sound. The room is gradually darkening, like a cloud passing over the sun outside.

My focus blurs.

Groggily, I realise that I'm losing consciousness. That's why everything is turning so dark…

I slump, and hit the floor seconds later, thrown aside as John grabs the door handle. There's a deafening bang. John yelps and swears.

Dimly, I guess that he's been shot. Yet somehow he's still on his feet, moving jerkily, disappearing out of the door with Natasha pursuing.

I close my eyes and let oblivion swallow me.

'Mummy?'

My eyes flicker open with an effort to see his worried little face staring down at me. How long was I unconscious? Minutes? Seconds?

'It's okay, Charlie,' I mumble, and slowly push myself up, my legs trembling with what is probably shock. 'Mummy just fell down, that's all. Come here, let me hug you.'

Back on my feet, I hug my son, ruffling his hair.

'Sorry, baby,' I whisper, bending to kiss his forehead.

The door behind me is still ajar.

I stagger over, intending to shut and bolted, but Natasha is there before me, standing in the doorway, the gun still in her hand.

'Quick, we go,' she commands me.

'Where's John?' I feel sick. 'Did … Did you kill him?'

'No, he got away.' She nods towards the back garden. 'Over the fields. So we go the other way. Out the front.'

Charlie drags free of my hand, staring at her and her lethal weapon. He seems fascinated by Natasha, which worries me.

'But the SUV. The men he said were coming from us… They're still out there. They'll be waiting for us.'

I grope for Charlie's hand again, but he dances just out of reach.

'I look in street. Nobody there.'

167

Surprised, my gaze snaps back to Natasha's face. Her delivery is so deadpan, I can't work out if she's lying and deliberately leading me out to those men, or if John was lying when he said the SUV was out there.

'Maybe they go away. Maybe they come back. Either way, we take chance. Better than stay and be killed.'

Natasha lunges for Charlie's hand and draws him to her side, more successful than me at catching him. Her smile is disconcerting as she bends towards my son, cloyingly sweet to the point of being sinister.

'You want ride in car, little boy?'

CHAPTER NINETEEN

'Yes, please.' Charlie beams and nods, looking up at our terrifying Russian visitor without fear, clearly entranced.

I itch to hustle him out of the room but don't want Natasha to become violent. She still has the gun, after all, and she's already shot John. I get the feeling she wouldn't hesitate to shoot me either. But perhaps I can slow her down by keeping her talking.

'Car? We don't have a car.'

'Woman next door has just pulled up. She has car.'

Woman next door.

She means Patricia Eagleton, I realise, my heart flooding with cold dread.

'Oh no... No, definitely not. She's my neighbour. And she's lovely. She's retired, for God's sake. You can't just …' I'm shaking my head. But she and Charlie have already left the house, my son skipping with glee at the thought of a proper outing at last.

I stumble after them, calling, 'C-Come back,' though I'm gasping and my voice is so faint, I doubt Natasha can even hear me.

There's blood on the step.

John's blood.

I blink down at it and my stomach heaves. I'm right back in Simon's house, staring at bloodstains on the rug, his corpse beside me with scissors sticking out of the back of his neck, like some grotesque ornament.

'Mummy? You coming, Mummy?'

I force myself to hurry, following Charlie's voice. At the mouth of the alley, I come face-to-face with Natasha talking to my neighbour across the bonnet of her car. Patricia looks bemused, even a little alarmed, but her face clears on seeing me.

'Ah, there you are, Sylvia,' she says with obvious relief, and reaches into the back of her car. 'I've just been shopping in town. I saw some juice packs and bought one for Charlie. I hope you don't mind.'

'Not at all,' I stammer automatically, and watch as she hands a pack of individual juice cartons to Charlie, the kind that come with mini-straws attached. 'That's very kind of you.'

'I didn't know you had someone visiting.' Patricia dives into the back of her car again, re-emerging with a pack of toilet rolls under one arm, along with a bulging bag of shopping. 'How lovely for you. I'm so glad you have some company at last.'

My heart hammering, I chance a look at Natasha. The gun has disappeared, presumably back into her capacious hoodie pocket. I look up and down the street. But there's no sign of the SUV I expected to find looking.

Was John lying?

Perhaps – and I shudder to contemplate it – he was never a friend, but always one of Them. In my mind, I'm capitalizing the word Them, which makes me feel like a conspiracy theorist.

That doesn't mean I'm wrong, though.

'Sylvia, why don't you help neighbour with shopping?' Natasha's smile is more a grimace.

'Oh no, really – '

'I insist,' Natasha says in a steely tone, and pats her hoodie pocket, throwing me a significant look.

'Yes, okay,' I say wearily, not wanting the Russian to produce her gun again and possibly shoot my poor, inoffensive neighbour. 'Let me help you with that, Patricia. No, please. It won't take me a minute.'

I take the shopping bag from her surprised hands, leaving her to carry the toilet rolls instead. Letting Patricia lead the way, I head indoors after her, while my neighbour innocently chatters on the weather and her scorched back lawn and wilting hanging baskets, and the difficulties of our current hosepipe ban.

Then Patricia asks abruptly, 'Are you all right, my dear? You seem a bit distracted.' She glances back at the front door and lowers her voice. 'That friend of yours. She's not causing you any bother, is she?'

I wish I could admit everything. But I dare not say anything that might force Natasha into a confrontation with poor old Patricia. The woman is clearly crazy, and she has a gun … and my son.

'Goodness no. Whatever gives you that idea?' I set the shopping bag on the counter and smile wanly at her. 'Though I should warn you,' I add, feeling responsible for her safety, 'we saw a man creeping around the back of the houses earlier.'

Her eyes widen. 'A man?'

'He looked dodgy. Maybe a good idea to keep your doors locked for a while, just in case he is looking to break in and steal something.'

'Thank you for the warning.' She pauses, watching me with concern. 'But shouldn't we call the police? If you think this man is up to no good.'

'No,' I say sharply.

Patricia frowns. 'My dear, are you sure everything's okay? Your friend … I'm sorry, but she is rather odd. She asked me how much fuel I had in the tank, before even introducing herself.' She pauses. 'Foreign, isn't she? That accent…'

A car horn sounds from outside, a loud imperious summons. We both jump in surprise and Patricia frowns, taking a quick step toward the kitchen door.

'Look, I have to go.' I touch her arm. 'I'm sorry. But thank you.'

'Whatever for?'

'For everything,' I say huskily.

Then I flee.

'Sylvia, wait,' she calls after me.

171

'I'm sorry,' I call back.

I find Patricia's small hatchback backed out onto the village street, engine running, both front windows open.

Natasha is behind the wheel.

'Get in, quick,' she shouts, and revs the engine, gripping the steering wheel with both hands.

I bend to look through the window. Charlie is already seated in the back. With no child seat, he looks so tiny and vulnerable, my heart breaks, watching him.

I have to get him out of there. Perhaps Patricia could look after him until it's safe to come back.

'Stop it right this instant,' I hiss at Natasha through the open window. 'You can't just steal a car.'

But the sound of an engine brings me upright. I turn, staring. Another car has rounded the corner near the Grange. A black SUV. It stops just short of the pub and sits there, idling, as though the unseen driver is eyeballing me the same way I'm eyeballing him.

I hear someone call my name, and turn the other way, startled.

Near the turn to the church, the Reverend Shearsman is crossing the road, some kind of plastic-wrapped bundle under his arm. He too has stopped, midway across the quiet street, and now raises a hand to me in greeting.

'I'm so glad I've caught you. Could I have a word, Sylvia?'

At my back, I hear Patricia's muffled exclamation as she comes out of her house to lock her car only to realise it's in the process of being stolen.

Natasha revs the engine again. Loudly.

'We go now,' she insists.

Caught between a rock and a hard place, I jump into the passenger seat and slam the door.

What else can I do?

Natasha has my son. I can't simply allow her to drive off with him, and it's obvious she won't wait a second longer.

'We shouldn't be doing this,' I say grimly, fumbling for my seatbelt. But it's too late. I'm knocked back in my seat as she accelerates with a squeal of tyres, roaring out of the village like a Formula One driver.

I catch a glimpse of the vicar as he jumps out of the way, his expression scandalized, and feel a bubble of hysterical laughter building inside me. Maybe I am mad, after all. Because only a mad person could possibly find this amusing.

'Whee!' Charlie shrieks, his voice high with excitement.

At least somebody is having fun.

Natasha stares straight ahead, eyes intent on the road, teeth bared in an animalistic grimace. In my wing mirror, I watch as the SUV accelerates after us, giving chase through the sleepy Devon village.

I grapple with my seatbelt, finally locking it in place. 'Where are we going?' I ask, gripping the seat a little too late as Natasha corners at speed and I'm thrown sideways.

'Away from *them*,' is all her reply, delivered through gritted teeth. Her gaze flashes to the rear view mirror and then back to the road ahead. 'You know road?'

'No,' I say shortly. 'I've only been this way once. I don't drive.'

'Ha!' The noise is contemptuous.

I stare at her profile, a series of urgent questions burning a hole in my mind. So far I've been coasting along, not delving too deeply into what's going on for fear of what I might find. But the thing with John has shaken me. I thought he was an average bloke, someone I could trust.

Clearly, I was mistaken, because John just tried to *kill* me. Or used me as a human shield, at any rate.

'Who are you?' I demand. 'Why did you come to see me? And who the hell are those guys behind us?'

'Later.'

They're still behind us, a few cars' lengths away but gaining ground all the time. There's a crossroads coming up, a few hundred yards away in full countryside. Fields to the left of us, fields to the right, and ahead of us, the winding, narrow lane the limousine driver took when he brought us here to Darkling Moreton from London.

'I think the main road is straight on,' I say helpfully.

We reach the crossroads.

She doesn't carry straight on.

Instead, she slams Patricia's hatchback down a gear and spins the steering wheel violently to the left.

The car skates sideways, judders and almost stalls. Then she forces it down the left-hand turn, booting it back up to speed and into the first corner so fast, I brace against the dashboard, fearing a head-on collision with any oncoming vehicles approaching around the blind bend.

The hatchback gets round the corner without incident, but only just, veering so close to the other side that her wing mirror snaps grasses on the opposite hedgerow.

'For God's sake,' I yell at her, thinking she must have a death wish, 'slow down, Charlie's in the back.'

'You want them to take him?' she demands, shifting her gaze from the road for a split-second to glare at me.

Them.

I don't know who *they* are but I know the answer to her question. I suck in a deep breath and shake my head.

'Of course not.'

'Then shut up and let me drive, yes?' She takes another corner at breakneck speed and the car almost lifts off the ground, or that's what it feels like.

The SUV is gaining on us.

Looking in the mirror, I catch sunlight bouncing off blacked-out windows as the large, dark car hurtles around the corner behind us, the driver flinging his vehicle about the narrow lane with almost as much abandon as Natasha.

'I feel sick,' Charlie whimpers.

I turn in my seat as much as I can without removing my seatbelt, and stretch out a hand to him.

He takes my hand and squeezes it. His skin is warm and clammy, and I feel like the worst mother in the world because I've allowed this to happen to my son. If I had simply given myself up, and let social services take Charlie into care, he would not be in this car right now, and his life would not be in danger.

'I know, darling, but just hang on... Mummy's here.'

Natasha slams on the brakes without warning, and our fragile contact is lost, my hand thrown clear of Charlie's.

The car skids, teeters and then she's dragging the wheel to the left again. We're turning down a dirt track.

A sign flashes past but I barely catch a glimpse before it's gone. A farm of some kind. It is twice as narrow again as the lane, with dried mud ruts forming a series of ridges the whole length of the track, throwing the car violently up and down at speed, everything juddering and shaking.

'Like rollercoaster,' Natasha shouts, and I realise that she's talking to Charlie, perhaps trying to reassure him or jolly him along.

'Please... don't crash... Patricia's car,' I somehow manage to say, every tooth in my head aching as we bounce up and down, though I have no idea if she can hear me or not.

The SUV must have lost us for thirty seconds or so after we turned down the dirt track. But now it's acquired us again and is closing in. Watching in the wing mirror, I see its large black wing mirrors slapping grasses and wildflowers in the hedgerow on either side, great gobbets of dried mud thrown in the air in its wake.

Natasha casts our pursuers a narrow-eyed look in her rear view mirror, and then scouts ahead for another exit. There's a high, shiny grey silo a few hundred yards ahead on the right. Grain storage, most probably. The dirt track opens out as we reach it, and Natasha goes off road, hurtling towards the silo, her speed barely slackening despite the very different surface under the tyres, now a mixture of rocky dirt and uneven rough grasses.

'Why would they kill us?' I yell at her.

Hunkered down over the wheel, Natasha spares me a brief, surprised glance. 'What?'

'Back at the house, you said we had to run away or they'd kill us,' I point out, my voice still raised above the noise of the rough terrain. 'Why would anyone do such a thing? I don't even know who those men are, or why they've been watching the house.'

'You are babe in wood.' More contempt and derision.

'So educate me.'

'No time.'

I glare at her, frustrated. She has answers but isn't willing to share them. We pass the large grey silo. There's nobody about. In the distance, I see dirty and dilapidated farm buildings. There's a sloping field between us and the farm. Something has been stored there, possibly multiple plastic-wrapped rounds of cut grass, all covered with black sheeting weighed down with old car tyres.

She flashes me a look, checking me up and down. 'Seatbelt on?'

'Yes. Why?'

I understand why a second later. The SUV is right behind us. I catch the roar of its engine, and am thrown forward as it impacts us from behind with a high-pitched scrape of metal hitting metal and the crunch of broken glass. They've rear-ended us.

Patricia's little car leaps forward, whining, and yet somehow, miraculously, we carry on.

I swear furiously.

She glances at me, eyebrows raised. 'Ah, what matter now? Only a little nudge.'

'Are you crazy? Or is that the vodka talking?'

She shrugs. The SUV 'nudges' us again. More of an almighty thump than a nudge.

I cry out, jerked forward against the restrictive choke-hold of the seat-belt.

In the back, Charlie moans. It's the noise he makes before he's going to be sick, as I recall from the time he went on a playground roundabout for a bare five minutes before chucking up all over my trainers.

Today, him being sick is the least of my worries. Charlie being killed in a car crash is a far more pressing possibility.

'We have to stop,' I yell at her, terrified for my son.

Natasha pays no attention.

I grab her arm. 'Are you listening to me?'

The SUV rear-ends us again, dislodging my grip. The whole car shudders and there's an awful clanking sound from beneath us now, like the undercarriage is dragging on the rough ground or maybe the rear bumper is hanging off …

'What in God's name are they trying to do?' I crane round in my seat, staring through the rear window of the hatchback, but the glass is speckled with mud. All I can see is the black mass of the SUV looming immediately behind us.

'Make us crash car,' Natasha replies, as calmly as though this kind of situation happens to her every day.

She changes gear with a violent gesture, and swings the wheel wildly one way and then back again. The car zigzags, and my body zigzags with it, my head wobbling.

'What the hell … ?'

'I swerve, they swerve. Maybe into pothole.'

She's clearly insane. I should never have listened to her and left the house. Charlie was safer there. I could have barricaded us in, found a defensible position, while we waited for my protector to show up. Instead, my little boy could be killed at any moment.

This is all my fault.

'You have to stop,' I scream at her, almost deafening myself in the tiny enclosed space.

She pays no attention. We've run out of grassland. She's staring ahead, her gaze flicking up and down the field, looking for an exit, for somewhere to go. At last, she gives a little cry under her breath, and I think, with some relief and trepidation, that's it. She's giving up, she's planning to surrender.

But I'm wrong.

She guns the engine for one last effort, making for some invisible point in the fencing that lies ahead. I get the feeling Natasha doesn't believe in surrender.

There's a tractor-sized gate in the fencing ahead, leading into a field of what looks like maize, growing lush and tall under the warm sun.

It's shut fast.

'You can't... You're not serious.' But I know she is. I brace against the dashboard again, shouting to my son in the back, 'Cover your face, Charlie. There's going to be a big ... a big bang.'

She slams her foot flat to the floor.

We hit the gate at speed. The driver's airbag deploys, hitting Natasha in the face and shutting off the engine. The steel gate doesn't appear to have been locked, merely closed, and thankfully it bounces open as we slam through. Unfortunately, it also bounces straight back again, catching the rear of the car with a sickening crack.

We veer sideways, Natasha hampered by the airbag as she wrenches at the now locked steering wheel, muttering what I guess to be Russian swear words under her breath.

The car stops dead.

Natasha bashes her airbag down with her fists, reaches around it and restarts the engine.

She accelerates again as though nothing has happened.

Behind us, the SUV, which had checked slightly before following us through, collides with the bouncing steel gate on its wild return trajectory, and also stutters to a halt.

It's an expensive, high-tech car and I imagine they must have airbags for everyone. Airbags in the front. Airbags in the back. And, hopefully, the airbags all deployed as a safety measure when they hit the gate. Maybe they won't even be able to restart the vehicle.

I find myself smiling grimly.

'Watch out,' Natasha warns me, her voice rising.

'Sorry?'

Simultaneously, the car slams into the four or five-foot maize crop that fills the field as far as the eye can see. There's no longer an air-bag to deploy but the jolt shocks me and I face forwards again, staring open-mouthed as Patricia's hatchback decimates row upon row of thick green stems with a rhythmic *phut-phut-phut*, leaving behind a car-shaped swathe of destruction.

Despite this barrage, Natasha continues to power the battered car through the farmer's crop, broken stems and leaves noisily spattering the windscreen. She flicks the wipers on fast as though it's raining, so the silky delicate leaves are swept away as soon as they land.

I can't see the SUV anymore but I can hear the engine, roaring somewhere behind us in the carnage.

We start to bump up and down, the field suddenly uneven, but she keeps on that bearing, looking hard right, and I realise she's seen an escape route. There's a road that way, bordered by leafy sunlit trees, and she's making straight for it.

I stare at the approaching road with fresh hope. Maybe we're actually going to escape these guys, after all. And I'm not alone in thinking that.

'Ha,' Natasha exclaims, her smile more of a snarl as she glances in her rear view mirror. 'Now we see who boss.'

I wipe perspiration off my forehead with the back of my hand. 'You … You okay, Charlie?' I call out, my voice wavering.

'Okay,' he replies.

Seconds before the road, we hit a concealed ditch.

It's like going over a cliff.

The hatchback tumbles headlong into the ditch, which accommodates a shallow, reed-strangled rivulet, and comes to an abrupt halt, the engine cutting out.

I'm thrown violently forward and then flung back again by the impact, hitting my head.

Stunned, I sit in a daze, hot metal ticking in the silence. My chest and neck are aching, maybe from the restraining strap of the seatbelt, maybe from some other impact I missed in the chaos.

I'm staring straight through the filthy windscreen into the bottom of the ditch. Above a gloomy trickle of water, soft banks of mud envelope the sides of the car, reeds and rough grasses thrusting up against the windows. A bright green grasshopper jumps from a blade of grass onto the windscreen, tiny antennae waving, and I stare at it blankly.

'Charlie?' I whisper, my brain like shaken jelly. 'You still okay back there, baby?'

'Okay,' he repeats, but his voice is high and unsteady.

'Mummy's going to get you out of here, don't worry.'

'Okay.'

Mummy just has no idea how.

I can't open my door. I try but it's jammed fast against the mud walls of the ditch. Hanging forward in my seatbelt, which has at least saved me from being catapulted through the windscreen on impact, I turn my sore neck to look at Natasha.

Pale and motionless, the Russian slumps far forward over the collapsed, pillowy remains of the driver's airbag, her eyes closed, a nasty cut weeping on her forehead.

She wasn't wearing a seatbelt when the car crashed, I realise. She told me to buckle up. But she didn't bother.

'Natasha?'

She doesn't respond.

'Natasha?' I try again several times, louder and louder. 'Natasha? Natasha? You've got to wake up. I … I need you.' I'm panicking now. My breathless voice gasps her name, my lungs hurting as they constrict. But there's still no reply.

She's out cold.

CHAPTER TWENTY

With shaking hands, I unfasten my seatbelt and turn, laboriously scrambling out of my seat and wedging myself between the two front seats. Charlie seems unharmed, physically at least. He stares back at me with wide eyes.

'Don't worry,' I say, trying not to look as terrified as I feel, 'Mummy's coming to help you.'

But even as I say that, a shadow falls across the rear window, and I glance up, mid clamber, to see a man's face. I recognise him at once. It's the swarthy, dark-haired man who chased me across the field to John's campervan.

Before I can react, he wrenches the back door open and reaches in for Charlie, who shrinks away.

'No,' I shout, 'leave my son alone,' and I lunge forward.

But he's already unsnapped Charlie's seatbelt and is lifting him out of the car. I make a grab for Charlie's leg and the man bats me away effortlessly. Charlie wails and kicks, but it's too late. He is being handed to a second man, only partly visible through the dirty, debris-flecked pane. And then he's gone.

'Charlie!' I scream and make a grab for the man, who is still there in the door crack, only to realise he has taken something from his pocket. It's small and sinister, glinting in his hand. Not a gun as I suspected at first, but a hypodermic needle. As I launch myself towards him, he thrusts it at my neck, and I recoil, a sharp pain there.

The man grins into my face.

'What the hell…?' I make another grab for him but my balance is off. His smile vanishes and then he's gone.

Charlie.

I have to get him back.

Somehow, I'm through the gap between seats and clambering out of the open front door. I hear a strange muffled banging outside. Again, and then again.

Gunfire?

Despite my fear, I keep going. But it's not easy. The car is wedged into the ditch at a steep angle. There's a tilting mountain of mud and weeds ahead, the sun is in my eyes, dazzlingly.

More bangs and thuds. A strange whining ricochet off metal. Is someone shooting at the car?

I'm terrified for my son.

But there's so much dirt to crawl through. The sun should be going down soon, yet I've never seen an afternoon so bright, light everywhere, spilling through decimated maize onto my upturned face.

Where's Charlie? Where the hell are they taking him?

Breathless and desperate, I dragged myself through a jungle of weeds, my hands digging in the dirt, my nails black with it, and finally come to my knees at field level.

I hear an engine close by and realise the SUV must be mere feet away, somewhere behind me, unseen in the towering green wall of maize.

Stumbling to my feet, I lurch toward the other car, shouting something like, 'No! Come back!'

A gun snout appears at the car window as the SUV roars past me, knocking me back into the reeds.

I hear gunfire again. They weren't aiming at me though, but in the direction of the road.

I lie on my back in the dirt, staring up at impossible blue. I've lost him now forever. I'm swimming in an endless sea, searching for Charlie, but my arms are so heavy, I feel exhausted, and it's all I can do just to drift and stare…

A face looms over me.

'Hello, Miss Smith. Do you need a hand?' It's the elderly gentleman in the Panama hat.

'I know you,' I say.

He looks down at me without expression, and then turns to someone else, out of my eyeline. 'She's out of it. They must have given her something. Put her in the car.'

While I am still trying to work out what he means, another man stoops to help me up from the ground. I struggle to get away but it's pointless. My arms and legs are made of spaghetti, no strength in them. They flop aimlessly.

'You're Robbie,' I say.

I know him too. He's the third man on our quiz team. The Clippers. The name makes me giggle.

'Clippers,' I remark, by way of explanation, and giggle again. I actually can't seem to stop giggling, which is worrying.

Robbie says nothing but heaves me up and over his shoulder in a fireman's lift. Rather impressive.

The world spins.

I stop giggling and hold my breath, fighting against a sudden urge to be sick. That would not be terribly polite; Robbie really doesn't deserve to be covered in my vomit.

Unless this is a kidnapping.

A crow sitting on a nearby fence post takes fright and flaps away, its wings a trail of undulating black smoke that slowly dwindles to a point of oblivion I follow with my darkening gaze …

Maybe an hour, maybe only ten minutes later, my mind briefly resurfaces to some hellish scene. Dogs are barking and snapping about my hands and heels. They're tearing me apart.

To my relief, it's a painless death.

I feel my extremities rip and sever under the dogs' razor-like teeth, blood spraying everywhere and skin flapping loosely back and forth, red and white, red and white, red and white, while the dark river of my life flows further and further away.

I wake in a dark, unfamiliar space to the deep rhythmic tick of a clock that makes me feel small and safe and cosy, like I'm a child again.

I listen to the comforting tick-tock of the clock with my eyes shut, enjoying the unaccustomed happiness this brings, before memory comes surging back.

And with it, fear.

I sit up too quickly, exclaiming, 'Charlie!' only to collapse again at once, closing my eyes and clutching my head. My mouth is dry and gritty as though I've been eating dirt. Which maybe I have. That laborious climb up out of the ditch, hand over fist, grasping at reeds, seemed to take forever. Suspiciously so, in fact.

'What on earth…?' I remember the flash of a hypodermic needle at my neck, and realise I've been drugged. 'What … What the hell did they give me?'

'Nothing wholesome, I'm afraid. Some kind of hallucinogenic by the things you've been saying.'

My eyes flash open again, startled by the deep male voice.

I'm not alone in the dark space.

A man rises from a nearby seat and comes towards me. I stare up at him in alarm, gradually picking out his features in the darkness.

Sir Philip Janus.

For once, he's not wearing his hat. But then, we are indoors, so that makes sense. Unlike everything else in my life.

I sit up more slowly, nursing my aching head. 'Charlie…'

'I know,' he says gently, 'and please try not to worry. We'll get him back, I promise.'

I don't believe him. But the state I'm in, there's not much I can do on my own anyway. As he turns away, I glance swiftly about the room, trying to get my bearings. But I don't recognise anything.

'Where am I?' I demand.

'My house.'

Sir Philip Janus's house. The big place with the tall iron gates and the snarling dogs. And Robbie weeding the flower beds. The man who hoisted me up back in the field and bore me away while the world turned dim. No wonder I dreamed about being torn apart by dogs in my drugged state. His two German Shepherds must have set up quite a baying when Robbie carried me into this house over his shoulder.

'Natasha... The woman who was with me.' My voice is hoarse. I clear my throat, horribly parched. The after-effects of the drug, no doubt. 'Where is she?'

'Safe.'

'She was hurt.'

'Natasha is safe,' he repeats firmly, 'and being looked after.'

'By Robbie?'

He says nothing.

I give up, deciding not to press it. Though I don't know why I care about Natasha's welfare. I only met her today when she barged into my home and terrified me half to death.

Sir Philip hands me a glass of clear liquid. His mouth quirks in a smile as I study it dubiously, recalling Natasha's penchant for neat vodka. 'It's only water,' he assures me. 'Drink. You've been out for hours. Your mouth must be dry.'

He's not wrong.

I drink gratefully. Plain tap water.

It tastes delicious.

Then what he said hits me. My stomach clenches like a man's fist has just slammed into it, winding me.

'*Hours*?' I stare up at him, numbly. 'But my son, Charlie … He'll be so scared!'

'They won't hurt him.'

'How on earth can you be so sure? And who are *they*? How do you know about them?'

The dapper gentleman moves away and flicks on a standard lamp beside the sofa. It gives out a soft, discreet light, just enough to light the space around us. We're in an elegant, book-lined room with luxuriously thick red rugs on the floor and a dark wood dresser decorated with flowers, pretty ornaments and a few photograph frames. There are no windows in the room, which strikes me as odd.

'You need to trust me.' His tone conveys absolute certainty.

I'm outraged by this blithe, privileged reassurance. It's madness. Charlie is only a little boy and he's been abducted. He needs his mother with him. The mere thought of those men, those strangers with guns, holding my son captive, free to do anything they want with him…

Panic rises inside me.

My first impulse is to run out of this house and keep running until I find him. Or call the police and let them put me in prison, I no longer care so long as my boy comes out of this alive.

But I see Sir Philip's ironic expression and know that he has read my thoughts. And he's right. Those men didn't strike me as the kind of people who would care much if the police were looking for them. Which means my best chance of getting Charlie back alive must lie with this man.

'Okay,' I say shakily, forcing myself to stay where I am, at least long enough to get some information out of him. It does seem likely he'll have some of the answers I've been seeking.

I heard gunshots too, I remember abruptly. I saw a muzzle flash from the SUV, yes. But someone else had been shooting back at them. The only other people I saw in the vicinity were Robbie and Sir Philip. Had they been the ones shooting? It's not a very comfortable thought. Besides, this man has to be in his seventies, at least. I can just about imagine Sir Philip clay pigeon shooting in his younger days, but not wielding a gun against a human enemy, especially at his age.

'Sir Philip Janus … You own the building where I live.'

'Yes.'

Fear floods me at this confirmation. But a mad kind of relief comes with it too. As though I'm about to discover the truth of what I've been going through these past few years.

'So why did you help us today? Why were you there?' My heart begins to thump. 'Are you *him*?' When he says nothing, looking back at me blankly, I add in a whisper, just to be clear, 'Are you my protector?'

'Your *protector*?' For a terrible moment, I think I'm wrong, and tense in apprehension, ready to lie in order to cover an awkward mistake. Then Sir Philip smiles, his face transformed. 'Yes, I suppose you could call me that.'

Not good enough. I need clarification beyond all doubt. 'Are you the voice on the phone?' I ask bluntly.

He nods.

No hesitation, no prevarication.

He's the robotic voice on the phone. The man who's been texting me instructions and couriering money and new identity papers to wherever I end up each time that …

I turn away from that sickening thought and take a minute to let it sink in. 'So why didn't you come to help us sooner?' My voice chokes. 'She turned up at the house. Natasha. I thought at first you'd sent her in response to my message. That's why I let her in. Otherwise I would never – '

'I didn't send her.'

'I know that now. But at least you sent John …' I gasp, a hand to my mouth. 'Natasha shot him! I'm sorry, I only just remembered. I still don't know why, but

188

John grabbed me by the throat and Natasha... Well, she had a gun, and I guess she thought she was protecting me and Charlie.' I search his face, horrified. 'She said John was wounded but I know he got away. Ran into the back garden.' I feel sick with apprehension. 'He may be dead.'

'He's not dead.'

My eyes widen, fixing on his face. 'You knew about him getting shot? So you *did* send him to help me?'

Sir Philip looks grave. 'I didn't send John either, I'm afraid. Robbie and I were not in the vicinity. I intended to send a trusted friend instead, but there was an unfortunate delay.' He pauses. 'John is working for the men who've been watching you.'

'*What*?' I'm baffled and suspicious. 'No, you've definitely got that wrong. John and Robbie were on a pub quiz team with me. They seemed to be good buddies. And Robbie works for you.'

He nods. 'I asked Robbie to keep an eye on him. He told me about the pub quiz. I'm sorry if that confused you.'

I can't take it in. 'But John can't be one of *them*. He's a good friend.'

The old gentleman meets my gaze mildly, his eyebrows raised. 'Is that so?'

My head may no longer be spinning, but it feels thick and woolly. I sit up straighter, trying to gather my scattered thoughts. 'Okay, not a *good* friend. He did try to grab me at the house,' I admit, speaking slowly while I wait for my brain to catch up. 'Maybe I read him wrong.' And thank God I didn't let John seduce me, I'm thinking, an embarrassed warmth in my cheeks as I remember how close I let him get to me. 'But who are these men you say he's working for? The same men who've been watching me?'

The old gentleman hesitates, a slight frown in his face.

I add anxiously, 'I haven't done anything wrong. Simon, Kurt ... I didn't kill them, I swear it.' When he doesn't look surprised, I suck in my breath, nodding. 'But you already know that. Why else would you have been helping me?'

seats himself beside me, his expression sombre. 'The men in the
⹁, my dear, are Russians.'

'Russians?' I blink, confused. 'I don't understand. They're after *Natasha*,
you mean? Not me?' I'm still lost, struggling to work out what's been going on.
'But no, that can't be right. They were watching the house long before she even
showed up.'

'Yes, I'm sorry about that. You were the bait, you see.'

'*Bait*?'

'Natasha has been in hiding for years. But wherever I moved you, she always
found you. She seems to have a sixth sense about it. Either that or she's a more
talented tracker than I gave her credit for.'

'You put me in that house deliberately to catch Natasha?'

'Things were getting out of hand. I needed to flush her out, once and for all.
The best way to do that was to bring you here, to keep you right under my nose,
where we could watch the house day and night.' He has crossed his legs and
places his hands restfully on his knee. Looking down at his hands, his eyes narrow.
'The only concern was the possibility that my enemies would notice you before
she did. And they did. I apologise for having put you in danger.'

I stare. 'Who is she?'

'I think you've already guessed, my dear.'

'Don't *my dear* me!'

His eyebrows rise again.

'Just tell me the truth, for God's sake. I'm sick of your hints and half
explanations,' I snap.

'Very well,' he says calmly. 'Natasha is your mother.'

Again, the sensation that I've been punched in the stomach. I struggle to
breathe.

'*What*?'

'Come now, don't look so surprised. You must have had your suspicions.'

I look away, fighting the urge to get up and run away from this madness. Because he's right.

Natasha is my mother.

I feel it in my bones now that he's said it out loud. I did have my suspicions. I just didn't want to confront them, to face the hideous possibility that *that woman* might in any way be related to me and Charlie.

My son.

I'm in freefall panic again. What's Charlie doing right now? Is he okay? Is he scared? I hope Sir Philip is right and those men won't touch a hair on his head. Because I'm so frightened he may be wrong. Am I ever going to see my little boy again?

I bury my face in my hands, wishing I could wake up from this nightmare that's become my life.

'Your real name is Marina,' he says softly, 'and you were born here in England to a Russian mother – Natasha – and an English father, Charles.'

My brain hears the words but I can't seem to follow them.

Your real name is Marina.

It feels both alien and oddly familiar. *Marina.* Yes, maybe that was my name as a child. I have a vague memory now of …

It must be a Russian name.

Unlike my father's.

Charles.

I look up sharply as I realise the significance of what he said, my hands dropping away in surprise.

An English father – Charles.

'Sadly,' Sir Philip goes on, holding my gaze steadily, 'things began to go wrong for your parents soon after you were born. It was not a happy marriage. They moved here to Darkling Moreton soon after they were married. But Natasha was homesick for Moscow, and your father frequently had to go away for long periods for his work. Your mother was never a very stable person, and when the

191

worst happened during one of his absences, she found herself unable to cope without him. She did something dreadful and ran away with you. You were given to friends to look after for a while, but they were not trustworthy people.' His face hardens. 'When Natasha was unavoidably detained and didn't come back to claim her child by the arranged date, they panicked and decided to abandon you at – '

'At a train station.'

'Yes,' he agrees, nodding. 'You remember that?'

'A little. No details.'

'By the time she was able to return for you, almost an entire year had passed. By then, you had vanished completely and her friends were both dead.'

My eyes widen. '*Dead?*'

'Drugs were involved, I believe.' His expression is cold. 'And that's how Natasha lost you. It took her years to find you again.'

I feel sick, as though the drug they gave me still hasn't properly worn off and the world is spinning again, a haze of light and shadows.

Natasha is my mother.

I can't understand how I didn't see it before, not since coming to live in Darkling Morton. So many clues right under my nose.

There was the tricycle Charlie found buried in the long grass; I somehow knew what it was even before we dragged it from its hiding place. Then the curious light-headedness I experienced when looking up at the house, or staring across the rough moorland at the end of the garden. Plus, I'd been so sure of the contents of the garden shed before wrenching the door open, only to find it empty except for a strimmer, and the jolt of surprise I'd felt, trying to reconcile the two images. Like looking in the mirror to find the wrong face staring back at you.

'I was the child on the red tricycle.'

He doesn't ask me to elaborate. 'Yes.'

She did something dreadful.

'She killed a man in the church. With a pair of scissors.'

'Yes.'

'She killed Simon too. And Kurt.'

'Yes.'

I'm suddenly desolate. I didn't kill those men and block it out. At least I can be sure of my innocence now. But they died because of me, all the same. Without even knowing, I caused their deaths.

'But why?' I demand, tears springing to my eyes. My voice is croaky. 'Why do something so awful?'

'I thought at first it was maternal instinct gone mad. But then I received a cryptic message from her and realised my mistake. She was protecting you, that's all. Just as I tried to do once I – '

I interrupt him, abruptly furious. 'She was protecting me? But from what? From men? From having *sex*?'

My voice rises and I struggle not to lose control. Sir Philip says nothing but looks at me with concern.

Bizarrely, his silence only makes me angrier.

'And what's your part in all this?' I demand. 'How do you know about my mother and father? Why have you been looking out for me and Charlie all this time, moving us on whenever Natasha kills one of my boyfriends, finding new places for us to live, even new identities, for God's sake?' I glare at him, tense and shaking. 'How on earth do you manage that, anyway? *Who the hell are you?*'

CHAPTER TWENTY-ONE

'I'm your grandfather,' Sir Philip Janus tells me, as calmly and evenly as though we're discussing the weather. 'My son Charles was Natasha's husband and your father. Which makes your son Charlie my great-grandson.' He pauses. 'So please trust me when I say I want him back safely every bit as much as you do.'

I'm stunned. 'My *grandfather*?'

'I'm afraid so.' Sir Philip looks down at his hands, and his lips twitch. 'I apologise if that's a disappointment.'

I ignore his ironic tone, slowly picking my way through the chaos in my head. 'And my father? He was your son? Charles, you said. So where – '

'He's dead. I'm very sorry.'

I swallow, taking that in. 'When?'

'It was after Natasha took you away. I suppose you would have been about six or seven at the time.'

'How did he die?'

'That's a very long story.'

Frustration roils inside me. 'I'm not going anywhere. I'd like to hear it, thank you.'

Sir Philip hesitates. 'We really ought to deal with the present before considering the past.'

'It seems to me that *my mother* is living in the past,' I snap, 'and I'm paying for that in the present.'

'Natasha is sadly unbalanced. She always was, I fear, right from the beginning. Your father found her alluring because of it, something I could never understand. I merely find her an irritant.' His voice is mild in the face of my anger. Apologetic, even. 'Natasha only knows one way to deal with a threat and that's to erase it from existence.'

I jump on that, trying to understand. 'You're saying she thought Simon was a threat? Kurt, too?'

'Yes, exactly that. I'm glad you're so quick.' He sighs. 'Obviously, I couldn't allow you to suffer the consequences of those deranged acts. You would have been accused of murder and probably found guilty, given the circumstances of those unfortunate deaths. Charlie would have been taken away from you, and you yourself would have gone to prison.'

I can't argue with that, so merely nod, hugging myself as I listen. I feel cold inside and very alone without Charlie.

'At the same time,' Sir Philip goes on, 'I was afraid to bring you here to Darkling Moreton any sooner than I did. To acknowledge you publicly as my granddaughter would have been the equivalent of painting a target on your head, as we now have ample proof. And at least I knew Natasha would never harm you or Charlie. The rest were … collateral damage.'

Collateral damage.

Those were human beings she brutally murdered. Doesn't he have any feelings? I have so many questions for him. But right now, only one is burning a hole in my brain.

'So I named my son after my father, Charles? Without even knowing what my father's name was? How does that work?'

'Maybe you did know,' he suggests, 'without knowing that you knew. After all, at the time you were abandoned and taken into care, you must have been about four or five years old. Surely old enough to retain some memory of your parents?'

'I remember almost nothing from before being taken into care.'

195

'Curious.' He eyes me speculatively. 'You must have blocked it out after Natasha went away, leaving you with drug-addicts for nearly a year. Too painful an experience to recall, perhaps.' His gaze is impassive. 'Yet somewhere in your head that memory was secretly lodged, ready to be retrieved when you later gave birth yourself and sought a name for your son. Unless you believe in coincidence, that is.' His smile is faint. 'Which, personally, I don't.'

'But Natasha found me again eventually, when I was training to be a hairdresser. Why not simply introduce herself?'

'I expect she didn't think she'd get a very warm reception. After all, she left you with strangers who abandoned you at a train station.'

I hug myself tighter, nodding, gritting my teeth. 'So, instead, she killed the man I was seeing. Nice … very nice.'

'I believe he was actually working for the Russians, if that's any consolation.'

I stare at him. 'What?' I laugh wildly. 'That's the most ridiculous thing I've ever heard. *Kurt*? Working for the Russians? He was a hairdressing tutor, for God's sake.'

'Oh, they'll use anyone they can bribe or blackmail into doing their dirty work for them. Though in this case, Kurt was genuinely a Russian agent. Long-embedded here in England and parachuted in when they first spotted Natasha and gradually realised she was watching you. If Natasha was hanging around, I expect they imagined you must be of interest in some way. So they sent Kurt in to, erm, get to know you better.'

'Kurt was a Russian agent? You mean, a spy?'

He nods, watching me.

My skin prickles with horror. I'd been an impressionable teenager back then, then. Kurt had so easily seduced me, making me feel like I was special to him. When all along …

Kurt was Charlie's father. A surprise baby, and one I didn't even know about for some months after his murder. That was how innocent I was at the time.

My stomach turns. 'I don't understand. I thought … Well, I just assumed when you kept talking about 'the Russians' that Natasha must be a criminal in Russia and they'd sent police or investigators to get her back. But you're saying she's a spy?'

'Absolutely.'

'I don't believe you.'

'I don't blame you. But it's all true. In fact, after she met your father and fell in love with him, she became a double agent for a while. He persuaded her to work for both our government and the Russians, though without the other side knowing. She retired after she had you, of course.'

'*My father* persuaded her?'

'He was a spy too.'

My eyes widen. 'Oh, of course he was.' For the first time, I begin to wonder if he's mad.

'After your father died, she went into hiding and we completely lost track of her. Such a pity. Natasha was good at her job. But she had a flair for the dramatic that made her a bit of a liability in the field.' He pulls a face. 'Using hairdressing scissors as an assassination weapon, for instance. So messy, so over the top. But she does like to make a grand gesture.'

I'm frowning. '*We* lost track of her?'

'Oh, didn't I say? I was a spy too, for many years. It's the family business, in fact.' There's the ghost of a smile on his lips as he registers my stunned expression. 'My wife, Alice – your late grandmother – was also in British Intelligence, though she'd retired long before Charles entered the service.'

'And … you're retired now too?'

It feels as though I'm having a fantasy conversation. Spies, Russians, double agents. Perhaps that hallucinatory drug still hasn't worn off, after all.

'Yes, though only quite recently,' he admitted, 'and under protest. For many years, I ran things at the service. Not quite the chief but I had my own parking space.' He smiles faintly. 'That how I was able to locate you, using discreet

197

contacts, and later to help you when Natasha started eliminating threats to your person, shall we say?'

'But why did she kill Simon?' Guiltily, I recall media reports about his death and how all that conflicting information about his identity had thrown me into chaos. 'I saw on the news that his real name was Tim Shaw. That he was a private investigator who used to be in the police. Was any of that true?'

'Once the Russian had you down as a person of interest, they were hard to shake off. And Natasha kept finding you, however well I covered your tracks. It would have been impressive if it hadn't been such a nuisance. Indeed, I had to pull in some favours to cover things up this last time, not being in the service anymore. Especially when the mark turned out to be a former policeman and there was a lot of media interest in the case. But I still have contacts.'

'His body was found in a burnt-out car.'

He nods. 'A good way to conceal DNA evidence from investigators. I didn't want you unfairly incriminated.'

'But my mother did?'

'I doubt if Natasha even considered that possibility. She's a creature of impulse, and she's spent her life getting away with acts that would have landed most ordinary people in jail.'

'But was Simon investigating me?'

'As far as I was able to ascertain, Tim Shaw was hired by the Russians through a proxy. It's unlike he knew he was doing the work of a foreign power by getting close to you. Unfortunately for your friend, Natasha had no qualms about dispatching him once he was reporting back to the Russians on your movements. If he was spying on you, then he had to be eliminated. Natasha can be fanatical like that. Unstoppable, even. It was one of her great strengths as a spy. But as a private citizen, it makes her very dangerous.'

I feel like I'm going mad. 'Okay, but why would the Russians be watching me in the first place? I'm a nobody. I'm not a spy and I knew nothing about my past. Explain *that*.'

'They were trying to find Natasha. She's a wanted woman in Moscow. An enemy of the state. She worked against her own government for British Intelligence and that means she's marked for death. But they'll want her back in one piece first, so they can interrogate her, find out what she told us, and make her suffer for it a thousand times over.' His face hardens. 'Just as they made my son suffer.'

I stare. 'What exactly are you saying?' My heart thumps uncomfortably. 'That the Russians killed my father?'

'Charles worked as an agent for several years after university, specialising in Soviet affairs. He was sent to Moscow for further training and that was where he met Natasha.' His face and voice betrayed no emotion, yet somehow I feel his fury and distaste. 'By the time I realised that he had formed an attachment to one of the enemy, there was nothing I could do. Charles was in love, and worse, she was expecting his child. Her handler realised something was wrong but before the Russians could pick her up, Charles got her on a flight to the UK. At the time, I'd recently bought this place is my retirement home, so I agreed to look after her at Darkling Moreton until his time in Moscow was at an end. We acquired a small house in the village for her, since Natasha didn't wish to live with me and Alice, and she ran a salon there. Being a hairdresser had been her cover back in Russia.' He pauses, a mere flicker in those composed eyes. 'A few months later, days before Charles was due home, he met a contact from the SVR – that's the Russian equivalent of our secret service, dealing with espionage outside the Russian Federation – and disappeared off the radar. We put out the usual feelers, of course, but heard nothing back. Natasha had just given birth and was … unstable. It was a very difficult time.' His face tightens. 'Finally, we heard from the SVR.'

My stomach plunges. 'What did they want?'

'You and Natasha for my son. The two together or no deal.'

I stare at him, speechless.

'You have to understand, this wasn't just about your mother. Not back then, anyway. The Russians had hated me for years and this was their chance to make me pay for some of the things I'd done to them, whilst also punishing a rogue agent.'

'What happened?'

'We refused to exchange, of course. Natasha was willing to go back and face the music alone, but they wanted the baby too. To really turn the screw for some of the decisions I'd taken during my time at the top.' He laughed grimly.' I imagine they also thought you might have strategic importance later, after they'd interrogated and disposed of Natasha. The grandchild of their enemy, a girl they could mould as they wished if brought up in Moscow by one of their own handlers.'

'That awful,' I burst out, shuddering.

'Exactly what I thought. And I knew Charles would have been furious with me if I had agreed to exchange. He would never have balanced his life against those of his wife and child. So we said no and awaited further developments.' His gaze meets mine. 'A few years later, via backchannel contacts, the news came. Your father was dead.'

Although this is the first time I have ever heard about my father, a and inexplicable sadness floods my spirits. 'How?'

'There was never any explanation. Though the Russians had never officially admitted that they were holding him, so of course it would have been impossible to give any details. The situation was too politically awkward. Instead, there was a cover story about him having been found in a brothel.' He sees my expression and shakes his head. 'All lies to discredit him. We buried him here in the churchyard.' He pauses. 'I'm very sorry.'

'And Natasha? You said she gave me to friends… What happened?'

'After we buried Charles, I'm afraid your mother had a nervous breakdown. She was determined to kill the people who were responsible for his death, and was sure she could find them, given the right resources. But we had your welfare to consider. You were only a small child and you'd just lost your father. Perhaps it was wrong of me but I refused to help Natasha return to Russia and seek out his killers. It seemed to me the height of madness.'

'But someone came looking for her, instead.' I recall the story about the dead man in the church. Village gossip. Yet surprisingly accurate, for all that.

He nods. 'He was a Russian agent.'

'She told me part of it. Though I didn't understand it at the time. He tried to kill her and take me away, didn't he? She stabbed him with her scissors and ran.'

'Close enough, yes. And that might have been an end to it,' he says severely, 'except that she took you with her. I had to deal with the fallout alone... A Russian agent found dead in Darkling Morton, for God's sake. Thankfully, I wasn't in the country at the time or suspicion might have fallen on me. As it was, I flew straight back to England and managed to keep Natasha's name out of it. But you were both in the wind by then. It took years and a great deal of money to find you again.'

'Why didn't Natasha simply leave me with you?'

'She didn't trust me. And perhaps she had good reason not to. That was my mistake. I told her Charles would be safe, that the Russians wouldn't dare harm him. Not my son.' He looks away. 'I was wrong.'

I follow his gaze to the other side of the room, where a framed photograph stands on a table next to a vase of artfully arranged flowers. The photograph is of a young man in a black university mortar board and gown, smiling proudly into the camera.

I cross the room to examine the photograph more closely. This is my father. He has my son's sweetness in his good-natured smile, but something else besides. An active, determined character suggested by his rugby players' build and the stubborn jut of his chin. I have a stubborn streak myself.

What did I inherit from Natasha, though? And why did I choose to become a hairdresser, just like her? Had there been some residual memory at work there?

'I want to see her,' I say firmly. 'I want to see my...' I can't get the word *mother* out. 'Natasha.'

'I'm not sure that would be wise.'

I stare round at him. 'I want to know how we're going to get Charlie back.' When he doesn't answer, I add angrily, 'You've lost your son. But you can still save your great-grandson.'

'It's in hand.'

'All right. Tell me how, then. What's your plan?'

My voice is shrill. But those men with guns – Russian agents, if Janus is to be trusted – have abducted my son, and I'm terrified they may hurt him. All I have is Sir Philip's story of being my grandfather and his reassurance that he knows what's going on. Which isn't enough. So far, it's been a fantastical tale of spies and hostile foreign powers and, frankly, I'm not sure how much of that I believe.

On the other hand, I've spent several hours in Natasha's company now, and I saw for myself how she was with Charlie. Firm but protective. She may well turn out to be my mother and Charlie's grandmother. At the very least, I don't believe she means him any harm, and will do whatever it takes to get him back unhurt.

So if I can hear Natasha corroborate Sir Philip's story to my face, maybe – just maybe – I might accept his version of events.

Before I can make my demand more forcefully, the door opens.

It's Robbie, Sir Philip's gardener.

He glances in my direction, gives me a nod of acknowledgement, and then looks towards Sir Philip.

'Sir? There's been a development.'

CHAPTER TWENTY-TWO

'What is it, Robbie?' Sir Philip has risen to his feet.

'I've just heard from Patty, sir.' There's a note of urgency in the gardener's voice. Assuming he really is a gardener, that is. 'She's lost John.'

Sir Philip frowns. 'What on earth does that mean? How can she have *lost* him? I thought he wasn't that badly wounded.'

'No, not lost him that way. I mean he's absconded.'

'Good God.'

'I didn't think he would be up to it, sir, or I would never have left him there. I found him and carried him into the house myself, and Patty saw to his wound. He'd been cleaned up and bandaged by the time I left, but seemed too weak to be a nuisance. She nipped into the kitchen for more hot water, and by the time she got back, he was gone.'

'You mean he *walked* out of there?'

'Either that or he was carried. Patty says the front door was wide open and she heard the sound of a car but didn't see anyone.' Robbie rubs his chin, once again glancing at me and then back at his boss. 'She wants to know what to do.'

'Nothing for now. Thank her for me, would you?'

'Of course, sir.'

I'm astonished by this exchange, turning to Sir Philip. 'Who's Patty? Is she your wife?' I'm confused. Is John an enemy or not? If he's working for the

Russians, why were they looking after him? 'Was he here in your house all this time?'

Sir Philip puts a hand on my shoulder. 'Please don't upset yourself, my dear. Patty is an old friend and a dab hand with a first-aid kit. She's been looking after John for us, but it seems the Russians have taken their man back before we could have a word with him.'

'Patty...' I blink. 'You're not talking about *Patricia*, surely? Patricia Eagleton?' When he says nothing, I stutter, 'But she's my next-door neighbour ... Why on earth would she get herself mixed up in something like this?' Then I remember what Patricia told me, and add slowly, 'She worked as a civil servant. For the government, she said.'

'That's right,' Sir Philip agrees smoothly. 'As did I.'

I'm stunned.

Nice, normal Patricia Eagleton with her beaming smile and kindly ways ... a *spy*?

Robbie grins at my expression and turns to leave, but stops short on the threshold and turns. A mobile phone is ringing somewhere in the room. It's not a ringtone I recognise.

'Sir?' he says. 'That's your mobile phone.'

We watch in silence as Sir Philip walks across to pick up his phone. 'Yes?' His voice is haughty and abrupt. He listens, and then says simply, 'I understand,' and ends the call.

I feel a surge of incredible impatience when he merely stands staring into space afterwards, saying nothing. 'Well?' I press him, trying to swallow my frustration. But it's hard. Those evil men still have Charlie, and every second I'm away from my son feels like a year in hell. 'Was it them? Was it important?'

'Yes, it was our friends the Russians.' He turns to Robbie. The big bloke has come back into the room and is standing still and tense, hands clenched into fists at his side, as though waiting to spring into action. 'They've set a rendezvous at St.

Hilda's. Forty-five minutes. I think the boy will be there. I'll need you to get him away from them and into hiding as fast as possible.'

Robbie nods, as though this is a perfectly normal request for an employer to make of his gardener. 'How many are we looking at?'

'Hard to say. Two, at least. Maybe three or even four.' Sir Philip flexes long fingers. 'I don't imagine they can have more than that available. Not at such short notice.' He shrugs. 'Let's hope for only three. That would help matters.'

'All the same, I don't like those odds.' Robbie shoots me a wary glance. 'Not given the delicate nature of the package.'

He means Charlie, I realise with a jolt.

'Me neither.' Sir Philip checks his wristwatch. 'But there's no time to consider calling the cavalry. Anyway, that could lead to some very awkward questions.'

'Agreed.'

'Hey,' I exclaim, grabbing Robbie's arm and refusing to let go even when he tries to pull free. 'I'm still in the room, you know. What are you talking about? What's this meeting about?' When both men merely look back at me, their lips stubbornly closed, I get furious. 'It's my son they've taken. Can somebody please explain to me exactly what's going on?'

'My dear,' Sir Philip begins, and then clears his throat when I glare at him, starting again, 'Marina … If you don't mind me using your real name … The Russians have your son. They want me to meet them at the church in forty-five minutes … Well, rather less than that now.'

Relief sweeps over me at his words. I release Robbie's sleeve, exhaling. 'You mean, they're going to hand him over to you? Just like that?'

'Not quite.' Sir Philip grimaces. 'There's something they want in exchange.'

My eyes widen as I take in his sombre expression. 'Is it Natasha? You said they were after her for information.' I hesitate when he doesn't answer. 'They want her in exchange for Charlie, is that it?'

Sir Philip raises his eyebrows. 'If only it were that simple,' he mutters, turning to the nearest bookshelf as though planning to hunt among the ancient leather-bound tomes for a good book.

'This is hardly the time to be choosing your next read,' I snap.

'Best stay out of it, Miss,' Robbie begins gruffly, but falls silent when I swing back towards him, my eyes blazing.

'Now you listen to me - ' But an eerie grating sound at my back makes me jump. I turn in shock, my fury forgotten, to see the well-stocked bookshelf has swung outwards to reveal a dimly-lit opening in the wall. 'What the hell?'

'Forgive the amateur dramatics,' Sir Philip says. 'But we're up against the clock on this one. If you'd care to follow me …' And he plunges through the opening, swiftly disappearing down a short flight of steps.

I stand staring after him, utterly bemused.

Lurking immediately behind me, Robbie nudges me to follow. 'After you, Miss.' I'm pretty sure I detect amusement in his voice. 'Mind the step.'

I duck through the opening and descend the short flight of steps into a narrow corridor with iron-grey walls and bare concrete floor. At the far end, Sir Philip waves me forward with a genial smile before stepping into another room just out of sight.

Off-balance, I follow him, Robbie never far behind me, and soon find myself in a room with slightly rounded walls, iron-grey like the corridor. Only this one displays a row of wall-mounted monitors showing grainy black-and-white images, along with several computer terminals at desks equipped with keyboards and swivel chairs.

'What is this place?' My voice echoes. I turn slowly, taking it all in. 'You said this was your house.'

'It's underneath my house, in fact. An old nuclear shelter, built in the fifties, modernised and converted for my needs.' Sir Philip nods towards the monitors, though his gaze is on my face. 'Surveillance, for instance.'

With a start, I realise I'm staring at an image of the outside of my house on the main village street.

Except it's not just an image. It's live. As I watch, a car passes slowly along the street and disappears. Someone walks past with a dog on a lead. A bird flaps past the camera.

'You've been watching me.'

'Only the exterior,' Sir Philip says smoothly, as though this is somehow reassuring.

I remember my laptop and phone being taken. 'You're sure you don't have a camera in the house? You took my devices.'

Sir Philip grimaces. 'Robbie's the tech expert. I'm afraid he hacked your devices so he could check you were following the rules. But it was only done to protect your new location. Because the Russians are even better than us at that kind of game.'

I swallow my rage. 'You didn't see Natasha coming.'

'Yes, I'm sorry about that. But she must have approached the house from the rear. The camera is only at the front.'

I study the fixed angle, frowning. I feel sick at the thought that he's been watching me and Charlie come and go. And yet, if what he's told me is true, it has been for my protection. I suppose I have to accept that as necessary, given what I now know about who we are and why all these appalling things have been happening to me.

'Where's the camera?'

Sir Philip glances at Robbie, who steps forward awkwardly. 'Ah, well, there's a nesting box strapped to a tree further down the street, you see. I adjusted the lens to telephoto and trained it on the front of the house. Not enough detail to be intrusive, but good enough to show any intruders.' He points to a few of the other screens, which show differing views of the village and church. 'Nesting boxes are useful for that kind of thing, as are lamp-posts and any railings with enough shrubbery around to conceal a micro camera.'

I'm not impressed. 'Natasha visited me at night once. Did you miss her that time too?'

'No.' Robbie looks embarrassed. 'I caught her coming out. Though it's true I missed her going in.'

'Robbie fell asleep on duty,' Sir Philip murmurs.

'And I apologised for that, sir.' His employee drew a deep breath. 'Anyway, once we were sure you and the boy were both safe, there wasn't much we could do except keep an eye out for any further visits.'

'And how were you so sure we were okay?'

'I saw you come out after her and look around, then lock up again.' He rubs his chin, his expression rueful. 'I did try to erect a camera out the back one day while you and the boy were out, under cover of doing some tree surgery work. But there was this one damn squirrel who didn't like it. Kept vandalising the camera. Chewing and dislodging it, you know.' He shrugs. 'So we gave up.'

While we've been speaking, Sir Philip has been busy in an adjacent room. Now he returns, holding two handguns.

I stare, horrified.

'No more guns.' I shake my head. 'They'll never give him back if we go in there so aggressively.'

There's a brief silence.

'I'm sorry to tell you this, my dear, but they'll never give him back if we don't.' With a quick glance at Robbie, my grandfather lays the handguns down beside one of the computer keyboards. 'Our only option is to take him back. Have you ever shot a gun?'

'No, thank God.' I shudder. 'But what do you mean? Are you saying the Russians are going to try double-crossing us? Why would they?'

'Because they want something in exchange for Charlie that we can't give them.'

I stare. 'Like what?'

I've been assuming up to this point that they'll ask for Natasha in exchange for my son, and although I don't want to hand my long-lost mother over to the enemy, I know it's a trade I'll agree to.

Natasha was never there for me when I was growing up in a series of unhappy foster homes. She abandoned me – presumably to search for my father – and left me to suffer unspeakable cruelty at the hands of monsters.

No, I won't blink at that trade. And I don't think my grandfather would either. I get the impression he doesn't like my mother very much. But Sir Philip is looking sombre again.

'Information,' he says.

I frown, not sure I understand. 'What kind of information?'

'The kind I can't give them.'

'For God's sake, your great-grandson's life is at stake. He could die if you don't give them whatever they want.'

'And two friends of mine could die, along with their innocent families, if I do.'

I'm baffled. 'What are you talking about?'

'The details aren't important – ' he begins, but I interrupt him, my temper flaring at his cool tone.

'Don't patronise me. We're talking about my son's life here. My *innocent* son. Charlie's only three years old and he's your flesh-and-blood. Or don't you care about any of that?'

'Of course I care,' he says impatiently. 'My concern for you and your son have motivated everything I've done in recent years. And believe me, it hasn't been easy or legal, tidying up after Natasha's dangerous behaviour and getting the two of you somewhere safe again,' he says, adding mildly, 'The problem is, there's also a small thing called the Official Secrets Act.'

'I don't give two hoots about the Official Secrets Act.' I wait for his response, breathing hard, my arms folded, shaking with fury and stress. 'Tell me now or I'm walking out of here and going straight to the police.'

It's a bluff, of course.

I might go to the police, risking everything to get Charlie back, but I don't imagine for a second that he and Robbie will actually let me leave. But I need to know what he's talking about. Otherwise, how can I judge for myself what kind of information he's withholding and if it's worth my poor son's life?

Just the thought of making that sacrifice, of giving up on Charlie and trying to get him back through a violent shoot-out instead, makes me shiver.

Sir Philip hesitates, glancing at Robbie again. Then he sighs, sinking his hands into his trouser pockets.

'Early in the Noughties,' he says softly, 'I created a group of twelve Russian informants in Moscow loyal to the British government. Twenty years or so on, most of that group have been discovered and eliminated. Some died in the natural way of things, while a few were allowed to come to Britain once their cover was blown. Only two still remain active and undiscovered. Both hold positions high in the Russian government and are not only essential to our Soviet intelligence gathering but are also friends of mine. Twenty years is a long time to handle a spy, especially one in such a precarious, high-exposure situation. Theirs are the identities the Russians want us to expose in return for your son's life.' He pauses. 'To betray either or both of them now, when there's an alternative choice before us … ' Sir Philip shakes his head, holding my gaze. 'I'm sorry, my dear. I know it must seem hard to you. But even apart from the consideration of personal loyalty to two very brave agents, I refuse to betray my country. Not even to save Charlie.'

I suck in a breath, hugging myself hard. There are tears in my eyes, blurring my vision.

'However,' he adds, his mouth twisting in an odd smile, 'there's no reason to despair just yet. We may not be in a position to call in additional help. But we have everything we need to fight back against these people.'

I glance from him to Robbie. 'You mean … You and him? Because I can't shoot.'

'Well, we'll see about that. I'm sure Robbie can manage to give you a crash course on how to handle and discharge a weapon while I make a few calls.' Before I can make any kind of protest, he turns away, heading for the door. 'And there's Natasha.'

I stare after him. 'What about her?'

He stops, looking back at me. 'You wanted to see her, I believe.'

'Yes.'

'Do you still want to see her, after everything I've told you?'

'Yes.'

'I'm sure Robbie can facilitate that once he's shown you how to load and shoot a handgun.' There's that faint smile again as my gaze returns with distaste and apprehension to the sinister metallic weapons lying beside his elbow. 'I know she had a whack on the head earlier, and I'm not her favourite person. But her actions in the past have indicated a certain zeal over keeping *you* safe. Plus, she was clearly trying to protect her grandson today, even if her decision-making was flawed and erratic.' He pauses. 'So maybe you could persuade her to lend a hand tonight.'

'In what way?'

'My dear, your mother has been a professional assassin since before you were born. Use your imagination.' Sir Philip checks his watch. 'You may want to hurry, though. We now have less than half an hour before we need to be in position at the church. Though keeping them waiting might not be a bad idea. To show them we still have the upper hand.'

'What, you want to make them *angry*?' My heart thuds. 'Are you crazy? You'd only be risking Charlie's life more.'

'They're professionals. They don't get angry.' His cool, intelligent gaze brushes my face before he nods to Robbie and turns to leave. 'But they might get rattled,' he says over his shoulder, heading out of the strangely echoing underground room. 'And rattled is good.'

211

I'm not sure I believe him that professionals don't get angry. Natasha is supposedly a professional. And she's hardly a calm individual.

Once he's gone, I study the two handguns with undisguised trepidation. 'I've never so much as picked up a gun in my life,' I mutter as Robbie scoops them up, one by one, and examines them with expert hands. 'This is insane. And illegal.'

'Yes,' Robbie agrees, with a lopsided grin, and hands me a gun, ignoring my expression of distaste. 'Now, Miss, just watch this … '

CHAPTER TWENTY-THREE

After a crash-course in how to aim and shoot a handgun – something I've never thought I would need – Robbie reassures me that I'm unlikely to be needed if it comes to a shoot-out.

'Sir Philip will have it well in hand,' he says, briefly showing me how the gun is loaded – too briefly for me to really take it in, so I have to hope he's right – before demonstrating how to tuck it into my jeans waistband at the back and pull my loose top discreetly down to cover the tell-tale bulge. 'This is just in case.'

'In case of what?'

'Things going south,' he mutters, thrusting his own handgun into the back waistband of his jeans.

'I'm not killing anyone.'

'Of course not.' But his eyes twinkle. 'Nobody ever wants to kill anyone. It's just, sometimes there isn't a choice.' He clears his throat. 'How about if someone was about to kill your boy, and you had a gun and a chance to stop them. You'd do it then, for sure, wouldn't you?'

I've never considered this as a situation, to be fair.

'I don't know. Maybe.' I pull a face. 'Probably.'

'There you go, then.'

'Only I'd be likely to miss and hit Charlie instead.'

'Hmm.' Robbie rubs his chin, something he seems to do quite frequently. Must be all the stubble he's cultivating there. But I doubt that shaving has been high on his agenda recently. 'In that case, best make sure you aim right, Miss.' He repeats what he told me during the aiming part of his tutorial. 'Remember, chest is best.'

'Why not shoot them in the head?'

I grimace at the thought of blowing someone's brains out. Though at least it can be done from a distance, without getting any blood and stuff on yourself. How my mother was able to stab someone with scissors, up close and personal, and probably getting heavily blood-spattered in the process, is beyond me.

'Head's a smaller target.' He checks the cameras one last time – everything seems dark and quiet in the village – and gestures me to follow him out of the surveillance room. 'Aiming at the chest gives you plenty of scope for hitting *something*, at least.'

We walk along the corridor with the iron-grey walls. There's a door to the right with a glass panelled window. Reinforced glass.

He peers through the window and seems satisfied by what he sees. He unlocks the door and ushers me inside.

Opposite me is Natasha, chained to a bed. Literally chained, like a dog. One wrist is attached to the bed by a thick metal chain. The bed itself has an iron frame, bolted to the wall and floor.

Very comfortable.

She looks awful. There's a bandage about her head, and she appears to have a black eye; at least, there's extensive bruising to one side of her face. Was all that damage from hitting the windscreen when the car plunged into the ditch? Or has Robbie been laying into her in an effort to get her to talk? Or Sir Philip, perhaps?

The thought repels me.

Though why would they beat her up … and then bandage her head? That doesn't make much sense. So perhaps it was the car crash that left her face so bruised and battered. The driver's airbag had already deflated by the time we plunged into the ditch, after all.

214

She studies Robbie first, cautiously, and then shifts her gaze to me. A strange look comes into her eyes. 'Ah, you betray me,' she states heavily, as though this is a fact she'd been sure of from the start.

'No.' I take a step towards her, and she sits up, nursing her head with her unshackled hand.

'Yes,' she grunts.

'Honestly, you were hurt. I tried to wake you but you were out of it. Then the Russians got in and took Charlie away. I started after him but one of them injected me with some bloody hallucinogenic drug.' It sounds lame, even though it's the truth. 'I don't remember much after that.' I hesitate. 'Did Robbie hit you? Did they hurt you?'

She gives a cracked laugh. '*Them*? No, I bang head on windscreen.' She closes her eyes. 'I'm sorry for boy.'

'Your grandson.'

Her eyes fly open and fix on my face. 'What?'

'I know it all. You're my mother.'

'*He* told you.'

'Of course he told me. The real question is, why didn't you?'

'You would have believed me?'

'Maybe not. But you could have tried.'

'Huh.' She shrugs with derision, looking away. 'You were safer not knowing. Boy too.'

Now that I have some understanding of the situation, I can see she's probably right. But that doesn't lessen my anger and frustration. There's so much I want to ask her. And so little time.

Slitty-eyed, Natasha glances at Robbie. 'So now we kill them and take boy back,' she says flatly.

'Not *we*,' Robbie tells her, his voice gruff. 'I think you should stay here. Can't be trusted.'

'This is my mess. I clean it up.' Natasha gets to her feet, stumbling slightly. The chain rattles in her wake, not allowing her to take more than one or two steps away from the bed. She jerks at the chain, throwing it an angry look. 'I am not wild animal.'

'Aren't you?'

'Ah, kinky Janus. He likes chains in the basement, yes?' Natasha laughs without humour. 'I can't help like this. Unchain me.'

'No can do.'

She gives a cry of frustration and drags on the chain violently, rattling it like a phantom out of an old ghost story. The whole bed shakes, dust puffing off the wall behind her. Thankfully the bolted-on structure holds firm.

I step carefully out of her reach, almost to the open doorway, and notice that Robbie has also taken a few steps back.

Chained up or not, this woman could still be dangerous.

'Why are you here, then?' she demands.

'I'd happily leave you here to rot.' Robbie grimaces. 'But Sir Philip, he needs your help with these Russians. He wants to know, like, how many there are likely to be, what kind of weapons they have, and if you know who they work for.'

Natasha stares at him, incredulous. 'He thinks I know these things? That I work against my own child and grandchild for Mother Russia?' She shakes her head vehemently. 'They want me dead too. Bastards.' She spits on the floor, making me jump in surprise. 'They take me for exchange, yes? I will do it.' She nods, chin raised proudly. 'No need for chains. I make exchange with boy.'

'That's not what they want,' Robbie informs her.

She looks mystified.

I say, 'They want information.'

'What information?'

'Something only Sir Philip knows. But he can't do it. Not even to save Charlie.' My voice breaks. 'So any help you can give us … '

She tugs on the chain again. Small puffs of dust fly off the wall again. 'Let me go,' she insists angrily. 'Give me gun back. I kill them. I kill them all.'

I drag Robbie out into the corridor. 'Why can't she come with us? You heard Sir Philip. She's an assassin. She could help us.'

'Because she can't be trusted,' he says doggedly. 'Sir Philip's wrong – '

'No, I can see that he's right now. She obviously hates them as much as you do, and we need all the help we can get,' I remind him in a whisper. 'I'll be no use in a fight. But she's happy to shoot people. You heard her. She's totally up for killing these guys.'

'Aye,' he mutters. 'But she's a Russkie too, don't forget.'

'She's also Charlie's gran.'

There's not much point trying to conceal the truth about my relationship to Natasha, and besides, I'm certain this man knows it already.

He meets my angry gaze and pulls a face. 'Well, yes, when you put it like that ... '

'How's our guest? Tearing the place apart yet?'

I turn to see Sir Philip coming briskly down the corridor. The cane I've seen him use is tucked under one arm, and I get the impression he doesn't need it for walking, it's just there for effect. For his doddering old gentleman act that goes down so well with the villagers. He may be seventy-odd, but he looks at least twenty years younger tonight, sharp-eyed and clean-shaven, a decisive look about him.

My grandfather.

I still can't take it in that we're related. I have a mother and a grandfather. My whole life has been spent seeing myself in the light of an orphan. To discover I have a family has been a shock and I'm still struggling to come to terms with it.

None of which is helped by the fact that my mother is a Russian assassin, and my grandfather was a British spymaster. And may still be, by the way he's carrying on tonight.

'Says she wants to help,' Robbie is telling him. 'Claims we can trust her.'

'About as far as we can throw her, yes, I agree. But needs must …' Sir Philip mutters. He steps into the room – though cell would be a better description for it – and looks Natasha up and down. His face is not friendly. 'Good evening, Natasha. Now, what makes you think I'm going to believe a word you say?'

This is the first time I've seen them together, and I'm immediately struck by two things. Firstly, how different they are in looks. Sir Philip is the quintessential English gentleman, even without his fetching Panama hat, his hair silvering, his face craggy with age. Natasha, on the other hand, has high cheekbones that could be described as Slavic, with an austere beauty that makes me wish I looked a little more like her.

Secondly, how much they hate each other.

A great deal, judging by the way their eyes clash as they square up to each other.

They're both rather aristocratic in looks though, I realise, glancing from one to the other in surprise. Autocratic too, stubborn and determined to have their own way.

Now, *that*, I may have inherited. I've always been stubborn. Along with more than a dash of my mother's fiery, impulsive temperament.

Natasha purses her lips and folds her arms. The chains rattle and clank. She jerks her head towards me. 'She believes me.'

'Of course she does. You're her mother. What could be more natural?' Sir Philip waits for a response that never comes, raising thin brows. 'But that state of affairs is unlikely to last. You were responsible for her father's death. She will never forgive you for that. And nor will I.'

I stare at him. 'What? You didn't tell me that before.'

'Your father was picked up by the SVR, the Russian secret service, because of her,' Sir Philip tells me in icy tones. 'Charles was a pawn in her game and he paid the price for trusting someone so flagrantly out of control. It's true that Natasha didn't kill him with her own hand. But if my son had never become involved with her, it's my belief he would still be alive today.'

218

'But then I wouldn't exist,' I point out. 'Or Charlie.'

He says nothing.

Behind us, Robbie fidgets. 'We need to set off soon. Time's nearly up.'

'Time?' Natasha's eyes sharpen. 'What is this?'

Sir Philip begins to turn away without answering her, but I grab his arm.

'We need her,' I say in a low voice. 'You said it yourself, you can't give them what they want. As soon as they realise that, Charlie's life will be in danger. And I haven't the faintest idea how to shoot someone. Or not without actually killing them.'

'Patty is meeting us on the way,' Sir Philip says. 'It's all arranged. We don't need anyone else.'

Robbie is frowning. 'With all due respect, sir, Patty was never an operative. She was your personal assistant and, to be frank, she's getting on a bit. I know she'll have had *some* training. But I don't imagine she's ever been in the field.'

'Field? What field?' I ask, bemused.

'He means she never kill anyone,' Natasha explains, watching Sir Philip through narrowed eyes. 'Who is this personal assistant called … Patty?' When Sir Philip looks uncomfortable, she throws back her head with a disbelieving laugh. 'Not old lady we steal car from?'

'Patricia can handle herself,' Sir Philip says stiffly.

'Ha!' Natasha shakes her head at him. 'So, you leave trained assassin chained up and take ancient secretary to fight instead?' She rolls her eyes. 'You will all be dead by midnight… And I will die of thirst, chained to bed, because nobody will ever find me in this hell place.'

'She's got a point,' I say, and can tell that Robbie at least agrees with me, even though all he does is grunt. But no doubt it's more than his job's worth to openly challenge his employer. 'You can't leave her down here.'

With a sigh, Sir Philip reluctantly nods to Robbie to release her chain, which he does with a key taken from his jeans pocket.

'Ah, much better.' Natasha rubs her wrist and smiles. 'Now, a gun?'

219

'You can have mine,' I say at once, and hand it over while Sir Philip is still protesting.

'For God's sake,' my grandfather mutters, taking a quick step back as though he expects her to start shooting us all.

Robbie also flinches as she accepts the handgun, watching the former captive with wide-eyed apprehension, his ruddy cheeks noticeably paler than before.

But Natasha merely checks the gun is loaded and then tucks it into her own waistband, but at the front, still smiling.

'So,' she says, 'what is plan?'

There's a staircase out of the underground bunker. It leads to a door that, when closed behind us, doesn't look like a door at all but a perfectly ordinary wooden panel in the wall. The camouflage is effective; I look back and can't even see where the door is any more.

'Wait here,' Sir Philip says, and jerks his head to Robbie, who follows him down the hall and into a room where they stand talking for a moment in hushed voices.

'I can't believe you spent all that time with me and Charlie, and didn't tell me to my face that I was your daughter,' I hiss urgently at Natasha.

'It was not important.'

'Not important?' I stare at her, angry and baffled, not for the first time today.

'It was long conversation. No time for long conversation.' She waves a hand dismissively. I can see myself in her face. It's unnerving. Those restless blue eyes, the eyes of a killer... That's not how I look, is it? 'Anyway, you know now. End of story.'

'Hardly.' I glance down the hall but the two men have still not re-emerged. 'Why did you do it? Why did you kill Kurt and Simon?'

'Simon was not his name,' she corrects me.

'Tim Shaw then. What you did to him ... He didn't deserve that.'

'He was working for them.'

'Your former employers? The … SVR?'

Her eyes narrow on my face, but all she does is nod.

'So you killed him?'

'He was not good for you.' Now she sounds like any other mother, strict and controlling. 'I did what was necessary.'

'Okay, but did you have to do it like … like that?' I push that horrible mental image away, the one of his scissor-pinned body covered in blood, the white rug spattered and spoiled by the dark rust-red of congealed blood.

Her smile is disturbing. 'Yes.'

I shudder.

'And Kurt?'

Her lips twitch. 'Kurt?' Her eyebrows tug together, as though struggling to recall who I mean.

'The hairdresser. I spent the night with him, and the next day … I found him dead.' I search her face for any signs of remorse but she's blank, almost matter-of-fact.

'Yes.' She nods slowly as though remembering. 'His name was not Kurt.' She hums, thinking. 'Ivan.'

'Ivan?'

'Yes, that was his name. I was watching you … It was first time I find you.' She half-smiles. 'So many years, searching, and there you are, still alive, and so pretty … '

I look away, feeling awkward.

'And then I see a man with you. This Ivan.' Her face tightens. 'And I recognize him.'

'What? You *knew* him?'

'He was Russian. Trained by SVR, same as me. Him and his brother. I forget name of brother. Both bad men.' Her blue eyes narrow. 'I see you together, and I know he is there to find me. So he must die. And afterwards, I tell Janus what I do.'

My eyes widen, fixed on her face. 'You told Sir Philip you'd killed Kurt?'

'He was right man to tell. He hide you from SVR.' She shrugs. 'From me too, yes. But I find you again in end, no problem.'

Sir Philip and Robbie are coming back.

I'm still struggling to process what she's said, my heart thumping unpleasantly. Everything Sir Philip told me is true. Kurt was a Russian agent, sent to seduce me, presumably in the hope of smoking Natasha out so they could grab her. Shaw was an undercover investigator hired by the Russians to do much the same. Which means the Russians must have been watching me for years, hunting for me each time I changed identities exactly as they've been hunting for Natasha, our two lives inextricably linked without me even being aware of her existence …

'Right, guns?' Sir Philip demands.

'Check,' Robbie says, patting the bulge in the back of his jeans.

'Check,' Natasha says, placing a proprietorial hand over the bulge at the front of her jeans.

Everyone looks at me.

'I gave her my gun,' I remind them, having nothing to pat or fondle.

'You need a gun.' Robbie is frowning.

'I'm fine without one, honestly.'

'People without guns get taken hostage and used as human shields,' Robbie tells me bluntly.

'I'll take that chance,' I say.

Sir Philip studies me, and then unstraps his old-fashioned watch and hands it to me.

'What's this?'

'A wristwatch,' he says unnecessarily.

'I don't need a wristwatch. I've got a phone … ' Abruptly, I realise I don't actually have my phone with me. The burner is back at the house. 'Anyway, why would I need to know the time?'

'To synchronize with the rest of us,' Sir Philip says mildly, adding, 'Besides, it's equipped with a tracker.'

'Oh right,' I say, and strap it onto my wrist, grinning. 'I suppose it acts as a mini-bomb too. Or a gigantic magnet. Like a James Bond watch.'

I look up to find them all staring at me.

'I was joking,' I mutter.

Sir Philip's phone buzzes. Or rather, his jacket buzzes.

Now we all look at him instead.

'That's your phone, sir,' Robbie points out politely.

'I know.' Impatiently, the old gentleman fumbles in the pocket of his smart, olive green silk-lined jacket and produces his mobile phone. He frowns down at the screen. 'Patty,' he says briefly. 'She's at the rendezvous. Wants to know what the hold-up is.'

I feel again that sick sensation in the pit of my stomach.

We're running late.

For rescuing my son from trained Russian killers.

Come on, come on, come on, I think in a spasmodic loop, both hands clenching to fists, even though there's nothing to lash out at. Not yet, I remind myself.

'Tell her, *you*, Janus,' Natasha says succinctly, and prods an accusing finger in his direction. '*We* have been ready ten minutes. *You* are the hold-up.'

Sir Philip pockets the phone again, and scowls at his daughter-in-law down the length of his refined nose. I imagine it's a scowl perfected over many generations of his aristocratic family.

I half expect him to say something unpleasant in return. To remind her of all the terrible things she's done or accuse her of being to blame for my father's death. Or perhaps to tell Robbie to lock her up again.

But he does none of those things.

It seems Sir Philip Janus is willing to put up with a great deal in order to fix the mess he made by bringing his granddaughter and great-grandson to Darkling Moreton to serve as bait for a ruthless killer.

'You should stay behind,' he says, turning to me.

What?' I glare. 'No way.'

'You're not trained for this. You could be killed.'

'I'm coming with you. Charlie is my son.'

He stares back at me, and then sighs heavily. 'On your own head be it, then.' He glances round at the others, an odd note in his voice. Suppressed excitement. 'We all know what we're supposed to be doing, I hope?'

Yes, it's excitement. Perhaps he's been missing this kind of thing in retirement. The doomed mission. The midnight rendezvous in the dark woods. The shoot-out in the country church. All of which appear to be part of our 'plan'.

I hope to God he knows what he's doing. Because my son's life is at stake here.

Robbie grunts his assent.

I nod.

Natasha rolls her eyes, and once again pats the handgun sticking out of her jeans. Lovingly.

'Good.' My grandfather whistles for his two dogs to follow him. 'Then let's get Charlie back.'

The two powerful German Shepherds rise from the floor in silent obedience and accompany us down the hallway towards the side door into the garden. As he told us when we discussed his plan, there's a concealed gate in the high wall that runs around the property, giving directly onto the rough ground between the old manor house and the stream. This is the way out he's decided we should use to avoid scrutiny from anyone watching at the gates.

Sir Philip opens the side door and we plunge, one by one, into the waiting darkness outside.

CHAPTER TWENTY-FOUR

The gate hinges must have been well oiled; they open easily, without any tell-tale squeaking or grating as I half expect. We're skirting around the village towards St Hilda's. Not to pray, though that might be a useful thing to do under the circumstances, but because the men holding my son want to meet at the church.

There's some logic to that. It's getting on for midnight and the churchyard will be deserted. The church itself should actually be locked but Sir Philip is a churchwarden and has a key. I don't know how the Russians intend to get into the church if they arrive before us, which seems likely given all the delays, but I can imagine one of those men kicking in the vestry door rather than waiting politely in the church porch.

To avoid detection, we're taking the long way round beside the stream, the same route I took the very first time I left Charlie at the Sunday school playgroup and went off exploring on my own. The path is beaten-down grass, with weeds and brambles brushing our legs and the stream running alongside us, unseen but tinkling in the darkness.

Avoiding detection is important, because Sir Philip is supposed to be going to the rendezvous on his own. So the three of us accompanying him is likely to put the wind up the Russians. Hence taking the long way out of sight of the road.

But what if the Russians aren't in their big intimidating SUV on the main road? What if they're on foot and taking the long route too?

Natasha walks close to my right, nearest to the bank of the stream and slightly in advance. Her eyes scanned the darkness ahead, her hand hovering close to the gun in her waistband. I get the feeling she's ready to protect me. Which is reassuring but also bizarre and terrifying.

My mother.

I'm still adjusting to all the information that's hit me in the past few hours. One of the weirdest things is that Kurt was a *Russian*. Yes, he had an accent. But he told me he was Polish and I believed him. No doubt he considered that I was the most average of ordinary citizens with no second language and no experience of travel beyond the UK, and would not know the difference between a Polish and a Russian accent.

In that, he was absolutely right.

I can see now, thinking back over what Natasha and Sir Philip have told me, that Kurt's death must have massively increased the Russians' interest in me. I was then not merely the daughter of a traitor but now potentially the person who'd erased their comrade Kurt.

No, not Kurt.

Ivan.

I shall have to get used to all this, to the uneasy shifting about of reality, of what I now know to be real, to be true.

We reach the edge of the woodland with Sir Philip leading the way, his dogs alongside us, low to the ground, sniffing and panting quietly. He doesn't use a torch to light the way. But there's a moon and stars shining faintly above, occasionally covered by scudding clouds, and maybe his profession has given him plenty of experience at walking without light at nighttime.

I have no such experience. I stumble several times, and once Natasha prevents me from falling into the stream, righting me without comment.

Robbie brings up the rear, his head turning from time to time, as though checking there is nobody behind us. Though it's so dark, this far from the road and the village streetlights, I can't imagine how he would be able to tell.

Once we are safely inside the woodland and under cover of its thick foliage, we come to a halt.

The path is narrower here but at least we are less visible to anyone who might be watching our progress. Though if anyone is watching, that's our plan out the window. Because the whole plan relies on the element of surprise…

Robbie, at a nod from Sir Philip, cups both hands to his mouth and makes what I consider a creditable impersonation of an owl hooting.

Natasha is less impressed. 'What is that? Owl?' She shakes her head. 'More like duck … with constipation.'

'Hush,' Sir Philip says reprovingly.

Robbie eyes her but says nothing, merely cups his hands and hoots again.

We wait.

After a few seconds, another 'owl' hoots to our left. Not far, by my guess.

Robbie replies.

Maybe thirty seconds pass, and then a shadow detaches itself from a thick, glowering tree trunk and glides towards us over the woodland floor, making little sound. A face gradually swims out of the darkness. A face I recognize.

'Patty,' Sir Philip murmurs, and goes to greet her. 'Thank you for doing this.'

'My pleasure.' Patricia looks past him to me. 'Anything to get that lovely little boy back. Those brutes… ' Then she sees Natasha and her body stiffens, her expression unfriendly. 'What's *she* doing here?'

'Helping us,' Robbie says.

'It is not ideal. But we need all hands on deck.' Sir Philip looks awkward though. 'So let's try to get along.'

I don't think I have ever seen my docile next-door neighbour so stern. It's alarming. She looks uncannily like a cat burglar, clad in black leggings, black top and jacket, a thick black woollen beanie drawn down over her hair and forehead so that not even her hair is showing.

'You stole my car,' Patricia says in an undertone to Natasha, 'and crashed it into a ditch. It will never be the same again. And how am I supposed to explain bullet holes to the local garage mechanics?'

'Mice?' Natasha suggests, the pale oval of her face disdainful.

The two women stand glaring at each other.

My head is reeling.

'You knew who Natasha was when you saw her in the street?' I ask Patricia, shocked and a little bit furious.

'Not really. But I'd seen photographs, so I was suspicious.'

'So why didn't you…?'

'Stop her?' Patricia gives me a hard look that makes me feel uncomfortable. 'Sir Philip asked me to keep an eye on you, that's all. He didn't ask me to interfere in your life. But I did try to warn you.'

'You did?'

'I asked if you were okay. I suggested your friend was acting oddly. You ignored me. Besides, I could hardly let on that I knew who she was. I had no idea she was about to steal my car, trust me. Or not with Charlie in the back.'

'I had to steal car,' Natasha puts in, sounding annoyed. 'It was steal car or be shot.'

We both ignore her.

I feel hurt and betrayed. My chest is heaving with sudden distress as I gulp back tears. Patricia has always seemed so harmless and ordinary and accommodating. The perfect next-door neighbour, in fact. Now I realise she knew who I was all along, or she was in Sir Philip's confidence at least. And has worked with Sir Philip in the British secret services.

Somehow, it's worse than discovering that Natasha is my mother.

'There there, love.' Patricia relents and drags me close for a quick embrace. It's not much of a hug, given the day I've endured and my fears for Charlie, but the familiar scent of her perfume settles my nerves. 'I'm sorry I deceived you, truly I am. But I was under orders from Sir Philip. He always knows what's best in these situations.'

She pulls back and gives me a wink. For once since I met her, she's not wearing lipstick or any garish eyeshadow. But perhaps Sir Phillip's phone call got her out of bed and she just changed into dark clothing and headed out.

'We're going to get your lovely boy back from those villains, don't you fret. All of us together,' she adds, and her lips purse. 'Even *her.*'

There's a ping, loud in the silence of the dark wood.

I look at Sir Philip, who is once again wrestling his mobile phone from the inner pocket of his silk-lined jacket.

This is my grandfather. He wears a silk-lined jacket. Okay, the olive green is pretty good camouflage in a wood at night. But I can't get over the fact that this posh Knight of the Realm is related to me. I want Charlie to meet him. To know who he is.

Charlie.

'Oh Christ.' Sir Philip is studying the screen, which lights up his face with a ghastly green-blue patina of light. If anyone's looking for us among the trees, we've just given away our position. But I suppose those men are not likely to shoot him. Not when they want him to divulge top secret information. Information that would save my son but kill two courageous, long-serving British agents.

'What is it?' I demand, feeling queasy again at the thought of all the things that could go wrong tonight. I'm not cut out for this spy business and I know it.

Reluctantly, he shows me the screen. Someone has sent him a photograph.

'Oh Christ,' I say too, and clap a hand to my mouth. Now I really feel sick.

It's a close-up photo of Charlie. He's seated in what looks like a low-backed blue chair with a plain red wall behind him. His little hands are bound with plastic ties and there's a strip of silver tape across his mouth. His eyes are wide and terrified, the camera flash a flame reflected in each iris. There's a dirty mark across one cheek. A developing bruise?

Fear crawls inside me, swiftly followed by a hot burning fury.

'I'll k-k-kill them,' I stutter, and my hand clasps for a non-existent weapon in the waistband of my jeans.

Of course. I gave my gun to Natasha.

She's leaning in with the others, all of them staring aghast at the image on the upraised phone.

'Give me back that gun,' I order her, my voice thick with anger and loathing.

The Russian shakes her head, but she's smiling coldly. 'You are my daughter. Yes. Now we see.'

'Let keep calm and stick to the plan,' Sir Philip tells me, but there's strain in his voice. 'It looks bad, yes. But there's no real evidence they mean to do him any serious harm.'

'Have you seen his face? The bruising?'

'The key thing,' he insists, 'is to keep negotiating with these people. To make them believe things are going their way, in the hope this makes them lower their guard.' Briefly, he puts a reassuring hand on my shoulder. 'Please try not to worry, Marina. We're going to get him back for you.'

His use of my Russian birth name sends a jolt through me, a reminder that I don't even know who I am. Not really, not at the core of things.

He continues, addressing all of us now, 'But remember, my chief aim is to get the boy away from them within the first few minutes. As a pre-requisite before I divulge any information. But it may prove difficult to persuade them to hand him over to me first.' He looks around at us all. 'So, to be completely safe, you need to wait at least five minutes before making a move. Is that understood?'

He turns away to exchange a few quiet words with Robbie. Then, the two men shake hands and Sir Philip orders his two dogs to stay with Robbie.

I don't like the way they shake hands. It feels somehow final. Like a goodbye. As though Sir Philip doesn't think he'll be coming back from this meeting. My heart thumps erratically as I watch my grandfather, whom I've barely got to know since discovering he *is* my grandfather, slope off into the dark alone.

We're not far from the church now. The four of us – Natasha at the front, me and Patricia in the middle, and Robbie bringing up the rear as before – follow at a discreet distance, avoiding the noisy gravel path and threading our way between gravestones instead, trying to keep out of sight of the church entrance, with the dogs padding alongside us.

I've never particularly liked churchyards. I expect that's quite a common thing. But churchyards at midnight are among my least favourite things ever, I now discover. I walk as lightly as I can, my ears straining for any sound, however small, that might indicate a threat.

I don't think I've ever been so frightened in my life, not even when faced with a brutal murder. But then, I know these men have guns, and Sir Philip and Natasha and Robbie have guns, while I have no weapon at all.

Add to that my heart-pounding fear that I may never see my grandfather or my boy alive again, and it's not a pleasant experience, tiptoeing at dead of night past gloomy stone angels and graves surrounded by Victorian railings, tensed for raised voices or the sound of a shot.

Natasha is almost out of sight, a faint shadow creeping from gravestone to gravestone, staying low.

She freezes, and then runs forward, disappearing round the front of the church.

Surprised, I glance back at Robbie to find he's running too, feet moving silently over the dark grass between graves, passing me without a word.

Looking ahead, I realise why.

Lights have come on inside the church, burning through stained glass to illuminate squares and arched oblongs on the grassy area ahead.

My nerves jumping, I hurry after them to the front of the church, moving as quietly as I can, Patricia at my elbow.

Sir Philip is not yet inside the church. He is standing outside the porch, staring up at the lit-up stained glass windows.

Natasha and Robbie have both stopped dead, watching him.

There's nobody else in sight.

Sir Philip doesn't turn at our approach. Maybe he doesn't hear us. Or maybe he doesn't intend to deviate from the plan, regardless. He simply squares his shoulders and plunges into the church porch…

I catch up with the other two. 'What the hell is going on?'

'They're already inside,' Robbie whispers, hustling us back into the shadows behind the church porch. Just in case anyone is on guard, I imagine.

'But how?' I whisper back. 'I thought the church was kept locked at night. That's why Sir Philip brought his key.'

Robbie nods.

I stare up at the bright interior of the church, confused. 'What? You're saying they broke in?'

'Or they have key,' Natasha says.

'Only the churchwardens have a key,' Patricia points out, still in a hoarse whisper. 'Sir Philip and Mrs Bloxley.'

Mrs Bloxley. The grey-haired woman who helps run the Sunday school playgroup. I can't imagine she would agree to come out and open the church at midnight for a couple of murderous Russians, especially not if they have my bruised three-year-old son in tow. Unless, that is, she was forced to do so at gunpoint.

Robbie frowns. 'And the vicar, of course.'

Natasha rounds on us both, her eyes snapping in the dark. 'What now, then? No sign of boy.'

'Yes, that's worrying,' Robbie agrees.

There's something in his voice… Filled with creeping horror, I can hardly breathe, my lungs hurting. 'What are you saying?'

'We don't know if Charlie is even inside the church,' Robbie explains. 'They may have left him somewhere secure instead. To be released once they're sure of the intelligence that Sir Philip has promised to give them.'

'But he's not going to give them anything useful.' I swallow, terrified for my boy. 'And the plan – '

'The plan is out of the window now.' Robbie grabs me by the shoulders and gives me a little shake. I've been whimpering, I realise, scared half out of my wits by the implication of what he's saying. 'Hush, they'll hear us. What we need is to check if Charlie is in the church with them, that's all. Okay?'

'Okay,' I mouth, shivering.

He releases me.' Good.' He turned in time to see Natasha slipping away from us, and swears under his breath. 'Come back here.'

But it's too late. Natasha has gone, already vanished inside the yawning mouth of the church which.

Robbie, Patricia and I wait, staring at each other and at the church porch in horrified silence.

What else can we do?

Half a minute later, Natasha returns as silently as she left.

'Did you see who's in there?' Robbie demands.

'Church door shut,' she tells us.

Frustration boils inside me at her matter-of-fact tone .'You should have opened it and looked inside,' I whisper, half tempted to do so myself, despite the obvious danger.

I need to know that Charlie is alive. I need to see him. Right now, nothing else matters.

'I know this door,' Natasha says, shaking her head. 'It will not open quietly. It makes noise.'

'So what now?' I'm painfully aware that the clock is ticking. We are running out of time to save my boy, and we don't even know where he is. 'We've got to find out what's happening in there.'

'Agreed.' Robbie takes a few steps back out of the shadows to stare up at the ghostly church façade. 'Is it possible to see through stained-glass, do you think?'

'I expect so.' I guess what he's thinking. 'But these windows are too high up. We'd never be able to reach them.'

He looks at Natasha and Patricia, sizing them up, and then eyes me speculatively. 'You can't weigh much.'

'I beg your pardon?'

'If I were to give you a leg up… '

I get his meaning at once, and nod urgently. 'Yes, I can try.'

'I keep watch,' Natasha says, dragging the handgun from her jeans. 'You climb.'

'Oh, my dear, do be careful,' Patricia whispers, eyes widening. 'Sir Philip would never forgive us if you hurt yourself.'

Robbie throws her a dry look and she throws up her hands, lapsing into silence.

Together, we creep around to stand directly below the large stained-glass windows that face the car park. These should give us the best view into the church.

Robbie halts below the middle window and crouches slightly, cupping his hands before giving me an encouraging nod. 'Hop up, and grab onto that ledge when I lift you.'

Fixing Charlie's image firmly in my mind, I step up onto his interlaced hands with one foot, balancing awkwardly.

In the same movement, before I'm quite ready, he jerks his hands upwards and I find myself hoisted at speed through the air.

Half blind in the dark, rough lichened stone scraping my face, I grab wildly at the window ledge above my head and pull myself up, holding that position for a few arm-wrenching seconds. My head rises to the level of the lowest glass section of the windows, and for that instant I'm able to peer in through misty yellow and green lead-seamed glass.

Two men all in black are side-on to the windows, standing by the last row of pews and facing the rear of the church.

One looks like the burly man who chased me through the field towards John's camper van.

The other is balding and shorter, but his face is concealed by the other man.

The burly guy has a gun trained on Sir Philip.

There's no sign of my son.

As my arms weaken and my brief grasp on the stone lintel slips, I cast one last desperate glance about the body of the church, hoping to see Charlie huddled in a pew or standing to one side.

But all I see is an empty church, wall lamps burning, nobody there but the three men …

I fall to the ground, winded and gasping, 'He's not there. Charlie's not there.'

CHAPTER TWENTY-FIVE

Natasha helps me up from the dewy grass, her face in shadow. 'Tell us what you see in church.'

'Only Sir Philip and two men,' I whisper, trying to make sense of what I saw in that one brief glimpse of the building interior.

'No Charlie?'

I shake my head, still dazed by my fall from the high window. 'I told you, he's not in there. There's no sign of him anywhere.'

Natasha mutters something in Russian. Probably a swear word, judging by her heavy frown.

I banged my head when I fell and it's thumping now. 'What … What do you think we should do?'

'Well, we can't go barging in there now, all guns blazing,' says Robbie slowly, thinking out loud. 'Not without Charlie on the premises. If they've left him somewhere secure, whoever is looking after him may have standing orders to kill him if the others don't come back on schedule.'

This is a terrifying thought.

'Don't,' I mutter, sickened by the idea of my innocent little boy abandoned to the care of some psycho killer.

'And if he's been left alone without a minder,' he goes on, 'maybe tied up or imprisoned… We may never find him again without their help. So we can't risk shooting them.'

Natasha makes a snarling noise and tightens her grip on her gun.

I look at her. 'This this is your fault. You did this to him.'

'Me?' My mother sounds outraged.

'If you hadn't come back here, if you hadn't kept interfering in my life, those Russians might never have found me or Charlie in the first place.'

'They had already found you,' she says coldly. 'This is why I interfere. To save your life.'

'But you didn't need to kill Kurt – ' I begin furiously, but she interrupts.

'I needed to kill him before he kill you,' she corrects me, and then nods at my silence. 'You were bait. I kill fishermen. Not worm.'

Baffled, I stutter something and then give up. It doesn't seem worth pointing out that the 'fisherman' had turned out to be Charlie's father, something I only discovered after my desperate flight to a new identity.

'Let's focus on the problem in hand,' Patricia interrupts us.

I feel queasy and desperate. '*She*'s the problem.' I step away from them both, dragging on my hair in frustration.

'I can't argue with that,' Patricia mutters.

'We have to do something,' I exclaim, fuming. 'This is ridiculous.'

Without any warning, Natasha grabs me from behind, clapping a hand over my mouth. 'Hush!'

I struggle with her, furious and protesting.

Then I see why she grabbed me.

The church door has opened while we were talking, spilling a dim golden light across the gravelled path, and they're coming out of the porch.

Sir Philip emerges first, his hands in the air.

The other two men follow, a few paces behind. The burly man still has his gun trained on Sir Philip, his expression murderous.

The third man is the Reverend Shearsman.

The angry protests die on my lips. We all stand frozen in place, watching, unsure what to do. It's pointless even trying to get out of sight now. We've already been seen. But it's awkward.

The burly man shifts his gaze to us, surprised. The gun muzzle wavers slightly, turning towards our little group while also trying to cover Sir Philip.

Patricia starts forward, concerned. 'Sir Philip?' Then she frowns, halting. 'Vicar? Is that you?'

The vicar stops and stares back at us, speechless. He's not in his usual black vestment and dog collar that mark him out as a man of the cloth. Instead, he's put on a dark brown jacket over a black polo neck and black jeans. Similar gear to the burly Russian, in other words. The only hint of colour are his white and blue trainers, that stand out like flashing neon in the darkness.

'Ah, Patricia,' Sir Philip says slowly, locking gazes with his former personal assistant. 'Yes, the vicar agreed to let our friends here into the church before us.'

I have to check, though I already know the answer in my heart. 'Is Charlie with them?'

'I'm afraid not, my dear.' My grandfather's face is unreadable in the shadow of the old church. 'But they've promised to let him go … as soon as they've been able to check the, erm, information I felt obliged to give them.'

Oh God.

His meaning is clear. He's followed the original plan, despite Charlie's absence, and given them dud information to play for time. The names of two undercover British agents operating in Moscow. Names that don't exist.

The other man from the SUV must be guarding my son somewhere nearby, waiting for this meeting to play out before deciding whether to release Charlie or kill him.

So as soon as the Russians check the false names Sir Philip has given them and discover that they've been duped …

I put a hand to my mouth, unable to hide my fear.

'No need to panic, my dear. We're just waiting for a return phone call from this gentleman's associate. The one who's sitting with Charlie and is in a position to verify my information. I'm sure everything will be all right.'

'Shut up,' the burly man says in a thick accent, threatening us all with his gun. 'Enough talk.'

'My apologies. I'm an old man and old men talk too much.'

'I said, shut up.'

'Quite right. We just need to wait.' Sir Philip takes a clumsy step to the left, swaying as though too doddery to walk straight. I check his face but he doesn't look unwell. Then I realise what he's doing. Covering Natasha, who's standing exactly along that line, gun raised. 'It's a question of timing, that's all.'

A question of timing.

Before I have quite processed what he means by that, Sir Philip drops to the gravel path and there's a sharp retort that echoes off the stone building. With a shocked expression, the Russian crumples sideways, the gun falling harmless from his hand. Robbie bounds forward to grab it up and stands over the man, pointing the muzzle down at his chest.

But there's no need.

The Russian gasps, chest heaving, staring wide-eyed at nothing. Then gives a strange wet-sounding gurgle and lies still.

'Get him out of sight.' Sir Philip has already risen to his feet and is dusting himself down, oddly limber for a man who was calling himself 'old' mere seconds before.

'What about the vicar?' Gun in hand, Robbie turns towards the other man, but the Reverend Shearsman has already taken to his heels, running around the other side of the church. A few seconds later he has vanished into deep shadow. 'Should I go after him?'

'No need. I think I know where he's going.'

'The vicarage?' Robbie asks.

'Too obvious.' Sir Philip has his phone in hand and is checking the photograph of Charlie again. He holds it up, turning to show me the screen. 'Is that the parish hall, would you say?'

I blink, my heart thudding hard, my attention still fixed on the horrible sight of the dead Russian. Natasha has taken the man's legs and Robbie his arms, and between them, the two are dragging him into the bushes on the far side of the church porch, leaving a rusty trail behind on the gravel …

Blood.

'Marina, I need you to focus.'

The use of my original name snaps me out of my trance. 'What? Oh …' I stare at the photograph, and force myself not to consider how scared Charlie looks, but to study his surroundings instead. The blue plastic chair, the dull red wall … 'Yes,' I say croakily. 'That's where they hold the Sunday school playgroup. That must have been where he was heading. Quick, it's round the back of the church,' I add, already starting to move when I realise everyone else has frozen into position. 'For God's sake, come on … We have to hurry.'

Then I almost walk slap-bang into a large, red-faced man in a baseball cap, T-shirt that doesn't quite cover his hairy belly, and long shorts. Summer clothes. He's got a large grey Irish wolfhound on a leash, who is staring up at our little group with mild interest.

He's just come from the direction of the parish hall, I realise, and is clearly amazed to see us all.

I step back, speechless.

Thankfully, Natasha and Robbie appear to have finished their gruesome task, emerging together from behind the church porch. But the whole thing must look deeply suspicious.

'Evening, Sir Philip,' the dog-walker says in a deep voice, eerily loud in the silent churchyard. 'Evening, Robbie.' He glances first at Patricia and me, and then at Natasha with a more dubious look, no doubt wondering what on earth is going on. 'Ladies.'

'Good evening, Ben,' Patricia says, perfectly naturally, as though she frequently hangs around churchyards at dead of night.

His troubled gaze goes to the porch and the lit-up church interior; the door is still open. 'Bit late for a prayer meeting, isn't it?' He laughs uncomfortably, clearly sensing tension in the air. 'Not had a burglary, have you?'

Sir Philip thrusts his hands in his trouser pockets, looking rueful. 'I'm afraid we have, yes.'

'Ah, that'll be why the vicar seemed in such a hurry. I just passed him on the path. Said hello but he didn't even look at me. Much taken?'

'Nothing we can't replace.'

'Such a nuisance though. Bloody thieves. Nothing's sacred these days, is it?' The man jerks his head towards the church. 'Need a hand, Sir Philip?'

'Thank you, that's very kind. But it's all being sorted. Police are on their way.' Sir Philip hesitates. 'Reverend Shearsman has just gone to check on the parish hall.'

'Ah, right you are. Yes, that makes sense. Vicar was headed that way.' He nods, and I finally realise who he is. The pub landlord from The Last Trump. 'Well, I'll leave you good folks to it, then.'

'Goodnight,' Sir Philip says politely.

'Goodnight, Sir Philip.' The pub landlord nods to Robbie. 'Night, Robbie.' He glances at me, Patricia and Natasha again, less certain. 'Goodnight, ladies.'

'Sleep well,' Patricia says, smiling.

I smile too.

Robbie nods. 'Night, Ben.'

Natasha says nothing but tugs on her top, which she's pulled down over the bulging waistband of her jeans. She must have stowed her gun there again. The gun she just used to kill the burly Russian, whose body is concealed in bushes behind the church porch.

'Come on,' Sir Philip says urgently as soon as the landlord is out of earshot. 'We need to get to the parish hall. Robbie, Patricia, you two go round the other side of the building. They may try to leave through the back door. You can be waiting for them.'

'Understood,' says Robbie shortly, and he and Patricia set off at a run, back the way we came, presumably to approach the parish hall from the other side as instructed.

Sir Philip, Natasha and I run around to the parish hall entrance by the main path. At least, Natasha and I are running, but Sir Philip isn't able to do more than walk briskly, and we soon leave him behind.

The door to the parish hall stands open. The lights are on.

I'm ready to plunge inside, regardless of what might be waiting for me, but Natasha grabs my arm in the doorway. 'No,' she whispers hoarsely in my ear. 'Me first.'

She pulls out the handgun again. Just looking at it gives me the shivers. But she's right. Our enemies also have weapons, and for all I know, they may be prepared to shoot my son. Barging inside without any thought for the consequences could be fatal.

Edging through the door, Natasha points the gun into the hall before taking one careful step inside, staring around the brightly lit interior.

Whatever she sees makes her go still, her eyes widening. She turns, gesturing me to enter the hall. 'Look,' she says in a low voice, 'they shoot vicar.'

Horrified, I push past her, staring. Sure enough, not far from the neatly stacked Sunday school toys, the Reverend Shearsman lies sprawled on the polished wood floor of the parish hall, blood slowly pooling out from under his body.

'Oh my God … We need to call an ambulance.'

'Why bother? He's dead.'

He's certainly not moving. But all the same …

'How can you be sure he's dead?' I whisper.

'With all that blood? If not dead now, soon.' She shrugs. 'You stay. I check the other rooms.'

With that, Natasha continues along the hall, gun still in hand, heading cautiously for the rooms at the other end.

I fall to my knees beside the vicar. He's been shot in the chest and it seems impossible, from the wound and the sticky pool of blood, that he could still be alive. But as I reach for his wrist to check his pulse, his small black eyes open and he stares up at me. There's terror in his paper-white face.

'You… ' he chokes.

I waste no time on small talk. 'Vicar, where's my son Charlie?' It seems hardhearted of me when the poor man is dying. But Charlie is all that matters to me right now. And for all I know, the Reverend Shearsman is up to his eyeballs in this horrible business. He was in the church with the Russian, after all. The only explanation is that the vicar is somehow involved.

'I… I don't know.'

'Tell me the truth.' I looked down at the dreadful wound to his chest, his black clothes sticky with blood. 'I'll get you an ambulance. But first, you have to tell me about Charlie.'

'Not my fault,' he manages to say. 'They said they would kill my mother if I didn't help.'

'Your mother?'

'Glenda … She lives with me at the vicarage.'

'I see.' There's blood trickling out of the corner of his mouth. I don't have a phone, but I could run back to Sir Philip and get him to call for an ambulance. I need an answer first though. I hate myself for it but what else can I do? This man's life is probably at an end. But my son may still be alive and I have to get him back if I can. 'Where's Charlie? Where's my little boy?'

'He … He was here,' he gasps.

'Well, he's not here now. So who's taken him?'

He struggles, frowning. 'John.'

'*John* took him? You mean, handy-man John, the one who's been camping behind the church?' When he nods feebly, I close my eyes in horror. God, what on earth made me trust that man? And of course Charlie will probably trust him, despite what happened at the house. He may even think I sent John to fetch him. 'Where's he taken him? Do you know? Please, Vicar, this is important. Charlie's life is at stake. Is there anything else you can tell me? Anything at all?'

But all he can do is shake his head and gasp, his eyes staring fixedly up at the ceiling. One of his hands lifts and he makes a vague and unsteady sign of the cross.

Where the hell is Natasha?

I glance up and down the hall but there's still no sign of her. She can't have found Charlie in the back rooms or she would have brought him out or shouted for me.

I lean closer, frowning, seeing the vicar mouth something weakly. 'What? Say that again, I didn't catch it.'

'Vicarage … Tell my mother … '

The Reverend Shearsman gives a great shudder. His eyes roll up, and he lies still.

'Good God.' Sir Philip has come into the hall, and I turn to see Natasha with him too. She must have gone out the other end of the parish hall and walked around to the front entrance again.

Robbie and Patricia appear in their wake, both holding guns and staring down in consternation at the body of our vicar.

'Bloody hell.' Robbie shakes his head, putting away his weapon after a quick glance around. 'This is a right mess and no mistake.'

Brows snapping together, Sir Philip turns sharply to Natasha. 'Did you do this?'

Her eyes flash at him. 'No.'

'He'd already been shot when we arrived,' I say quickly, getting to my feet. 'He must have run back here to warn them. Only they shot him for some reason.' I run a hand through my hair, frantic with worry for my son. 'He said it was John. That John was here and took Charlie away.'

'Nice to know my first aid skills are good enough to get a wounded man back into action so quickly,' Patricia snaps. 'Horrid little man. I should have tied him up.'

My mother shoots me a narrow-eyed look. 'I *tell* you to let me kill that John person,' she says in a low voice. 'Now you see the trouble he cause.'

I ignore her.

'We're all a little bit to blame for this,' Sir Philip says. 'Our plan hasn't gone well so far, has it?'

Patricia looks down at the vicar. 'Poor Reverend Shearsman. He was such an excellent fund-raiser too.' She glances round at Sir Philip. 'I imagine the Russians no longer had a use for him once he'd opened up the church for them tonight. And all done to gain some paltry advantage over us. What dreadful people they are.'

'Yes, and dead men give no evidence,' Sir Philip agrees. 'Bold of them, all the same. I doubt they were granted dispensation to leave a trail of dead civilians behind them. The Russians are usually more discreet in their operations on foreign soil. Which makes me wonder ...' But whatever he's wondering, he doesn't share it with the rest of us. Instead, he takes out his mobile phone. 'No chance of keeping this quiet now. I'd better call London, get them to send a team down to Darkling Moreton asap to contain this.' His brow furrows. 'I'm not looking forward to having to explain what happened here. For the second time, too.'

To my surprise, Patricia doesn't seem particularly upset by the vicar's violent death. She's looking at me instead, concern in her wide eyes. 'Was the Rev already dead when you found him, my dear?'

'Not quite.'

'And did he say anything useful?'

I'm shaky, finding it hard to focus. Where the hell is Charlie? 'Erm, he said they'd threatened to kill his mother. And that's why he helped them.'

'Glenda.' Patricia pulls a face. 'Yes, of course, he adored his mother. Spent every spare minute of his life with her. No wonder he so readily fell in with these jokers, if they were holding his mother hostage.' She pauses. 'Did he give any indication of where John might have taken Charlie?'

'No. Just something about the vicarage and his mother. I suppose he wanted us to rescue her.'

Sir Philip, about to make a call, looks round at me sharply. 'The *vicarage*?' His gaze shifts to Robbie. 'Get round there straightaway, would you? If that's where they've been holding the vicar's mother, maybe they'll take Charlie there too. Though now the Reverend is dead, I expect they'll abandon that post and move the boy somewhere safer.'

'Come on.' Robbie nods to Natasha on his way out the door. 'Vicarage is three minutes from here. If we run, we might still catch them.'

'Yes, you two go,' Sir Philip agrees, returning to his phone as Patricia pockets her gun and stoops to examine the vicar's body. 'I'll sort things out at this end. Call me as soon as you have news of the boy.'

It's gone midnight. Charlie will be tired and hungry. He must be so scared and unhappy, wondering why his mother doesn't come to rescue him. But we're so close to getting him back now, so close …

'Wait,' I shout, 'I'm coming too.'

Sir Philip calls my name but I ignore him.

I must find Charlie.

Breathless, I run after the other two, following them through the dark churchyard, across the hushed village street, and towards the vicarage, a Victorian red-brick house set back from the road in its own grounds with high railings surrounding it.

CHAPTER TWENTY-SIX

Just as at the parish hall, the front door to the vicarage stands ajar. Like an invitation to enter. There are no lights on inside the house, or none visible from the front, at any rate. But that doesn't mean nobody is home.

'I'm going round the back,' Robbie whispers, pushing through a side gate. It creaks ominously in the silence of the night and then he disappears from view.

We go up two broad steps and peer through the open front door. The house is mostly in darkness, but a thin strip of light is showing under a door at the far end of the downstairs hallway.

I'm in a hurry to get inside and find Charlie at last.

But Natasha shakes her head, holding me back with her arm. 'Me first,' she repeats with ironic emphasis, and steps into the dim hallway ahead of me, gun held out, as she'd done at the parish hall.

I follow cautiously, remembering what we found at the parish hall, but still listening out for any sound – a cry or a whimper – that might tell me where my young son is being held.

The hallway is decorated in an old-fashioned way. Polished red floor tiles, dark wood panelling, a grandfather clock ticking steadily, and a silver-edged oval mirror near the hat stand that takes me unawares, so that I jump ludicrously at our reflections. Natasha's white-blonde hair reminds me of my own blonde hair, though my natural shade is less emphatically platinum. Not quite peas in a pod, especially now my short hair gleams red, but there's no mistaking the relationship between us.

There is a creaking sound from upstairs. Natasha's head snaps around and she stares up the shadowy staircase. 'Wait here.'

'Natasha, no… Wait for Robbie,' I urge her in a whisper. 'It could be a trap.'

'You stay. I check for trap.'

And she moves away, pivoting one way and then the other, gun held out, staring into each dark corner of the hallway on her way to the staircase.

I watch in trepidation, sure that she must be walking into danger.

She puts a foot on the first step, peering upwards into darkness, gun raised to shoulder level. The creaking sound comes again. I recall the vicar's mother, Glenda, the old woman in the wheelchair who baited me in church that time. Could this be her, perhaps moving about on her bed, the mattress springs protesting?

She might be tied up or gagged. The Russians wouldn't have wanted her making any noise that could attract the attention of neighbours or passers-by.

Or maybe someone is in the room with her, babysitting the hostage, pacing back and forth or periodically checking the windows. Someone who may have seen us creeping through the gate and into the house a few minutes earlier and is now waiting behind the old lady's bedroom door, weapon in hand.

It could be John up there, working with the Russians, armed and dangerous. He's already killed once tonight.

'Natasha,' I hiss, taking a few more steps into the house.

But my mother's already halfway up the stairs, listening intently to those little creaks and rustles from above, and pays no attention.

As she vanishes round the bend in the stairs, I hear a dull thud somewhere in the distance. Inside or outside the house? It sounds like someone closing a door.

A car door.

That's what I heard.

A car door being slammed shut somewhere nearby.

248

I hear it again a few seconds later.

Thud.

Definitely a car door.

Or rather, a second car door being shut.

But where?

I go to the bottom of the stairs but my mother is nowhere to be seen. I catch creaking again but now can't be sure if it's her I can hear, moving stealthily along the upstairs landing, or the sound we heard before.

'Natasha?'

I wait.

A faint creak above my head.

I hiss her name again, staring up into shadow.

Still no response.

Frustrated, uncertain, I back off slowly and control the urge to yell for her. If John or the other Russian is up there and I give away her position by yelling, I could get her killed.

Instead, I thread my way cautiously along the dark hallway until I reach the door with the narrow strip of light showing beneath it. The door has one of those round, brassy handles that are a bugger to turn unless you're used to them. I grip the handle gingerly and begin to turn it as silently as I can, and feel the mechanism yield and the door begin to open.

It's the kitchen.

The fluorescent strip lighting is on overhead, illuminating large, surprisingly modern kitchen cabinets, white goods and green Aga cooker.

There's nobody in the room.

But there's a cool draft, and as I tiptoe lightly into the kitchen, I see that the back door is wide open.

I catch movement outside in the dark vicarage garden and freeze. There's a knife on the kitchen table, next to a chopping board. One of those sharp slender blades used for paring and chopping. I snatch it up and hurry to the door, determined to protect my boy if those bastards have got him out there.

Creeping out of the door, knife in hand, I almost smash straight into Robbie, who was coming into the house, gun first.

'Jesus Christ,' Robbie explodes under his breath, and steps back, lowering his gun, shock on his face. 'Be careful, would you? I nearly blew your head off.'

'Sorry.'

He stares at the kitchen knife. 'Glad you didn't stick that into me. It looks sharp.'

'It is.'

'What the hell are you doing with a knife?'

'I thought you were one of them.'

'Uhuh. So, what, nobody's inside the house?' Robbie demands, peering past me.

'Natasha's gone upstairs to check out a creaking noise.'

'And you thought you'd take a walk in the garden?'

'I heard a car door shut somewhere close by. You know, that kind of dull thud …'

'Yeah, I heard that too.'

Somewhere over on the other side of the house, a car engine starts up, loud and unmistakable. We look at each other.

I know that deep, throbbing note. It's the SUV.

'The Russians,' I gasp.

Robbie's face changes. 'They're trying to get away. There's a covered parking area through here … Quick.'

Without waiting for me, he launches into what looks like an impenetrable cluster of bushes, and I hear the clang of a gate, buried somewhere deep in the shrubbery.

Hastily following, my face whipped by spiny branches in the darkness, I stumble through the concealed gateway and into some kind of enclosed space with brick walls and a tin roof, presumably the covered parking area, and hear a gunshot.

'Robbie?' He's too far ahead of me on the vicarage drive to hear, a dark silhouette outlined against the red glow of rear lights, and the engine roar from the SUV must be drowning out my voice anyway. There's another gunshot; the sound ricochets horribly in the enclosed space. Robbie staggers backward, clutching his shoulder. 'Oh my God!'

Seeing the driver's door open, I dart sideways into shadow, creeping along the wall of the parking area until I'm on the driveway. The SUV is a few feet ahead.

Gun in hand, the driver heads towards Robbie to finish him off. Except Robbie can't be too badly hurt, thankfully. He's down, but he's already dragging himself back into darkness, towards the gate shrouded by bushes.

There's someone in the front passenger seat of the car. I can see the shape of a head. A man, I think.

Is Charlie in the back?

My heart thumps violently as I consider dragging open the back of the SUV and rescuing my son if he's in there.

But I can't watch this Russian thug shoot Robbie dead while I do nothing. I don't know the man well but he's been helping me get my son back, for God's sake. Risking his own life for a stranger's.

I owe him.

The kitchen knife is still in my hand.

I launch myself out of the shadows, knife raised in my shaking hand, ready to plunge it into the Russian's back if necessary ...

I see the man more clearly now. There's something oddly familiar about the way he moves and holds himself, the shape of the back of his head, his broad shoulders.

Perplexed, my brows tug together. What the hell... ?

251

Maybe I make too much noise as I leap forward. Maybe I even shout out loud. Some kind of war cry. Whatever it is, the man spins away from Robbie, staring round at me instead.

I can't take my eyes off his rugged face, illuminated like a devil's mask by the red glow of the SUV rear lights.

'K-Kurt?' I stammer, unable to believe my eyes. 'But … you're … you're dead. I saw your body.'

The Kurt lookalike smiles. It's not a pleasant smile.

He reaches for me.

Horrified, I take a few hasty steps backward, the paring knife still raised as he comes towards me, though my hand is shaking. He has a gun; I have an itty bitty knife. It's not much of a contest. Laughable, really. Except I'm not laughing. This isn't about me. This is about Charlie. And I'm going to do whatever it takes.

'Stay back!' I warn him.

Then a heavy weight comes down across the back of my head; I stagger, and my legs crumple under me into darkness.

Gradually, I come to again, huddled foetus-like, still in darkness, with a throbbing head and a sick sensation in the pit of my stomach. Some kind of rough material has been drawn down over my face like a hood so I can't see a thing. But I can still hear and feel.

I'm swaying awkwardly back and forth, wedged tight on my side.

My body aches.

I try to shift position, groaning, and my head hits something unyielding. I turn, automatically questing that way. My cheek, my jaw … Not hard enough for metal or stone. A wall of tough plastic beside me, the vibrating thrum of a powerful engine running through it and jarring my teeth. My knees are drawn up, my feet lodged against another wall that's stopping me from stretching out. My hands are tied behind my back, shoulders complaining at the uncomfortable imposition of constantly being pulled back.

Full consciousness follows, and with it understanding. I'm in the back or boot of a car, presumably the Russians' large SUV with the blacked-out windows, travelling at speed.

The car slows abruptly, rounding what feels like a sharp bend, and I'm thrown first one way and then another.

I listen intently.

There must be a driver. But nobody is speaking, so I have no way of knowing how many other people are in the vehicle.

Slowly, painfully, I try to piece together what happened and how I've ended up a prisoner in this car, heading God knows where.

The Russian.

I stiffen, remembering again with the same fundamental shock of disbelief how the man turned in the darkness to look down at me and I froze, recognizing his face …

'Kurt,' I whisper.

But that's impossible. Kurt is dead. I saw his lifeless body myself, stood over it in horror, frightened and trembling. Though it's also true that Kurt simply disappeared off the face of the earth after I fled. I spent months searching for his name online, expecting to see reports of his gruesome murder, or at least some reference to a man found stabbed with scissors, and turned up nothing. Nothing whatsoever.

Was it possible that I was duped? That someone – Natasha? Sir Philip? the Russians? – staged that man's death? But for what purpose? Why go to so much trouble just to make me think I'd killed someone when I hadn't and he was in fact alive and well?

But no, he would have to have been the best actor in the world to play dead that long, to lie there with fake blood congealed on his body and never breathe or blink or so much as twitch ….

That man was dead.

Kurt.

Kurt is dead. No doubt about it.

So who was that man with the gun in the vicarage grounds? And where is my son?

I stir, cranking round to listen. But I can't hear Charlie in the vehicle. Though he could be asleep, I suppose.

I want to shout to him, to call his name. Just to hear him respond, and also to let him know his mother is there, close at hand. But what if nobody answers? Maybe he's not in the car. And they may even stop once they realise I'm awake, and decide to interrogate me or perhaps to knock me out again for the duration of this journey.

And what if Charlie hears me, but is terrified even further by knowing his mother is a prisoner too and can't actually help him?

Maybe he's in the SUV and witnessed me being trussed up and thrown in the luggage space at the back. He may think I'm dead. He may start to cry and incur the wrath of his captors.

No, I won't do it. I refuse to cause my innocent little boy any more risk than I already have just by being his mother. So I shut my mouth and glare at nothing in the darkness of my rough, musty-smelling hood.

I'm going to kill them, I think, infuriated by my own impotence. I'm going to rip their heads from their shoulders and …

The car takes an abrupt turn to the right and brakes sharply, slowing as it goes over what feels like a cattle grid. The whole vehicle shudders and I shudder with it, unable to brace myself. Then we're driving again, but more slowly, as though approaching the end point to our journey.

I brace myself for more violence, wondering if the Russian killed Robbie before we left the vicarage or if he managed to escape and get word to Sir Philip. And what of Natasha? She was checking the upstairs of the vicarage. Was John waiting for her up there?

My heart cramps up at the possibility that my mother could be dead. She's not exactly good mother material. But she's all I have, and I've barely had a chance to speak to her …

The car stops abruptly, and the engine shuts off.

The car ticks in the silence.

I strain my ears and hear a faint kind of roaring, like distant traffic or a plane somewhere far away.

Where the hell are we?

Two car doors open and slam shut, almost simultaneously. I hear several pairs of footsteps on rough ground. Then a cool draught as the tailgate is dragged open. Through the coarse fabric over my face, I sense a bright light shining in my direction.

A torch?

I lie tense and unmoving, waiting.

A hand grabs at the hood covering my face and pulls it off.

I blink, staring up into the blinding bulb of a torch. Two men are looking down at me, the velvety night sky behind them. One holds the torch, his broad-shouldered figure familiar. It's the Russian who looks exactly like Kurt but can't be. So I didn't imagine that. Which is a relief, but barely.

The other man is John.

CHAPTER TWENTY-SEVEN

'Get out,' Not-Kurt orders me, his thick Russian accent also strangely familiar, as is his face. And yet I don't speak Russian. Maybe my mother spoke Russian to me as a small child. Yet if she did, I have no memory of that nor any understanding of the language. So how can his voice sound somehow recognizable?

I switch from staring at John to stare at Not-Kurt, angry and baffled. My hands are tied behind my back and he expects me to climb out of the high back of this SUV under my own steam?

John grabs my arm and drags me to the edge of the tailgate. 'Come on,' he says. He was smiling faintly before, as though amused by my predicament, or maybe my shock at seeing him there. Now his face is blank.

I'm furious with him. I'd been secretly hoping there was some reason why he helped the Russians by holding Charlie captive and shooting the vicar, like they were blackmailing him or holding a loved one hostage, just as they'd threatened the life of the vicar's mother to force his cooperation. But it looks like John is just one of their creatures, after all. A true believer.

'So,' I croak through dry lips, 'you're working for the enemy.'

'They're not *my* enemy,' he says coolly.

Not-Kurt hands his torch to John and lifts me out of the car as though I weigh nothing, setting me down on uneven ground. The faint roaring I could hear has to be the sea, though it's pitch-dark and I see nothing but shadows around us.

The ground sinks softly beneath my feet. I sway, trying to regain my balance, and nearly fall. Are we standing on … *sand*?

'Careful.' John steadies me.

'You were shot.'

'Yes,' he agrees with a grimace. 'Courtesy of your bitch mother.'

So he also knows that Natasha is my mother.

It's hard to get my head around the fact that John has been working with my enemies all this time. That he was only pretending to be my friend, to try and seduce me into giving up information …

'I'm sorry.' I struggle to conceal my fury and bitterness behind a strained smile. I may need this man to help me. To keep me alive. Charlie too, if they still have him. 'Natasha shouldn't have done that. Honestly, I didn't know she was going to shoot you.'

'Of course not.'

John winces, growling under his breath as he turns to close the SUV tailgate, and I realise he's not as steady as he looks. He probably ought to be in a hospital, in fact. But I suppose gunshot wounds must come with an automatic police alert, and these guys can't afford to have the police involved.

'Your neighbour fixed me up. Patricia, isn't it? I might have been more grateful if she hadn't been working for Sir Philip. Still, she did a good job.' John pats his shoulder, which I can see now has been bandaged bulkily under his top, the white edge of a bandage taped to his neck. 'I'll do.'

Not-Kurt has taken back his torch and moved out of sight, rummaging in the back seat of the SUV by the sound of it.

I wonder what he's planning to do with me.

'It's not too late to help me,' I whisper to John, aware I may only have seconds to persuade him. 'Where's Charlie? Is he with you?'

He says nothing, looking away to our right. There's a low, brooding shape there, set against a lighter rise. Some kind of building? Is that where they're taking me?

My heart thumps as I add in an undertone, 'You know Sir Philip will be coming after you, don't you?'

'Sir Philip won't have a clue where we are.' John seizes me by my arm. 'Come on, time to take a little walk.'

It's not cold. In fact, it's quite a warm night, though there is a breeze blowing my hair back, and I get the impression of a wide-open space somewhere away to our left. Definitely a beach. I can smell salt now, and that rhythmic roaring must be the tide rushing in over to my left, unseen in the darkness.

Despite the warm breeze, I'm shivering.

Fear.

'Wait,' I cry, stumbling as he pulls me across dark ground towards the small, shadowy building. My feet are still sinking into something damp and soft which has to be sand, my hair whipped up in the sea breeze. 'Please tell me that Charlie's safe. Give me that at least,' I beg him.

John's sneer becomes more pronounced. 'Oh, he's safe enough. So you can stop bleating about the boy.'

A familiar sound behind us brings my head round in shock and delight. 'Charlie?'

'Mummy … Mummy!'

So that's what Not-Kurt was doing in the back seat of the car. Getting my son.

'Hang on,' Not-Kurt growls and drags Charlie towards him. I see the flash of a blade in his hand and choke, 'No!' But all he's doing is cutting the plastic ties that bound Charlie's hands together. Then he pushes my son towards me. 'Go on, get moving.'

The sight of my little boy tottering towards me from the car, his short chubby arms held up in entreaty, nearly brings me to my knees. It's only the unhappy knowledge that Charlie needs me to be strong that keeps me on my feet. I lurch back towards him, my hands still tied, wishing I could grab him to me and hold him tight.

Charlie grasps my legs and lays his head against them. 'Mummy!' He's crying. 'Mummy!'

I'm crying too. Tears fall freely down my cheeks as I stand, head bowed, eyes closed, sobbing his name shamelessly.

I thought he might already be dead. That I would never see him again. The fear had tormented me ever since he'd been taken.

'Charlie, my baby... My wonderful, perfect baby boy.'

'Oh, for God's sake,' John mutters.

I ignore him. 'Did they hurt you?' I ask my son, my voice quavering. 'Are you okay, Charlie?'

'Okay, Mummy.' He wipes the back of his hand across his wet face, looking up at me. 'Home, please?'

'Darling, I want to go home too. But we can't just yet. I'm sorry.'

'Hug,' he moans, holding up his arms.

Oh God.

Despair floods my heart at his plaintive cry, the yearning in his gorgeous little face.

'Mummy can't ... can't hug you just yet.' I stumble over the words, furious and weeping. 'Mummy's hands ... See? They're tied up behind me. But I'll hug you soon though. All right, little man?'

Charlie's lip trembles but he nods.

'That's my brave boy,' I manage to say, fighting my sobs.

Not-Kurt has locked the SUV and catches up with us now, the bright torch beam streaming ahead of him, my paring knife stuck in his jeans belt. 'Here, kid,' he grunts, scooping Charlie up under one arm like he's so much luggage. 'Let's go.'

'Okay, you heard the man.' John spins me to face the shadowy building ahead and gives me a shove to get me moving. 'Hurry up. We're on a schedule.'

'A schedule?' I'm panicked now. 'What does that mean?'

'Stop talking and move.'

I follow Not-Kurt over the uneven sand, sniffing and horribly off-balance, wishing my hands were free so I could wipe my face, at least, or save myself if I fall.

In the glimmering half-dark, I can see him a few feet ahead, his torch beam bouncing over sand dunes and patches of coarse, tangled grass. Under his arm, Charlie is crying again and struggling. I'm afraid that evil man may hurt him if he makes too much fuss.

'Please don't cry, Charlie,' I call to my son. 'We're nearly there, okay? Mummy's right behind you.'

But my gaze is darting around on every side, trying to get a feel for our surroundings, even in the dark.

Sir Philip won't have a clue where we are.

My heart sinks, knowing how unlikely it is that my protector will find me out here in this isolated place. Clearly, we're on the coast, of course. But which coast? Is this Cornwall or Devon? Or even Dorset, perhaps?

I have no way of knowing how long I was unconscious. It could have been an hour or only ten minutes. My best guess would be a beach in North Devon, which would put us less than twenty minutes' drive from the village of Darkling Moreton.

But the real question is, why are we here?

The building turns out to be a single-storey, stone-built cottage tucked below sloping sand dunes that rise out of sight. Not-Kurt's torch picks out thick grey walls, a thatched roof and chimney stack, and a blue door set under a low stone lintel at the front. He puts down Charlie, who stands mutely, staring up at him, and digs into a pocket, producing a large iron key on a string. This he inserts into the lock and turns it, his torch beam swaying, illuminating a shuttered window and a sign that says SMUGGLERS COTTAGE.

Not-Kurt pushes the door wide with his foot. 'Inside,' he tells Charlie gruffly. When Charlie hesitates, Not-Kurt gives a harsh laugh and shines his torch beam into the cottage. 'Nothing bad in there. See? Go on, inside.'

With one hesitant glance back at me, my son slips into the cottage and is swallowed up by darkness.

'You too,' Not-Kurt tells me.

I don't need to be told twice. I follow my son into the dark cottage and stop on the threshold, shivering and sucking in a breath.

It's shelter of a kind. But the whole cottage is cool and damp and stinks oddly of fish. Are we about to be locked in here?

But Not-Kurt and John enter too, pushing the door shut behind us so we're all standing in darkness.

Using his torch, Not-Kurt locates a large lantern on a side table and switches it on. It's surprisingly bright in the small space. Battery-powered, I guess.

'No electricity,' he tells John.

'Great,' John says.

I check for any possible exits first. It's not very promising. An internal door to the rear of the cottage may lead to a bedroom or perhaps just a toilet. There are only two windows, both curtained. One by the door, the other facing the sea. Both look too small for anyone but Charlie to slip through.

Though if only Charlie could escape, that would be something …

But the sea is so close, and perhaps the tide is out and will come in later, coming up the beach. The fear that he might drown out there in the dark is enough to make me push that possibility to one side for now.

Without knowing what lies beyond this cottage, I can't risk encouraging my son to escape without me. Not unless the alternative is certain death, and while I'm sure Not-Kurt wouldn't think twice about executing me, I can't quite believe either of these men would shoot an innocent three-year-old in cold blood.

I turn to study the rest of the cottage. It's quite cosy now the door's shut. There's a blue rug on the floor, and a two-seater sofa-bed with plump blue cushions set against the opposite wall. A round pine table and two matching chairs stand in a narrow kitchen area with a sink and two-ring gas stove below bare shelves and a wall cupboard.

Not-Kurt takes my paring knife out of his belt and slams it down on the table, then heads straight for the sea-facing window. He drags back flimsy blue curtains, opens the window, leans out to unfasten the shutters and push them wide, and then stands looking out.

I hear the roaring of the sea again, unseen in the distance, while the salt breeze whips at the curtains.

Charlie shivers, peering up at me hopelessly. His wrists still bear the marks of the plastic ties, red and raw. But at least they tied his hands in front, not behind.

'Poor boy,' I say soothingly, and nod him towards the sofa-bed. 'Go and lie down. I'm sure we won't be here long.'

'Want to go home,' Charlie whines, but drags himself to the sofa-bed all the same, rubbing his eyes.

'We will, I promise,' I say as he makes himself comfortable on the blue cushions. 'Soon.'

I hate myself for lying to my son. I've had to lie to him so frequently in his short life. Yet what else can I do? He's already exhausted and scared. Explaining that we may never go home again isn't going to help him feel better.

Charlie isn't the only one who's tired and in need of a rest. John has dropped heavily into one of the chairs, breathing fast. Now I can see him more clearly, it's obvious from his pallor and the perspiration dotted on his forehead and upper lip that he's suffering and unwell.

The gunshot wound, presumably.

John's hand is clapped to his hurt shoulder, pressing down hard, and when he adjusts his hold, wincing, there's a tell-tale red tinge to his fingers. It seems whatever Patricia did to patch him up, it was only a temporary fix, and he's bleeding again …

Not-Kurt closes the window again but remains where he is, staring out across the darkness towards the sea.

What is he looking for?

He turns towards me, the spitting image of Kurt, and I take an instinctive step backwards, faced with a look of such furious malevolence it's hard not to imagine he's about to murder me.

'You ...' he says, his voice grating, and adds something in what is presumably Russian, almost spitting the guttural words at me.

'I d-don't know what you're saying,' I stammer.

'Do you know who I am?' he demands, his dark gaze fixed on my face.

I study him, my heart thumping. *Not Kurt*, I think.

'Speak,' he barks.

'You look like someone I knew once,' I whisper, 'a long time ago.'

'Who?'

'His name was Kurt.'

He shows his teeth. 'No, it wasn't.'

A cold feeling creeps over me. How does he know that?

'What do you mean?'

'His real name was Ivan and he was my brother.' He comes right up to me, inches from my face. 'My *twin* brother.'

So that's it.

Not-Kurt is dead Kurt's twin brother.

And he hates me.

CHAPTER TWENTY-EIGHT

I stare at him in horror. No wonder he's been so persistent in coming after me and Natasha. It was never business, it was always personal.

I had been hoping to strike some kind of bargain with this man, to keep him talking at least. But now I see it's hopeless. Our chances of getting out of here alive have just sunk below zero.

I'm not giving up though. I'm probably dead. But he holds no grudge against Charlie, surely? So his life might still be saved.

'I … I'm so sorry,' I babble. 'I didn't kill him, please believe me. I had nothing to do with his death.'

'No, but you ran away, like the coward you are,' he spat out. 'And my brother vanished. Your people took his body and disposed of it. No body, no crime. We all knew Ivan was dead and who killed him, but we couldn't prove it and we couldn't bury him.' He shows his teeth again. 'I had to explain to my mother what happened to her precious boy. Because there was no body, she wouldn't believe it. She would watch the door every day for him to come home. She got sick and died, still not believing he was dead, but thinking he no longer wanted to see her.' His voice cracks, becomes hoarse. 'I loved my mother, and I had to watch her fall apart, and all because of *you*.'

This man wants to kill me. I read it in his body language, his clenched fists, his vicious glare. Not just kill me but make it last. Torture me before he executes me.

I swallow, groping for the right words, the right facial expression, to appease him. 'What happened to your brother,' I whisper, 'it was awful. It was … totally wrong. But I didn't do it, I swear. It wasn't my fault.'

'*Da*, it was your fault,' he insists.

'No,' I say, but he slaps my face and I stagger back, falling awkwardly against the sofa-bed, unable to defend myself with my hands still bound.

'Shut your mouth, whore.' He stands over me, his eyes wild. 'Your crazy traitor mother killed my brother. And he wouldn't have been killed if he hadn't been following orders, setting a trap for Natasha by watching you. Ivan was sent here to get that bitch back onto Russian soil, to make her pay for betraying her country, for turning against her own people. We never forget traitors in Russia. So yes, this is *your* fault as much as hers.' His dark eyes fix me, burning with vengeance. 'And now it's your turn to die. You and your son together.'

Tears running down my face, I struggle back to my feet, panting, instinctively standing between him and my son.

'You can't … It was nothing to do with Charlie.' I shake my head, sobbing again now, my chest heaving. 'He's only a little boy. Please, don't do this.'

'I only wanted to kill Natasha at first, it's true. Natasha burnt out my mother's heart with pain until she could no longer bear to be alive. She did this to me, to my whole family. But when we took the boy, I began to see how I could make her suffer a little of what my mother suffered. So yes, this way is better.' His smile is feral. 'I watched her try to save your lives, driving that stupid little car through the corn. So I know what it will do to Natasha to find your bodies mutilated, barely recognisable. And to know how much you and the boy must have suffered before you died.' He laughs, a chilling sound. 'Yes, I like this way better.'

I'm shaking, cold inside. 'But … what about Sir Philip?'

I glance at John, who's slumped in his chair, listening to all this without a word, one hand still clamped to his bandaged shoulder, his face like wax. Begging and pleading haven't made any difference to these men so far, but perhaps common sense is worth trying.

'Sir Philip won't give you the information you want if you kill us,' I try to insist. 'The names of those two agents –'

'I don't care about that.'

This alarms me. 'You … You don't care?' My heart thuds harder as I realise what that means. That he won't feel accountable for his actions. That he'll do whatever he wants here and shrug it off as unimportant. Unless I can scare him. 'I doubt your superiors will be very happy about that.'

'My *superiors*?'

Not-Kurt shakes his dark head, showing his teeth again, his voice mocking. He reminds me of a rabid dog, out of control, enjoying his moment of madness.

Though if Kurt was actually Ivan, I should probably try to think of this one as Not-Ivan.

I can't quite manage it though. Kurt will always be Kurt to me. Which makes *him* Not-Kurt.

I feel like I'm losing my grip on reality.

He says, 'You still don't get it, do you? I wasn't sent here to get those names for my government. I came to kill Natasha.' He sneers at my shocked expression. 'I've been looking for that bitch traitor ever since she killed my brother. Find you, find Natasha, that's what I was told, again and again. But she's good, I'll give her that. She covers her tracks well, as do you.'

I shake my head helplessly. 'That wasn't me … I'm not one of them.'

'Your grandfather, then.' He nods grimly at my silence. 'The names of those agents would have been useful to get the SVR off my back after I go back to Russia. But maybe I don't go back to Russia. My mother is dead, my father is dead, my brother is dead, my sister is married to a fool.' He spits on the ground, and shrugs. 'I have cousins in Estonia. I go there, maybe. Change my name, my appearance … It will be worth it, to know how Natasha suffers. How she regrets not being able to save you and the child.'

'Please, there's something I need to tell you,' I say desperately.

He raises his eyebrows, waiting.

'My son, Charlie.' I suck in a breath, hoping Charlie won't understand what I'm about to say. 'He's your nephew.'

The Russian stares at me.

'After Ivan died,' I whisper, 'you're right, I ran away. But later, I realised I was pregnant. With his child.'

'Lies,' he says dismissively.

'I'm telling the truth. My son is all that's left of your brother. And you want to kill him?'

'He's Natasha's grandson. That's all that matters to me.'

I put a hand to my mouth, shaking.

'She's right though. Do you really have to kill the boy?' John interrupts this back-and-forth, and the Russian's head swings in his direction instead, a dangerous look in his eyes.

'This is not your business,' the Russian snaps back at him. 'You were not paid to have an opinion but to get close to this girl, to tell me when Natasha appeared … Easy work. Any fool can do this. But you even made a mess of that. Got yourself shot.'

John frowns. 'I'm okay,' he insists, looking far from okay.

'Mind your own business, then. So maybe you live to walk away, huh?'

'With the money that was promised me, yes.'

That explains a lot. John was offered money to do this, to keep tabs on me from the inside, while they watched from a discreet distance in the SUV. So he isn't working *with* the Russians so much as *for* them, like Tim Shaw was. Like a paid mercenary.

Deep-down, I'm still trying to believe he's a good person, despite knowing he can't possibly be. He shot the vicar, presumably to stop him from spilling the beans about where they were holed up. Or perhaps Reverend Shearsman got cold feet and threatened to call the police, even though they were holding his elderly mother hostage. So John put a bullet in him and fled.

267

Killing a man of the cloth is hardly the act of a good person. Now he's going to sit idly by and watch while I'm tortured and executed. And my three-year-old son with me. I'm not sure if I despise John more or less for that, knowing that all these deaths are just a paid job to him.

Though he's making a case for the Russian not killing my son. That's what it sounds like. If he succeeds, I may forgive him the rest.

Charlie must live. Nothing else matters.

Not even me.

'What?' Not-Kurt is frowning at John.

'The fee you're paying me,' John explains, looking annoyed now. 'That's what I'll be walking away with tonight.'

'I don't have it.'

'You don't … ' John sits up, his eyes narrowed on the other man's face. 'What do you mean by that?'

'Are you stupid as well as useless? The money you're owed. I don't have it. In fact, I never had it.' Not-Kurt shrugs. 'Dimitry was running the finances.' I suppose that must be the name of the burly man who died at the church. 'He was supposed to wire the fee direct to your bank account as soon as the job was over.' He shrugs. 'But he's dead now, so … No money for you.'

'Now listen here,' John begins hotly, but stops when the Russian produces a gun from his jacket pocket.

'Better stop talking if you want to live.'

'Woah, okay,' John says in alarm, putting out a blood-stained hand. 'Calm down. There's no need to – '

He gets no further, because the Russian shoots him in the chest. Just like that. Pulls the trigger like it's nothing.

The shot is deafening in the enclosed space. I jump, gasping.

Behind me, Charlie whimpers.

Slowly, with a groan and an astounded look on his face, John slips off the chair onto the floor. The chair topples backwards and John lies there, a motionless lump on the blue rug, his head and torso turned away from us, his legs sticking out.

'Now for you,' Not-Kurt says without a flicker of remorse and turns the gun on me. 'Though I think I will rape you first. In front of the boy. I have time, so why not?' He considers me thoughtfully. 'If I untie your hands, will you be a good girl and lie down without any trouble? Or must we do this the hard way?'

I'm shaking so violently it's amazing that I am still conscious. But I have to stay conscious. I have to stay calm and keep thinking up ways to delay the inevitable. To give Sir Philip time to find us and come to the rescue. In the deepest recesses of my mind, I know he's not going to find us. We're not going to be rescued.

And it's my fault.

People without guns get taken hostage and used as human shields.

That's what Robbie told me, and I brushed it aside as ridiculous, then tried to attack this experienced killer with a pathetic little paring knife from the vicarage kitchen. And got taken hostage.

Except we're not hostages.

He's not going to barter us for anything or anyone. He's just going to kill us. Purely for revenge.

I push those dark thoughts to the back of my mind again and focus on hope, on delaying tactics, on pure bloody survival.

Because I must. Because that's all I can do.

For Charlie's sake.

I need to come up with a distraction.

But I stare at the Russian and can't think of a single thing to say or do that will stop him from raping me and then killing us both.

Not a single bloody thing.

'Well?' he demands, the gun still pointing directly at my heart. 'Don't make me wait. It will only make things worse for you.'

'Yes, I … I'll be good,' I whisper.

'Okay.' He is matter-of-fact, putting the gun down only to pick up the knife I brought from the vicarage kitchen. 'Turn around.'

I turn slowly, looking down at Charlie in despair. 'Close your eyes, baby,' I tell my son, who's shrinking against the cushions, pale and trembling. 'Whatever happens, don't … don't watch, okay?'

Charlie nods and closes his eyes.

I feel the slide of a blade between my bound hands, sawing at the plastic ties, then I'm free.

The blade prods into my back, sharp and sinister.

'Don't do anything stupid,' the Russian reminds me. 'Come over here, take off your clothes and lie down on the rug.'

I half turn, my teeth chattering, my brain numb with fear as I watch him put down the knife and reach for his jeans belt, beginning to loosen the buckle.

Think, think, think …

Then I see it.

Out of the corner of my eye.

A light, flashing.

I stop where I am, staring through the dark window. The blue curtains have been drawn back and the outside shutters pushed open for the widest view. And out there, deep in the vast pitch-black expanse of the Atlantic Ocean, a light is flashing.

'What's that?' I whisper, pointing.

His eyes narrow, as though suspecting a trick, but he risks a quick sideways glance at the window. And he too sees the light.

Not-Kurt gives a triumphant cry, as though this is what he's been waiting for all along.

He refastens his belt buckle, grabs his gun and sticks it into his jeans waistband, and then collects his torch and mobile phone from the table before heading for the door.

'Stay here,' he orders me.

About to turn the key in the lock, he stops and looks round at me, frowning. Hurriedly, he turns back towards John's prone figure, rummages in his pockets and finds John's gun too, then returns to the door.

'Don't try anything stupid,' the Russian warns me, unlocking the door with his gaze still warily on my face. 'I'll be back in a few minutes, and there's nowhere to run anyway.' There's an excited look to him, his face flushed and elated, as though Christmas has come early. 'If you're a really good girl when I get back,' he adds, half-smiling, 'maybe I'll let the boy live after all, okay?'

I nod, but I know he's lying.

As soon as Not-Kurt has locked the cottage door behind him and I've heard his footsteps retreat, I run to the sea-facing window and fumble to open it. But it's too narrow for me to fit through and, leaning to look down, I see there are jagged rocks immediately beneath the sill. Charlie could climb through and jump down, though he would probably be hurt, but I could never hope to squeeze through that tiny gap after him. So he'd be alone out there on the beach, a scared three-year-old in the cold and the dark, with no idea which way to go or where to hide when the Russian finishes with me and comes looking for him.

'Impossible.' I drag the blue curtains shut to hide us from that flashing light out to sea, and rock back and forth, paralysed with fear. 'What am I going to do? What the hell am I going to do?'

'Don't cry, mummy,' Charlie tells me, hugging my leg. Now that my hands are free, I'm able to hug him back. I bend and hoist his small, fragile frame into my arms. He clings on tightly, arms about my neck, half squeezing me to death. 'Love you, mummy. Please don't cry.'

'Oh, my baby,' I sob, burying my face in his warmth. 'I'm sorry, I'm so sorry. This is all my fault. I wish I knew what to do.'

A groan behind me brings me round with a startled jolt.

It's John, on the blood-soaked rug.

271

I stare across at him in hope and astonishment. He's not dead. Badly wounded but … He's rolled over onto his back, one hand flung out from his body, groping for something… Or maybe trying to get my attention.

Carefully, I set Charlie back on the sofa-bed. 'Stay there, baby,' I whisper, and bend to kiss his forehead. 'I have to check on John.'

I kneel beside the dying man - at least, he must surely be dying, given the amount of blood saturating the blue rug - and stare down into his face. His eyes are closed, but when I check his pulse, which is faint and sluggish, his eyes flicker open and he looks up at me.

'Hey,' he mouths, his voice a bare thread of sound.

'I thought you were dead.'

It's a cold thing to say, under the circumstances, but I know the Russian could be back any minute and there's no time to waste on polite lies. I don't trust John, but he can't be feeling much loyalty for his former employers right now, one of whom just shot him rather than hand over the money he was due. Which means he may be open to helping us.

Given how close to death he looks, there's not much chance of him protecting us against that bastard when he gets back.

But there are other ways he could help…

'Me too.' He tries to smile but only grimaces. 'Where's our friend?'

'He saw a light flashing out to sea and got excited. He's gone outside but said he'd only be a few minutes.' I lay my hand against his cheek, which is icy-cold to the touch. 'He's going to kill us. Even little Charlie.' I see his eyelids flicker, and gasp, 'Can you help us? Please, if there's anything you can do … '

'Boat,' he croaks, his gaze flicking towards the window. 'His ticket out of here.'

It takes a second or two to get his meaning. Then my eyes widen. The boat out there in the bay has come for Not-Kurt. The flashing light was a prearranged signal. Telling him they've arrived and to be ready to come aboard.

272

'That's why he took the torch,' I say slowly. 'To signal them back. Like the old smugglers.'

He gives a tiny nod. The effort to speak must be exhausting him.

'Do you have a phone?'

'No.'

'How about a key to the cottage door?' I ask.

He shakes his head, and his eyes begin to blink and close again. I stare down at him, frightened that he's about to die.

'Don't go to sleep. You mustn't go to sleep.' It's horribly cruel of me but I slap his face, saying sharply, 'Wake up, John!'

His eyes open in response to my slap, but his gaze is cloudy and unfocused, looking vaguely up at the ceiling.

'John?' I speak quickly and urgently before he can slip into unconsciousness again. 'The window's too small for me to get through and Charlie wouldn't last five minutes on his own. I need to get us both out of here before the Russian comes back.' I wait but he says nothing. I'm suspicious he's not entirely there and force myself to slap his face again, relieved when his gaze snaps back to my face. 'Stay with me, okay? I'm sorry, but … Is there another way out of here?'

He draws breath, a terrible gurgling in his throat and lungs. 'Shower room,' he manages to say, indistinctly, and blood trickles out of his mouth, running down his chin. 'Window… Bigger.'

'Thank you,' I say shakily, and on impulse, lean forward to kiss his cheek. But his gaze has already drifted away, his breathing shallow and laboured, and I know the end can't be far off for him. 'Goodbye.'

He doesn't respond.

Jumping to my feet, I pick up the lantern and then collect the paring knife on an afterthought too, threading it gingerly into my jeans waistband just as the others did with their guns.

I only hope I don't somehow manage to stick it in myself …

'Come on,' I say to Charlie, who jumps off the sofa and runs with me to the door at the back of the cottage.

I hold up the lantern.

It's a sparsely decorated shower room with a toilet and pedestal sink. Nothing much else except a freestanding wooden towel rail positioned beside the sink, a grimy-looking white towel draped over it.

The door doesn't lock.

Behind the toilet is a single-frame window. John was right. It's larger than the one in the main room. Not huge but probably big enough for me to climb through, just about …

'Okay, this is good.'

I put Charlie down, balance the lantern on the sill where it throws grotesque shadows up the walls, and try to open the window.

It's locked.

'No, no, no … '

I wrestle with the handle, jerking it back and forth, trying to open it with sheer brute force. But it refuses to budge.

'Oh God.'

For a horrible moment, I start sobbing again, thinking, *this is it*. We are going to die here. And all because this stupid bloody window is locked …

Then I spot the window key on the sill and wipe my eyes, feeling like an idiot. Thrusting the key into the lock, I turn it and feel the mechanism release.

I throw the window wide open, the cool night air rushing in, and turn to Charlie, who's been studying the shower room with interest.

'You first,' I whisper, holding out my hand. 'Quick, we need to hurry, and don't make a sound, okay?'

'Need wee-wee,' he says, staring longingly into the toilet.

'You'll have to hang on, baby.' I see a flash of rebellion in his face and say more firmly, 'I need you to be a brave boy. Can you do that for Mummy?' When he still doesn't budge, I force myself to take a hard line. 'You don't want that … that nasty man to catch us, do you?'

Charlie shakes his head solemnly.

I feel guilty at using the traumatic events he just witnessed to scare him into obedience. But anything's better than watching him die at the hands of that vile monster …

'Let's go, then. And remember, not a sound.'

Picking him up, I stand my son on the sill and then lower him gently out through the window.

As soon as his feet touch ground, I release his hands and he staggers but does not fall. 'Well done,' I gasp. 'Mummy's going to climb out now. Stand well back … That's a good boy.'

I push the wooden towel rail up against the door and switch off the electric lantern, plunging the shower room into darkness. That may gain us a few extra seconds when the Russian comes back and starts searching the place for us.

I throw down the paring knife first, just in case I manage to stab myself by accident. Then I climb awkwardly out of the window, without waiting for my eyes to adjust to the darkness.

It's not as big a space as I'd hoped, but by turning sideways and slipping one leg out, then basically tumbling into the sand on my head, with my other leg naturally following after, I'm able to escape the cottage.

Dusted liberally with sand, my eyes and mouth gritty with it, I slip the paring knife back into my waistband, grab Charlie's hand and grope my way along the rough uneven stones of the cottage wall until we're facing the dark expanse of the sea, wind in our hair and the smell of salt in our faces.

I check but can't see the Russian anywhere, and the light out in the bay has vanished too. Which means he's either on his way back to the cottage or there already, discovering our flight.

We might have only seconds.

'Now we run,' I whisper to my son, and scoop him up, balancing his light body on my hip.

I set off at a loping pace, Charlie bouncing and hanging on to me, dodging deep puddles and black shadows of ribbons of submerged rock as we head out across wet sands to God knows where …

CHAPTER TWENTY-NINE

We haven't gone more than three or four hundred yards across the beach before I hear a sound behind me, and glance back, still fleeing, to see the cottage door wide open and Not-Kurt's torch beam lighting up the interior. The moon has come out above us, peeping occasionally from behind cloud, and I can see now what a tiny place the cottage is, huddled under sand dunes, not far from the end of a rough, sand-covered track winding back inland between slopes of dunes …

The SUV is parked further up the shore, empty and silent. If only Not-Kurt had left his keys on the table too, I could have stolen the car and got us far away before he even heard the engine.

There are no lights visible further inland, which makes it unlikely that anyone lives near enough to have heard us arrive. Though it must be the early hours of the morning by now, so any neighbours would have their lights off anyway.

No, the Russians chose this place for a reason. Because nobody lives out here. There's nobody to see the boat coming into the bay. To witness the signal flashes. To hear any gunshots and report them to the police, or perhaps to spot a dingy coming in to pick up Not-Kurt and his prisoners …

Except he's not planning on taking anyone back to Mother Russia, is he?

He's just going to kill us and leave our bodies to be swept away by the next high tide. Which could be within the next few hours, judging by the rising roar of the waters.

Is that what they're waiting for? For the tide to be higher? I'm a city girl at heart. I can barely swim, and I know nothing about boats and sea travel. But I guess high water is better than low water for a quick getaway.

I hear a shout behind me, faint and inaudible, the words snatched away on the tide.

Glancing back, my grip tightens on Charlie.

Not-Kurt has emerged from the cottage and is shining his torch frantically up and down the dunes and across the beach. But the beam only reaches so far, and he hasn't even looked in our direction yet.

He'll probably be expecting me to head back to the road, hoping to find a house or stop a passing vehicle. But I know there'll be nowhere to hide on the road, whereas out here, in this vast sandy wilderness, there are rocks to duck behind and shadows to linger in …

I slow down to a walk, not wanting to catch his eye with any sudden or fast movement.

He's a small figure beside the cottage door, shining his torch beam across the sands now. Almost towards our position.

I look away, blinking.

He shouts again, sounding so angry and vengeful, my heart leaps and I start running again, unable to help myself.

'Please, God, please … ' I'm breathing hard, clutching Charlie tight, staring ahead to where rocks rise from the sand, crooked black ribs shining in the moonlight, some of them higher than a man, others low, or forming plateaus that gleam with crevice pools. I could hide us there among the rocks, and wait for the tide to come in, and hope not to drown before he shoots us.

Reaching the first dark outcrop of rock, I glance back, and have to stifle a sob of terror. He must have seen me despite the distance. He's running straight towards us across the sands, the torch beam swinging wildly.

Then something ricochets off rock a few feet away with a sharp crack.

He's shooting at us.

Thankfully, it's too dark and he's too far off to get lucky.

But next time …

I weave between the black rocks for protection, running hurriedly on another fifty feet towards the next undulating ribbon of rock.

I'm tiring now, weighed down with Charlie, feet sinking into thick wet sand, my heart pumping, lungs hurting.

I need to stop and rest, to get my breath back. But how can I?

Further on, the rocks stand tall, maybe four or five foot in places. I duck down behind them, legs burning, panting like a dog and staring crazily about for somewhere to hide.

'Bad man,' Charlie whispers, still balanced on my hip.

'Yes, baby, he's a very bad man.' I'm almost crying. 'But I'm not going to let him anywhere near you, I … I promise.'

I'm lying to him.

The Russian is going to catch up to us, and kill us both. Put a bullet in my innocent little boy. Then escape in his horrible bloody boat and not give a damn that he's just executed his own nephew.

I look into his trusting blue eyes and know I have to save my child.

Whatever it takes.

I get moving again, slipping between rocks, hunting for somewhere suitable, and eventually find one with a sandy crevice low down.

There, I drop Charlie off my hip and wedge him into the crevice. With any luck he'll be all but invisible, as long as he keeps his fair hair out of sight.

I crouch down to his level, hugging him tight. 'I need you to do something, Charlie.' I point directly up the beach, where dunes meet the pebble-strewn sand. In the light of the moon, clumps of coarse grasses can be seen growing along the shoreline, high and thick, waving gently in the sea breezes. Perfect for a small child to hide in. 'See those tall grasses? You're going to run up there and hide in them.'

'With Mummy?' he asks hopefully.

'No, darling.' My heart is breaking. 'I … I have to go on to the next bunch of rocks. That way.' I nod down the beach. 'Listen, as soon as that nasty man goes past you, you have to run up there and hide among the grasses. Understand?'

He shakes his head, his lip trembling.

'Charlie, it's a … a game. I need to see if you can run up there and hide without being seen. Just don't move until he's gone past you.' I kiss him on the forehead. 'And don't come out for anyone but me.'

'Mummy,' he moans, holding out his hands.

'No,' I say as firmly as I can, and straighten up, my vision blurry with tears. 'You're a big boy now. Nearly four years old. So, don't spoil the game by being seen.' I ruffle his hair one last time, gasping, 'And not a sound, okay?'

Then I turn and start running towards the next cluster of black rocks, probably the largest grouping of rocks on the beach, not bothering to hide, fully aware that I'm visible in the pale patch of moonlight lying over the strand.

I need to draw his fire.

It works.

I hear the Russian shout something, and the thud of his feet across the damp sands, and then he shoots again, because I hear the crack of a bullet hitting rock.

The moon goes behind a cloud.

He fires again, and misses again in the darkness, yelling furiously now.

I keep running, zigzagging here and there to avoid being an easy target, and lurch down behind the next group of rocks, panting and with a stitch in my side, badly out of breath. I rest for maybe three or four seconds, and then force myself to keep moving, sidling between the ragged cluster of rocks, staying low and trying not to make too much noise.

How long can I keep him distracted with this game of hide-and-seek before he finally manages to hit me? And will that be long enough for Charlie to have reached safety? I want to turn and check that he's obeyed me and is running to hide among the sand dunes, but I dare not let the Russian catch me too soon.

The longer I can give my son to get away, the better. Every second counts.

Of course, I know I'm going to die tonight. But my death was probably inevitable from the start of all this. I just couldn't accept it before now ...

My foot trips over something half-buried in the sand and I fall clumsily, unable to stop myself from crying out. I scramble hurriedly back to my feet and glare round at the object in the sand. The moon comes out again, and I see something gleam.

It's metal. A long, thick, metal bar of some kind, sunk in the wet single-like stretches of sand between rocks.

'Come on, where are you?' Not-Kurt has stopped at the head of this large black cluster of rocks. I catch his shadow moving as he rounds the first outcrop and peers along the passage between rocks. 'You're dead, bitch. But your son can still live ... If you come out now and stop *pissing me off.*'

He sounds demented.

Quickly, I drop to my knees and begin to dig out the metal bar, scrabbling and spattering myself with sand in my hurry, trying to hold my breath so my pursuer doesn't hear me gasping.

At my back, the roar of the incoming tide has been steadily increasing. Now a tiny pale ribbon of foam flicks at my heels, and I pause, staring down at it in shock.

The tide has reached me.

I feel a moment of panic, not for myself but for Charlie. Has he done what I told him? Has he run up the beach and hidden among the sand dunes? Because, if he hasn't, if he is still where I left him among the black rocks, the tide will soon have reached him too. And although it's low now, wetting my feet, it will rise quickly, and anyone caught here amongst the rocks will be drowned.

The metal bar is almost free from the sand now. I wrench at it, grunting with effort, and stagger back as it comes loose, the heavy weight trailing from my hand.

'There you are ...' Not-Kurt has found me. 'Now I'm going to hurt you,' he yells above the sound of the tide. '*Really* hurt you.' His voice rises. 'Nobody kills my brother, and makes a fool out of me, and lives to boast about it.'

I see him turned to face me, standing motionless, maybe ten feet away amongst the rocks, one half of his face and body in shadow. Moonlight silvers the other half, touching that side of his dark head with a white sheen too, as though he's aged forty years since I saw him in the cottage. Then he moves, and the illusion is broken, a young, well-built, dark-haired Russian clambering over rocks towards me with murder in his heart.

He's panting, hurrying over an uneven expanse of damp, limpet-encrusted rocks, and as I back away, the metal bar in my hands, he slips and falls, exclaiming in Russian as he goes down.

While he's picking himself up, I dart around the next cluster of rocks and duck out of sight, crouching there in the darkness. But I'm further down the beach now, and when the tide rushes in again, it soaks my trainers completely, the white foam ankle-high.

He's roaring, furious. 'Where the hell … are you now?' He's hurt, I guess, judging by the hoarse note in his voice. And slower too. His footsteps are more dragging. Has he twisted his ankle? 'I'm going to kill you, bitch, and make you suffer. You and your brat.'

I have to kill him.

The thought crystallises in my mind.

It's awful, and I'm not a killer, but I have no choice. If he kills me, he's going to go looking for Charlie. And he'll probably find him too. Charlie is so young. It's cold and dark and he's seen some terrible things tonight. A man like this could coax him out of hiding with false promises, with offers of food and warmth, with the lie that his mother is waiting for him.

The only way I can ensure that my son survives this night is to kill the Russian.

The metal bar is cold and slippery and hurts my hands. Gritty sand rubs awkwardly under my fingers, and the whole thing weighs a ton.

I'm not strong. I'm not a trained fighter. And this man has a gun. Two guns, in fact. But I'm determined, and I still have some element of surprise on my side. Because he isn't quite sure where I am.

And I still have the little paring knife, stuck snugly in my waistband. It's not exactly an effective weapon, unless my target is an onion or a carrot. But I should imagine it could do a lot of damage, if I stick it into him in exactly the right place.

I remember what Robbie told me back at the manor house. *Nobody ever wants to kill anyone. It's just, sometimes there isn't a choice.* He was right too about how my perspective on killing would change if it was my child I needed to protect …

He's nearer now, still yelling threats, dragging himself between rocks.

My legs are aching from the unaccustomed exercise of running across such a vast expanse of beach, with Charlie's weight on my hip, and then all the ducking and hiding, the crouching, the desperate need to stifle my loud breathing.

But I need to make one last big effort. And if I fail, it's all over.

Slowly, I straighten, balancing the metal bar in both hands, tightening all my muscles…

He's only a couple of feet away now. This big rock is all that is between us, a dense shiny monolith crusted with tiny shells. I hear him mutter something in Russian, and then he rounds the top of the rock, and is standing straight ahead of me.

I lurch forward with a wordless cry and swing the metal bar at the same time, putting all my strength behind it.

The bar smashes into his chest. I was aiming for his head but didn't have quite enough strength to keep the heavy metal bar lifted so high through the swing.

He staggers back at the blow, crying out, but doesn't fall. Despair floods me. I was too weak, I've failed. Failed myself, failed my son … The metal bar spins away, clattering among the rocks, and I collapse sideways against the black, monolith-like rock, fighting to keep my balance on shifting sands.

The Russian charges me.

We fall backwards into the oncoming tide, wrestling each other, rolling over and over, his large hands at my throat, trying to choke the life out of me, my arms flailing, legs kicking wildly…

'Stop fighting me, you bitch,' he shouts into my face, 'and just fucking *die*.'

A shock of icy-cold water dashes over us both as another rolling wave sweeps in, splashing off rocks and streaming violently back seconds later, dragging shingle under my back so forcibly that it moves us several feet back into the shallows.

I splutter, struggling against him, salt water in my mouth and eyes. But he's too strong. He's on top of me, holding me down in the onrush of tide, determined either to strangle or drown me, or both at the same time. It's like being waterboarded, only the sea is high enough here to threaten him too, water crashing into his broad shoulders and face, silencing his furious obscenities.

Another roller ploughs into us, deep and cold and rushing.

I'm underwater.

I struggle, thrashing violently about, but he just keeps pinning me down, his face swimming above me, a grey-black shadow with glinting eyes and teeth. My heart pumps manically, almost bursting out of my chest, and then stutters. My body stiffens, like it's going into shock, and I stop thrashing.

The roaring in my ears begins to dim, and I'm staring up at him through a long dark tunnel, his face growing smaller and fainter …

Charlie.

He's killed me and he's going to kill Charlie next.

And it will be my fault.

The tide pulses in again, sudden and lethal.

Now he's underwater too. His grip loosens as the tide rolls over us both, and he thrashes against me, then pushes upwards and away, frantic to get out of the water, to breathe air again.

My hand drags the paring knife from my waistband and I roll over, half-sitting, half-lying, gasping for oxygen.

Not-Kurt is right above me, huge in the dark, face silvered with moonlight, head thrown back, shaggy hair dripping and his mouth stretched wide for air.

With superhuman strength, I push myself upwards, plunge the knife into the pale exposed flesh of his neck and wrench it sideways, slicing deep and wide at the same time.

Then I drop the knife and fall backwards into the water, gasping and sobbing.

It all happens in an instant.

One minute he was drowning me and the world was turning black above the billowing waves of water, and the next I'm being washed back and forth in the churning tide, watching jets of bright red blood spurt from the puncture wound in his neck.

His dark eyes widen, looking beyond me and out to sea. He says nothing, one hand clamped to his throat, blood pouring freely through his fingers and into the water, a scarlet torrent.

With a horrible gurgle, the Russian tumbles forward, pitching face-first into the water beside me.

Grimly, I begin to crawl away through the rushing tide, not looking back but heading up the beach to where I left Charlie …

I find my son among the coarse grasses on the sand dunes, shivering and hugging his knees to his chin, his eyes wide and blank.

'It's okay, Mummy's here,' I say again and again, holding Charlie close and rubbing at his skin to get some warmth back into him. 'You're safe now. We're both safe.'

I only hope I'm right.

'G-Go home,' he stutters.

'Yes, baby, we're going home.' Though I have no idea how to achieve that. I have no phone and there are no lights visible anywhere along this stretch of coast. 'But I need to get a blanket round you first. You're so cold.'

Charlie says nothing, shivering violently. I rub harder at his back, and stare back down the beach towards the faint outline of the cottage. It's still in darkness but there are probably blankets there. There's certainly a towel.

I could dry Charlie, wrap him up, and keep him sheltered in the cottage until the morning, when I could walk for help.

Only it's not that simple.

John's lying dead in that cottage. He must be dead; it's unlikely anyone could have survived such catastrophic blood loss. And I don't want to inflict that horrible sight on my son again. A man he knew and once trusted, murdered in cold blood in front of his eyes, his lifeblood soaked into the rug. The poor boy's already been caused untold harm by what he's seen and heard in the past twenty-four hours without adding further trauma.

Yet I ought to check that John's dead before leaving his body there … Just in case.

And then there's Not-Kurt.

His body could be washing away by now. Or it may be thrown higher up the beach by the incoming tide, perhaps to be dashed against the black rocks. An unpleasant thought.

But that's not what's worrying me.

Whoever was signalling the cottage from that boat out to sea will be expecting him to turn up for the rendezvous. Because they came here to rescue him, didn't they? At least, that's what John seemed to be saying. His 'ticket out'. So maybe more Russians will be coming ashore at any minute, and when Not-Kurt isn't at the cottage as planned, they may come along the beach searching for him.

I stare back along the beach. There's the cottage. And a short distance away, his black SUV, parked where he left it.

The car keys.

Not-Kurt had them, didn't he? In his pocket, perhaps. I don't recall him putting them down in the cottage.

If I could manage to drive the car …

286

I don't actually have a licence but I had a handful of lessons from a would-be boyfriend in college, so I know the basics. And I bet his expensive car has an automatic gearbox. What my friend used to call 'point and shoot' driving. Just put it in Drive, turn the wheel in the right direction, and press the accelerator.

But even for that I would still need the car keys.

I stare back at the black rocks where I crawled away from his lifeless body. The water is swirling about the rocks, maybe knee-deep now or higher, and rising swiftly.

'Stay here a minute,' I tell Charlie, but he clings to me, moaning and shaking his head. 'Darling, I need to do something. I'll only be a minute.'

'No, don't leave me,' he cries feebly, his hands like little pincers on my arm. 'Please, Mummy.'

I give up and we sit hunched in miserable silence, staring at the incoming tide, its frilly foam driving past the nearest black ribbons of rock submerged in the sand. Charlie seems mesmerised by the sea. But then, he's never been to the seaside before tonight.

I guess from the ragged barrier of large stones and pebbles choking the sand twenty feet away, cast up the beach by previous storms, that even the highest tide never comes this high, so we should be safe enough on the dunes.

The sound of the sea is oddly comforting. There's also something familiar and haunting about being here, looking out to sea, the salt breeze lifting my wet hair …

Did my mother take me to the beach as a small child, perhaps? I have a vague memory, only now surfacing, of building sandcastles on a sunny day while the sea roared and rushed behind me, a maternal presence watching me from a deckchair. But as soon as I try to see beyond that memory, it dissolves like smoke, and I'm left with the cold dark of the Atlantic Ocean at night.

I hear shouts, and stiffen, my heart beginning to race again. Some kind of light is bobbing up and down on the sea, a small boat or dingy approaching the shore.

Not-Kurt's people, coming to find him.

And he's dead.

'Quick,' I whisper to Charlie, 'we have to hide. Maybe higher up the dunes.'

But even as I gather my failing strength for a climb up the shifting dunes, a brighter light appears in the sky to the south-west, coming inexorably closer and closer.

The whirr of blades grows louder, Charlie and I both staring into the night sky.

'Wassat?' he asks, mouth open.

'I think ... it's a helicopter,' I say slowly, and then with greater conviction. 'Yes, a helicopter.'

I get to my feet, unsure whether I should wave at the pilot and risk drawing the attention of those men on the boat, or if I should use its passing as cover while Charlie and I dash up the dunes to a safer position.

But the small boat has turned and seems to be retreating. Seconds later, the light winks out. The moon shows only a shadow on the water, slowly receding into nothingness as scudding clouds cover its silver face again.

The helicopter circles and then touches down on the sandy foreshore near the cottage, high enough to avoid the incoming tide, the blades churning up dusty sand clouds.

As I watch, hugging Charlie against my leg, a group of men jump out of the helicopter and fan out, some with serious-looking guns, others speaking urgently into phones.

One man waits apart from the rest, surveying the scene. The cottage with its open door, the SUV standing silent and motionless, and the dark sea beyond.

How on earth ... ?

'Oh my God,' I say, and glance down at my wrist watch. Sir Philip's wrist watch. 'I thought he was joking when he said there was a tracker in it.'

I doubt his watch will ever work again though. The glass is cracked and it's been in the sea. I hope he won't mind.

'Mummy?'

'It's okay, baby.' I start to descend the steep sand dunes, skidding and half-running, holding him firmly by the hand. 'Everything's going to be okay.' As the helicopter blades begin to slow, I wave my hand and shout, 'Over here! We're over here!'

The man turns sharply at my voice and raises a hand in greeting, starting towards us.

'Who's that?' Charlie asks plaintively, dragging his heels a little, perhaps fearing that another Bad Man has arrived.

'That's your grandpa,' I tell him, my voice shaking. 'And Mummy's very, very glad to see him.'

EPILOGUE

'So,' I say, combing through Patricia's fine, towel-dried hair, 'what's it to be? Feathery layers? Or an easy-to-maintain bob?'

'Actually, I'd like something daring,' Patricia tells me seriously, meeting my gaze in the salon mirror. 'I met a nice man at the library yesterday, you see. He's taking me for coffee at the weekend.'

I stifle my laughter, reaching for a pot of hair thickening gel. 'Coffee, eh?'

'He's a bit younger than me,' she confesses. 'So I fancy a walk on the wild side. Take a few years off my look. And maybe a new colour. Black?'

'Okay.' I pick up my scissors and study her hair speculatively. 'I think I know what you mean. Liza Minnelli in *Cabaret*?'

'Yes ... short and sleek, but sort of spiky too.' Patricia winks at me. She's wearing her garish green eyeshadow again today. 'Just a touch of decadence.'

A car pulling up outside the salon catches my attention.

'Here,' I say, handing her a hairstyle brochure. 'Why not take a look through these and let me know if any styles leap out at you? Just in case you change your mind about the Liza Minnelli look.'

She starts to flick through them, humming happily to herself as I open the door to the salon.

Darkling Moreton was glowing with mid-October sunshine earlier, but the sky is darkening now as we head into late afternoon. It's been a bright autumnal day, fallen leaves littering the streets, and the short walk through the churchyard that I still take every Sunday morning so Charlie can attend playgroup and see his friends.

Sir Philip's BMW has drawn up to the kerb with Robbie behind the wheel and my grandfather already outside, releasing Charlie from the back seat. I'm glad to see that Robbie is looking well, despite having been shot, his right arm lying along the open car window. The sling is long-gone and he's been declared fit to drive again, but I doubt he's doing much gardening work at the moment.

My son bounds towards me, school rucksack on his back, grinning from ear to ear. He's really enjoying his new school and has already made several good friends among his class-mates.

'Mummy, I painted this today!' He holds up a floppy piece of paper with a smushy rainbow on it. 'It's for you.'

'Thank you,' I say, with due reverence for his art skills, and carefully secure it to the salon wall with a piece of Blu Tack. 'It looks wonderful.'

'I'm starving,' he announces, and heads straight to the back door into the kitchen for a snack.

'Hey, mister,' I call after my son as he heads through the sliding partition between the salon and our living quarters, 'how many times have I told you? Side door for the kitchen. No traipsing through the salon every time you come home from school.'

There's no reply.

With a chuckle, I turn back to my grandfather. 'Thank you for picking him up again. Though I'm sure he'd be fine on the school bus.'

'I enjoy the run out,' he insists as always, though adds, 'Once the boy's settled in properly, he can travel on the school bus with the other kids. But until then, humour an old man, would you? He's my great-grandchild and I've never had a chance to get to know him. I'd like to make up for lost time.' Standing on the salon threshold, he nods to Patricia. 'Ah, you've got a customer. Apologies, Patty, I'll only be a minute.'

'Don't hurry on my account,' Patricia says politely, and looks at herself in the mirror, tweaking her hair.

'Marina, I'd like to invite you to dinner tonight,' Sir Philip says in a lower voice, after a quick glance up and down the street to make sure nobody else is within earshot. 'To meet your, erm, *mother*. As we arranged last week.'

He doesn't mean Natasha.

Part of the explanation he gave the secret service for the Russian 'incursion' of Darkling Moreton, as he now refers to it, is that I'm Sir Philip's granddaughter, and the Russians took me and Charlie hostage to blackmail him into giving up secrets, but were ultimately foiled by him and Robbie. Which is pretty close to the truth.

We all agreed not to mention Natasha or her part in all this, as his old bosses would have made it a priority to hunt her down, and Sir Philip felt it would be safer for everyone if that didn't happen.

Only he told them that my mother is actually his *daughter*, Sarah, who works in banking in Bahrain, and who has reluctantly agreed to pretend she had a daughter in her twenties, as a single woman, whom she gave up for adoption. Apparently, I had come to Darkling Moreton to track down my true family, and unfortunately came to the attention of the Russians, who just happened to be keeping tabs on Sir Philip.

This rather unlikely story seems to have satisfied the powers-that-be. Either that, or they are reserving judgement and watching us all in the hope we may slip up in the future.

Hence the need for continued secrecy.

Personally, I think his daughter Sarah sounds like a saint for agreeing to go along with this story of a 'secret' teenage pregnancy. But then, with Sir Philip for a father, perhaps she's used to subterfuge.

Either way, I'm dying to meet her.

The necessary paperwork has been arranged and yet another identity procured for me. This time the name on my papers is my real one, Marina, and my surname is Janus. But Sir Philip claims this is the last time he'll be using his old contacts in the underworld to organise new ID for anyone, as it's so expensive and, besides, he's getting too old for such 'shenanigans'.

'Sarah flew into London this morning from Bahrain and should be here in an hour or so.' He checks his watch. The cracked glass has been fixed, the leather strap replaced, and it still works. I guess he's sentimental about it. 'I'd like her to meet Charlie too, but maybe tomorrow after school? This dinner looks likely to go well past his bedtime, and it is a school night.'

'I'll babysit him,' Patricia calls. 'He can stay at mine tonight and you can pick him up for school in the morning, How's that?'

Sir Philip gives me a look from under frowning brows. 'Ears like a bat, that woman,' he murmurs, then says more loudly, 'Thank you, Patty.'

'I heard that,' Patricia tells him, head bent, still studying the hairstyle brochure. 'Ears like a bat was part of the job description for your P.A., as I recall.'

Sir Philip clears his throat, looking embarrassed.

'I'll be there,' I promise him, smiling, and squeeze his arm. 'I can't wait to meet Sarah. And thank you again for *everything*. I'm sure I don't deserve all the help you've given me.' I gesture to the brand-new signage above our heads, quirkily announcing SNIP SNAP alongside a pair of scissors and my mobile number, plus the simple but smart salon interior. 'I could never have afforded all this without your generosity.'

'You're my granddaughter, and it's my pleasure.' But he's beaming. 'Dinner at seven, remember. Best bib and tucker.' He pauses, his eyes turning more serious. 'Any word from Natasha, by the way?'

My mother vanished soon after Charlie and I returned from that cottage by the sea, leaving a brief note for me, apologising that she couldn't stay in Darkling Moreton any longer but would 'keep in touch'. It's taken me a long time to accept that she's gone. I even suspect my grandfather may have threatened her in some way. But at least she took some time before she left to talk to me about my father, and explain how it was between them in the early days, how they'd fallen in love and how fate had been against them.

That was her exact turn of phrase. 'Fate was against us from start,' she said in her husky voice, downing more neat vodka as we drank together late one evening in my little kitchen. 'But Charles, he would have been proud of his little Marina. You kill that pig on the beach. You save your son. Yes … Proud, very proud.' She nodded sombrely. 'I was angry with my friends for losing you. You had bad time as child without mother, father … I'm sorry.' Putting her hand on mine, she added, 'But I cannot stay. You understand, yes?'

I suppose there are simply too many bad memories for her in Darkling Moreton. Not to mention uncomfortable links to the British government, via my grandfather. She's still a murderer and a wanted woman on both sides. And I suspect Sir Philip would gladly hand her over to the authorities if she spent much more time hanging about in this quiet Devon village.

There are limits, after all.

'Don't worry about that business with the private investigator, Tim Shaw,' my grandfather told me recently, meaning Simon's death. 'They'll never track it back to you. I've seen to that.'

Which means they won't track it back to Natasha either, I suspect.

Despite her murderous streak, it's hard to consider my mother truly *wicked*. She only had my best interests at heart in killing those men. But the way she'd done it …

No, definitely unhinged.

But maybe one day she'll turn up out of the blue again, to see Charlie and maybe get a good haircut. I'll be keeping a bottle of Russian vodka in the cupboard for that day, just in case.

I shake my head at Sir Philip. 'Not a whisper, sorry. But I'll let you know if she gets in touch.' I smile and change the subject. 'And how's Glenda doing?'

The late vicar's elderly mother had made a surprising recovery after her hostage ordeal that night.

Natasha, finding her trussed up and gagged upstairs in the vicarage, had released the old lady, who had instantly suffered a nervous attack that required my mother to carry her to the bathroom, so missing all the excitement happening outside, much to her annoyance.

Though Natasha had got downstairs in time to drag Robbie to safety before Not-Kurt could go back and shoot him, unaware that they'd already knocked me out me and bundled me into the SUV. Since I regained consciousness in the boot with my hands bound, I assume they must have stopped along the way to the beach cottage to tie me up. Safer for them away from the village, I guess.

'It must have been a severe shock to lose her son like that. No more nervous spasms, I hope?'

'Mrs Shearsman fleeced me at bridge last night,' Sir Philip admits. 'Definitely not allowing her bereavement to affect her too badly. Says she's looking forward to moving into a retirement flat in Barnstaple, using his life insurance payout.'

Locally, the tale Sir Philip had come up with to explain the vicar's violent death was that a band of robbers from 'upcountry' had taken his mother hostage and forced him to help them turn over the church and parish hall, but when he bravely fought back, they'd shot him before absconding.

This story had satisfied most villagers, with the help of the landlord's testimony that he'd seen the vicar acting 'most peculiar' that night, and Sir Philip had also somehow come out of it looking like a hero, having generously replaced the 'missing' church goods so that life could continue as usual.

The new vicar is a stout, constantly smiling lady from a neighbouring parish, who even popped into my salon in her first week for a quick trim.

I still feel bad about John.

He was found dead in the beach cottage, as I'd feared. It haunts me that I left him to die alone.

But, as Natasha pointed out at the time in her usual dry manner, he would have left me to die alone if he'd been paid to do it, so I shouldn't waste too much time grieving for him.

All the same, I prefer to think John might have helped me escape anyway, money or no money.

John had such a lovely smile; I refuse to believe he was utterly bad through and through.

His caravan disappeared and I have no idea what happened to his body. All that was taken care of by Sir Philip's former colleagues in the secret service.

But a few weeks after that awful night, I took a walk out to the field where his caravan stood, and laid some wild flowers on the site, in memory of the man who helped me and Charlie escape before that vile man got back.

Without him, we would probably have died, as it took Sir Philip over an hour to pinpoint our location using the tracker in his wristwatch and scramble a secret service helicopter to fly out there in time.

So I'm grateful for John's help that night, regardless of his other bad deeds.

I sat down with the others after we got back to Darkling Moreton and wearily explained everything that had happened to us in exact detail. Sir Philip took down details of the boat with its flashing light and passed them to the authorities, though it was long gone by then.

I even admitted that Kurt – or rather Ivan – had been Charlie's father, stammering a little over how that had come about.

Thankfully, nobody seemed to blame me for my impulsive behaviour, and I slept the deepest sleep that night, curled up with Charlie, the pain of my past slowly pushed away to make way for a happier future …

I wave off my grandfather and Robbie in the BMW, check that Charlie is seated in front of the telly with his favourite new after-school snack of peanut butter sandwiches and milk – ready prepared and left on the kitchen table for him – and head back to Patricia, who's been waiting patiently.

'Sorry about that,' I say, smiling shyly as I meet her eyes in the mirror, 'but this is all new to me … Running my own salon, having a kid in school, being part of a real *family* at last. I'll get better organised soon, I promise.' I plump Patricia's hair, scissors poised. 'So, what's it to be? Liza Minnelli?'

'Yes, thank you.' She grins at me in the mirror. 'Make me a new woman.'

Thank you for reading this novel. Your reading supports authors.

Other thrillers by Jane Holland

GIRL NUMBER ONE (#1 UK Kindle Chart Bestseller)

LOCK THE DOOR

FORGET HER NAME

ALL YOUR SECRETS

LAST BIRD SINGING

WHY SHE RAN

THE HIVE

DEAD SIS

KEEP ME CLOSE

TAKE MY PLACE (a short story)

UNDER AN EVIL STAR (Stella Penhaligon Thrillers 1)

THE TENTH HOUSE MURDERS (Stella Penhaligon Thrillers 2)

THE PART OF DEATH (Stella Penhaligon Thrillers 3)

Printed in Great Britain
by Amazon

16447488R00171